Praise for Mackenzie Ford's

GIFTS OF WAR

MACKENZIE FORD

GIFTS OF WAR

Mackenzie Ford is the *nom de plume* of a well-known and respected historian who lives in London.

GIFTS OF WAR

GIFTS OF WAR

A NOVEL

MACKENZIE FORD

Anchor Books
A Division of Random House, Inc.
New York

FIRST ANCHOR BOOKS EDITION, JULY 2010

Copyright © 2008 by Mackenzie Ford

All rights reserved. Published in the United States by Anchor Books,
a division of Random House, Inc., New York. Originally published in
paperback in Great Britain as *The Kissing Gates* by Sphere, an imprint of Little,
Brown Book Group, London, in 2008, and subsequently published in
hardcover in the United States by Nan A. Talese/Doubleday,
a division of Random House, Inc., New York, in 2009.

Anchor Books and colophon are registered trademarks of Random House, Inc.

The Library of Congress has cataloged the Nan A. Talese/Doubleday edition
as follows:
Ford, Mackenzie.
Gifts of war : a novel / Mackenzie Ford.—1st ed.
p. cm.
I. World War, 1914–1918—Fiction. I. Title.
PR6I06.O73G54 2009
823'.92—dc22   2008037259

Anchor ISBN: 978-0-307-45615-1

Book design by Songhee Oh

Printed in the United States of America
10 9 8 7 6 5 4 3 2 I

To: K.

CONTENTS

A Confession

The Majestic Hotel, Paris, May 1919

IT IS TWO A.M., RAINING HARD, and the cobblestones on the Avenue Victor Hugo are glittering like a thousand silver spoons. Vast puddles are forming in the gutters, black as ink. There are more cabs battling the rain than you would expect at this hour, the hides of the horses shiny and sleek. The clatter of their hooves is muted by the hiss of wind and rain. Oblivious to the weather, two lovers embrace under a tree. I hear dance music faintly from the ballroom several stories below me. How far away the war seems already.

The war. Some people are already calling it the Great War, not because great moral issues were settled—not at all—but because of the number of young men killed: a whole generation has gone. I survived the war. In fact, and ironically, paradoxically, the Great War—if that is what it was—brought me the greatest happiness I have known.

By now, I suppose, everyone has heard of the Christmas truce of 1914. From Christmas Eve to Boxing Day, all along the Western Front, some six hundred miles from Belgium to Switzerland, ordinary soldiers on both sides of the war, and in marked defiance of orders from High Command, laid down their arms, hauled themselves from their trenches, and clambered into no-man's-land to fraternize with the enemy. In some cases, the truce had been prepared with the exchange of messages, scribbled on paper and thrown across the barbed-wire defenses in used tobacco tins: "You no shoot, we no shoot." In other places, the truce was more spontaneous. Soldiers suddenly appeared, without weapons, carrying a white flag tied to a broken tree branch or, on our side, a cricket stump. The other side responded in like manner, and men met in the middle, to exchange cigarettes, swap buttons or badges, and complain about the higher-ups.

A week or so later the newspapers were full of it. Ordinary "Tommies" and "Fritzes" had written home to their parents, and some had forwarded their sons' letters to the press. I remember one headline that read "THE TRUCE OF GOD," which I thought missed the point. Why had God allowed this damned war in the first place?

No one knows my story, though, which began during the Christmas truce and would not—could not—have happened without it. This has been my secret for nearly four long years; I have guarded it more closely than any of the innumerable military, political, and economic secrets with which I have been entrusted in that time. But now something has happened and I must set down my story. You will see why.

The Photograph

HAD IT NOT BEEN FOR THE WAR, Christmas 1914 would have been straight out of a fairy tale. On 24 December the weather changed abruptly. Along the Front it turned bitterly cold, and the sun that shone all afternoon was too weak to unfreeze the puddles of muddy water that stretched everywhere. Rats and rabbits skittered on the ice, and even the lice—as dug in as we were, in our hair and clothing— seemed lethargic in the cold conditions. It was a better day than most for scratching. That night a thin cloud cover formed but the temperature didn't ease up and a light snow fell, dusting the desolate landscape with a fine layer of crystals. The branches of dead trees—what trees remained standing—became lit in an unnatural way, rather like actors onstage are lit from reflected light below. What was beginning to be familiar terrain suddenly took on a strange, eerie appearance and I remember wondering whether I had, in fact, been shot and killed and was now looking onto the other side—a version of hell that had indeed frozen over.

But no, the eeriness was all too real. That night, as midnight approached, when it was already Christmas by their time, but not with us, we heard movement in the German trenches. Where we were, they were about eighty yards away—no more—so sounds carried. First one, then another small fir tree was hoisted on to the lip of their trenches, lit by candles. One of our sharpshooters fired at one of the trees, and knocked it back down out of sight. This normally would have brought a burst of answering fire from the Germans, but not this time. All was quiet. I barked an order, the sharpshooter made no attempt to fire at the second tree, and we waited. After a delay, there was a small commotion on the German side and another candelit tree was positioned on the lip of their trench. This time we left it alone.

Again we waited. Some minutes afterward we heard the strains of a mouth organ, a trembling, unassertive—even vulnerable—sound, which only just carried across the distance. Its tone was plaintive, melancholy. The musician played a few bars and then voices joined in. The song, which I recognized, was "Die Wacht am Rhein," "The Watch on the Rhine," based on a nineteenth-century German poem. The clouds had gone by now and the Front had a stark beauty in the clear moonlight. On our side we had all but forgotten the cold.

As the song ended, one of our men shouted, "*Guten* singing, Fritz!" or something very like it. We all laughed and cheered. After a short silence, the mouth organ started up again, and the Germans gave us "*Stille Nacht,*" "Silent Night," which of course allowed us the opportunity to join in with English words. What a scene! Two groups of men, in ditches eighty yards apart, who hours before had been doing their level best to slaughter one another, singing in unison. Well, almost.

Everyone sensed that this was something historic. It was one of those moments in life when everyone—everyone—raised his game, and no one who was there will ever forget it.

I was twenty-three then, and a second lieutenant in the Forty-seventh Gloucestershire Rifles. I was born and grew up in Edgewater, a tiny Cotswold hamlet not far from Stroud. My school career had its moments—mostly wrong moments. I was good at languages but that was about it. I was caught smoking twice and fighting twice. These fights weren't brawls but midnight bare-knuckle knockout bouts in the school ring—this is how arguments were settled in my school, and highly illegal.

Twenty-three was a little old for the rank I held, that being mainly due to the fact that I had delayed my degree at Cambridge, to spend two years in—of all places—Germany. My father had been more impressed by my facility with foreign languages than I was myself and at his expense I spent one year in Berlin and another in Munich, brushing up my German (though not only that). The prewar years in Germany, in Munich especially, were the great years of modernism. The birth of abstract painting took place there, the first forays into cabaret; the great novels of Thomas and Heinrich Mann were written in the city. What a time! It was in Munich that I learned to drink and to swear. I dabbled in painting, song writing, and I lost my virginity. I played the tables, lost my allowance, worked as a bouncer in the casino to pay off the debt (the boxing came in handy). I visited hermaphrodite strip shows, learned to nurse a drink for hours on end in all-night piano bars, and took part in everything the new century had to offer. I never knew whether this is what my father had intended for me, but I loved most of my time in Germany and silently thanked him all the same.

So I didn't go up to Cambridge until I was twenty and therefore didn't come down until May 1914, just before I turned twenty-three. I'd been working in publishing in London for all of six weeks when war broke out.

Despite my Munich-inspired sophistication, my familiarity with abstract art, continental women, foreign food, and fashion, like so many others I didn't see the Great War coming. And, like so many others, I volunteered immediately. My father was half-pleased. He was always a rather distant man, whom I respected rather than loved. We never really talked about it, but I think he understood the danger more than I did. I suspect he thought that I would get a better—and maybe safer—commission if I volunteered early. He thought my German would help to get me a billet in intelligence, away from the front line. He was wrong: what was most wanted in the early days was infantry, fighting men—or, as the skeptics in the newspapers insisted, "cannon fodder."

My mother was against the war from the very beginning and didn't want me to have any part of it. She would, I think, have even been prepared for me to be a conscientious objector. My mother was a ferocious figure of respect, too, rather than love. I don't want to give the impression that my parents were cold people—they weren't—but the distance they kept was their way of allowing my sister and me to develop our own personalities. Anyway, my mother distrusted authority—any authority. She had no belief in God, loathed the church, and thought the army High Command little better than a bunch of brutish, emotionally stunted pigs, as intellectually vapid as a flock of geese (her very words). Men, she said contemptuously to anyone who would listen, make mistakes in life that women would never contemplate. When I left the house to join up she kissed me on the cheek but said nothing, not even "Good luck" or "Good-bye."

My sister, Isobel, was different again. Two years younger than me, Izzy was the archetypal younger sister (or so I thought then), adoring of her elder brother, looking up to him, taking his lead in everything. I didn't ask for it; she just grew up with her attitude without thinking. For me it was as much a burden as it was a pleasure. And it made me underestimate her.

I obtained a commission in the Forty-seventh Gloucestershire Rifles, based at Tetbury. As a second lieutenant—the lowest commissioned rank—I did a month's officer training, and just three weeks basic training. There's not much to say about Tetbury but, about halfway through the course, we got a weekend pass and several of us took the train down to Bristol. Bristol was to play a walk-on part in my story in a number of ways, and the first time was that weekend.

I traveled with a couple of other second lieutenants; we had been primed by the adjutant on the general staff not to miss a certain "establishment" (as he put it) near the docks, called the Baltic Wharf, and to use his name. Not to mince words, the establishment, while a perfectly serviceable pub on the ground floor, turned out to be a brothel on the floor above. All was revealed when one of us, in ordering some drinks, mentioned the adjutant's name. Apparently, the owner of the Baltic Wharf had been a company sergeant major earlier on in his life, and still had a soft spot for khaki. None of us knew whether we would be allowed out of the camp again before our training was completed, and it didn't take a genius to see that, once we were in France, or Flanders, or wherever we were going, women would not be very high on the army's list of priorities. Add to that the fact that each of us had had no chance to spend our pay for several weeks, and the Baltic Wharf began to seem like a little splash of color in a very gray-and-khaki world.

I remember that the girl was called Crimson—not her real name, obviously—and that she was from Halifax in Nova Scotia. She had lived in Bristol for some months, having been smuggled aboard a ship in her hometown in Canada to service the crew, then been too frightened to sail home, because war had broken out and the North Atlantic had suddenly become very dangerous.

The Wharf was a very civilized place for a brothel (at least, I imagine it was; I am not too qualified to speak, Munich and Bristol being my only experiences in that direction). Besides a number of bedrooms on the first floor, the Wharf had a sitting room, a place where you could relax, put your feet up, have a smoke and a drink, read the newspapers. It was quite clever in its way. The idea was not to rush the men away, once the main business was finished, so to speak, but to persuade them to linger, perhaps try another girl after a suitable break. Anyway, I was relaxing in the room, alone with a drink and a cigarette, waiting for the others I had traveled down with and leafing through that day's *Morning Post*, when another man joined me. He nodded, poured himself a drink, and began to light a cigarette.

I was a bit preoccupied, to tell the truth. There was a piece in the paper about some of our ships being sunk off Ireland. Crimson wouldn't be going home yet awhile.

Just then we heard a commotion below, and raised voices. A look of fear crossed the other man's face and he rushed to the door. He stuck his head out, left it there for a moment, then slammed the door shut.

"Jesus!" he growled.

"What is it?" I asked. "Police?"

"No," he breathed, more quietly now. "Worse. Curfew."

"Curfew? It's not late."

"Not that kind of curfew. Enlisted men aren't allowed by the harbor. Officers only."

"Oh! Why?"

He shrugged. "I don't make the rules. There've been a couple of fights, a knifing."

"Are you going to run for it?"

He shook his head. "It's all up."

"What's the penalty, if you are caught?"

"The penitentiary, bread and bleeding water. Loss of privileges for weeks, more. I could even lose my stripe."

I got up, went to the door, and looked out. A lieutenant was moving toward the stairs that led to the bedrooms and the room where we were waiting. I closed the door again.

"What's your name?"

"Meadows, sir."

"I mean your first name, and don't call me 'sir.' "

He nodded. "John, sir." He made a face. "John."

I took off my jacket. "You're in luck. I know the officer on the stairs. Only slightly, but he'll recognize me."

"How does that help me?"

I held out my jacket. "My first name's Hal. Put this on and sit over there. Try to look relaxed."

"You want me to impersonate an officer?"

I still held out the jacket. "It's your choice."

He took it.

I lounged in an easy chair, trying to look as relaxed as I could.

Meadows hesitated, looking me straight in the eye. Then he slipped his arms into my jacket and slumped onto the sofa.

The door burst open and a man I knew as Lieutenant Ralph Coleman came in. He stopped, looked at me, nodded, and then looked at Meadows.

Meadows coughed.

"John," I said. "Can you spare another cigarette, please? I think I must have rolled onto mine." I grinned.

He did his best to grin back. "Sure, Hal. Here." And he threw the packet in my direction.

Coleman took a step further into the room. What now? He looked from me to Meadows. "Can I bum one of those cigarettes, do you mind? I've run out."

Meadows nodded and I threw the pack toward Coleman.

He lit the cigarette, dropped the packet on a table, blew smoke into the room. "You lucky bastards," he said softly. "I was told there were some enlisted men in here today, but I've found no one so far." And, as he backed out, he grinned. "Don't tire the girls out, you two. My turn tomorrow."

I never saw Crimson or the Baltic Wharf again. Toward the end of October, we shipped out to France. We arrived at the Front by motorbus. Two thousand of them, driven by reservists, had been sent out by the government. You can imagine the jokes that circulated about arriving at a war by bus. In no time, in November in fact, we saw heavy fighting around and along the Marne River and our strength was reduced so much that the minimum height restriction for recruits was lowered from five foot eight to five foot three. Christ, we were taking a battering. I was directly affected by this because my immediate superior, a full lieutenant who was from Bath and all of six months older than me, was killed in the push on Nieuport and I had to take over.

And so, with the war only weeks old, my unit was—in terms of personnel—already 80 percent different from the one that had left Tetbury. Almost no one under my command was out of their teens, and some, I am fairly sure, had lied about their age to get into the infantry and should by rights have been at school.

By Christmas Eve we were all, in a way, tired old men. The mud, the danger, the constant bombardment, the sight of so many bodies, and so many *bits* of bodies, not to mention the blinded, the maimed who had lost arms or legs, the quantities of blood sluicing through the mud, the screams, in the middle of the night, of men who could not be rescued from no-man's-land ... this was a very different kind of experience from Munich. We learned to sleep standing up, to ignore cold and damp, to forget about sex, to accept the insect life on our bodies, to stop thinking beyond the next day. In my first letters home I tried to describe the horror, but after a few attempts I gave up. No words could describe what we saw. In the trenches, we stopped talking about it.

The Christmas Eve carol singing lasted for about half an hour. I thought our side stole a march on the Germans because we had a young man in our lines who had been in the choir at Gloucester Cathedral (and, given his probable age, should still have been there). He sang beautifully and had teamed up with an older man who was a bit of a virtuoso on the mouth organ. The young man, the boy, sang a sad lament—composed for a soprano voice—from one of Handel's operas, *Rinaldo*, I think. I don't remember the Latin title, but in English the lament was called "Let Me Weep," which I thought no more than appropriate. An English boy singing a German song in a Flanders field. Handel, I know, had found real fame only in London. The aria was doubly suitable.

When the boy had finished and the strains of the mouth organ subsided, leaving only a faint whisper of wind, we all knew that there would be no more music that night.

"*Gute Nacht, Fritz!*" shouted our linguist. "*Schlafen Sie gut.*"

"Good singing, Tommy!" someone shouted back. "Merry Christmas."

The mood of the men in the trench that night was different. "Maybe we'll get some proper sleep," one man growled.

"I hope so, too," I replied. "But the guard will be maintained, as always. We're taking no risks."

"Do you think that's really necessary, sir?" said one of the men.

"I don't know, but I don't want to lose anybody for the sake of elementary precautions. In any case, whoever is on duty will have me for company, at least to begin with. I have letters to write."

They didn't like it, but they could see the sense in what I said.

The men designated as guards took up their positions and I settled down to my letters. I say "my" letters, but they weren't really. Besides being underage, a handful of the "men" in my unit—as in all units—were unable to read or write. Most of them had never anticipated the importance of letters at the Front—letters received from home, and letters they sent to their families. I hadn't foreseen this problem either, but it quickly became apparent where the solution lay. Many of the men who *could* read and write could do so only with difficulty, and by Christmastime writing letters for the men, and reading aloud the replies they got from home, was one of my more important duties, crucial so far as morale was concerned.

My routine was simple. I read the men's letters to them as soon as they arrived, usually late at night. The men told me what they wanted to say in return, I made notes, and spatchcocked their personal details together with an account of what action our unit had seen in the previous few days. They made their mark at the end of whatever I wrote before it was sent off. In this way I got to know far more about the men under me than I had ever anticipated—who had missed the birth of their infants, due to being abroad, whose brothers had already been killed, who supported which football team, who expected their girlfriends to stay faithful and who didn't, the names of their dogs, what brand of beer they missed most.

It was amazing how quickly we slipped into the routine, and how much the men came to rely on these exchanges. Even though they couldn't read them, they carried their letters from home in their tunic pockets and would take them out from time to time. "Here, sir, read us that bit about our Lily telling the vicar his sermon was defeatist." "Sir, can you just read that part about my mother's prize at that garden show?"

"Oh no, don't, sir," others would complain. "Jee-*sus*, we had all that garden fête stuff nonstop yesterday—and the day before. Give us a break." But they didn't mean it. For men who had seen what we had seen, even in our short time at the Front, normal news from home— about a garden fête, or a vicar's sermon, or a terrier who had had puppies by caesarean—was as near sacred as it got.

There was lots of sad news, of course, especially for the men from large families with several brothers away in the war. I read those quietly, and in private, warning the men what was to come. That helped me know whom to give leave to, and when.

I don't know when I did fall asleep that evening, but eventually the letter writing was done and I nodded off. When I woke up it was just getting light. A weak sun was lifting itself over the Caillette hills in the east. Yawning, I sneaked a look across to the German lines. Never was a landscape so pitted and pockmarked with shell holes, flats of mud, and disfigured by twisted shards of shrapnel as our section of south Belgium. Nowhere, in the entire history of the world, was loved less than this bloodied patch of land. The mud flats remained frozen; the thin layer of white crystals that had fallen the afternoon before still formed a translucent sheet, glistening like the stubble on an old man's beard. Dead trees, their leaves blasted away, were outlined in white against the mud. Stenciled against the landscape, they had no right to be so beautiful.

But the mood of the men that day was like that of the night before—somehow different from usual, and right from the beginning, from first light. You have to remember that in 1914, in the British army, we had no helmets—they were not introduced until 1916. So although the trenches were, in theory, supposed to be deeper than the height of a man, meaning one was always protected, in practice this was nowhere near true everywhere. Infills, underground streams, rocky outcrops all meant that, in many places, one had to stoop, or even crawl, to prevent one's head from showing and presenting itself as an easy target to the enemy snipers.

But not that day. From daybreak, both sets of soldiers moved around freely, allowing themselves the luxury, for once, of standing up straight to shave, placing a mirror on the lip of a trench, in full daylight and in full view of the Germans, who did the same. We cooked breakfast, whistled our heads off, shouted "Happy Christmas" across the barbed wire, and those who could wrote letters home.

Around half past ten, one of their men stood up on open ground. He raised his arms, to show he was carrying no weapons, and held aloft a metal rod of some sort with a white handkerchief tied to it. I ordered that no one on our side should fire. Instead, we watched as he made his way forward, through the shell craters and frozen mud, to the German line of barbed wire. He stopped and beckoned.

I sent out the company sergeant, a carpenter from Bath called Frank Stephenson. He too was unarmed. He returned a short time later with a message.

"Their C.O. would like to meet you at noon, sir, noon our time. For an exchange of gifts and a discussion about burying the dead."

Gifts? What on earth did the Germans have to give us and, more important, what did we have to give *them?* Was the exchange of gifts even appropriate? But I liked the idea of a discussion about burying the dead. Corpses, or parts of corpses, lay all over no-man's-land. The stench of decaying bodies, and the shrill squeaking of the rats as they gorged on the remains, never let us forget that, at the Front, death was not the end. Each and every one of us had lost good friends, even relatives, and a decent burial—any kind of burial—was the one thing we could do for men who were beyond all other forms of aid.

But what gifts could we exchange? Our men had nicknamed the trench the Great West Road, and Bond Street it wasn't.

"We've got plenty of plum puddings, sir," said Stephenson. "How about them?"

By God, he was right. "What's your idea," I said, chuckling. "To poison the Germans?"

Stephenson grinned.

Back in London the *Daily Register* had organized a campaign to see that all units at the Front were supplied with plum puddings for

Christmas and, because the *Register* and the rest of the press were watching, the puddings had got through, in huge numbers. Boxes of the stuff occupied as much space as our ammunition dump.

"Brilliant idea, Sergeant," I added. "Let's kill them with kindness. Make the puddings ready, will you." I hated the *Daily Register* and its hysterical jingoistic war coverage, and the idea of off-loading its Christmas gift onto the Germans appealed to me.

If the Germans opposite wanted to discuss burying the dead, we would have to make the most of the time available, so I instructed the men to bring together all our shovels and told Stephenson to start looking for wood, for crosses. It was such a change from my normal type of order that the men set to it with something approaching gusto.

At noon, I was the first out of the trench. It was unnerving to show myself but, after those first heart-stopping seconds, when any one of three hundred Germans could have riddled me with bullets, the fear vanished, to be followed by exhilaration as I stared across the landscape, viewing it like an ordinary person would in peacetime, the sort of ordinary person I had forgotten how to be.

The cut of my uniform and the outline of my cap would have been easily visible from the other side, marking me out as an officer. I walked forward a few paces to our line of barbed wire and stopped. After weeks and months of trench warfare, I can't begin to describe the sense of freedom that being above ground gave me. I felt light-headed. I took out my cigarette case and lit a Craven "A." It was a casual gesture—the kind you made on a London street all the time—but out there it felt ... well, nonchalant, flamboyant, extravagant even. It was a momentary return to an earlier life that we had suppressed. Apart from anything else, the smell of burning tobacco helped kill off the stench of decaying bodies that the intense cold couldn't quite obliterate.

The other officer climbed out of his trench and splashed toward me. He was good-looking, slim, blond, with a straight nose, a well-defined jaw, and he wore a white silk scarf around his neck. Compared with me he was positively dashing.

As he moved forward, I turned and motioned to my men. In a line, they too clambered out of the trench. The German line soldiers did the same.

I had stopped when I had reached the barbed wire but my German opposite number didn't. Many gaps had been blown in the wire, but he found one where a tree had fallen across it, and he stepped into the very heart of no-man's-land. I followed his example.

We had almost come face-to-face, nearly within hand-shaking distance, when a commotion broke out to my left and slightly behind me. I turned quickly, noticing fear on his face, a fear that I felt too. What had happened to interfere with our careful choreography—was it going to be turned into chaos, or even mayhem?

What had happened was that two rabbits in no-man's-land, disturbed by the unexpected presence of so many humans, had suddenly broken cover and bolted. This was too much for the men on both sides. Rabbits—fresh meat—were difficult and dangerous to capture under normal circumstances, but today was not normal circumstances. Today the rabbits did not have the war shielding them. Men on both sides gave chase, shouting and cheering, slip-sliding in the mud, diving this way and that.

The rabbits, of course, were no respecters of barbed wire, still less of no-man's-land, and in no time the men were scattered right across the landscape, so splattered with mud that it was difficult to tell who was who. More to the point, both sides were now *collaborating* in corralling the rabbits, cunningly shepherding them into an unusually large shell crater. Two loud cheers went up as first one, then the other rabbit was captured and held proudly, imperiously aloft by the ears, wriggling and squealing. True to the spirit of the chase, the Germans took one of the rabbits and we claimed the other. I have often wondered what would have happened had only one rabbit appeared.

After that joint success, however, there was no stopping the men. They formed small knots all over the ravaged terrain, shaking hands, swapping tobacco, buttons from their uniforms (strongly forbidden, at least in theory), and showing one another photographs from home.

I turned back to the German officer. We grinned at each other and shook hands. I told him who I was, speaking in German. "Lieutenant Henry Montgomery, Forty-seventh Gloucester Rifles." He replied, to my surprise, in perfect English: "Oberleutnant Wilhelm Wetzlar, Thirty-second Saxon Infantry. Happy Christmas, Henry. I have a present for you." Whereupon he took from the breast pocket of his gray tunic three juicy cigars, each fat as a thumb and about six inches long.

"I can't accept them," I said. (Throughout, I spoke German and he spoke English.) "I have nothing for you, except this." And I shame-facedly produced the box with the plum pudding in it. I felt we British were losing this war of gifts.

"I accept with pleasure," he said, reaching forward. "Tonight, Christmas night, I shall feast on rabbit and Christmas pudding." He laughed. "It will be a dinner I shall never forget."

What could I do in the face of such charm? I took the cigars, smelled them, rolled one next to my ear, before placing them in the breast pocket of my tunic, making myself the silent vow that I would smoke them on special occasions.

"Your English is very good," I said as I buttoned my pocket.

He smiled. He had brown eyes, and his lips were more brown than red too. "Until June I was a teacher in your country."

"You *were?*" I was flabbergasted. "Where?"

"Stratford-upon-Avon. Shakespeare is very popular in Germany—he translates very well. Falstaff called Prince Henry 'Hal,' right, in Shakespeare?"

I nodded. "It's what my family call me."

"Hal it is then." He continued, "I was on an exchange scheme—I taught German in Stratford and my exchange partner taught English in Göttingen, where I work. I was born in Mannheim but I grew up in Göttingen—that's an old, very beautiful university town, like your Cambridge. Where did you learn German?"

I told him about my years in Berlin and Munich.

"Did you ever go to the Paris bar?" he asked.

"On Kantstrasse? But of course. Never before two o'clock in the morning, though."

He laughed again. "I know what you mean. Is there anywhere like that in London?"

"I don't know," I replied. "I worked in London just before the war started, but only for a few weeks. I know Berlin and Munich better than I know my own capital city. And I did a Goethe course in Weimar."

"Well, what's Munich like? I've never been."

"If you're a bohemian it couldn't be better. There are more painters, more playwrights, more musicians, more cabaret performers than anywhere I've ever been. To think I may have killed a few, over the past few weeks and months . . ." I trailed off. "It doesn't bear thinking about. Did you like Stratford?"

He nodded. "The river is very beautiful. Smaller than rivers in Germany, but so many swans. They can be quite aggressive, swans, especially if you get too close to their young. And there are cricket games by the river—such a lovely idea for everyone to dress in white." He smiled. "As Shakespeare has always been popular in Germany, so Stratford is popular too. You know it?"

I shook my head. "No. I've never been. I'm ashamed to say that you are probably more familiar with Shakespeare than I am."

"What a pair we are," he said, grinning again. "You're English and know more about Goethe than I do, and I'm German and know more about Shakespeare. Maybe we should swap places?"

Dare I say it but I liked him. I certainly liked him a good deal more than many of the officers of our own side that I had encountered in Flanders, not all of whom one would want to spend time with back in London.

Nevertheless, I thought it right to bring the conversation around to the business of the bodies. We agreed that we would spend the rest of the day on this task, each side burying its own, and not interfering with the other. We also agreed that we would each repair, as best we could, our own barbed wire, if time allowed. Wilhelm—I think of him as Wilhelm—then asked if the truce should be extended to the following day. I said I couldn't guarantee it, and added that I thought he couldn't guarantee it either. Both sets of top brass were vehemently against fraternization, he and I were disobeying orders as it was, and if word came down later that day from further up the chain of command, both of us would have no choice but to obey. He agreed, but we told each other that we would wait out the night, enjoy our Christmas dinners, and take the morning as it came. I then added that we British would not be the first to fire, unless explicitly instructed to do so by superior officers, and that so far as I was concerned the truce would last until midnight British time the following evening.

He accepted that, and agreed.

We knew the men would take their lead from us, so we prepared to part, to set about the supervising of the burial parties. Just before he turned away, however, he said, "Are you married, Hal? Do you have children?"

"No, twice over. Not married, no children."

"Engaged maybe?"

"No."

"I am." He reached into another of his tunic pockets and took from it a photograph. He handed it to me. It was a portrait of a very beautiful blond woman—a girl really. Clear skin, wavy hair but swept back and held in place by an Alice band. A shy smile of someone who hadn't quite discovered yet what effect she had on men.

"You're lucky," I said. "She's very beautiful. What's her name?"

"Sam."

"Short for Samantha?"

"Oh, no. Her real name is Sally. Sally . . . Ann . . . Margaret Ross, so she's always been called after her initials—S.A.M."

I looked at him.

"Yes, she's English. She's a teacher, at a school in a small village not far from Stratford—that's how we met, when I was on the exchange course. We got engaged just before I was recalled to Germany, in June—I was in the reserve." He took back the photograph of his girl and pulled another from his tunic.

"I have a favor, Hal," he breathed softly. "This is a photo of me in uniform. Sam, of course, has never seen it—she hasn't heard from me since war broke out." He turned the photo over and held it out to me. I shied back, but he kept his hand out. "Her name and the name of the school she teaches at are on the back. Can you see she gets it? It would mean such a lot, to her and to me. I can surely never send it, but you can. I haven't written anything, like a note. That *would* be dangerous, if it were found on you. Or if it were intercepted in any post that you sent to her."

When he saw that I looked doubtful, he took a step forward. "We were very much in love—but will our feelings outlast this war? Will *I* outlast this war? She didn't fall in love with me when I was one of the enemy, and if she had a photo of me, as I am now, maybe that will help clear her mind. She will have to keep the photo secret, of course. How could she live in England if she had a German fiancé? If the photo—the uniform—frightens her, turns her against me . . . well, that's cleaner, honest, we will know where we stand, she can start putting me out of her mind. But I shall never forget her and the first thing I will do when this war is over is go looking for her. This photo will tell her all she needs to know."

He still held out the snapshot. "Will you do it? Will you see that she gets this? Please. As a Christmas favor."

He put the photo of his girl into his tunic pocket, and as he did so I was reminded of the disparity between Wilhelm's gift—the three cigars in *my* tunic pocket, which I had accepted—and the pathetic plum pudding. Agreeing to do as he asked would make up for the disparity, a gesture that would reclaim some British honor in this exchange.

So I took the photograph and put it in my tunic pocket alongside the cigars.

Hospital

THE TRUCE LASTED THROUGH BOXING DAY, though there was no more fraternization, not in our sector anyway. At midnight, however, the war resumed. To begin with, it was weird, shooting at men you'd enjoyed a smoke with. But then the bombardment started up again, the whistle of bullets filled the air at other times, and, inevitably, blood began to flow. The horror and madness resumed where they had left off.

A week later our unit was ordered to make a push for the small village of Plumont. We advanced under cover of dark and, at about eleven forty-five P.M. on Sunday, 3 January 1915, I took a bullet in my groin and the shooting war ended for me. The bullet that found me fractured my pelvis, I went down in a mudflat, and later I was told that I might have drowned but for a lance corporal who found me, saw that I was still breathing, and pulled my unconscious head out of the freezing water. I had passed out from loss of blood and pain and only came to hours later in a hospital tent outside Douai.

"It wasn't easy for that lance corporal," said the medical orderly who told me all this when I recovered consciousness. "But he said he owed you one. Man called Beddoes, or Meadows."

The blood loss was stanched, the pain was stultified with drugs, and I was invalided home, via Calais, Folkestone, and Farnham, to a hospital in the Vale of Evesham called Sedgeberrow. There, my pelvis was reconstructed—to the best of the surgeon's ability—and when the pain was under control my parents were allowed to see me. They had been to the hospital just after I had arrived, as had Isobel on a separate occasion, but I had been too sedated to realize I had visitors.

I didn't know what to expect of my mother and father on their second trip. After all, my injuries were hardly life-threatening. Was my mother, who had been against the war from the start, going to give me the "I-told-you-so" treatment? Would my father be disappointed that I was not more of a hero, and hadn't had any impact on events—that all my "preparation" in Germany had been wasted? They had never shown much emotion when Izzy and I were growing up, so I didn't expect them to gush. We would all have been embarrassed.

In the event, they were surprisingly gentle and took me for a walk around the grounds in a wheelchair. Being in the Vale of Evesham, the grounds of Sedgeberrow were full of fruit trees—apples, pears, and plums mainly, though it was too early in the year for there to be much sign of life. But there was also some market gardening going on— vegetables mainly—so there was plenty to look at and talk about if you liked that sort of thing.

I asked about life back home in Edgewater, inquired after the vicar (whose family was always the subject of much gossip in the village) and my sister. I was told she was in London finishing her training to be a nurse and would come and see me again in due course. At some point, I remember, my mother made an excuse and left my father and me alone. I was in the wheelchair and he was sitting on a bench, and we were watching some ducks meandering about—they seemed to have lost the patch of water they lived on—when my father suddenly burst out, "Hal, I have something to tell you."

This was very unlike him, to be conspiratorial. Though distant, he was usually the most straightforward of men. He was taller than me, and always stooped when he addressed me, so that his hair flopped down over his forehead.

I was aware that I had picked up a few mannerisms from my father and one of the things that he did, which had rubbed off on me, was to set his lower jaw to one side when he was preparing to say something awkward or difficult. He did that now.

What was coming? Was he or my mother ill? Were they getting divorced? Had some disaster befallen my headstrong sister?

"The doctors told us . . . and, well, we elected to tell you, rather than have them do it." He leaned forward and put his hand on my leg. "When that German bullet entered you and smashed your pelvis, it also destroyed your prostate gland. You've been very unlucky, Hal, cruelly damaged, but . . . well, my sad task is to tell you that you'll never be able to have children." He looked straight at me. "This is all painfully personal, but it's better coming from me than from a stranger. You will still be able to have erections and there will be some ejaculate, so I've been told. But no semen and therefore no children." He withdrew his hand and looked away. "I am terribly, terribly sorry."

I didn't say anything.

I didn't say anything then, and I didn't say anything for the rest of the day, for that week. I can't fully explain it even now, but that was the last news I was expecting and, perhaps because of it, perhaps because I was so used to death itself, a profound depression settled over me that I was quite unprepared for and was unable to do anything about. All the descriptions you read about depression are completely inadequate to the task. A black cloud? That doesn't come close. A huge weight pressing down on you? Not at all. If you can imagine such a thing, if such a thing could exist, depression is like being alive in a coffin, down a mine, six miles deep under the ocean, with no light, no air, and, above all, no possibility of escape, no possibility of any other living thing being anywhere near you, where no sound can reach you, no smell, where nothing has any meaning. Think of what you can see behind you—it's not black, is it, but nothing? No color, no texture, no form. That's what depression is—nothing, six miles down.

I don't remember my parents leaving that day and I don't remember them coming to visit me again for weeks on end, though I am sure that they did. I lost interest in everything, even the war. Especially the war, which was responsible for the way things had turned out. I suppose that my depression interfered with my recovery but I don't know that for certain. I do remember that, after a while, a pretty nurse came to see me every day and took me out in the wheelchair and tried to get me walking and talking again. But, though I did start walking, I remained universally, unalterably, dismally morose and mute. Pretty girls were the last thing I wanted to see: what earthly *use* could I be to a woman, pretty or otherwise?

The only woman I wanted to see, the only woman I could be any use to, was Isobel, my sister. She still adored me, the more so now that I had a war wound, which to her made me a genuine war hero. She wrote me a couple of letters from London before she could get away for a visit. "Poor you," she said in one of them, resolutely refusing to hide from my problem, as others were apt to do. "But I've been reading this new book by a doctor, a head doctor—Sigmund someone, a German of all people, or an Austrian, one of the enemy anyway—and he says that people who can't have full sex often channel it into other areas, intellectual, or sporting, or social. That's what you can do— become some big shot at the War Office. You speak fluent German and you have a war wound. Soon as you are up and walking—well, up and limping—they'll have to do something for you."

Sisters can get away with that sort of crack and I looked forward to her letters. They, more than anything, helped me over my depression. And when, eventually, she came to see me, toward the end of May, she worked her magic even more. She was dressed in her nurse's uniform—pale blue—and looked very fetching, my little sister now all grown up and Miss Efficiency herself. First, she refused to take me out in the wheelchair, saying, "No, you can walk the whole way, come on."

"Do they teach you cruelty in that hospital?"

"Come *on!*" And she marched off down the corridor.

I followed.

That afternoon we toured the whole grounds, the first time I had done so on foot. I told her as much. "Good," she said. "Great. But you've got to get better quickly anyway—they need your bed for people who are worse off."

Worse off. She was right. Feeling sorry for myself, turning my back on the war, wallowing six miles down, I had never stopped to think of the people who had had rather more than their prostate destroyed. I had almost forgotten the people I had buried. Izzy's sibling "cruelty" shook me back to the real world.

But what finally caused me to shake myself free of Sedgeberrow was when Isobel screwed up her courage that day and said, "Hal, can I ask you something really, really personal?"

Oh dear. She sounded like our father on the day when he told me about my paternal prospects. Now what? Was Izzy pregnant? Was she secretly married to someone our parents thought undesirable? Did she want me to intervene, to soften the blow?

"You can ask, Izzy," I replied. "I'm not promising to answer, if it's too personal, but fire away. I've never been a spy, if that's what you're going to ask."

"No, no, nothing like that," she said. "If you *were* a spy, I shouldn't expect you to tell me, unless it was in a note, to be opened only after your death."

I couldn't help but grin. My sister always had a gruesome and romantic imagination, which for her were pretty much the same thing.

"Go on, then, what's your question?"

I remember that we were sitting on a bench, near the ducks, which—I had decided—commuted between some distant patch of water and the garden vegetables that grew on the hospital grounds.

"Now, you're not to get angry—promise?"

"How can I—?"

"*Pro-mise!*"

"All right, all right. I promise."

"Okay," she said. "Okay. Here goes." She took my hand in hers. "I couldn't say this sort of thing to Ma and Pa—they would *die*—but . . . well, you've been in Munich and Berlin, and war . . . Are you, are you . . . you've had this depression, I know, so it's unlikely, but—"

"Say it, Izzy, say it. Am I what?"

"I mean . . ." It came out in a rush: "You're not homosexual, are you?"

"Good grief, Izzy!" I jerked my hand away from hers and groaned. "Of course I'm not queer. You've seen how depressed I've been, and you know why. What *on earth* makes you think I'm queer?" I groaned again. "Jee-*sus!*"

"Well, I know it's silly," she said, giggling out of relief, I think, that it was now all out in the open. "You could have been depressed because you couldn't have children . . . that would matter as much to a homosexual as a normal person."

"Izzy," I hissed in what I tried to make a menacing tone. "I repeat that I am not, *not*, queer—but what made you think I *was* homosexual in the first place?"

She took back my hand. "Well, when you were really, really ill, at the very beginning, remember that I came to see you and you were heavily sedated—completely torpedoed. Remember?"

I nodded. "I remember not remembering you were here. Uh-huh."

"Well, I was a bit bored, hanging around for you to wake up—

which you didn't. And I couldn't leave, because I had to wait for the taxi to come back for me."

"Y-e-e-s . . . Get to the point."

"So, well, for something to do I started going through your things—"

"Izzy—!"

"I know, I know, I shouldn't have. Don't get mad—you promised. But I *am* your sister and I did it. I'm too old for you to twist my ear off, like you used to, so *there.*" She grinned.

I didn't grin back.

"And . . . well, in your wallet I found a photo—"

"Jesus Christ!"

"Don't blaspheme. Or think of a new swear word. I imagined it might be a photograph of your girlfriend and I wanted to see what I thought of her, see how pretty she was, that sort of thing, but . . . well, it was a man, a very good-looking man, I have to say, in some sort of uniform." She made a face. "I thought you'd fallen in love in the army— with a man. The photo had a name and address on the back, Sam someone if I remember right. I even thought of writing to him, but I didn't—*I didn't!*" she cried out as my eyes grew rounder and she could see that my temper was beginning to cook.

I took my hand from out of hers, and instead cupped her hands in mine. "That serves you right, Izzy, for sticking your nose—your stumpy button of a nose—where it doesn't belong. And no, you're not too old for me to twist your ears." But I didn't try.

What I did do was tell her the story of the Christmas truce, and my exchange of gifts with the German officer, Oberleutnant Wetzlar.

"Crikey, Hal," she said when I had finished. "I mean, can you do that, act as a sort of messenger? I mean, it's very romantic—I wonder if anyone would take such a risk for me—but isn't it . . . well, *treason?* Will they shoot you if you get found out?"

"Well, I haven't delivered my message yet, have I? And the authorities will only find out if a certain nurse tells them."

But by now Izzy's romantic side was moving into a higher gear, and she was ahead of me.

"Stratford's not far from here, is it?"

It simply hadn't occurred to me, but Izzy was right. I'd been so self-obsessed that I'd forgotten my geography. But she was on the ball; Stratford was not far away at all.

Theft

LEFT TO HERSELF, Izzy would have driven to Stratford the very next day, in our father's car, but I didn't want that. I wasn't sure what I did want but I knew I wanted to move more slowly, and all by myself. What Izzy *had* done, however, was convince me that I preferred to hand over Wilhelm's photograph in person, not entrust it to the post. In that way there would be no chance of me being found out, for passing on something from the enemy, but—more important, I think—Izzy's romanticism had persuaded me that the physical hand-over of the photograph, the actual event, would be an emotional moment that I wanted to experience for myself. That encounter would be wasted if I just slipped the photograph in an envelope and slid it into a postbox. Also, in delivering the letter in person I could describe the Christmas encounter between Wilhelm and me, without setting down anything incriminating on paper. Finally, I have to admit, there was also the fact that Sam Ross was an attractive woman—or she photographed well. I wanted to see her for myself, to talk to her but also to see whether, in the flesh, she lived up to her image in the photo. She had become engaged to a German—how did she feel about him now? Was she still in love with him? The more I thought about it, the more interesting the handover of that small photograph became.

By this time—the time of Izzy's second visit—I had been told by the medical authorities at Sedgeberrow that I would probably always walk with a slight limp. Although the reconstruction of my pelvis had gone well, small bits of bone were missing—shot away; the connection with my left leg was less than perfect, so that, in one way and another, my whole hip area was a good deal less than 100 percent. That wasn't quite as depressing as the news about my prostate, but it wasn't wholly unexpected either. When I reported my medical progress to my commanding officer at Tetbury, he too said he wasn't surprised. "But don't worry, Montgomery," he went on. "We can't let you and your German go to waste. I'll inform the War Ministry—I'm sure they'll need you somewhere in intelligence. Stand by."

So I might get a job that my father approved of after all.

The upshot was that in mid-June the Sedgeberrow medics said I was free to leave their care but would not be suitable for "active duty"—whatever that meant—for two to three months. I told the C.O. and then went home, to Edgewater. But I felt uneasy, back in my old room, with its books and fishing tackle, and cricket bits and pieces. There was a war on, after all. So after three days I wrote off for some German-language books, to make sure I didn't get rusty. The bookseller in London who sent back the books included with it a flyer from the War Ministry that he said he had been instructed to give to all people who bought German-language material from him. It was aimed primarily at women, not at men, and it asked anyone who thought they were proficient in German—"proficient" was the word used, I remember—to consider working for the war effort. It said that if candidates passed a language test, tuition would be provided free of charge, with free board and lodging, in specialist subjects—technology, economics, geography—and it listed several places where these courses were given: Carlisle, Doncaster, Nottingham—and Stratford-upon-Avon. I couldn't believe it until I realized that the school where the tuition was given was probably the self-same language center where Wilhelm Wetzlar had worked before the war. It made sense.

Stratford was the closest anyway, so I applied there, via my commanding officer, and was duly summoned for a test. I borrowed my father's motorcar and, more to the point, his petrol allowance and, in early July 1915, I set out one Sunday for the forty-five-mile drive from Edgewater to Stratford. I put up at a hotel and, at nine-thirty the next morning, presented myself at the school. The test was entirely oral and in my case lasted for all of twelve minutes, as it should have done. My German was near fluent and it was quickly apparent to the examiners that I was supremely qualified for their course. They said I could start the following Monday, and I accepted.

I was killing two birds with one stone on this trip and had driven up from Edgewater relatively slowly so as to conserve petrol for the next part of my journey—a side excursion to Middle Hill, the village where Sam Ross taught. Outside the exam room it was a beautiful day and I opened all the windows in the car as I found the Alveston and Wellesbourne Road, which led east, away from Stratford and toward Middle Hill. The road ran alongside the Avon River for a bit, then through a deer park and part of a sewage works. I passed a construction site, where there was digging and scaffolding. There were hills ahead of me but the road veered off to the left, north. I found Middle Hill easily enough—it was a collection of attractive, red-brick cottages, with a main street that widened at one point, sufficient (as I later found out) to accommodate a market there every Tuesday, at least in peacetime. As you came into the village, the road rose, to form a bridge over a canal and a railway line.

The school wasn't difficult to find either. It was at the far end of the main road, but once I had found it I turned the car round and parked near the village pub, called the Lamb. A small change of plan was beginning to revolve around in my brain. I walked back in the direction of the school. My limp was quite pronounced (and moderately painful) in those days and, since I was in uniform, I attracted appreciative glances from the various people I passed who drew the conclusion that I had been wounded at the Front.

The school was next to the church and built to a much bigger scale than the other village buildings. It had been erected in a more forceful, assertive, bulky style, with stone gables and runnels and architraves. In case there should be any doubt about its purpose, one word was carved in capitals above the main entrance: SCHOOL.

I walked past and went on into the churchyard. A stream skirted the edge, the gravestones reaching all the way down to the sloping bank, where moorhens patrolled in a line. Beyond the stream there was an iron fence with a kissing gate and beyond that what looked like a cricket field. Here it was difficult to believe that we were at war, so peaceful and pastoral was the panorama, so far from Flanders in every way. A woman tidying the graves looked up as my shoes scuffed the gravel. She took in my uniform and smiled, though she didn't say anything. Neither did the vicar, who appeared just then in a black cassock, scurrying like a large moorhen himself out of the church porch. His expression seemed abstracted and I hoped he wasn't the figure of fun and gossip that our vicar back in Edgewater was. He was surprised to see me, I think, and a brief smile unraveled along his lips. But then he scurried on to the woman tidying the graves and engaged her in conversation.

I entered the church. It was small. A large brass cross glistened on the white cloth of the altar. Two bunches of flowers stood on either side of the cross. As I looked around, I could see that there were flowers everywhere, on the pulpit, next to the organ, and the table where the hymn books were stored—this was a much-loved, much-used place. Two rows of pews at the front of the nave were closed off by small wooden doors: private pews, no doubt belonging to the more important personages or families in the area. I hated that sort of thing—my own family had its pew in our village—but I had never done anything about it.

I sat farther back and thought for a bit. I can't say that I had been very religious before the war but, by now, after I had seen what I had seen, whatever residue of faith I might have had had been shot to pieces, like my pelvis. At the same time, the Christmas truce had shown me the power of Christianity to influence some men to behave well. Those with faith behaved better at Christmas, but how could I have faith?

But it wasn't faith that concerned me most that morning. I took out the photograph of Wilhelm. I smiled, recalling Izzy's misunderstanding and her earnest questioning. It was, I supposed, an easy mistake to make.

Sitting in the pew, I also took out my handkerchief and polished the toe caps of my shoes where they had scuffed the gravel outside. This was another mannerism inherited from my father that I couldn't shake. He was obsessive about the shininess of his footwear.

The vicar came back in, wished me a polite "Good afternoon" as he went by, and began taking the hymn numbers from yesterday's service from out of their holder.

With a start, I realized that it must have gone noon. I confirmed it with a glance at my pocket watch. Turning over in my mind the thought that was forming, I got up and went out into the sunshine.

As I approached the school I could see a small knot of mothers gathered by the gate. In the country, unlike the city, many children went home for lunch.

And then, across the playground, I saw her. Sally Ann Margaret Ross. There was no mistake. The same blond hair, the familiar Alice band, the same eyebrows and cheekbones. She was stooping and, from the expression on her face and the stern cast of her mouth, she was ticking off a young child, who had clearly done something wrong, but not very wrong. Maybe Sam Ross wanted the child's mother to see the infant being rebuked, so the punishment would be reinforced at home. At any rate, the lecture didn't last long, for she stood up and shooed the child across the playground, toward its mother. She put a whistle in her mouth and her gaze raked the playground for any other infringement. Apparently, Sam Ross—at least on playground duty—was a strict teacher.

All this flashed through my mind—I remember now—but it was soon gone. For the fact is that my head was awash in other thoughts, thoughts I had had the night before, again in the car on the way to Middle Hill, and again in the church. Sam Ross was taller than I had imagined and she also had a figure that Wilhelm's photo—a portrait only—had not even hinted at. But most of all there had been her manner, when stooping, admonishing the child. It was an amalgam of firmness and tenderness, tempered and graceful—here was a young woman of considerable presence. Her movements matched her beauty. I could easily understand what Wilhelm had seen in her.

For all these reasons and, I told myself, because she was so obviously on "playground duty," I didn't approach her there and then. Instead, I walked on and reached the Lamb. It had opened at noon. There weren't many in the pub and they all fell silent when I entered. It was an appreciative silence, though, not hostile. In fact, after I had ordered a pint of bitter, the barman told me that the first drink was on the house and this, I later discovered, was not unusual for war veterans. (He actually said, "The Kaiser's paying," and grinned.) I thanked him, raised my glass to the others, and then retreated to a table in an alcove to consider what I was going to do. I took out Wilhelm's photo one more time, and then put it away again.

While I was sipping my bitter two things happened that affected my plan. First, I gathered from the general conversation in the bar that a couple of people were billeted in the pub, helping to build an airfield near Wellesbourne, the construction site I had seen on my way there. Then an older man came in. The barman poured him a pint and took from behind the bar a plate with a chunk of bread and some cheese on it. The older man accepted all this and sat near me, reading that day's newspaper. He nodded to me affably and bit into his cheese.

Later, when the cheese and bread were finished, the barman came across to take away the empty plate.

"When's the hearing?" the barman said.

"A month from now," replied the older man.

"And who comprises the jury?"

"The board, you mean? It's not a jury, strictly speaking. It comprises me, as headmaster, one of the teachers, elected by the staff, two school governors, and a school inspector from Coventry—five in all."

"And what are her chances?"

At this, the older man drew a finger across his throat.

The barman disappeared and the headmaster went back to his paper.

Later, I asked the barman for a sandwich but he didn't have any. The headmaster, he said, had a special arrangement. So I ordered a half pint of bitter and sat on, thinking, long after the headmaster had gone back to school for the afternoon lessons.

Eventually, an hour or so later, I drove back to my parents' house. I didn't wait for school to finish, as had been my original intention, and I didn't approach Sam Ross with Wilhelm's photograph.

When I got back to Edgewater, the first thing I did was to buy a secondhand motorcycle going cheaply in the village garage and which my father paid to have renovated (fortunately, the kick-start was on the right side, the side of my good leg). Then, a couple of days later—in what I thought was my niftiest move—I said good-bye to my parents, rode the bike to Middle Hill, and rented a room in the Lamb. They seemed happy to have me, the food could have been worse, there was a garage for my bike, and I could run up a tab at the bar. My course at Stratford was forty minutes away.

It took only a day or so to put my half-formed plan into operation. One evening, when he came in for a late-night whisky, I engaged the headmaster in conversation. He was avid for news, as everyone was, as to what the Front was actually like. He came into the pub most nights and, in less than a week, he had done what I hoped he would do—he invited me to give a short talk at the school, about life at the Front. I said I would be delighted.

And so, the following week the whole school was collected together in the gymnasium, which doubled up when needed as a school hall. The children sat cross-legged on the floor, the staff sat on the stage at one end, and a few parents turned up and stood around the walls. I shook hands with all the staff beforehand, so I was introduced to Sam.

The headmaster had asked me not to frighten the children with too much gore and reality, and so I did not dwell on the atrocities I had seen, the bodies blown to smithereens, the unrecognizable lumps of flesh and hair caught up on the barbed wire, the pitiful screams of grown men beyond the pale and beyond rescue in the shapeless darkness of no-man's-land. I did mention the devastation—I didn't think I could avoid it altogether—but with luck, I thought, the war would be over well before the young children in that gymnasium were old enough to fight.

They were young children who couldn't sit still for very long, and would most likely need to go to the lavatory at any moment. So I talked mostly about the Christmas truce, which was popular with the headmaster and the staff. The children were surprisingly upset about the capture of the rabbits; I think that from where they were sitting, they would have preferred it for the men to have gone hungry than for two rabbits to be killed and eaten. Everyone knew "Silent Night," of course, and could relate to that. I mentioned my meeting with a German officer, and our exchange of gifts—everyone thought the plum-pudding business was very funny—but, and here's the thing, I didn't mention Wilhelm by name or the business with the photograph. And I carefully avoided looking in Sam Ross's direction during that part of my talk. Instead, I moved quickly on to our agreement about the burial of the dead—a suitably uplifting theme for a school environment.

And then it was over. The children gave me three cheers and scampered off. The headmaster invited me and some of the staff back to his office for a sherry, and there I made a point of talking to Sam. I asked her if she lived in the village; she said that she did but she didn't volunteer where. I asked her if she was married; she blushed and shook her head. I said I was staying at the Lamb, that that was where I had met the headmaster, and asked her if she ever went there. Again she shook her head. I asked her what the highlights of Stratford were but she said that, apart from Shakespeare's house, she wasn't sure if there were any.

Wilhelm's photograph of her had been in black and white, of course, but in the flesh, in the blaze of sunlight that swept in through the open French windows of the headmaster's study, she was not so much black and white as gold and white. Her hair, the fine down on the lobes of her ears, on the angle of her jawline, on the smooth expanse of her arms, glowed gold, formed a frame of gold dust against the ivories and creams of her flesh and her open-necked shirt.

I can't say that our first meeting was a resounding success in terms of conversation, but I remember the word that came into my mind to describe her. She was mouthwatering.

I did notice that she seemed a bit cold-shouldered by some of the staff, but I thought nothing of it, not then anyway.

Although our first meeting was not all it might have been, I thought I had time on my side and was not unduly worried. The authorities at Stratford had been a bit miffed when I had told them that I was taking that Tuesday off and most of the time the rules were pretty strict. After all, there was a war on and the government was paying for the course. But when they had found that I was giving a talk at a school, about the war, their attitude softened and I was forgiven.

We worked long hours—nine till six-thirty—but we did get Thursday afternoons off and so the next Thursday I sat in the smoking room of the Lamb, reading. Although the bar was closed, so far as the sale of alcohol was concerned, we residents could use the room to read in, or write in, to talk in, or even doze in. The smoking room had a bay window that enabled you to look along the street. I was thus conveniently placed to keep the school entrance under surveillance and to observe, unnoticed, all comings and goings. I took the opportunity to taste the first of the cigars I had been given by Wilhelm at the time of the truce.

It was raining that day and the knot of mothers waiting for their children outside the school was smaller than usual. The news from the war was not encouraging just then. This was the time when the Czar in Russia had dismissed his chief of staff and tried to run the army himself—catastrophically. I'd had a letter from my sister in London. She was threatening to come and see me in Stratford. "You can't help win this war in the boondocks, you know. There can't be many German submarines in the river Avon. Come to London . . . there's room in the flat and it will be just you and <u>four</u> girls!!!!!" Izzy had always been fond of exclamation marks. "It's my <u>favorite</u> punctuation!!!" she would say when she wrote to me at school. Underlining came a close second.

Three-thirty arrived. The children emerged, and the knot of

mothers dissolved. Ten more minutes passed. I recognized one or two teachers hurrying home, a brave one on a bicycle.

Then I saw Sam. She was wearing a navy blue raincoat, not so very different from those a lot of children wear, and a navy blue sou'wester hat. She looked very young. But the blue of her outfit emphasized the blond of the hair that fell about her shoulders.

I let her go by the Lamb before I slipped out the side door. I stood under the arch at the side of the pub, out of the rain, and watched as Sam stepped into the grocery shop halfway along the Wellesbourne Road. She emerged a short time later, carrying a small parcel, but as she left the shop she turned and shouted something I didn't catch. Although I didn't hear clearly what was said, I sensed that Sam was upset as she hurried off, running across the road and turning right beyond the fountain where the market stalls were pitched on Tuesday mornings.

I followed at a distance. The rain was insistent rather than heavy, but there were few people about. I reached the corner and looked down Newbold Lane. There were houses on either side and at the far end the lane rose where it crossed the canal and then the railway line—the station was at the far end of the village, beyond a warehouse belonging to a local brewery.

Sam was on the bridge and disappearing over it. As soon as she was out of sight I hurried forward, not easy in the rain and given my limp, though the pain was getting easier day by day. Just as I reached the bridge a train rattled by, its smoke and steam billowing out either side of the engine, like a set of old-fashioned whiskers. The locomotive was slowing on its approach to Middle Hill station and for a moment the carriages obscured my view ahead. As they disappeared westward, however, I suddenly saw Sam again. She was standing on the far side of the canal at the door of a lockkeeper's cottage, and she had inserted a key into the keyhole. She had turned, to watch the train, but that meant she was facing away from me and didn't see me watching her. Then she let herself into the cottage and disappeared.

I walked on. I could have asked almost anyone in the Lamb where Sam lived—it was a small village—but I didn't want to advertise my interest in her. Beyond the canal and railway, Newbold Lane became much more of a lane than a road, narrowing to accommodate single-file traffic only, and its surface was more primitive, too—loose gravel. The lane led, I knew, to a pig farm and very soon would become lathered in mud and worse. The rain was heavier than before but I was well wrapped up and I resolved to walk as far as the mud before turning back. I was going to knock on Sam's door—no time like the present—but I wanted her to get home, get out of her wet clothes, and relax first, before I arrived. I didn't want her preoccupied when I made the little speech I had planned.

My mind went back to the war. Recently the French had made a series of attacks on the Germans but had been rebuffed. One of the problems was an overall lack of strategy. General Joffre, commander in chief of the French forces, was a law unto himself and that only meant that the Allies, as a fighting unit, were less than the sum of their parts. It couldn't go on and a summit was planned. The sculptor Henri Gaudier-Brzeska had just been killed in a charge at Neuville-St.-Vaast.

The mud on the road was thickening, as was the smell of pig. The shine on my shoes was definitely under threat, so I turned round. I was now walking into the rain, which sliced against my face like grains of shrapnel. As I came within sight of the bridge again, my heart did a somersault in my rib cage. A woman was walking along the towpath, away from the lockkeeper's cottage. Was Sam going out again so soon? Had I missed her on my way to and from the pigs? Then I realized that the woman on the towpath was not Sam, and was probably no more than fifteen. In fact, I recognized her as one of the girls who sang in the Middle Hill church choir.

She had her head down because of the rain and didn't see me. I let her get well out of sight; then I climbed down the steps off the bridge and continued on to the towpath. In the distance a narrow boat was gliding slowly toward the lock gates but it was minutes away. The raindrops pelted the surface waters of the canal in tiny explosions.

I reached the cottage and pushed at the low gate. The hinge complained in a soft whine.

I stood for a moment at the door before knocking. Did I really want to do what I was about to do? I heard a kettle whistling and I thought I heard a baby crying somewhere. Suddenly the smell from the pig farm wafted across the meadows and shook me into action.

I knocked on the door.

After a delay, Sam appeared. "Oh!" she gasped, obviously as surprised as I hoped she would be. "Oh."

"I hope I'm not intruding," I said softly, taking off my hat, despite the rain. Cold water sluiced down the back of my neck.

"No, oh no." She had on a striped apron. "Put your hat back on, please, you'll get soaked. How did you know where I lived?"

"They know everything at the Lamb," I lied, putting back my hat.

I noticed that she didn't ask me in. Was someone else there? I'd come too far to pull back now.

"I wondered . . . there's a dance in Stratford on Saturday, I thought you might like to go."

She looked at me without blinking.

"Well," I said, "I know dancing is not exactly my strong suit, not with this leg, but . . . there'll be lots of people, a bar, music . . . it's a change from village life. What do you think?"

She bit her lip. "I can't go out, not at night anyway." Then she added in a half whisper, "No, not nights."

What did she mean by that? That she didn't want to go out *at all?* That she didn't want to go anywhere with *me?*

The pig smell intensified.

I tried again. "We could always go to Stratford for lunch, walk by the river. Visit Shakespeare's grave—though I'm sure you've done that." It sounded lame.

But she was nodding. "Yes, yes, I'd like that. The river there . . . it's where—" She trailed off, but I knew what she'd almost said. It was where she and Wilhelm had courted, back in the spring of 1914.

That told me . . . not a lot, exactly, but enough for now. Don't rush your fences, I reminded myself.

"How are you on motorbikes?" I said.

"What?"

I raised my voice above the rain. "I have a motorbike."

"Oh no, far too dangerous. I mean, I've never been on one, but I've seen them. They go so fast—thirty miles an hour even. Oh no. Especially now that—" She checked herself, and I didn't press it.

"Let's take the train," she said. "I'll meet you at the station at eleven-thirty."

"You don't want me to come for you here?"

"No. Meet me at the station at half past. Don't worry, I won't be late." She half-closed the door. It was clear that this was a dismissal. She smiled, closed the door fully, and immediately opened it again. "Thank you," she said in a whisper. And then the door was closed a second time.

I have said next to nothing about my German course at Stratford. Housed in an old agricultural college on Wood Street, the language school had been operated as a private outfit in the days of Wilhelm Wetzlar, when its chief job was to teach German and other languages to graduates who had obtained a scholarship to study at European universities, such as Göttingen, Heidelberg, Paris, and Bologna. And to teach English to foreigners. On the outbreak of fighting, the War Ministry had taken it over. The school now taught interpreters, interrogators, propaganda people, translators, budding spies, would-be diplomats—anyone with a gift for languages whose talent might come in useful at some stage (there was no *strategy* so far as I could see). There were fewer women in the course than I'd expected after reading the Ministry of War brochure I had been sent by the London bookseller. The men were mainly army, with a few naval types thrown in. One or two were, like me, injured.

The "Ag," as it was called, was built on three floors and must have been quite old, for it was very short of staircases. In fact, had it not been for the war, I am sure it would have been closed down as a fire risk. There were, naturally, no lifts and only one of the new telephone machines: in the office belonging to the director of studies, so it was hardly accessible. Built of stone, the whole building echoed—a cough barreled down the corridors like the clap of a shell at the Front. The canteen, on the ground floor, stank of brown food—brown soup, brown meat (though that's being kind; it was often gray), brown onions, brown sausages. Fortunately, Stratford was well endowed with pubs. A cricket team had been formed but my limp ruled me out other than as an umpire, which didn't appeal.

Because of my two years in Germany I was entered in the senior course of advanced technical German, learning specialist scientific, economic, geographical, and military terms. The idea was that, with my military experience and my language proficiency, I would eventually be attached to the general staff of some forward unit, translating captured documents or even interrogating prisoners. I didn't object: it would impress my father and seemed useful enough work for a wreck with a limp.

I settled in fairly well, the only problem—which we all faced—being a certain Major George Romford, second-in-command and director of studies. He had a blue chin where, however close he shaved, the follicles fought back, giving him a stubble that never quite went away. He had a mustache like a brush, which, I suspect, camouflaged a harelip. And he had the largest Adam's apple I have ever seen—it must have been the size of a duck's egg. Whenever he spoke, it did a jig in his throat and I couldn't take my eyes off it, except to notice that his shoes could have been shinier.

Major Romford was an old-fashioned class warrior who had been born into a docker's family in the East End of London and, to his credit, had worked his way up. He had obtained a brilliant degree at London University, spoke three languages other than English, and looked upon anyone who hadn't been born in the rough end of town and gone to his beloved "school of hard knocks" as a weakling in need of building up through a regime of being pulled down. The translations, pronunciation, and sentence construction of someone like me were never good enough for George Romford, even though we both knew that I spoke German with a better accent and a greater natural fluency than he did, which was a cause of bitterness on his part. (He had learned his German in school and had never been abroad, so it wasn't surprising that I had the better accent and usage, but that of course never came into his calculations.) He particularly hated me, not only because of my superior accent and because I hadn't grown up in a tenement or the workhouse but also because I had my own transport and so could get away from the college (and him) with unparalleled speed and efficiency. I spent my time at the Ag dodging Romford and avoiding his eye whenever he gave a class. He was particularly smarmy in his dealings with women, and that didn't endear him to me either.

Despite this drawback, I did learn some technical German on the course, enjoyed it, and even found some books on German science and history in the Stratford library that helped fill me in on the general background to the technical terms I was learning.

On Saturday morning Sam and I met as arranged on the platform of Middle Hill station. (There was only one platform for both the "up" and "down" trains.) She was on time as she had promised; I bought the tickets and we stood awkwardly together, waiting for the train. The sun was out, the birds were near deafening, and though I felt awkward I was in a good mood. I'd been for a walk that morning (my limp was improving all the time) and had picked a buttercup for my buttonhole.

Sam looked a picture. She wore a pale blue woollen coat, with a matching Alice band. If anything, she was more beautiful than on any of the previous occasions I had seen her.

Before I could say anything, two young children—who had spotted her before I had—rushed up to her.

"Miss! *Miss!* We're going to Bristol, like you said," shouted one breathlessly.

"Our Colin's a sailor on a boat," chorused the other.

"He's going off somewhere secret and we're saying good-bye."

Sam was sitting on her haunches, down at their level. "Now calm down, Maureen. Don't shout, Brian."

She was back in her playground role, as I had seen her the very first time. Friendly, but firm.

She looked up at me and smiled, as she listened to what they had to say. They had obeyed her instantly, crowding closer to her and talking away nonstop, but much more quietly now. As the signal clanked down and the hiss of the train could be heard, they broke off and ran back to their parents, along the platform.

Sam stood up.

"What was that all about?"

She took a handkerchief from her bag and wiped her lips. "I have a thing about travel. I've always wanted to visit every place on earth and now, with this war on, it's not going to happen anytime soon. I was reading to the class the other day, from a travel book, and we were talking about far-off places. I said everyone should travel, as soon as they could, as far as they could. They have the chance to go to Bristol—that's a long way for them—and they wanted me to know."

"They're going to Bristol and back by train?"

"Yes." She nodded. "Poor mites—they'll probably fall fast asleep in class on Monday, but they'll have seen Bristol. All the other children will want to know what it's like. Maureen and Brian will be . . . what's the word, what do they call Mary Pickford? A star, that's it. They'll be stars for a day." She smiled again.

The 11:38 moved off at 11:48 and, soon after we left the station, the train passed the lockkeeper's cottage where Sam lived. I was surprised to see, standing outside the cottage and waving, the young girl I'd observed when I'd called on Sam, the girl who sang in the choir. That set me thinking.

The train wasn't busy and we had a compartment to ourselves. Sam unbuttoned her coat and sat back in her seat. As the train picked up speed and the smell of smoke from the engine came at us in wafts, she pointed out various villages we passed: Charlecote, Littleham Bridge, Avoncliffe. The line crisscrossed the green-dark waters of the Warwickshire canals a few times, and she knew their names as well. Her body, under her coat, was more than a match for the countryside.

"Have you been sailing on the canals?"

"Of course, many times. But it's a bit slow for me. I like speed."

Why hadn't she wanted to go on my motorbike, I wondered.

At Stratford we got off and Sam waved to the children who were going on to Bristol. Away from the station, we decided to have a walk around town to begin with, to work up an appetite, then have lunch at a pub we both knew, the Crown, and take a longer walk by the river in the afternoon. I knew the main streets of Stratford pretty well by now, but Sam knew the back alleys and mews, the secret yards and dead ends where many of the older establishments were to be found—blacksmiths, stables, foundries, saddlers. The road led us by the ferry, past a church and a water mill. I noticed the high proportion of women working in the blacksmiths and in the foundry—the men, I assumed, were away fighting. It may sound odd, but at times I was grateful for my limp. It explained why *I* wasn't abroad, doing my bit.

At one point we stopped off at a small mews house that, according to the sign outside, was a woodworker's shop. "Come on, look inside," said Sam. "This is where to come if you ever need a new walking stick—or a wooden leg." She flashed me a grin.

I did as I was told.

Inside, there were three men working—one man and two boys, really. But they were not what drew the eye. What you couldn't help but notice was what was on the walls. Those walls, made of old, long, brown bricks, were covered in every type of tool you could imagine. All pegged to the brickwork in a neat arrangement, each with its place—where the workmen knew how to find them—were the most beautifully crafted implements: planes, in shiny polished wood, bradawls, bodkins, drills, awls, hammers with different kinds of heads, prongs, small pickaxes, knives of varied shapes and sizes, chisels, spokeshaves, cleavers, adzes, whittles, naked blades, and rasps. The overall effect was like the huge abstract collages I had seen in Munich.

"How did you stumble across this?" I asked.

"There's a woodwork teacher in school. He brought me here. I love tidiness. Have you ever seen anything like it?"

"Not in Stratford," I said. "Someday I'll tell you about my time in Munich. But this is stunning, stunning."

We waved good-bye to the three men.

Gradually, we worked our way back to the Crown. Sam knew one of the waitresses there, who was introduced to me as Maude, and she gave us a good table with a view of the yard, where, in the old days, the coaches would have unloaded. The yard contained a number of barrels—empty, I presumed—which were waiting to be exchanged for full ones the next time the brewery made a delivery.

There wasn't much choice on the lunch menu—it *was* wartime, after all—but it was a good deal less brown than the canteen at the Ag and I remember the hotel actually served a fish course after the soup: very civilized.

I don't remember too much about the Crown itself on that occasion because by now I was totally smitten with Sam. I have only fallen in love once in my life and it happened immediately, totally, and right there in the back alleys and dead ends of Stratford. Sam, I realized, was trying to keep her distance even as I was trying to get closer. As we had poked about the hidden side of Stratford she'd spoken as if she were a guide and I a paying tourist. Had she given Wilhelm this treatment to begin with? I put it out of my mind. During our "tour" there were no intimate little glances or smiles, there was no squeeze of my arm, no physical contact of any kind. But I could tell she was not indifferent to me either. She was seeing how I responded to what she had to say, how I dealt with the difficulties she was putting in my way. And yes, she was a bit shy. I was just glad to be with her.

Before lunch we both had a sherry. With the food I had a pint of bitter and she drank shandy—half beer, half lemonade. By now she had taken off her coat, to reveal underneath a white frock, buttoned down the front. When she shook off her coat, she also released more perfume. This, plus the fact that the frock was a shade—though no more than a shade—too small for her, was the most alluring experience I think I had ever had to that point, not excluding the Eleven Executioners cabaret in Munich, or Crimson. It was, conceivably, the most erotic moment of my life.

During the first part of lunch she said it was my turn to talk, that she was talked out after our tour of the town. I wasn't sure that was the truth—she was still keeping a distance from me—but I was happy to let it go. So I did what lovers (or would-be lovers) do at times like that. I gave her my life story, or an edited version of it, designed to make her think well of me.

I told her how I had grown up in the Cotswolds, not on a farm exactly—we lived in a large house next to the church in a small hamlet—but otherwise surrounded by farmland and the beech woods of the wolds.

"So, from an early age I was familiar with which mushrooms could be eaten and which toadstools were poisonous, where the badgers came out at night, and where the bluebells formed their plush, iridescent carpet in spring. I remember even today the damp smell of bluebells in the beech woods in late April—I was so familiar with those beech woods, and so familiar a sight there myself, that even the foxes learned to recognize me and stopped being afraid.

"In the summer the foliage of the beech trees formed great cathedral-shaped spaces high above, bathed in a green-golden light, through which sunbeams sliced down in dramatic diagonal shafts. At other times of the year, when it was cold and it rained, my sister and I would bend twigs into a hoop and collect wet—or, better still, frosted—cobwebs from the hedgerows, so that they formed intricate, beautiful lacework patterns that we held up to the light. Endless streams cut through the wolds, in deep, secret folds, where water rats, moorhens, and the occasional snake could be glimpsed.

"Everyone—all the local children, anyway—knew in which field the farmer kept his bull and for us younger ones—admonished sternly to keep away—that only made that field seem lusher, greener, more mysterious, and altogether more desirable than all the other fields put together. The iron fence to the field contained a kissing gate. This kept the bull in but didn't keep us children out when there weren't any adults about. We devised a daring game in which the aim was to see how long we could stay in the forbidden field before the bull saw us, or smelled us, and came looking, first at a trot, then, as he got closer, at a rush (we called the game 'Bullrush'). Then you scampered back through the kissing gate and taunted the bull from safety. I remember we once stayed in the field until we had counted to four hundred and forty-four, a magic number for my sister and me ever afterward. Then I was given my first pocket watch and we timed how long we could remain in the field. It wasn't the same, and soon afterward we began to lose interest.

"The vicar in our village had five daughters and a big scandal arose when one of them was made pregnant by a local farmhand." Sam's cheeks reddened, but I pressed on. "She was fifteen at the time, a year older than me, and my secret shame and embarrassment was that I had once kissed her, in the back corridor of the dark and rambling vicarage. I later found out that she kissed anybody and everybody, but at the time I remember being worried sick that *I* had made her pregnant by that illicit kiss. But the police never came looking for me and after a while my guilty feelings subsided. The daughter was taken away and I never saw her again, much to my regret. I had enjoyed that kiss and would have risked it again.

"My sister was two years younger than me and we always did everything together—well, she didn't kiss the vicar's daughter, obviously. I was the leader in all games and expeditions and she was content to be my trusty lieutenant."

"What's your sister's name?" said Sam, between mouthfuls.

"Isobel. Izzy."

"Was she a tomboy?"

"Not really. Why do you ask?"

"One of my sisters was a tomboy—always bullying the rest of us and leading us into scrapes."

"No, Izzy was—is—really quite feminine. Not a tomboy at all. She's become a bit of a bully now, though. She's a nurse, or training to be. Bossiness seems to go with the job."

"Will she join up? You can travel as a nurse, especially in wartime. Teachers don't get to travel." She made a face. "Sorry for interrupting. Go on."

"I don't know what my sister has planned. She's been living in London and we've lost touch a bit. But we used to be close."

And I told Sam about the first expedition my sister and I embarked on, if you can call it that. It occurred when I was about seven and Isobel was five, when we were allowed to sleep out in a tent in the garden overnight. "We lit a fire, with the aid of our parents, and cooked—or, rather, burned, cremated, sacrificed, *incinerated*—some sausages, which we then nibbled and pretended that we were enjoying. Isobel was a bit frightened by the owls later in the night and, to tell the gospel truth, so was I. But I played the big brother role to perfection, and we fell asleep with our arms around each other, inside the same sleeping bag.

"Our biggest expedition was to watch the Severn Bore. The river Severn was about ten miles from where we lived and at certain times of the year, especially in the spring and autumn, when tides were strong in the Bristol Channel, a wave, about four feet high, was produced by the sharp narrowing of the channel, and moved steadily up the river, certainly as far as Sharpness and maybe even farther, for all I know. People traveled for miles around to see the bore, but for children the game was to sit somewhere on the bank where you were at risk of being caught by the wave, and then play "Chicken." You sat or stood on the bank until the last possible moment, before the wave got you— and then you ran. Oh, how you ran! The last person to move won.

"Of course, our parents would never have let us play this game, had they known, but Isobel and I sneaked off as soon as we had bicycles. It wasn't hard to cover the ten miles to the river, even though there were some hills in the way. When the tide was right, we could get back easily before dark. Our parents were very strict about us being in the house before nightfall at all times of the year, which meant we couldn't play the really dangerous game of beating the bore at nighttimes. We heard the older children talking of this, when we reached the river, and we were both truly in awe of them. To wait by the river, without being able to see the bore coming, and to judge its speed and distance only from the sound it made was truly impressive. People occasionally got it wrong, of course, and sometimes drowned. There were children we saw by the river every time we went who we didn't see at other times of the year. They were curious friendships, but intense for the short time they lasted."

"We had big tides in the Bristol Channel," said Sam, chewing hard. "That's where I grew up, Bristol. The tides occasionally caused floods. Afterward, my sisters and me would go down—when we were allowed to—and look at the fish and eels that had got trapped when the water receded. Ugly things, eels." She shuddered. "Untidy things, floods."

I nodded. "But village life in the Cotswolds was not all owls and bluebells. In Edgewater we had an epileptic who had regular fits, and all of the children were taught that if we saw Martin having a convulsion, we had to take out our handkerchiefs—we were not allowed out of the house without a handkerchief in our pocket—and hold his tongue with it, so he didn't swallow it and choke to death. Then another child ran for help. No one laughed at epileptics in our village, nor were we frightened of them, as some people are in towns."

Sam wiped her lips with her napkin. "I know what you mean. We have two children in Middle Hill who are epileptics. It's just an illness, but fits frighten young children. It upsets the whole class for the rest of the day when Alice or Barry has a fit. Poor tykes." She swallowed some shandy. "I think we should teach more medical knowledge than we do."

I cut into my food. "There were poor people who lived in our village too. They were called tinkers and we weren't allowed to play with them, not officially anyway, but we knew all about them, especially how infrequently they washed, and how badly they treated their emaciated ponies.

"And we had a murder. The tinkers liked to trap animals in the woods with those metal contraptions that snap shut when you tread on them, and grip you in an iron jaw with zigzag teeth. They were always being told how dangerous the traps were but they didn't listen. And then one day, or more likely one evening, a man stepped on one and a metal tooth sliced through an artery in his leg. He must have screamed and screamed but no one heard him and, overnight, he bled to death. At the trial the tinker pleaded guilty to manslaughter but not to murder—the local paper was full of nothing else for days on end. However, the Crown—the prosecution—wouldn't accept it. They argued that the very fact of the trap being placed in the woods meant that the tinker intended harm of some sort. And indeed the tinker was found guilty of murder and sentenced to death.

"On the strength of it all, the children from our village became celebrities at school. And we became amazingly familiar while we were very young with the legal difference between manslaughter and murder. For weeks we discussed nothing else—that and the difference between an artery and a vein. We had all been scared by the murder—though we would never have admitted as much—but we must have known more about first aid than any other children in the land.

"The tinker was hanged a few weeks later. I shall never forget the Tuesday it happened. Most people thought he should die, but our village lived that day in silence.

"Sorry," I said after a moment. "That's all a bit dark."

She nodded, smiling. "I'd like to hear about your family, your parents."

"Well, I was not especially close to my father but I respected him. My grandfather—who I never knew—had started a book publishing business and it had been very successful. Montgomery & Mann published novels, history, and science books mainly, and by the time my father joined the family firm the company had offices in Edinburgh and New York as well as in London."

"Have you been to New York?"

"No. Not even Edinburgh."

"I'd *love* to see New York. I'd risk those submarine things if I had the chance."

"You *would*?"

"I told you, I've got this . . . this wanderlust. I'm just sitting out the war. Once it's over, I'm going to travel, travel, travel. But I'm interrupting again—sorry. You were telling me about your father—he *must* have been to New York."

"Yes, a couple of times, I think. To see how the business operated there. He once told me he had had the idea in the back of his head to emigrate but then he met my mother and she hated the idea. So no move was ever made—my mother is quite unlike you in that respect."

Sam smiled. "Go on."

So I explained that when my father was about forty-five, and I was

fifteen—as I pieced the story together later—*his* father received an offer from a big conglomerate, an offer that was, as the saying goes, too
good to turn down. "Six months later, my grandfather died of a heart
attack and my father inherited the money. He stayed on at the firm for
a while, although he didn't need to work, but he gradually lost sympathy with what the conglomerate was doing with the company, and so,
around the time I was in Germany, he left.

"He was, therefore, a bookish man. And he was, I think, more interested in ideas than in people. There were books everywhere in the
house and for that reason, among others, he didn't feel the need—as
so many of his friends did—to send his son away to prep school. One
effect of this was that Izzy and I had from an early age a life independent of our parents, making us self-reliant. At the same time, we had
a content family life. Christmas, Easter, and birthdays were celebrated
but not ostentatiously—one gift was enough for anyone, in my parents' opinion. My sister and I were made to play outdoors in most
types of weather but this wasn't cruel, and when either of us was genuinely ill our parents were very solicitous.

"I did go away to boarding school when I was thirteen. But even
then I didn't go far off. It was at boarding school that my first interest
in Germany began to form. One of my father's jobs when he was still
in publishing was to keep up with German scholarship, which was
then the equal of—and in many respects superior to—both British and
American scholarship, in history, medicine, engineering, and chem-
istry, for example. So I always took an interest in the German language, German history, and German science.

"I'm talking too much," I said, suddenly noticing that Sam had
long finished her lunch, whereas mine was eaten less than halfway
through. "Sorry," I added. "Why don't you talk for a bit while I attack
this fish."

"Okay." She smiled. "If you can run to another shandy."

My glass was empty too. I waved to Maude, the waitress, and ordered more drinks.

"I'll bet your life was more interesting than mine," I said.

She bit her lip, in a way that I had noticed her do before. "Yours sounded idyllic, as family life should be, reserved but content, not disfigured by war. But I'm sure you left out lots of bits that weren't idyllic."

I shrugged, chewing. "Epileptic fits, gypsies, murder—it's the best I can do."

"I'm one of four girls," she said after a pause. "A family a bit like your vicar's. I grew up in Bristol. My father was in the merchant navy so he was away a lot. Maybe that's where I got my wanderlust, but I'm not so sure. When he was home my father drank and we learned to dread it. He hit my mother. She never did anything in retaliation, not then. But one time, when he went back to sea and she knew that he would be away for weeks, if not months, she simply packed up all our things, and we moved out. We lived in a rented, furnished flat, so it wasn't difficult. She took us to London, where she had a sister—we're a family of women," she sighed, with a smile.

"My mother was a seamstress and so was Ruth, my eldest sister, a good few years older than the rest of us, and they found work easily enough—we other girls were too young. We moved to a flat near my aunt and we were all much happier than we had ever been in Bristol. At weekends, we visited all the museums, Buckingham Palace, the Tower of London, the Houses of Parliament. Then our mother was taken on as a jacket maker for one of the tailors in Savile Row in the West End—you know, where all the rich people have their clothes made. She used to go there, to deliver and pick up work, twice a week, and on one visit she met one of the customers. She was pretty, my mother, and this customer—his name was Mortimer Stannard, *Sir*

Mortimer Stannard—was very taken with her. He started inviting her out for dinner, to the theater, even one time to the races. She made her own clothes and of course looked lovely."

She paused. "You can probably guess what comes next."

When I shook my head, she added, "Why don't we continue this by the river? We're missing the best part of the day and you are not getting the share of fresh air your parents would want."

She was teasing me but she was right about it being the best of the day, so we skipped pudding and coffee, I paid the bill, and within twenty minutes we were strolling by the Avon. The river at Stratford is wide, the banks are flat, making the river seem wider still, and at that time of year the water meadows were choked with dandelions, like a vast spread of butter.

Because it was Saturday, the river itself was quite busy. Men and boys sat fishing, punts and rowboats chased ducks off the water, and there were even one or two hardy souls swimming. Compared with the Severn Bore it was all very tame.

After a few hundred yards, however, the fishermen began to thin out, the punters and rowers had all turned back, and, for the most part, and not counting the wildlife, we had the Avon to ourselves.

"That's Luddington in the distance," said Sam, pointing to a church spire showing above some lush trees.

"No," I said, stopping for a moment and putting my hand on her arm. "I can't guess what's coming next."

We resumed walking.

"Our father found us," she said. "He knew where Mother's sister lived and threatened her with violence if she didn't reveal where we had all gone. He arrived, drunk as usual, in a foul temper, and set about my eldest sister because our mother wasn't at home."

Sam stopped again. "See that?"

I looked. On the river was a swan with two small, dirty brown cygnets. We had chanced upon them and we were, in fact, a little too close for the mother swan's comfort. Her long neck was lowered and she was hissing in our direction.

We eased away and the swan relaxed. Hadn't Wilhelm said something about the swans at Stratford?

"People are no different from other animals," Sam whispered, as if her full voice might disturb the swan all over again. "My sister, for instance. Ruth is not my mother. She is—or used to be—the tomboy I told you about. Anyway, when my father set about her she set about him back—with a kitchen knife. She cut him in the arm, that enraged him still further, he lunged at her and, being drunk already, clumsily stumbled on something—and fell onto the knife Ruth was holding. None of us knew what to do, and he bled to death on the kitchen floor."

She stopped, bent down, and tugged at some long grass.

I didn't know what to say. I could see why she thought I'd had an idyllic upbringing.

"My sister was never charged with anything. When Mortimer Stannard found out what had happened, from my mother, he was marvelous. He employed a lawyer, who took a statement from my mother's sister, which confirmed that our father was belligerently drunk that day, had threatened my aunt with violence, and we sisters all testified that he had hit Ruth first and had fallen onto the knife."

I wondered whether that part was true.

Sam threw the clump of grass she was holding into the air and the breeze took it away. "Anyway, our father's death left our mother free to marry Sir Mortimer. She did, but not immediately and even then quite quietly, on a ship, and after he had paid for the three younger girls to be sent to boarding school, and from where I won a scholarship to teacher training college."

"I'm relieved the story has a happy ending."

She looked at me without blinking. I noticed that her eyes were watering. "My mother and Sir Mortimer were married by Captain Edward John Smith, master of the *Titanic*."

Pause.

"You mean—?"

She bit her lip and nodded.

So much for a happy ending.

We had come to a fence, an iron fence with a kissing gate.

"Shall we turn back?" I said as softly as I could.

She nodded.

I gave her my handkerchief to dry her tears.

We walked most of the way back in silence. Halfway along the bank, however, she slipped her arm through mine. Now, what did that mean? Affection? Too early. More likely she just needed some human contact after the emotional effort involved in telling her story. I squeezed her arm with mine.

I didn't say much until we were sitting in the train, waiting for it to leave Stratford station. "What happened between teacher training college and Middle Hill?"

"The college was in London, and in 1913 I came to a Shakespeare conference in Stratford." She bit her lip again. "Shakespeare's tragedies were my thesis subject at college. At the conference I met two teachers from the Middle Hill school, we got on, they mentioned there was a vacancy—and here I am."

"So it's your first teaching job?"

"Oh yes. I'm not . . . you know . . . that ancient."

I grinned. "Do you like it?"

She didn't say anything for a moment. Then the whistle sounded, the train juddered forward, and we were leaving the station. Amid all the steam and smoke and fuss of leaving, my question was never really answered.

The train wasn't so empty on the way back, it was difficult to talk about personal things, and we both dozed off for a bit. The sunny day was turning cloudy and my mind, even when I dozed, was fastened on whether or not I could risk kissing Sam on the cheek when we parted. Was it too soon? I didn't want to be rebuffed.

I walked her home from Middle Hill station, but when we turned off the bridge on to the canal towpath, Sam actually *offered* her cheek to be kissed. It was a dismissal but I was thrilled, and didn't attempt to go further.

"Will you be at church in the morning?" I asked.

She shook her head.

"How about a walk in the afternoon?"

She nodded. "I'd like that. I'll meet you at two-thirty in front of the school."

Once again she didn't seem to want me to pick her up.

She turned and walked on down the towpath.

I touched the cheek where she had kissed me.

So, there we have it. I had not mentioned Wilhelm and now had no intention of doing so. I was, so far as I knew, in love with Sam and at that point would probably have concealed any inconvenient fact, told any untruth—any lie—to have ingratiated myself with her. To be honest, I didn't go into the rights and wrongs of it all very much, not then. The war might last a long while.

The moment Sam and I parted, by the canal, that Saturday, I missed her. Though I had just spent hours in her company, I wasn't sure that I remembered her features properly. Yes, I recalled her smell exactly and vividly, the characteristic way she bit her lip, the way her Alice band shaped her face, how she held her knife and fork, the way the muscles in her throat moved when she swallowed her shandy. But I needed to see her face again, and soon.

The next day it rained. It rained as if it were winter, with a cold, insistent intensity, as if it were trying to stunt the growth of all the vegetation rather than make it possible. I went to matins, to help pass the time, because although I had no faith I still enjoyed singing the hymns I had been brought up with, and because I hoped that when the service was over the downpour would have ceased. If anything it was worse—low clouds, gray and somber as a German's uniform.

Those of us resident at the Lamb took our weekend lunches in a back room where we had dinner during the week. This was a sort of conservatory, and that day the rain rattled on the glass panes like staccato machine gunfire. I was on edge the whole time because I was apprehensive in case the rain would cause Sam to cancel our walk.

At two twenty-five precisely I let myself out the side door of the Lamb, eased into the street, and set off toward the school. I was wearing my raincoat, the collar turned up against the weather, and a tweed hat that Isobel had given me. My face got wet but I could live with that. Given the rain, I was not surprised to find that the high street—Wellesbourne Road—was deserted. An automobile went by, one of the newfangled Lanchester types, but the windows were steamed up so I couldn't see if it was being driven by anyone I recognized. I reached the gateway to the school and stood where the wall offered some small amount of shelter.

Would she come? There was no sign of her at two-thirty, or at two thirty-five. (I still had the same pocket watch I'd been given as a boy, the one I had used to time how long Isobel and I had stayed in the field with the bull.) From where I was standing, I could see as far as the church graveyard and I watched the flowers on the graves being pelted by rain.

When I turned back to look up the Wellesbourne Road, past the Lamb, there she was. The navy raincoat, the matching hat, her unmistakable figure. *She had come.* In no time she stood before me, offering a rain-soaked cheek to be kissed. I reveled in the pungence of her perfume. Raindrops were caught in her eyelashes.

"I thought you might not come."

"Because of some rain? Silly! Didn't it ever rain in your golden childhood?"

"Where would you like to go?"

Without hesitation, she pointed. "If we go down here, then follow the canal to the north, we get to Hampton Gorse after about thirty-five minutes. With any luck the tearoom there will be open."

We set off.

"Did you get to church?" she asked.

"Yes, I saw Katharine in the choir."

She nodded.

The rain was as insistent as ever and when we reached the canal we could see that the wind swept the waters into minuscule waves, the tips of which were whipped white in fury. No fishermen today.

"And you had lunch at the Lamb?"

I nodded.

These were seemingly innocuous questions but I knew enough now to understand where she was going.

"Sam . . . I know about the baby."

She didn't react in any way that was obvious. Her step never faltered; she didn't turn toward me but held her face steady into the wind and the rain.

I had finally put two and two together that morning in church, and fleshed out my inferences in the Lamb at lunchtime. Sam had a baby son. Very young. The tall girl, Katharine, whom I had seen in the vicinity of the lockkeeper's cottage, was her babysitter, and that's why Sam couldn't go out at night—Katharine, though she had left school, was herself too young to be allowed out after dark. And it explained why Sam hadn't been in church that morning: Katharine had to sing in the choir, and Sam didn't want to take the child out too much in public.

These details also put into context the conversation I had overheard the very first time I had visited the Lamb, between the barman and the headmaster. The fact that Sam, a schoolteacher, had had a child out of wedlock was regarded by some in the village as wicked, very wicked, unforgivably wicked, the work of the devil himself and an appalling moral example to the young children in her charge in class. I have to admit that, to begin with, I was shocked myself. It didn't fit with the image I had of Sam, or with the kind of woman I'd hoped she was. She didn't seem loose or promiscuous; quite the opposite, in fact. It wasn't *tidy*.

I had also learned that, in a few weeks, the local school board would consider whether Sam should be dismissed. She had held her place so far only because the relevant committee took time to be assembled, because she was a popular teacher, a good one and, owing to that, had the support of many on the staff. And because there was a war on and teachers were in short supply. The scandal was, of course, the talk of the village but not to outsiders like me. Only when I started asking, and because I was now living at the Lamb, did I learn the details.

After the penny had dropped, and I had broached the subject in the pub, I had been interested to observe that, in the Lamb at least, opinion was sharply divided. There was no shortage of those who were convinced that what Sam had done was evil, wicked, shameful, indefensible morally, and a sin beyond redemption. But there were others who agreed with the majority of the school staff that Sam was a superb teacher, an otherwise clean-living, upright young woman who was adored by the children. No less important, and perhaps the most significant factor of all, it was accepted that the father of the child was a soldier at the Front who might be killed at any moment, and that he had left for the war before Sam or he knew she was pregnant, and couldn't get back to marry her. Therefore, on this reasoning, Sam's "sin" was entirely pardonable.

I, of course, was devastated by this development. However, unlike everyone else in the Lamb, in the village, I knew who the father was. I also knew that the gossips who supported Sam were right in one respect at least: the father was at the Front and did not know he had a child.

It was some time before Sam spoke again. We trudged on, our faces set into the wind and rain, following the towpath, until we came to a bridge, where a lane crossed the canal. We walked into the shadow of the bridge, and for a moment we had a break from the weather.

Now Sam stopped and I felt her turn toward me. I say "felt" because, with the weather outside being so bad, it was dark and dank under the bridge and I couldn't see her features properly. Perhaps she intended it that way. When she spoke, her words echoed against the damp bricks of the underside of the bridge.

"I wanted to tell you myself but . . . yesterday . . . you made me feel so safe . . . I didn't want to spoil it. I'm sorry . . . ," she sighed. "I'm damaged goods."

"Is it so bad," I whispered. "I know that gossip in the Lamb isn't the most reliable testimony . . . but half the people are on your side, and they think you'll be acquitted."

She brought her face closer to mine, so I could just make out her features. "Because the boy's father is a soldier at the Front, is that what you've heard?"

I couldn't speak.

"It may be true." Her voice had dropped to a whisper. "It may be true, it may not be. I can't be certain." She turned away, then turned back again. "You know why I can't be certain? I'll tell you why I can't be certain. I can't be certain because *he's German!*" She almost spat these words. "He was a teacher here, in Stratford I mean, but he went back in the summer, and then war broke out. He promised to write but I suppose there wasn't time." Her eyes glistened in the dark. "I felt sure he'd get in touch some way. I don't know if he volunteered or was called up—nothing. He was in the reserve: I know that." She sobbed. "There ... you know something no one else knows, except me and him—Wilhelm, that was his name."

Her breaths came in large gasps, as if she were chewing the thin air under the bridge. "I shouldn't say this—" She fought for breath. "But it's a mercy my mother is dead. Imagine what she'd think—me getting pregnant without being married *and* to a German. My mother—" She faltered. "My mother would have spat at me—that's how she was when ... how she showed her disgust."

She breathed out. "She would have spat at me and I would never have seen her again."

She was in tears now; I could see them glinting silver on her cheeks as they caught what light was going. "What do you think people's opinion of me would be if they knew what you know? They think I am wicked enough as it is—evil, they call me, godless; they say the Antichrist is in me! Do you think I would keep my job if they found out what you know?" She caught her breath, to stop herself from sobbing again. "I'd be lucky to keep my *life!*"

I still didn't speak. Words were too dangerous for me.

She wiped the tears and the rain from her face. "Are you shocked?

Are you angry? Do you despise me, hate me?" She pointed back along the canal, and as she spoke her voice finally broke. "You—you can go back if you want to. Leave me here, I'll manage."

She was broken and she had taken a terrible risk in telling me. But she'd had to tell someone.

I didn't move. For a moment the only sound under the bridge was the water dripping from the bricks of the arch.

Should I tell her what I knew? She was broken and the photograph I had could help put her back together again. She thought she had been abandoned but I knew ... I knew otherwise. It was within my power to lift her spirits.

She was broken, yes, but under that bridge, in the half-light, she was more beautiful than ever.

I waited till her breathing had calmed; then I slipped my arm through hers, just as she had done with me the day before, by the river in Stratford. And I said, "Tea, that's what we both need. Come on."

She let me lead her out from under the bridge, back into the wild weather. We walked on, with neither of us speaking, letting the rain and the wind wash over us, each blown around by our thoughts. I was still fighting shy of too much talk, uttering words that I might regret.

We saw a few moorhens, miserable in the rain; we skirted puddles on the towpath, and smelled the bitter tang of wet cow parsley. We saw no one. We reached Hampton Gorse and, yes, the tearooms were not only open but, because of the terrible weather, almost empty. We found a table in the window and were brought a large pot of steaming tea. Despite rationing, there were scones and jam on the menu. We couldn't believe our luck and Sam cheered up a bit.

"Tell me about him," I whispered after the tea had been poured and we had absorbed the smells and the coziness of the room. "How did you meet?"

This was wrong of me, I know, very wrong. But it is how it happened. I did what I did.

The scones arrived. Sam buttered one, put dollops of jam on the butter, and handed it to me. I still remember the taste and wiping excess butter and jam from my lips and chin. The windows of the tearoom were steaming up.

"He was—is—called Wilhelm. He comes from Göttingen and was a teacher at the Ag, where you are now. Before the war it was a private outfit—but I suppose you know that. We met at the Stratford Mop last year; that's a big fair—swings, roundabouts, coconut shies, candy floss." She smiled at last, thinking back to that day, that meeting.

I had to ask. I couldn't help it. "You fell in love?"

Her mouth was full of scone, crumbs all over her lips. I even loved the way she chewed. She nodded and her eyes grew rounder.

Not the reaction I wanted.

"Wasn't it obvious he was German?" I asked. "To the other villagers, I mean. Couldn't they put two and two together?"

She shook her head. "He never came to Middle Hill—we always met in Stratford. And the woman I was with when I met him—another teacher—left at the end of the term and volunteered in the war." She wiped her lips with her hand. "At that time I was living with Mrs. Foley in the high street, in Wellesbourne Road, and she didn't allow gentlemen callers—as she put it. So I only ever saw Wilhelm in Stratford." She smiled again. "That's why I know the times of the trains so well.

"He wanted to come here, but I said no. Some people are *so* jingoistic. Stratford isn't London but they do get a lot of visitors—foreigners—because of the Shakespeare connection. So we were happy enough there, while it lasted."

She smiled, relieved to be able to talk to someone about him.

"He had a brother, and we used to joke about Dieter—the brother—falling for one of my sisters. This horrid, beastly war has spoiled everything. I was looking forward to going to Germany, to seeing Göttingen—that's a university town."

"You'd live in Germany?"

"I would have done, yes. But he said no. He said there is as much anti-British feeling in Germany as there is anti-German feeling here. Our plan was to emigrate and live in New York. He wasn't—isn't— as obsessed with New York as I am, but he did—does—think that America would suit us."

I pressed on, knowing the answers to the questions I was asking, but asking them all the same.

"He doesn't know about the baby?"

She shook her head. "He left quickly, meaning to come back quickly, but the war broke out so suddenly, so unexpectedly . . . he must have been trapped."

"And you don't know where he is?"

"No!"

That "No!" sliced through my heart. It was little more than a sigh, a soft sound, but it was as if some part of Sam were escaping, and she seemed to subside in her chair and grow smaller.

She gave me another half of a scone. "He said he'd write and put his address on the letter, so I could write back. That was the plan." She sighed again. "It doesn't matter, I suppose. Even if I had his address, anything I wrote wouldn't get through, because of the war. I just wish . . . I just wish I knew if he was . . . safe." She poured more tea. Her face had more color now, from the warmth of the room and from the relief in talking about him at last. "You know a funny thing? When you came to the school and gave us that talk about the Christmas truce, on the Front, I thought how extraordinary it would have been if you had met Wilhelm—that the German officer you talked with, and exchanged gifts with on Christmas Day, had been him." She handed me a fresh cup and saucer. "But, of course, coincidences like that don't happen."

Again, I said nothing for a moment. My face had more color, too. Then: "What is your son called?"

She shook her head. "Nothing yet. I call him 'baby'—he's not quite five months, after all. I can't call him Wilhelm—as well as being his father's name, it's the Kaiser's, and think of the problems *that* could raise, both now and later." She shrugged. "And I won't name him after my father." She poured herself some tea. "In any case, I'm by no means certain that if I took him to the vicar in Middle Hill he'd consent to christen a bastard. So I've let it drift. Have I upset you, saying I'm still in love with Wilhelm—the enemy?"

I stirred my tea.

"I'll take my chances," I whispered, swallowing some of the hot liquid to disguise my discomfort. "The war may last a long time—and who knows what will happen or how it will end?" I raised my cup to her. "We've come a long way since eleven thirty-eight yesterday morning."

She leaned forward and put her hand on mine. "Would you like to see . . . the baby?"

"William," I said suddenly as it came to me. "I'm going to think of him as William. It's a good, traditional name, strong, the name of the one man who conquered us. It's not too far from Wilhelm, and I can't just call him 'baby.' Yes, I'd love to see him."

"William?" she whispered thoughtfully. "No, too . . . too formal. And it always gets shortened to Bill. I hate Bill."

"Make it Will, then," I said. "That sounds informal, the link to Stratford is obvious—and it can't be shortened."

"Will? Will?" She tried it out. "Yes, all right . . . why not? I like Will, and you're right, it does recall Wilhelm without giving the game away. People will think the baby's named after Shakespeare. He'll have to know about his father someday, of course, but not yet, not until we see how the war turns out.

"Will?" She tried out the name again. "Yes, I like it." She smiled. "Thank you. If he ever does get christened, why don't I call him Will Henry?"

The next day, Monday, I was back in Stratford, at the Ag. It was, however, a day with a difference, for that Monday we in the advanced German course—there were about a dozen of us—had a lecture. It was given by a Colonel Pritchard, a slight man with unruly pepper-and-salt hair and a mass of broken capillaries that covered his cheeks like an elaborate wiring diagram. His talk concerned Germany's prewar capabilities in coal mining, steelmaking, and shipbuilding insofar as it was relevant to her ability to wage war. The point of the lecture was to familiarize us with the sort of intelligence material we would be dealing with once we had finished the course—subject matter, words, concepts. His sources included books, newspaper reports, interrogation transcripts, aerial photographs.

Now it so happened that Montgomery & Mann had published some of Colonel Pritchard's raw material and I knew several of his sources very well. So well, in fact, that I spotted what I thought was a small but significant error in the colonel's argument. When he came to the end of his lecture and asked for questions, I put up my hand.

He nodded affably.

"Sir, in your discussion of German steelmaking capacity, you say that Germany overtook Britain in 1908. I don't know whether you think this is important, but in Trevor Kennedy's survey—the work you quote—it says they overtook us in 1903, five years earlier."

Total silence in the room. Except that I could hear a train far away.

Then Pritchard spoke: "So you're saying I am wrong."

I reddened. "It's easy to confuse a three and an eight, sir. It's probably a misprint."

"Good grief!" growled Major Romford. "Apologize, Montgomery, for pity's sake! Who do you think you are, Winston bloody Churchill?"

When I didn't immediately do as he said, he exploded a second time. "Well, if you won't have the grace to apologize, I will do it on your behalf—and I'll see you later . . . in—my—office!" He turned to the colonel but the colonel waved him down.

"No, no. Let's have this out." Pritchard faced me. "Because it's not a small matter, is it?" He passed his stubby fingers through the waves in his hair. "You're saying, if I understand you correctly, that our estimates of German capacity are five years out—and five years in the wrong direction. Which means we may have seriously *underestimated* their capacity."

I nodded. "If I'm right, sir. If it's not a misprint."

"Jee-*sus!*" breathed Romford. "You cocky bastard—"

"Well, it's checkable," said Pritchard, rubbing his jaw. "And I'll certainly check it, just as soon as I get back to the ministry in London." He shifted in his seat. "But I'm interested to know how you are so well informed. When I asked for questions, I must say I didn't expect that kind of question."

"Exactly!" growled the major. "Quite out of order. I won't *have* this kind of—"

"*Shh*," said the colonel. "Just a second. Let's hear the young man's answer."

I told the colonel about my family's publishing history, my interest in science, my two years in Germany, the books I had borrowed from the Stratford municipal library.

When I had finished, he nodded. "What were your impressions of Germany—did you like it?"

"Yes, I did. I know they're the enemy but—"

"That's all right," he interrupted. "Any differences between us and them? Differences you think are—or were—important?"

I thought for a moment. "A couple of things struck me. Germany's just as snobbish as Britain—more so in some ways. But they do give more respect to scholars and, in particular, to engineers. When I was there the engineers were just getting organized, into a professional group."

"So?" snarled Romford.

"Yes," said Pritchard, much more quietly, "why do you mention that?"

I shrugged. "Make engineers respectable and you get better-quality people becoming engineers. That means their ships and industry are going to improve, and they are going to invent new and more terrible weapons."

"Any ideas?"

I nodded. "This new automobile technology . . . combine that with their steelmaking. Once you solve the problem of how an automobile travels over open country, you're bound to get armored vehicles."

Pritchard hadn't stopped rubbing his jaw. "Anything else?"

Romford's gimlet eyes bored into me. I didn't care. "The German navy is much more popular than the German army."

"Why should that be?"

"The German army was originally the Prussian army, so all the other parts of the country have reservations about it. But the German navy was only formed since the unification of the Reich, so it is German, not Prussian. At least to most people."

"And from which you conclude?"

"That the German people will stomach a war at sea longer than a stalemate on land, which you have at present."

"You're reading an awful lot into very little," hissed Romford.

"That's what intelligence analysis is, sometimes," answered the colonel softly. "Sometimes we have very little to go on, sometimes nothing at all." He cleared his throat. "You've seen service at the Front?"

"Yes sir. I was shot in the groin just after New Year, during an attack on Plumont. My pelvis was shattered."

"That's why he has a *limp*," barked Romford. He made it sound like something that was catching.

"Well," said the colonel, straightening his tie, "I'll check the facts and let you know what I find."

There were no other questions—no one dared risk Romford's wrath—so the colonel picked up his briefcase, stood, we all saluted, and he left, with the major in his wake. Just before they exited the room, Romford turned and hissed in my direction: "God protect you, Montgomery, if you're wrong."

That night I went to meet Will. Sam hadn't let me meet him on Sunday because, she insisted, the lockkeeper's cottage was so untidy. I said I didn't care but she said she did and that was that.

I arrived at the cottage at about seven, laden with some shortbread I had bought on the black market in Stratford, as well as two bottles of beer and one of lemonade, for mixing shandy.

Will, I was surprised to see, was a shade on the tubby side— "bonny" as the Scots say—but otherwise it was all I could do to restrain myself from remarking that he was the image of his father. It was so true: save for his disconcerting lack of blond hair, his features recalled Wilhelm's, from the shape of his face to the angle of his eyebrows, to the curl of his lips. If he thinned out as he grew up, he would become a good-looking boy.

He gurgled a bit, burped a lot, smiled a gummy smile, and contorted his features into a massive yawn. And that was it. There is, in my experience, a limit to the amount of time that you can spend talking to a five-month-old baby, but in any case soon after I arrived Will fell asleep. Sam put him to bed, I mixed her a shandy, and we sat down to dinner—pork, one of the advantages of living near a pig factory at a time of shortage, a sort of quid pro quo for being with the smell all the time.

We spent most of the evening talking about the hearing, when Sam's immediate future would be settled. I reported that opinion among the gossips in the Lamb was still divided but that the news from the Front was so bad just then (the Germans had advanced all of three miles near Ypres after releasing chlorine gas) that many people were saying that if the father really was fighting at the Front, then Sam shouldn't be abandoned by the village—that she might be abandoned by her man, permanently, at any time. Some of the more energetic Christians among the drinkers in the pub pointed to the Christmas truce, now receding into memory, as an example of what could be achieved by goodwill, and urged a similar goodwill in Sam's case.

She was having none of it and was not at all hopeful. "You should see the way I'm treated in the shops. Like something that slid out of the canal."

I thought back to that first day when I had followed her in the rain, when she had left the shop in the high street in such a hurry. Had the other women been having a go at her then?

"What will you do if the verdict . . . if the decision goes the wrong way?"

"If it comes to it, I'll probably go back to London—"

"To live with your aunt?"

She shook her head. "Oh no. She's churchgoing and wouldn't allow a bastard under her roof in any circumstances. So I haven't told
her. Not yet. I'll stay with one of my sisters."

"Do they know about the . . . about Will?"

She nodded. "I wrote and told them. They came to the hospital
when Will was born."

"And what's going to happen? Long-term, I mean."

She poured more lemonade into her beer, to weaken it. "It's early
days. If the unthinkable happens, if Germany wins the war, if Britain
is invaded, then Will's parentage might help. What a thought *that* is."

"You don't . . . you can't want that to happen, surely?"

"No, no, of course not. But it's opened my mind. War does that to
you, makes you think things you don't want to think." She looked
toward the stairs of the cottage, as if she had heard Will move. Then
she turned back. "I don't feel any hatred toward the Germans, do you?
I don't know why we are at war anyway."

I thought back to the Christmas truce, the fellowship of feeling
among the men in no-man's-land when they had caught those rabbits,
the exchange of gifts, the universal hatred of the common soldier for
the higher-ups. Wilhelm's photograph burned a hole in my wallet, in
my conscience.

"You've never thought about adoption?"

She shook her head and smiled. She was convinced Wilhelm
would be back someday.

We sat on, talking companionably, Sam getting up every so often
and standing at the foot of the stairs, to be certain that Will wasn't
stirring. She told me that Katharine, the chorister, babysat two nights
a week, and at weekends when she was wanted, save for Sunday mornings, when she had to be in church. It appeared that her family was
more sympathetic than most because Katharine herself had been born

out of wedlock, though her father, a bosun in the Royal Navy, had married her mother as soon as he had returned home on leave.

From what Sam said, it also appeared that the vicar led the opposition to her, even going so far—so she had heard—as to preach against "fornication" from the pulpit. That was another reason why she didn't go to church.

Thank God the vicar wasn't on the school board, I thought, and thank God he didn't know about Wilhelm.

"Are you religious?" I asked.

She shook her head vigorously. "Are you kidding? How could a God allow someone to behave as my father behaved, or allow the *Titanic* to sink? Do you think a God would allow this war?" She shook her head again, less vigorously, more sadly. "How about you?"

I drank some beer before replying. "When you've seen what I've seen at the Front, it's hard to believe in anything. Some of the men, though, had the opposite reaction—the carnage only convinced them there has to be a better world somewhere else." I sat back in my chair. Outside, the light was beginning to go. "When I came to talk to the school, the headmaster asked me not to frighten the children, not to dwell on the atrocities."

"Did he? Well, I don't blame him, do you? Children have plenty of time to be frightened, after school." She shifted in her seat. "What was that officer like, the German you met in the truce? Did you get on with him?"

Did my reaction give me away? I couldn't help but redden, I was sure of it. Did Sam know whom I had met—had she guessed, had she worked it out, did she understand how and why I had found my way to Middle Hill? She couldn't have.

"Young. We were all young. He was from Berlin." That was safe enough. "Did I like him?" I hid behind my beer; I wanted to escape this conversation, now, right now, and with a minimum of lies. "In another life I could have liked him."

"Did you discuss family, girlfriends, did he have children?"

Would she never stop?

"Neither of us was married. He had a sister, like me. Then we discussed burying our colleagues."

"Didn't you discuss girlfriends? Did he have a photo maybe?"

I was reddening again. Reddening and sweating.

But then, on cue and mercifully, Will suddenly started to yell. Sam disappeared upstairs in a flash and returned soon enough with the young man in her arms. He was already falling asleep again. She laid him on the sofa.

I rose to go. It was safer than having the conversation continue. Outside the door, I stooped to kiss Sam on the cheek. At the last moment she changed the angle of her head, and our lips met.

Her mouth opened. Our tongues engaged. Our bodies pressed against each other's. I was swamped by her smell, of soap, of perfume, of Will. I took the lead but she allowed me to do so. We stood for a long moment. When I opened my eyes, hers were closed, the skin on her eyelids smooth and pale.

I stepped back. Her lips closed, her tongue just showing between them. Had she felt the same rush of fire along her skin as I had felt? She had not cut the kiss short.

I turned without speaking. I went out onto the towpath. Lights were coming on in the distance. As I climbed the brick steps to the bridge over the canal and the railway my mind was in a whirl. What had that last gesture meant? Sam had told me she was still in love with Wilhelm.

The next night, Tuesday, I stayed in Stratford. Part of me would have preferred to be in Middle Hill but I had a visit from Isobel and the rest of me was anxious to catch up with her news. She was just about to leave for the Front.

I can't say I paid much attention in class that day. At any rate, I have no recollection of what we covered, what the weather was like, or what form of brown food was served in the canteen for lunch. I spent the day revisiting that kiss of the night before, turning over in my brain what it meant, whether it meant anything, whether Sam was having the same thoughts, thinking of me as much as I was thinking of her. And of course I was silently thanking Will for his brilliantly timed interruption, just as the conversation was getting sticky.

Izzy and I met in the bar of the Crown, where we had both re-served rooms. By the time we'd finished dinner, the last—the only—evening train to Middle Hill would have been long gone, and the petrol rationing meant that my motorbike was "dry" that week.

She looked splendid in her pale blue uniform and gray cape. My sister was by now a formidable person. Even as her brother, I could see that she was immensely attractive to men: long brown hair, deep brown sleepy eyes, a creamy skin. And she was already, at the age of twenty-two, a nurse, and a fairly senior one at that, thanks to the exigencies of war. The ambition to become a nurse had apparently overcome her when she was very young—while I was away at school—and she had started early. My being sent to the Front, and then being wounded, had only made her more determined. I had no doubt that she would do well. Izzy was a ferocious organizer and, in wartime, there was an obvious demand for nurses.

We had a sherry at the bar before eating. I noticed one or two envious glances being thrown in my direction by other men, who couldn't be expected to know that I was Izzy's brother, and off-limits. I was surprised to see her knock back her sherry in no time. Then she said, "I'll have a G and T now, if you don't mind. Sherry glues up my liver."

I did as she asked, adding in a whisky for myself. (There was more alcohol in those early days of the war than there was food.) When the drinks arrived, Izzy brought me up to speed about our mother and father. Mum was not so good, apparently. She was a heavy smoker and had a bad cough; Dad was worried for her. I promised to get home more often.

We picked up the menu cards and I was just opening mine when Izzy asked, "How's the war wound? Not the limp—I can see that's improving. I mean the other thing." Sisters can be direct with their brothers.

"That's not improving. Nor will it."

"Do you . . . can you . . . I mean, do you go out with girls, Hal? Do you still *feel* . . . you know, do you get . . . *aroused*?"

I have to confess, I blushed. "God protect us from sisters who are nurses," I blustered. "Yes, Izzy, I get aroused."

"Good," she said with a bland smile. She ran her finger down the menu. "I'll have the plaice." She groaned. "Everything else is fattening."

I signaled to a waitress, who took our order, and then Izzy waded in again.

"Do you have a girlfriend?"

"I might have."

"Well, I mean, you're not bad-looking, in a craggy, dark-haired sort of way, all cheekbones and cleft chin, a war hero, a limp—very *simpatico*, as they say in Italy. A lot of girls I know would come over all woozy with someone like you."

"Someone like me? I'm a type, am I? Thanks."

"Don't be so grouchy. I'm your sister—it's my duty to keep you in your place. Can I have another gin?"

"Do you think you should?"

"I'm twenty-two, you brute. Tomorrow I leave for London, then in a few days for France. Who knows what will happen there? Yes, I should have another gin. I plan to have several more before the evening is out." She blew me a kiss.

I signaled the barman to bring another set of drinks. "But you're not going anywhere dangerous in France, are you? The hospitals are well back from the front line."

"Oh, I won't be in a field hospital," she replied airily. "I'm part of an experimental unit, developed at the Lister Clinic in London. There's this new science—it's called blood transfusion. It was developed by a Czech, in Prague. I take blood, from some civilian's arm, say, I syringe it out into a bottle, mixed with some sodium citrate, to stop it clotting. We analyze it into four groups—O, A, B, and AB—and then we syringe it back into the veins of men at the Front who have been injured and lost a lot of blood. So long as they are the same blood group, you'd be amazed at the effect it has. This all happens before they are shipped back."

"Izzy, that sounds dangerous."

"Risky perhaps, but very useful—life-saving useful. Just because you're a man doesn't mean you get to be the only family hero. I'm going to be making a real contribution—and it's all settled, so don't try to stop me."

I couldn't think what to say. "Do Mum and Dad know?"

"Not yet, no."

"I thought as—"

"And don't you dare tell them! Promise?"

The waitress came to lead us to our table.

"Pro-mise!" Izzy hissed.

"Yes, yes, all right. Just be careful."

We went through into the dining room. Being as it was Tuesday, the place wasn't very busy. The walls were covered in watercolors, scenes from Shakespeare's plays. As we sat down, Izzy went on. "Don't look so glum, Hal. I know what I'm doing. I agree it's a bit more frightening than sneaking into a field with a bull in it and counting to four hundred and forty-four, but it's what I want."

"It's just . . . I thought you'd be getting married about now, having babies."

"Oh, babies can wait. As for sex, I've done that. I'm not a virgin, you know."

I stared at her. Fortunately for me, the food arrived, and we busied ourselves with vegetables, sauces, pepper and salt.

"You're looking glum again, Hal. Don't be shocked because I'm not a virgin. None of my friends are virgins either." She drank some water. "Am I being too frank? Nursing has that effect, I think. Can you stand the shock?"

"It's true what they say about nurses then? You are all sex mad?" I couldn't believe I was having this conversation with my sister.

"What kind of life do you live up here?" she asked, taking hold of her knife and fork. She looked at me earnestly, her brown eyes shining like dark honey. "There's a war on, Hal, people can get sent to the Front and be killed at any moment. You should know, for pity's sake—you've been there. So you've no choice but to *hurry*, experiment, try everything in case this is your last opportunity. I don't only live with other nurses, you know. One of my flatmates works in the Ministry of War, another is in the theater. We're all out every night—dancing, drinks, smoking, flirting." She leaned forward, lowered her voice. "And yes, *doing it*."

She ate some fish and leaned forward again. "Does that shock you, appall you, that your little sister actually *likes* doing it?" She waved her knife. "Who knows when it's going to stop, Hal? The war, I mean. God knows, we may lose. How would Ma and Pa get by if we were overrun with Germans, if their house was commandeered?"

She sat back as our water glasses were refilled. "You're living out here, with ducks and swans and cows, drinking *sherry*, of all things. You should get back to London. Yes, it's dirty, noisy—more than ever with these automobile things and motorbuses clanking around everywhere. But that all adds to the pace, the pulse, the urgency, the very *beat* of what's happening. Play while you can, play hard, try everything— even drugs if you want. Playing hard shows you are not defeated, not dead, not even down. It's your *duty* to play, because tomorrow it might end."

"You're drunk." I wished I hadn't said that. I sounded like a prig.

"No, darling, I'm not drunk. Tipsy, maybe, but flying, mainly because I'm with my lovely brother, who looked after me all those years, and now I am shocking him rigid with my vulgar language and unfortunate behavior." She leaned forward again and her voice changed, quickened. "I'm a nurse, Hal. I've seen lots of men naked. I've taken out their false teeth, put tubes down their throats to wash out their stomachs when they've tried suicide. I've smelled their awful smells and held their hands as they died, frightened. I'm more familiar with blood, urine, and excrement than I am with sherry, for pity's sake. I treat people who haven't washed for a month or haven't changed their underwear since the damn war started." She fingered her water glass. "We had a lovely childhood, Hal. The worst experience was hearing owls at night, when we slept in a tent on our lawn."

She gulped her water.

"But I wouldn't go back. Being an adult beats being a child any day. We had a young mother in the clinic the other day. She'd taken an overdose—and given the same drug to her young baby. We put tubes down their throats and pumped out their stomachs. The baby survived but the mother died. Think of that. We saved a life but we created an orphan."

Now she attacked what was left of her gin. "Don't you think our childhood was too tidy, too safe? Don't you think that Ma and Pa were too protective when we were very young? They wouldn't let us mix with those gypsy children, they were very strict about climbing trees—remember the time they found out we had been scrumping and made us return the bloody apples, for Christ's sake? That farmer had two *hundred* apple trees—more—and would never have missed what we took." She grinned. "Remember how stolen apples always tasted better than ones you bought?"

I nodded and smiled. "It was embarrassing taking the apples back, I remember that."

"I didn't speak to Ma and Pa for a week." Izzy chewed her food. "And they made *such* a fuss about keeping us away from that railway line. I mean, couldn't they see that we would never have done anything really dangerous, like playing Chicken when there was a train coming. I feel . . . I feel . . . I know why they did it, of course I do. And I know they loved us. But . . . well, it was scary running away from that bull, yet at the same time I *loved* it. We should have had more times like that, more *danger.*"

"You're going off to the Front, Izzy, that's dangerous. Don't get addicted to danger. I've seen that."

Her brown eyes shone again. "Don't worry. Your sister's not a fool. But I was never as bookish as you. I *like* how untidy life is, adult life. The surprises, the shocks, the confusion, the messes we get ourselves into. I like it because I know—understand—that chaos is the natural order, but that in being a nurse I can bring order—and calm— into at least one part of people's lives. Teachers can do that, and priests maybe. Even writers." She sat back and smiled. "Am I being pompous?"

"No." I grinned. "That's my job." I reached out and took her hand. "I've seen you covered in chicken pox, remember. All red and blotchy. And I still remember when you once wet yourself. I'll never think of you as pompous."

She moved her fingers and dug her nails into the skin at the back of my hand. "Brute!" she whispered again. But she was grinning too.

"What newspaper do you read, Hal?"

I frowned. "The *Morning Post*—why?"

"I was reading the *Times* in the train on the way here. With this paper tax and paper shortage it was very thin and ninety-nine percent was about the war. But on page five they have one or two paragraphs, usually without any headlines, that are designed to take your mind off the carnage."

"How do you mean?"

"Well, in today's paper, for instance, there were just five lines about the guardians of the workhouse in somewhere called Milton-next-Sittingbourne, in Kent, who took a two-year-old—a two-year-old, mind—away from its mother, because it was swearing, using the most terrible curses, and because, when asked if it wanted any milk, asked instead for beer or whisky."

"You're making this up!"

"I swear I am not. Obviously, it's not very funny if you are the mother or the workhouse guardians concerned, but for the rest of us, the other thousands of readers the *Times* has, it provides us with some relief from the war on all the other pages. I always look out for page five now. They quite often have a paragraph simply called 'Longevity,' in which they draw attention to the fact that, out of so many deaths reported in that day's 'Deaths' column, alongside all the mere boys killed in the war, that so-and-so lived to be ninety-five, someone else was eighty-nine, a third eighty-five, that the news isn't all bad and lots of people are living out their normal life span. I like that. It's propaganda, of course, in a way, but gentle and it shows the right spirit."

She finished her gin.

"Tomorrow I'm giving a party at the flat in London, where I shall be surrounded by all my friends. Nurses, theater types, American spies, soldiers on leave, strippers and croupiers from seedy nightclubs, painters, writers, doctors, black-market spivs. What will happen? Something certainly, because a few days later I leave for France and"—she snapped her fingers—"who knows?"

She smiled—a tender, sisterly smile that took me back again to our childhood. "I'm a bit light-headed, Hal, but that's because it's all so intense. But this is an intense time—and if you're not part of that intensity you . . . you're missing out."

Izzy's eyes shone, her skin glowed, and her hair had a sheen to it. She was fired up, all right. She was not my younger sister anymore.

I'd been overtaken.

The next morning I walked Isobel to the station, for the early train to London. We hugged on the platform.

"Thank you for the lecture last night," I said.

"Was I overbearing? Oh Lord. It comes from having to order patients about. I'm not quite the loose hooker I made myself out to be." She turned her brown liquid eyes up to me.

"Izzy," I said softly, kissing her forehead. "I'm proud of you. Make sure you write."

"Make sure you get to London," she whispered back as she kissed me. "You're wasted here. I'll get leave in about six months and we can have a party at the flat. I'll show you off to all my friends. That sexy limp, your craggy looks, all that book learning. Who knows what might happen?" She kissed me again and was gone.

Sam agreed to go out with me again on the following Saturday, only this time she chose where we went. I was to meet her at the station at noon exactly, and was told nothing more. When I arrived, she was already there with Will, a pushchair, and a picnic basket.

I took the basket from her and asked, "Where are we going?"

"It's a surprise," she said. "Though don't get carried away—it's not a very *big* surprise."

We took the 12:15 train, which headed south, to Walton Hill, Lower Lea, and Hookend Halt. We got out at Hookend, and were the only people to do so.

"Can you manage that basket?"

"Yes, of course."

"It's about a ten-minute walk from here." She strapped Will into the pushchair.

"What is?"

"The river Irwell. Then you'll see."

There was only one lane leading away from Hookend railway station and we took it until we came to a bridge over a stream. This, I assumed, was the river Irwell, for we turned off the road and onto a path, a mud path through the grass alongside the water. The meadow next to the river was very bumpy. The grass was lush, but only grass grew here. The banks of the river were marked by weeping willows, some of which had been pollarded, interspersed with other trees and bushes, which formed a green tunnel over the river.

Sam struggled with the pushchair until we were about halfway between the bridge, where we had turned off the road, and some buildings I could see in the distance. She seemed to know the place she was looking for.

"That's Blacklands Abbey," she said, indicating the buildings. "It's actually a monastery, still going strong."

We had reached a clearing between some trees where there was a small natural beach formed by the river. She parked the pushchair, took Will out, and gave him to me to hold. I put the basket down and Sam took a blanket from the pushchair that Will had been sitting on and laid it out on the grass. She took back Will, set him gently on the blanket, kneeled down herself, and began to unpack the picnic.

"Corned beef," she said. "It's all I could get." She had a tin, some bread, margarine and tomatoes, two apples, two bottles of beer and one of lemonade.

"Why didn't you let me bring something?"

"You did your bit last week. Fair's fair."

"Independent, aren't we?"

She looked up at me. "I have a child. I have to be."

I took off my jacket and sat on the blanket. Will stared at me.

"Is this the surprise?"

"Not yet. Be patient."

She got the food ready and I poured her a shandy and myself a beer. There were a few insects about—flies and wasps—and she fitted Will with a hat with a brim. He seemed happy enough.

"How did you find this spot?"

"I'll tell you in a minute—let me just finish these sandwiches."

After a moment, she held up an enameled plate with a corned beef sandwich and a tomato on it, and a hard-boiled egg.

"A feast," I said, and it was. "The open air always seems to make food taste better."

She nodded, her mouth already full. "I'm starving."

We munched and sipped our drinks in silence.

"Now," she said after a while. "Let's see how observant you are. What's unusual about this river?"

"Ah! The surprise."

"Come on, it's easy enough."

But I couldn't see anything unusual. "It looks like any other river to me."

"Look up and down it. Tell me what you see."

I did as I was told. I stood on the small beach and looked upstream and downstream. "I still can't see anything unusual."

"All right, then. How *far* can you see upstream?"

"Half a mile, I suppose."

"And downstream?"

"About the same."

"And why can you see all that?"

She had lost me. "I don't know. Because the river is straight?"

"*Yes!* At last. If you can see upstream for half a mile, because the river is straight, and you can see downstream for half a mile, that must mean the river is straight for a whole mile."

"So?"

"So? *So?* Have you ever known any other river that is perfectly straight for a whole mile?"

"I don't know. I don't suppose so."

"You don't *suppose* so? I can tell you it's *very* unusual."

"So is this the surprise?"

"No, not yet." She wouldn't let up. "Why do you think this river is so straight?"

"Something geological?"

"No, look at those bumps in the meadow: see? Didn't you notice them when we were walking here?"

"Well, yes, I did."

"And what do you think they are—or were?"

"Aha! I see now. The old riverbed."

"At last, the penny drops." She let out a sound somewhere between a chuckle and a sigh. "These bumps are old oxbows from medieval times. The monastery over there"—and she nodded—"has been here since the eleventh century, when waterwheels first came into use. The monastery has a big waterwheel and, so as to drive it faster, the eleventh-century monks straightened the river for a mile upstream, to speed up the flow of water."

"Okay," I said. "Okay. Is *that* the surprise?"

"Not yet," she said. "Not yet. We have to wait for Will to fall asleep. It has to be quiet. Let's just lie here softly talking for a bit."

We lay down, digesting our lunch, finishing our beer and shandy, listening to the gurgle of the water in the river, the *zzzz* of the insects, Will babbling to himself, and the occasional birdsong.

"So," I said. "How *did* you find this place?"

"Wilhelm, of course. He had come here with others from the school where he taught, in Stratford, locals who knew all the interesting places. There are trout in the river, though we never caught any."

I wasn't sure I wanted to talk about Wilhelm, but Sam obviously did.

"Did he like Stratford?"

"I think so. Before he worked in Göttingen, he had grown up in big urban sprawls, so he liked the ease with which he could get into the countryside here. And he liked the small scale of everything, especially the small churches—not so imposing as in Germany, he said, but more human."

"I think Will is asleep."

"Uh-huh. We just keep lying here, talking quietly. You'll see the surprise soon enough."

I said nothing.

"Wilhelm didn't get on with his father, but he is close to his brother, Dieter. They both took up mountaineering in their teens— you know, roped together, for safety. He said they had both saved each other's life. What a thing that must be to have happen. It's strange," she said and looked up with a sad smile. "His whole family are An- glophiles—they all speak English. I was looking forward to— Well, now all this has happened." She tugged at a clump of grass with her fingers.

"Tell me more about your sisters."

She wiped crumbs from her lips. "Ruth is the tomboy, I told you that. Or she was. She has turned into a very good seamstress and works in a uniform factory in London. She's a bit forceful, but that's no bad thing—it's a responsible job that she has. Faye is the wild one. Very attractive—blond, good figure—all the men chase after her, and she loves staying out late at night. In Bristol she was always down at the docks, where there are clubs and bars, even though we weren't al- lowed there. Faye knows how to live—she has the wildness of our father."

She sipped her shandy.

"Lottie is the dreamer. She always wanted to go on the stage, she likes dressing up, always has us playing charades at Christmas and birthdays. She and Faye got hold of makeup long before I did, even before Ruth did."

"And you, where does your—"

"Look! There! Now! *Look!*"

Sam was pointing upstream.

It took me a while to focus, to grasp what she was pointing at, what she meant. And then I saw it, understood why she had brought me to this place: a flash of blue glinted brightly as it struck a shaft of sunlight slicing through the foliage—and a kingfisher zoomed down the green tunnel, barreling along about four feet above the water, fly- ing straight as an arrow and faster than a train.

Before I could breathe twice it had gone.

"That's what I *call* a surprise," I said. "I've never seen that before."

"Kingfishers like a straight river—that's what Wilhelm told me. So they can let themselves go. Isn't it a marvelous sight? And they like silence, and stillness, which is why we needed Will to be asleep. He'll be back before long. We just sit tight."

"Okay. I'll try not to fidget. I was about to ask where your wanderlust came from. Your father, difficult as he was, must have had something to do with it."

"I suppose so." But she sounded doubtful. "My father did come from a family of sailors but my mother's father was in the army and served in India—it could have come from there. She had some lovely old photos of India—you know, those sepia prints showing elephants and tiger hunts, and the crowded Indian trains, with people sitting everywhere. But she had them on the *Titanic* and they all perished with her."

She patted Will's head. "I haven't done any real traveling yet but I love trains and ships. I love the bustle and busyness of big railway stations, the smell of engines, all the ropes and rigging and clutter you get in the docks. It's all so full of . . . *possibilities*." She removed her Alice band and shook her hair free. "I love luggage in shop windows—it always makes me want to start packing. I just adore being *in* trains, on the move, rattling along, on the way to somewhere, anywhere. But there are such exciting-sounding places—Valparaiso, the Irrawaddy, the Orinoco. Imagine having *been* to the Orinoco. I read somewhere that the native Indians there can tell what river water comes from just by the taste. Imagine seeing a volcano erupt—spit fire high into the sky— or listening to a glacier crack and creak. I know there are oxbows *miles long* on the Mississippi." She refitted her Alice band. "I know, I know, I'd probably get yellow fever or malaria the minute I set foot somewhere exotic. But I'd love to risk it."

"You sound dissatisfied with Middle Hill." My beer was finished. "Do I want to travel? I can't say I've thought twice about the smell of railways, but I did like being in Germany—"

"Look! Here he comes again—"

Sure enough, the blue flash zoomed past us going in the opposite direction.

"What is he doing, do you think? Collecting food for Mrs. King-fisher or just letting off steam?"

"I'm sure there's an answer. I'll get one of the children at school to look it up."

"Do they always do your dirty work?"

She grinned. "Just one of the perks of the job."

I was going to ask her if she would miss teaching if the verdict went against her but decided against it. Maybe another time. In any case, Will was stirring, so we began to pack away the picnic things and prepared to return to Middle Hill.

Life at the Ag gradually got harder—and that was fine by me. After a few weeks, it was no longer good enough to translate accurately and in detail: we were forced to translate faster and faster without losing accuracy *or* detail. Clearly, in a war, efficiency and speed matter. Accordingly, after we had been in the course for about a month, examinations were introduced on Friday afternoons. We had to translate increasingly technical pieces and we had to do it in a specified time; the time varied with the length of the piece and the difficulty of the vocabulary and syntax.

Because I had spent two years in Germany I had no difficulty with this segment of the course, and neither did two of the others I had by then got to be on nodding terms with. Bryan Amery and Rollo West had both suffered from TB, which is why they weren't at the Front.

Like me, both had been in Germany before the war, Bryan in, I think, Frankfurt, and Rollo in Hamburg. Rollo knew quite a bit about shipping and had an even better vocabulary than mine and an almost native accent.

"Are you sure you're not a Fritz?" I used to tease him.

"I might easily have been," he replied once. He explained that he came from Southampton and his family had some ships and his mother had traveled with his father—and had nearly given birth while the ship was in dock in Hamburg. He had three brothers and three sisters and between them, he said, they spoke fourteen languages. He was a little too earnest for my taste, and worked harder at the course than he needed to have done, given his proficiency with the language. But he had plenty of money and spread it around in the pub. That made him popular.

I suppose he was agreeable enough—just—but we did exchange words on one occasion, over the examinations. Three or four of the others on our course were having a little difficulty in keeping up with the new speed requirements and Bryan and I offered to give them extra tutoring. Nothing special—half an hour a day during the lunch break, an hour on Thursday, when we had the afternoon off. To be frank, one or two were beyond help, but some of the others were more inexperienced than slow and they responded well. They seemed less intimidated by Bryan and me, more relaxed than they were with the formal teachers, and they improved.

But Rollo took Bryan and me aside at one point and asked us what we thought we were doing.

"What kind of question is that?" said Bryan. He had grown up on a farm in Shropshire and there was still some loam in his voice. "If they get through the tests, they don't get thrown out, they have a career, help the war effort."

But Rollo was shaking his head. "Wrong, wrong. What do you

think is going to happen the minute you two Girl Guides aren't there to hold their hands? I'll tell you what will happen—they'll drop behind all over again. What you are doing is a complete waste of time. In fact, you are actually hampering the war effort by ensuring that incompetents get promoted. These people are stones and you two are trying to get blood out of them."

"Nonsense," I replied, a touch too forcefully. "You've been to Germany, Rollo; so has Bryan and so have I. We're used to talking German fast, and we have learned to think as fast. The others will catch up—they are not stupid, just inexperienced. Most of them, anyway."

"And one of them's quite pretty," chimed in Bryan.

Rollo grinned and nodded. "I'll grant you that. But I still think you're wasting your time, and hampering the war effort."

"Let's see what happens at the exam," I said. "It's not long to wait."

"That's not my point," insisted Rollo. "Yes, some of them might pass—great for you if they do. But once we go our separate ways they'll fall by the wayside all over again. And we'll be worse off. The war effort, I mean."

We agreed to differ and Bryan and I went on coaching as we had been doing before Rollo's broadside. And, not to make too much of it, we had the satisfaction of seeing all but one pass. Moreover, the father of one of the group—the pretty one, at that—turned out to be a wholesale grocer, and she brought Bryan and me some jam as a thank-you for our troubles, plus a kiss on the cheek.

I don't know which Rollo was more envious of, the jam or the kiss.

No thanks to him, all but one of the class moved up a level.

———

I have left out one important point. After our return from our picnic by the Irwell River, when we had seen the kingfisher, Sam had allowed me to kiss her again, as we parted. On the cheek. A small thing, yes, but important for me. The trouble with falling for someone when they haven't fallen for you (as yet, anyway) is that you read their behavior like an archaeologist reads the remains of a site that hasn't been inhabited for hundreds or thousands of years, trying to construct a scenario based on very thin and often ambiguous evidence.

I didn't exactly have a scheme as to how to push our relationship forward—I was not, after all, very experienced. But I did think that our next outing should be without Will. There could be no advance in our intimacy with him there, much as I was coming to like him.

That, however, was easier said than done.

Then I had a brain wave. With archaeology on my mind, I suddenly remembered that a few miles away from Middle Hill was the famous Roman road the Fosse Way, amazingly straight—in the Roman manner—for miles on end. Not too far down the Fosse Way was Quinton Villa, a sizable Roman villa that, I knew, had been well excavated. What was interesting—or, more accurately, useful—for my purposes was that the villa was too far away to be reached on foot and the railway went nowhere near it. It could be reached only by bicycle.

I checked that I could borrow two bikes from the Lamb before broaching the idea of the trip to Sam and she leapt at it. "I can tell all the children about it at school afterward. Hal, *what* a good idea. Thank you."

So, with my idea having a better reception than I'd dared hope, we set off the following Saturday, which turned out fine, weatherwise. We both kissed Will and left him with Katharine. I had been told there was a pub in Quinton village itself, so with luck we could get something to eat and didn't need to load ourselves down with a picnic.

We rode out along the Loxley Road in the first place, then turned off to Ettingley and Whitfield. There were a few hills and we rested after about an hour at Blackwell quarry. I remember that a wind had got up, which didn't help, but there could have been a gale blowing for all I registered it that morning. I had fallen for Sam in the back streets of Stratford but, on our bicycle ride that day, I experienced something on top and equally disturbing: sexual longing. Seeing Sam straining at the pedals as we climbed the hill at Oakham, seeing the wind blow her skirt well above her ankles, almost up to her knees, registering the way her shirt clung to the outline of her breasts, the tightness of her skirt stretched over her hips, the elegant way her long fingers curled around the handlebars, I felt a stirring of unprecedented intensity. Riding behind her, downwind, I caught tantalizing snatches of her perfume. On her bicycle she was as sexual from behind as from the front. I wanted her.

When we reached Quinton Villa it was immediately clear that she knew more about ancient Britain, and ancient Rome, than I did. She pointed out all the salient features—it was a peristylar villa, apparently on two floors, with a colonnade around a courtyard, kitchens and stables, under-floor heating, and a dead canal that had once linked it to the nearby river Stour. After we had explored every facet of the villa itself, she led the way up Bush Hill, at the top of which we sat and looked down at Quinton.

"That's the Fosse Way over there." She pointed.

We could see cars and a van speeding along, doing fifteen miles an hour at least.

"Let's go back that way," I suggested, "for a short while anyway. You and I seem to specialize in straight things—rivers, roads, canals."

She smiled. "Good idea. Okay, time for me to play schoolteacher. How long is the Fosse Way and where does it go to and from?"

"This is a day out."

"You don't know?"

"If you want me to buy you lunch, go carefully."

She grinned. "Didn't you do *any* research about Quinton?"

"I thought you had pupils to do that. Perk of the job."

"Beast." And she gave me a playful punch.

"No, I don't know where it goes from and to."

"One hundred and eighty-two miles, from Ilchester in Somerset to Lincoln."

"Show off. I know what *Fosse* means, though."

She nodded. "Your ignorance is redeemed. But do you know why Quinton is interesting?"

"I didn't know it was particularly interesting, just that it has been well excavated and it's near Middle Hill."

"It's because it's interesting that it has been well excavated." She lay back in the grass, her shirt stretched tight again over her breasts.

I could have made love to her right there and then.

"At one point the Fosse Way was the western border of Roman Britain. That's probably how *Fosse*, meaning 'ditch,' got its name. It started as a ditch that was turned into a road."

"And Quinton is to the west of the Fosse—"

"Correct. So it was probably part of the advance defense system. There's probably a lot more to discover here."

I lay down next to her. Her perfume still wafted over me at intervals. To think that Izzy had once questioned whether I still got aroused.

We remained on Bush Hill for half an hour. From there you could see the Stour River—a dark strip between the meadows—yet another quarry, and Holberrow Orchard, with its regimented lines of fruit trees undulating down to Bevington Marsh.

I could have leaned over and kissed Sam at any time on that hillside, but I didn't. That day by the villa I felt uncertain. I was inexperienced—inexperienced at being in love—and two kisses on the cheek, interspersed by a proper kiss, had me flummoxed as to what to do next.

Sam lay on the grass, looking up at the sky, tugging at clumps. Her blouse was open at the neck and it fitted her tightly. She was as three-dimensional as ever. She must have noticed my eyes raking over her body, registering its increasingly familiar contours. I saw her swallow heavily once or twice.

Just after one o'clock I stood up and held out my hand, to help her to her feet. That was our only bodily contact.

We walked back to our bicycles and rode on into Quinton proper. I had been told there was a pub in the village and there was, the Royal Oak. There was very little in the way of food—cheese, cheese, or cheese, in fact—but there were benches outside in the warm air.

After I had brought the drinks and the cheese and bread, we sat for a moment enjoying the almost accidental beauty of Quinton village. I say "accidental" because, like many English villages, it did not appear to have been designed but had just grown haphazardly, and in doing so it had acquired its character and beauty.

I stepped across to my bicycle and took from the basket on the handlebars a package. I handed it to Sam.

"I wondered what you had," she said. "Is this a gift?"

"Well, yes and no."

She looked at me, puzzled, and began opening the wrapping paper.

"It's a book. But it's a library book, a book I found in the Stratford library, that I thought you would like to read but . . . well, I have to return it in two weeks. So you can't keep it. Sorry about that."

She had the paper unwrapped and was turning the book over so that she could read the title.

"*Kosmos* . . . ?"

"It's actually only part of a book. It's by a German explorer—but it's an English translation," I hurried to add. "He wasn't the first person to discover the Orinoco but he did travel along it farther than anyone else, and there's a whole chapter on his observations. I thought . . . in view of what you said last time . . . I thought you might like to read—"

"But *yes!* I know about this. Wilhelm mentioned it. Yes—Alexander von Humboldt, the great German explorer. Oh, Hal. You are so kind, so thoughtful. What a wonderful thing to have done. Don't worry, I'll read it in no time." She leaned across the table and kissed my cheek.

On the way back, the wind was behind us, which made riding considerably easier. There was little other traffic and we could pedal side by side and talk. I asked Sam what I'd meant to ask her the week before, how she fitted in with her sisters.

"Well, I'm not sure I do really. Because I've been to college and they haven't, they call me names, like 'Egghead' and 'Professor.' And 'Head Girl,' that's what Lottie likes. But I'm not a head girl, am I?" She turned her face to me. "I'm nowhere near as bossy as Ruth."

"Are they jealous?"

This clearly flummoxed her. "I've never thought of that. Why would they be jealous?"

"*Because* you've been to college."

"But only teacher training college, not a real university."

"Even so, you've had an education. But they only tease you, yes? Nothing more serious?"

"Oh no. We're quite close."

"Have they been supportive—over the baby, I mean?"

She didn't answer straightaway. We were freewheeling down a hill just then and she pedaled on, ahead of me. I let her go.

When we got to the bottom of the hill and she let me catch up with her, she was more composed. "Do you mind if I don't answer that, not just yet anyway. It's not exactly easy for me, and I haven't known you very long. Sorry."

"I'm sorry for prying."

She shook her head. "You're not prying. It's a natural question. But easier to ask than to answer. My sisters are . . . there are good and less good things about sisters, beastly things sometimes."

We came to the bridge over the canal, near where Sam's cottage was. We stopped and dismounted. I took her bicycle from her. I had to return it to the Lamb.

She came round the bicycles and stood close to me, clutching the library book and offering her cheek to be kissed.

I kissed it, smelling her smell, reveling in it, aroused all over again.

"I enjoyed today, Hal. Thank you. I loved it, all of it. Will doesn't know it yet but he is going to bed very early tonight. Then I can get started on the Orinoco."

At the Ag, on the course, the class I was in was gradually beginning to coalesce. We had more or less given up on the canteen, so dreadful was the food, and at lunchtime we walked over to the Crown, for a sandwich and a beer. In this way I got to be on nodding terms with Maude, the waitress Sam had introduced me to. After lunch, a few of us usually took a quick walk by the river and sometimes watched makeshift cricket games in the field next to the water meadow. We were leaning on a five-bar gate one day when one of the women in the course, a brunette in her late thirties and called Blanche, said, "What would a wicket be in German?"

"Do you mean the stumps or the grass between them?" said Bryan Amery.

"Either," said Blanche. "Both."

"A stump would presumably be *Stumpf*," replied Bryan.

Rollo shook his head. "Too literal. They use the word *Tor*."

"But," I said, "doesn't that mean 'gate'? Don't they use it for 'goal' in football?"

Rollo nodded. "Yes, it's a general-purpose word, but that's what they say. And the grass between the wickets is *Spielbahn*."

"So what is LBW?" asked Blanche.

"What?"

"LBW—you know, leg before wicket."

Rollo didn't reply straightaway, so I said, "Literally, it would be *Bein davor Tor . . . BDT*—"

"But," interrupted Rollo, "the Germans would probably use the English expression—LBW. Hal's right about *Tor* meaning gate and it being used for 'goal' in football, but they use the English word a lot too—'goal,' I mean. And 'run,' in cricket, is *run*."

"So 'wicketkeeper' would be . . . ?" Blanche wouldn't give up.

"*Torwächter*," said Rollo.

"Umpire?"

"*Schiedsrichter*."

"Silly mid on—?"

"No!" cried Bryan. "Spare us, please."

"Shut up, Blanche," said someone else. "Come on, let's get back."

We walked two abreast along the bank of the river and I found myself next to Rollo. "How come the Germans have all these terms for cricket, when they don't play the game?"

"But you're wrong, Hal. Cricket's been played in Germany since the middle of the nineteenth century, mainly in Berlin. A German cricket federation was set up a couple of years ago."

"I can't imagine it's very popular now."

"You can say that again."

We walked on. Germany never failed to surprise me. Cricket in Berlin! Hadn't Wilhelm mentioned the game at the Front? I couldn't recall his exact words.

We were just coming into Stratford when I felt a tug at my sleeve. I looked round, and there was Blanche. "Hal, can I have a word, please."

We stood and let the others walk on.

"Yes, Blanche, what is it?"

"I can't pay you back the pound I owe you. Not this week, anyway."

"I thought—"

"Yes, I know, I said I would. But I can't. I'm sorry."

I had lent Blanche money two or three times. She had a sister in the hospital in Worcester and didn't always have the cash available for the train fare to visit her. She had always paid me back before.

As gently as I could, I said, "When do you think you can pay me back?"

She looked at me and I could see there were tears in her eyes. "That's just it, I don't know."

I gave her my handkerchief. She wiped her eyes and blew her nose, hard.

I thought for a moment. "What are you doing on Saturday night?"

"Nothing." She shook her head. "Nothing special, anyway. Why?"

"I may need a babysitter, for about three hours. If you could . . . it would pay off what you owe me."

She brightened. "Oh, Hal, I'd love to do that. And would it really pay off my debt?"

I nodded and smiled.

She stood on tiptoes and kissed my cheek. "Thank you. You've made me feel *much* better. I thought you were going to be angry." She held up my handkerchief, in a ball in her fist. "I'll wash this and iron it and you can have it back tomorrow."

The fact that Blanche was free to babysit was a godsend for me. The cycling trip to the Roman villa with Sam had been a great success, but I knew that Sam wouldn't be easy to pry away from Will again, not for a cycling trip anyway. I had noticed, however, that in Stratford, on the following Saturday night, there was to be a performance of *King Lear.*

"Don't be silly," she had said when I had first raised the subject. "I can't get away, not with Will needing to be looked after."

"I've spoken to Maude, your friend at the Crown," I replied. "There are two rooms free on Saturday, and a woman from my course has agreed to babysit. Come on, we can have a proper night out: theater, dinner, no rush to get home. A proper hotel breakfast the next day. Some people might call that civilized."

I could see she was tempted.

"How long is it since you have been to the theater? *King Lear*—a tragedy, with daughters. It couldn't be closer to home."

We were walking by the canal in Middle Hill when the subject came up.

She paused, obviously turning things over in her mind.

"What would the sleeping arrangements be?"

I shrugged. "Two rooms. Will and you in one, me in the other. We'd share a bathroom. Think you can risk it?"

She ignored the last bit. "And who is this babysitter? I can't leave Will with just anyone."

"Blanche Brodie. She's in her thirties. I lent her some money—not much—so she could visit her sick sister in the hospital and she's having a problem repaying me. I'm doing her a favor and she's doing me one in return."

We walked on.

"If this woman, Blanche someone, doesn't babysit, what happens to her debt?"

"I don't know. She will still owe me, I suppose."

Sam agreed. The three of us caught the Saturday afternoon train from Middle Hill and were in the hotel by four-thirty. The rocking of the train sent Will to sleep almost straightaway, which meant that, as we left for the theater, just after five-thirty, in time for the six o'clock performance, he was wide awake and voicing his displeasure at the novel company he was being required to keep.

But Sam was firm. She liked what she saw in Blanche and shoved me out of the door right in the middle of one of Will's crying bursts.

"He has to get used to the fact that the world doesn't revolve around *him*," she complained as we hurried downstairs and out of earshot.

"But I thought it did," I replied. "For now, anyway."

She punched me lightly on the arm. "Beast! In Middle Hill, it's natural. But this is the first night out I've had since he was born. It's new for me and it's new for him. Am I being a bad mother?"

My answer got lost as we negotiated the lobby of the hotel and found our way to the theater—it was a fifteen-minute walk.

I had never been to King Edward VI's school before, but Sam had and knew the way. The school consisted of some black-and-white timbered buildings, long and low, though the Guild Chapel looked more like a conventional Norman church, square and squat stone with a stocky cube for a tower, and stained-glass windows. It had room for about three hundred and was packed to overflowing.

Having safely descended the steps down from the chapel for the interval, we found the rim of a stone fountain to sit on and wait. "What's your verdict so far?" I asked. "You're the expert."

"How I hate that word. But it is one of my favorite plays," replied Sam. "It places such demands on the man who plays Lear. Although Lear is old, most old actors don't take it on—it's too draining."

"Do you see anything of your family—your sisters—in Regan and Goneril?"

She smiled. "Oh no, we get on much better than they do. The psychology is different: we never had a kingdom to fight over."

"What *do* you fight about?"

"Who says we fight?"

I had half a bottle of whisky with me and offered it to her. She shook her head. I took a swig.

"It was just a question. Most families fight about something."

But she was shaking her head again. "My father was so awful, that drove us together. Solidarity. We were always watching out for each other. Our mother was *so* pretty, she and our father must have been in love at the beginning, before we girls came along. She had such plans for us. Meeting Sir Mortimer gave her hope for all of us, though she would never say bad things about our father, not after he—he died. 'He gave me four lovely daughters,' she would say." Sam paused. "Three lovely daughters now and one black sheep, one tart. She would hate the way I've turned out."

"Sam!" I said.

She shook her head. "You didn't know her. She was pretty, bustling, busy, always moving, restless, like these new automobile things when they've been cranked into action—you know, the way they rattle, shake, throb with energy and power. Our mother had an engine inside her—but, *but,* even with Sir Mortimer, she didn't ... you know ... they had to wait, until they were married. She told Ruth that she was looking forward to it, but that they had to wait till Captain Smith had married them, all legal. My mother would have closed up after I got pregnant. I would have been shut out, shut out of my own family; my life would have been colder, narrower, the color she brought to the lives of all us girls would have been gone for me." She looked up at the sky. "I feel out of breath just thinking about it."

"And your sisters? How are they? How have they been?"

She bit her lip. "Ruth and Faye were a bit shocked when I got pregnant—what I mean when I say a 'bit' shocked, is that they were very shocked. Shocked, upset, embarrassed, to be frank."

"And Lottie?"

Sam thought for a moment. "Lottie was more understanding. This will sound harsh, Hal, but . . . Lottie is . . . well, she is the plain one among the sisters. I know I shouldn't say that—it sounds cruel and arrogant all at the same time, and I would never say it to her face, *of course*—but . . . the fact is she rarely has had boyfriends. The fact is that Lottie loves it when Ruth and Faye have boyfriends—she lives through them, I suppose, enjoys the good times and suffers with them when they get thrown over. And she was the one who most kept in touch when I was pregnant. If she lived nearer she would have babysat tonight."

Just then we were called back in for the second half of the play. I didn't get a chance to follow up until later that evening when we were seated in the hotel dining room after the performance. Quite some time after the performance, as it turned out, since Sam had insisted on going upstairs to check on Will, who was fast asleep, with Blanche beside him, also fast asleep. Sam came down looking contented.

The dining room was quite busy—it was Saturday night, after all—and the service could have been quicker. But we were staying in the hotel and so were in no hurry. I ordered a bottle of wine and asked Sam what she had thought of the play now that we had seen all of it.

"Well, I'm glad they had the traditional ending."

"What do you mean?"

"The ending of *Lear*—the king dies and his favorite daughter dies, after the other two have killed each other—was never very popular in the early days, and used to be changed, so that Lear doesn't die and Cordelia marries Edgar, who of course loves her."

"But why?"

"Oh, history. English royalists didn't like what happened to Charles I and then James—1688 and all that—and Lear reminded them too much of the harsh reality. The traditional ending wasn't reintroduced until Victorian times. They were certain of their own monarch, so Lear's ending wasn't threatening to them."

The wine was brought, and the menus, a handwritten card. There was no choice: it was fish, then chicken.

"You prefer Shakespeare's tragedies to his comedies?"

She nodded her head and picked at some bread. "I suppose I do. Tragedy is more real, somehow. It's not the only mood for the theater, but the dominant one, the most classic. What did *you* think of the play?"

"I enjoyed the acting. I can't imagine Isobel or me ever falling out like Lear's daughters do."

"As I said, you don't have a kingdom to fight over."

"Does that make so much difference?"

Sam chewed some bread. "Land, money, power . . . it's all the same. It corrupts. I'm sure that if my sisters and I hadn't been so poor, we'd never have got on so well."

"You were going to tell me about Lottie."

"Was I? What was I going to say, I wonder?"

I refilled our wine glasses. "You said she was plain—"

"Oh yes! I shouldn't have said that. It's not a nice thing . . . I shouldn't have said it."

"Do you get on?"

"Oh yes . . . it's more . . . complicated than that."

The fish arrived. We sat back and allowed it to be served.

"How was it complicated?" I asked when we were starting to eat.

She chewed for a moment. Then: "Let me ask you a question. Are you your parents' favorite, or is it your sister? Have you noticed?"

"No, I can't say I have."

"Then you are the favorite."

"How can you say—?"

Sam's eyes shone. She was suddenly fired up. "Trust me." She separated some fish from the bone, chewed, and swallowed. The muscles in her throat moved back and forth. "Believe me, growing up in our family was a lesson to everyone." She brandished her fork at me. "I'm going to be very honest now. Lottie never noticed it, but she was our parents' favorite. She got all the little treats, far more than her fair share, anyway. She got more praise than anyone else, the best bit of meat at Sunday lunch—when we *had* meat; she sat next to our mother on the omnibus, and she was always given that extra something at Christmas. She was never punished as harshly as the rest of us. We used to steal her treats—and then it was us who got punished, for picking on Lottie! It was monstrous, but that's the way it was."

Sam cut into what was left of her fish. "All the other sisters noticed it—and it hurt. We used to talk about it, to each other, never in front of Lottie, of course, we couldn't lose face in that way. We would make sarcastic remarks, but she never seemed to take it on board—she just sailed through the early years, and the rest of us swallowed it. Our parents had a soft spot for Lottie and that was that."

She drank some water and poured a little more sauce from the jug.

"Now, here comes the weird bit—and maybe you will have a view about it. As we got older, as first Ruth, then Faye, then Lottie turned ten, and then twelve, boys came into our lives and these things began to matter more and more. And...I know I shouldn't say this, but Ruth and Faye and, yes, me, though I was still barely eleven, were all reasonably attractive, but Lottie wasn't. The rest of us didn't speak about it; nobody spoke about it in the family. But now Lottie started to hurt. And this is my point, or one of my points anyway . . . that when you are winning, or on the winning side, or in some favored position, success or winning is never as good a feeling as losing or being unsuccessful is horrible. Have you ever noticed that? People who lose feel that loss far more than winners relish winning."

"You think that's true?"

Sam was nodding. "Yes, I do. I remember my first boyfriend—he could hardly be called the name, we were so young. But I fell for someone else and didn't think twice about throwing him over. Yet when I was thrown over myself, by boyfriend number two and not so long afterward, I was inconsolable." She grinned. "Not for very long, I have to admit, but my point is that losing is much more hurtful than winning is pleasurable."

"What did you all do about it?"

Sam speared the remains of her fish with her fork. "We all handled it in a different way. Ruth, from having been a tomboy as a girl, now became quite feminine and took Lottie under her wing. Faye was always rather histrionic and rather flaunted her success with boys."

"And you?" I had almost finished my own fish.

"I suppose I was always the shyest of the three—of all of us, really. It came from being the youngest. It crossed my mind that, although we sisters had never noticed how plain Lottie was as a child, our parents *had*, and although they never said anything, they had realized early on that she might have a harder life as a grown woman than the rest of us. *And that was why they had made her their favorite.*"

Sam drank more water. "It had a big effect on me, that insight, their understanding of family psychology. I understood that parents aren't so stupid, that you don't always say what you know, that you think ahead, weigh up what is likely to happen and act on it, that what appears cruel in one light is actually kindness and thoughtfulness in another light. It made me like my mother even more than I did."

She put her knife and fork together.

"But it had another effect on our lives, too. When I got pregnant, Ruth and Faye tried to be understanding but ... well, they were shocked, I could tell, no matter how they tried to hide their feelings—Ruth especially. They were shocked. I repeat that I don't think they thought I was wicked—more foolish. But yes, they were shocked."

The fish plates were taken away and the chicken served.

"But Lottie ... Lottie was different again. It was as if ... as if *I* was now the plain one, the fourth of the four, the one everyone else pitied, the one with life stacked against her. I won't say she was pleased ... she was more ... well, *relieved* is how I would describe it." She smiled but it was a thin smile.

"And how did you react? To Lottie, I mean."

Sam made a face. "I was grateful, to be honest. I felt so ... so *alone* with Wilhelm gone, so cold, so exposed. No one had betrayed me but, yes, I felt betrayed."

I let a long pause go by. There was a table of six diners across the room complaining about the food. The noise they were making left us in an anonymous corner of relative silence. The staff had enough on their hands and would come nowhere near us for a while.

We chewed on our chicken.

"Why did you do it, Sam?" I said this after a long silence but I had to get it out. It was a natural enough question. "I can understand you sleeping with Wilhelm—of course I can. But ... why take the risk of getting pregnant? There are ways ... ways of doing these things ... You've been to college ... you must have known ... Did he—?"

"No! Stop!" It was a sigh, a cry, a sob, and a choking sound in the same breath. She snatched at her wine glass and held it to her lips, hiding as best she could for a moment.

A long pause, longer than the one I had let elapse. Tears glistened around the rim of her eyelids. "It wasn't him. *It wasn't him!* He didn't force me, I mean. Not at all. Oh no!"

She took a deep breath, swallowed a huge chunk of air. Again I watched the muscles of her throat ripple and the upper, visible parts of her breasts swell.

Like her mother, Sam had an engine inside her. Her skin glowed.

"We had rented a long boat—a narrow boat, whatever they are called—and were sailing for a weekend on the canals. Nobody asks if you're married or not in that world. It had been a gorgeous day, a day of birds and buzzing insects and the sound of running water as locks opened and closed, the smell of the other boats' exhausts as they chugged past, with all their brightly painted weird names. We had stopped for lunch at a pub next to a lockkeeper's cottage and we did the same for dinner—another lock, another lockkeeper's cottage, another pub next to it.

"This one was quite rowdy, however. It was late, people had been drinking, and they started arguing, arguing about the Germans, about how belligerent and militaristic they are, how they were building up their forces, their navy, how the Kaiser was a tyrant. You can imagine."

She bit her lip.

"I was angry, fearful, and embarrassed all at the same time, for Wilhelm. No one knew he was German, of course; he had the sense not to say anything but gave me a sign, and we left. We didn't speak until we were well out of earshot of the pub and nearly back at the boat. I started to apologize but he stopped me. He said it was just the same in Germany, that the Germans were just as anti-English as the English were anti-German, and that we should ignore it.

"There was a moon and we went for a walk along the canal bank, to calm down. We eventually returned to the boat and sat inside for a while, having a last whisky and talking. We were amazed that we could feel the way we did about each other, when everybody else in Britain and Germany was at each other's throats. I must say, Hal, it was wonderful, bewildering—and, yes, anxiety-making all at the same time."

The upper half of her breasts swelled again.

"After a while, Wilhelm went onto the deck for a smoke. I changed into my nightdress. Then he called to me. 'Sam,' he sort of whispered. 'Come out here. Come and look at this.'

"I went out on deck. While we had been talking, the moon had risen in the sky but, more than that, a mist had formed over the canal. It was as if the canal was steaming and the steam was shining—it was made silver-yellow, silver-gold, by the glow of the moon. And the best part is: we were cut off by the mist. It had closed in around us, silently, secretly, and when you blinked you felt its wetness on your cheeks and eyelashes."

She bit her lip again, thinking back.

"Wilhelm put his arm around me, and as we stood there, enveloped in the mist, we suddenly heard a flapping, a beating, a leathery sound, and two swans flew straight past us, very low above the water, and very close. They came out of the mist—and were gone back into it in no time.

"Wilhelm didn't say anything. He didn't need to. The mere sight of the swans, the fact that there were just two of them, was enough.

"He kissed me. I was wearing just my nightdress, very thin. He put his mouth on mine—and then he put his mouth on my breast. *Oh, Hal!*"

Those words went through me.

"What did I feel? No one's ever written about what I felt. Ever. And no one told me what to expect, not my mother, not Ruth or Faye or Lottie, not *anyone*. You read poetry and they make feelings, feelings of love, of tenderness, of intimacy, seem so beautiful, so . . . lovely. But they are . . . observing, they are outside, their words can be so . . . *limiting*."

Now she let out a breath.

"That's not what I felt that night. 'Lust' is a horrible word, I think. I had been in love with Wilhelm for some time by then, but that night, that night . . . that night, for the first time, I *wanted* him. When he put his mouth on my breast, I remember that I cried out. To begin with it was surprise, but it immediately turned into something else. A wave swept through my nerves, my flesh was flushed with blood, gorged, and I wanted to wrap my arms and legs around him and squeeze all the juices out of his body and into mine. No one's ever written about *that!* I wanted him to put his hands and lips and tongue all over me. I was sweating, crying—but in pleasure. I had sensations, more like *anticipations* in my body, in parts of my body that I had never felt before, or even known I *could* feel."

Sam was blushing now but her eyes still shone: she had to tell someone. This had been bottled up for too long.

"We lay on the deck of the narrow boat. The mist was all around us, but because of the moon it was a source of light as well as a cloak. My body was filled with fire, but fire as a tide—it rose through my body, swept across my skin. And then, and then . . . I was released."

Her breathing quieted.

"I don't think any of my sisters have been through that."

"Have you told them?"

She shook her head. "I tried. Faye listened, but not the others, not really. They probably thought I was being sentimental."

A waitress came at last to clear the plates away. It was getting late and we both decided to limit ourselves to coffee, though I also asked for a whisky.

"So, in a sense, you were unlucky."

"Yes, but not in the way you mean."

"Oh?"

"I became pregnant that night—yes. But that wasn't unlucky in it-self. We planned to get married and everything would have been—well, aboveboard. And we'd had what we'd had—this amazing evening of . . . sensual love. It was only when Wilhelm had to go back to Germany, and then war broke out, accidentally almost, that our luck changed. We didn't know on the narrow boat what was about to happen. Nobody did. It's not as if . . . as if Wilhelm tried to take advantage of me. It wasn't like that at all."

The coffees arrived.

"But isn't the result the same?"

"Not at all, *don't say that!* If I'd just gone with Wilhelm for one night, acting like a slut, and got pregnant, yes, it would have been disgraceful, cheap, tawdry—all those things. But Will is the fruit of that night, that beautiful night . . . when . . . well, I've told you." She closed her eyes, then opened them again. "When everything was perfect."

We both drank our coffees. The waitress brought my whisky.

"And you've not heard from him at all?"

She lowered her eyes. "No." A short intake of breath. "I felt sure . . ." She looked at me. "No."

I swallowed. Wilhelm's photograph was in my wallet, virtually in Sam's direct line of sight. My own chest heaved. I took a gulp of water to buy time, so I wouldn't be tempted to blurt out what I knew.

"What would you like to do tomorrow?"

She was still drinking her coffee and put down her cup. "You will never guess, never in a month of Sundays. You might have some idea if you knew, as you do know, that I love travel, and the *idea* of travel, and you might work it out if you knew, as you do know, that we only have tomorrow at our disposal, but—"

"I'm lost," I said. "Put me out of my misery."

"I enjoyed the play this evening, very much, but I know Stratford all too well. Since you ask, I'd like to spend tomorrow in Birmingham."

I was a bit flummoxed. I was *very* flummoxed. Who ever heard of anyone wanting to go to Birmingham as a *tourist?* But Sam explained: "I've never been, we can do it easily in a day without exhausting Will, it's a big city, with hundreds of small firms, many helping the war effort, and it's *industrial.* I've been living in rural peace and seclusion since before the war started and I want to see the grime and the soot, the overcrowding and the slums, the endless factory buildings and the acres of concrete without any trees, and the forest of chimneys spewing black smoke. That's what's fighting this war for us. In some ways, it's as foreign as the Orinoco."

So I agreed. We finished our coffees, went upstairs, and, since it was so late, I walked Blanche back to her lodgings. When I returned to the Crown and knocked on the door to Sam and Will's room, she appeared in her nightdress. It was very thin.

She held her finger to her lips. "Will's asleep." Then she stood on tiptoe and kissed me lightly on the mouth. "What a lovely night, Hal. I love it how I can talk to you, about anything. Even . . . you know."

I left it there, and turned in.

The Birmingham trip was a surprise, for me at least, and far more interesting than I could have imagined. We couldn't do too much because we had Will with us, and since neither of us knew the city, I negotiated with a taxi driver at Snow Hill station for him to drive us around for half a day. He thought it was pretty odd that we didn't want to go to any of the great hotels, or the theater district, or the cathedral, or the museum, or any of the better neighborhoods, but sought out Wilmot and Breedon's wire factory in Balsall Heath and the British Small Arms depot in Aston. But, once he realized we weren't joking, he entered into the spirit of things. And, like a true taxi driver, he certainly knew his own city.

We began at the inland port just off the Bristol Road, where several canals conjoined in a large basin and where there could be found several ship's chandlers, selling everything from carved tillers, to brass propellers, to ropes of all lengths and thicknesses, to waterproof paint, to paraffin lamps. Will loved all the strange shapes and colors and smells.

We visited metal foundries in Longbridge, paint factories in Neachells, panel beaters in Acocks Green, the new RAF factory in Castle Bromwich, Saltley Dock, the James Motorcycle works in Harborne, the Waterloo coach works in Selly Oak, and the psychiatric hospital in Rubery.

We got back to Snow Hill station around midafternoon and found we had to wait about an hour for a train to Stratford, where we would make our connection for Middle Hill. It was going to be a long day, especially for Will, who was already fast asleep.

There was a barrel-vaulted roof over the station, made of fancy wrought iron and glass, and next to the main platform a restaurant with a chrome contraption that made tea. There were soldiers everywhere. We bought our teas and found a table. Sam stirred sugar into her cup and put her other hand on mine. "What do you think? Do you see now why I wanted to come?"

"I can see that it's prosperous—despite the slums and the grime. That it's full of life, activity, full of *things,* many of them new things. I would never call it beautiful and I wouldn't want to live here."

She squeezed my hand. "Someone has to live here. Someone has to make the things we live by, fight by."

"I know that, Sam. What's your point?"

She sipped her tea. "I'm one of four sisters. One is in the theater, one is a gardener, I'm a schoolteacher—only Ruth is involved with the war. Is that right? Seeing everyone here, making guns, ammunition, boots, wire and screws and paint that go *into* weapons—is teaching enough, close enough, *involved* enough?"

"You sound like my sister. Is that why you wanted to come?"

She sat back. "It was one reason. But Wilhelm's in the war—he must be. You've been in the war and someday soon you'll go back into it. Is my family doing enough?"

Now I put my hand on hers. "You can't take the whole war on your shoulders. Teaching is not a waste. Your sisters are grown up; you can't think for them."

She nodded. "I understand all that, of course I do. But you see my point about travel. Even a short trip like this, even a day out in a new place, a grimy place, a smoky industrial no-man's-land, an ugly place, gives you a fresh perspective, makes you think—"

"—and makes you unsettled."

"Oh, I've been unsettled for a while."

I drank more tea.

"Sam, what if the war lasts a long time? They said at first it would be over by Christmas. It's about stalemate already. What if it lasts another year, two . . . more?"

She closed her eyes. "I've thought about that too, about little else. What about if Wilhelm is in the war—as he must be—and he is killed? What if the school board goes against me and I find I'm out of a job next week?"

A train was steaming in. People were getting up from their benches. It wasn't ours.

Sam looked miserable but visibly tried to brighten. "That could be a blessing in disguise. It would force my hand, force me to change, get more involved in the war."

"Do you really want that?" I said. "What about Will? And, in a sense, in a very real sense, you'd be fighting Wilhelm."

She was watching a group of children being shepherded onto the train. "It's a dreadful possibility. But war does that to us. Wilhelm had read that famous German military historian, Clausewitz. Clausewitz fought one war himself on the opposite side to his two brothers. They could have killed each other and it was accepted then. The same is true now. I'm in the same position." She smiled. "Not that I'm comparing myself to Clausewitz."

She placed her hand on mine again. "Don't mind me. I can talk to you and I like human contact. All our family like touching and feeling; it came from our mother, I think. What I'm really saying is: what a mess, what a mess my life is in, what a mess my emotions are, what a mess my future is, what a jumble my thoughts are. Everyone else is so black and white about this war, but I'm not. How can I be?" She drank some tea. "Which is where you come in."

She squeezed my hand again.

"You must think me terribly self-centered, talking in this way. But . . . well, it's been a wonderful two days for me, Hal. Will is a lovely baby but his conversation isn't much above gurgles and burps and his main interests are food and what happens at the other end of his alimentary canal." She grinned. "It's not just that you've been a wonderful listener, which you have, but the play last night, and now Birmingham, in all its grimy glory, its sheer filthy *usefulness* and practicality, which I half-anticipated, has done wonders for me. Strange as it may seem, sitting here in this vast station, surrounded by all this soot and squalor, I feel *cleansed.* And I have you to thank for that."

She lifted my hand and kissed it. "You've helped me see that, whatever the school board says, it's not the end of the world."

I didn't see Sam for a couple of days after our weekend with *King Lear* and the grime of Birmingham. She said she wanted to spend her evenings preparing for her ordeal before the school board later in the week, so I stayed overnight at the Crown in Stratford and attended two other plays being put on at the Guild Chapel—*Coriolanus* and *Julius Caesar.* By Tuesday evening I wasn't quite as expert on Shakespeare's tragedies as Sam was, but I was no longer a complete novice.

In the second play, there was an actress who reminded me very much of Izzy—same hair, similar figure, same high level of energy in her delivery. I couldn't sleep that night, my thoughts switching between my sister and Sam, so I got up early and revisited the river where we'd walked on our first time together. The swan with the cygnets was still in a bad mood.

Sam had at least confessed that her life was a mess. That was something from my point of view. From the way she had talked to me, the intimate details she had let surface, her self-absorption, I began to see that she was feeling the strain of living alone with a young child, with no one to share the burden—psychological, financial, practical. And her future was bleak.

A gust of wind swept in a flurry across the surface of the Avon.

As for Izzy, she would be arriving at the Front by now. I felt a mild anxiety on her behalf but she, I knew, would be all fired up and excited. I couldn't help grinning at the river. The Germans had better look out.

I thought back to our last evening, our dinner at the Crown and the "lecture" she had given me. The news from the war just then was mixed. Five thousand Austrians had been killed in defense of Galicia and the Australians had announced they were going to make munitions to help us. Various schemes to enable British companies to trade with the enemy via China had been exposed and stopped. On the other hand, Venice had been bombed—why on earth had the Germans done that? Poison gas had been used against the Russians, and British losses, so far, the government said, amounted to 258,000. In London a free buffet for soldiers had been installed at London Bridge, Emmeline Pankhurst had held an impassioned meeting about what women could do for the war effort, and there had been a big meeting of children in aid of Serbian relief. Concerts were being held at the Aeolian Hall in aid of the French. Several art galleries had organized exhibitions of war art, in aid of the troops.

That all seemed to emphasize Izzy's point of view: London was the place to be.

Later that morning, in class, we were given some German newspapers to read, papers that were several weeks old and, we were told, had reached us via Switzerland. We were to read with two aims in mind: to be aware of words, terms, and usages that we were unfamiliar with, and to see what we could analyze and predict about German civilian morale, from the tone of the articles. The last part was an interesting exercise but, at about eleven o'clock, I was called out of class and asked to report to Major Romford's office, and at double-quick time. Oh God, I thought, now what?

His office, lined with box files and stinking of tobacco, was near the main entrance on the ground floor. It had a door made of frosted glass. The door was partly open but I knocked anyway. No point in getting off on the wrong foot.

"Come in!"

He was sitting there, all mustache and uniform, writing, but looked up immediately. He glared at me but said nothing. Instead, he nodded, down and to his left. I could see that the telephone was off the hook.

I picked up the receiver in trepidation. Use of the telephone was new to me. Izzy had said during our dinner at the Crown that our mother wasn't well. I could think of only one reason for this call.

"Hello?"

"Montgomery?" barked a brisk voice. "That you? Pritchard here. Remember me?"

"Oh, oh. Yes sir, of course. Yes." It wasn't what I'd been expecting at all.

"These bloody phone things can be unreliable, so I'll come to the point. Two points, really. You hearing me all right?"

"Yes sir, loud and clear."

"Right. Well. Point one, you were right about the German figures. Spot-on. I've checked and I've double-checked and you were bang on the button. I would have phoned before but we've had a flap on. Fortunately, it was a misprint in my lecture, so it's not a mistake we've made in our actual policy. Thank the bloody Lord. But that's not the point. You spotted a mistake, an important one, and I owe you a vote of thanks."

I said nothing.

"You there?"

"Yes sir. Thank you."

"But I can do better than a vote of thanks. That's point two. Am I right in thinking that you are learning very little in Stratford?"

"Well, there are a lot of new technical words I'm learning, new scientific concepts, that sort of—"

"Yes, yes, but you can learn all that down here."

"Sir?"

"I want you down here, Montgomery, and I want you P.D.Q. You can start Monday—yes?"

"At what, sir, and where?"

"Now, don't be obtuse, man. You've been too long with the cows. I'll be doubting my own decision if you go on like that. I want you *here*, in the Ministry of War. Northumberland Avenue, just off Trafalgar Square. As an intelligence analyst. We need people with your experience and wide reading and attention to detail. Your German will come in handy as well. You'll get a promotion, of course. Captain, I should think. I'll fix it with your C.O. That good enough for you?"

"Yes sir." That seemed to be all I could say as I fought to keep the grin off my face with Major Romford less than three feet away. "Where will I live?"

"You're being bovine again, man. In a bloody hotel, of course. To begin with, anyway. You're on a captain's pay as of this conversation. A hotel won't ask you for money till you've been there a week. Now, do you know where the ministry is? Do you know London? Do you know Northumberland Avenue?"

"I'll find it, sir."

"That's something. Eight o'clock Monday. Ask for me."

"Very good, sir. And thank you."

"Be warned: you'll be worked hard, a damned sight harder than on that course. So have a couple of days off now. You may not get another chance for a good while." The line went dead.

I replaced the receiver.

Romford looked up. "Well?"

"That was Colonel Pritchard, sir. To say that I was right about the steel production figures. And to say that I am to report to the Ministry of War on Monday. Intelligence analysis."

His eyes narrowed. "Cocky, aren't we?"

"Sorry?"

"Things come easy for you, don't they? Always have, I expect. Doors open for people like you—I suppose Daddy's in the same club as Pritchard, eh?"

"Don't be so—"

"Our paths will cross again, Montgomery, and when they do . . ." He smirked. "Your class are all alike. Now, *verpiss dich!*"

Nothing too technical there.

———

At seven o'clock sharp that evening, I was at the lockkeeper's cottage. I was carrying a bag but I had a suggestion as well.

"There's a cricket game in that field beyond the church." I held up the bag. "Liquid picnic. Let's take Will. The fresh air will do him good."

Sam was hesitant. She handed me the library book I had given her and which she had finished reading. "There will be dew soon. I don't want him to catch a cold."

"Come *on!* It's a lovely night. We'll only go for an hour. If he falls asleep, fine."

"I was planning on staying in, working at what to say at the school board tomorrow."

"You've had ages to do that and it's too late now. You're either ready or you're not." I picked up Will's shawl and took a blanket from Sam's laundry basket by the fireplace. "Come to the cricket. Let them see you've stopped hiding."

"Hal! I haven't been—"

I silenced her with a look, and she relented.

The cricket field backed onto the church graveyard, beyond the stream and its family of moorhens. We passed through the iron fence at the kissing gate. When we arrived the game was already well under way with a "crowd" of about fifty people grouped around the "pavilion," otherwise a white-painted wooden shed with a green corrugated iron roof and a few rusty hooks where the numbers for the score hung. I could make out a crate of beer near where the scorer sat. He perched his scorebook on a second, upturned empty crate.

We lay on the grass on the side of the field opposite the pavilion, where we could be seen but not heard. I spread out the blanket and Sam laid Will on it. He began wriggling in an attempt to crawl. Sam watched him, enthralled.

I took a package from my bag and handed it to her.

"For me? What is it?"

"It's a gift, of course, a surprise. Open it and see."

She looked doubtful.

"I found it in Stratford," I said softly, trying to reassure her. "I couldn't resist it—you'll see why."

She took off the wrapping, pulling at the string with her fingers. Applause rang out across the field as someone hit a four.

"It's a map," breathed Sam, taking the wrapping away and holding up what was inside.

"I found it in a bookshop, framed. It shows the Amazon and the Orinoco, but it was made in the sixteenth century, before the course of the rivers was fully known."

"Hal, what a wonderful idea."

"I thought you could start collecting—maps, I mean. It's travel of a kind. Something you can do while the war is on."

"Of course, of course. Hal, you *are* thoughtful." She raised herself onto her knees and kissed my cheek.

I took from the bag some metal tumblers I'd borrowed from the Lamb. Then, with a flourish, I took out a bottle of champagne that I'd persuaded the barman at the Crown in Stratford to part with.

"*Voilà!*"

The tumblers sparkled in the evening sun and Will tried uncertainly to focus on one, his eyes big and round.

"How *do* you feel about tomorrow?" I said, offering Sam some champagne. She set down the map and took the tumbler.

"Nervous, of course." She swallowed.

"You like it here, but you're unsettled?"

She nodded. "You know how I feel. You know so much already." She brushed Will's cheek. "You've unsettled me even more."

A shout went up as a wicket fell.

"Sam, a lot's happened to me in the past few days, more than I dreamed possible. There's something I must say and I must say it tonight."

She eyed me. "You're not going too fast, are you?" She bit her lip.

"I have no choice," I said. "You'll understand when I tell you."

She picked up Will and hugged him to her.

My heart was racing. This time it was me who was fired up. This moment, this picnic of sorts on the cricket field, this pastoral English scene, this slow, beautiful green-and-white world, was important to me, but for now I put it to one side. I could hear my pulse throbbing in my ears. My throat was dry. Would I be able to get the words out, the words that I planned to say? I felt like I'd felt at school when I was waiting for the results of an exam.

"As of now, there are two things you don't know about me—two important things anyway, two *relevant* things." I smiled and laid a hand on Sam's knee, where she was half-sitting, half-kneeling and hugging Will. "First, when I was wounded in Flanders, my prostate gland was hit and in such a way that it is beyond repair." I paused. "I can never have children." I waited, to let that sink in.

A shout as another wicket fell.

"Second, today, this very morning, I was offered a job, a new job, a good job, a fantastic opportunity. As an intelligence analyst at the War Ministry in London." I paused again. I *was* in a rush but I wanted Sam to assimilate these two bits of news.

"If the board goes against you tomorrow, why don't you move to London and live with me? I know you don't love me but I don't mind. I have come to adore you and maybe, over time, you could learn to love me. We can get married, or let people think we are married, whichever you prefer. We can raise Will as 'our' son, even have him christened. You could get a job as a teacher in London. You say you are unsettled, want to be more useful. Come to London, give it a chance."

I let Will curl the minuscule fingers of his hand round one of my thumbs.

"Of course, it would mean . . . giving up on Wilhelm. It would mean hiding the truth from Will, certainly for now, maybe forever. But if you're unsure, we could try it, not get married immediately. We'd have to pretend, of course. No landlord would rent us anything, anywhere, if they thought we were living in sin. But, if we did that, you could wait . . . see how the war turns out, how long it lasts, what sort of peace there is afterward. It wouldn't be an ideal life but it might be the best, from Will's point of view. He'd have a father, a man to model himself on. I'd look after you—financially, I mean. My family has enough. More than enough."

She didn't say anything, just hugged Will to her.

"It's a good job I've been offered," I added after a moment. "Using my German, analyzing intelligence reports. I'll be nearer the center of things. Useful."

She looked away, then turned back.

"You'd do this for me?"

"I'm doing this for me, too. In a way, I'm trapped—trapped in my medical . . . condition, predicament, ailment, call it what you will. You're trapped too, I think. In a different way, of course, but you don't . . . you can't . . . you know what I mean." I stroked her knee again. "I know it hasn't been long that we've known each other, but I adore you."

She kissed Will's hair. "We'd need to live in London?"

"Yes. Not as safe as here, I know, but more interesting."

Another shout as another wicket fell.

"And you're going to take the job anyway?"

"Yes. I can't turn it down. It's . . . it's a second chance for me to be useful in the war. You can see that."

Will was growing sleepy and she wrapped him more tightly in his shawl.

"It's fast, isn't it?" The expression on her face was serious. "It's what—less than a month since our walk by the river in Stratford."

I said nothing.

Out of the corner of my eye I saw a cricketer running in our direction. The ball had been hit toward us. He picked it up and threw it back to the wicketkeeper.

"I'm touched by your offer, Hal. Very. But . . . the fact that you made it seems to suggest that I'm going to lose tomorrow. Do you know something I don't?"

I shook my head. I wasn't going to mention the gesture I'd seen the headmaster make on my first visit to the Lamb, when he had drawn his finger across his throat. "No, not at all, I swear. It all fell into place for me today, after the job offer. That's why I've splashed out on champagne. Also, I had dinner with my sister in Stratford some time ago. She's a nurse in London and just off to France. She helped me to see that I can't stay here. My wounds are as mended as they are ever going to be and . . . a job in the War Ministry . . . I can't say no."

Another commotion and the players began to leave the field. One side was all out.

Will was now fast asleep, his mouth wide open in exhaustion. I was growing fond of him.

"I don't know what to say," she breathed. "Until a moment ago, all I could think of was the school board. Now you throw in London, intelligence, raising Will as one thing when he's another. Marriage even." She waved her free arm, the one that wasn't cradling Will. "Good-bye to all this."

I still didn't speak. Someone was using a roller on the wicket.

Sam shook her head. "I can't give you an answer now. I told you my life is a mess, you've unsettled me even more, and now I'm more confused than ever. Having Will in the way that I did . . . it wasn't easy. If I lived with you, shared a flat or a house, pretending to be married . . . what kind of life is that? What would my sisters think? What would my mother have thought? She'd have said . . . it was sinning twice over." She shook her head. "The worst thing is—I don't know when I *can* give you an answer. Wilhelm came into my life suddenly, then disappeared just as suddenly. You look like you're doing the same."

Two other spectators, walking the boundary of the field between innings, went by. I nodded to them but they glared back at me. As they moved on, I heard the word "bastard" used. So did Sam.

She gasped and pulled Will closer to her. She raised her head and looked me square in the eye. "I don't love you, Hal, not now anyway."

I took her hand and kissed it. "The offer still stands."

She picked up the map and held it and Will close to her.

"Take me home," she whispered. "I need to be alone."

And so we packed away our things and trudged back around the edge of the field. She stopped at the kissing gate and turned toward me. "Remember the gate by the river at Stratford? That's where Wilhelm asked me to marry him. He was enchanted by kissing gates— they don't have them in Germany. He slid the gate across, so he had me trapped. He said he wouldn't let me go until I gave him an answer."

She smiled—a sad smile, I thought—then turned again and led the way over the narrow bridge across the stream into the church graveyard. In silence, we made our way back to the lockkeeper's cottage.

That night I didn't sleep, even though I stayed up drinking in the Lamb with the cricketers after the game in the hope that the alcohol would tire me out. Apart from the cricket, people talked about the school board meeting the next day, though some of the regulars had observed that I had befriended Sam and didn't bother to ask me whose side I was on. I went to bed at about a quarter to midnight and fidgeted my way through to two-thirty, when I finally dropped off.

I was awake again at five. I lay in bed reading, got up at six, and went for a walk along the railway line, to think. So long as I didn't push myself, my leg now gave little trouble. What would I do if Sam said no? I'd known her for only a few weeks, though it had been months since I first saw her photograph. She couldn't blow such a hole in my life in such a short time, surely? A German bullet had had a pretty permanent effect, and that had taken an instant, but that was different, wasn't it? I wasn't sure my analogy worked.

She was still in love with Wilhelm; that much was very clear. I had to be prepared for the worst.

What had happened to Wilhelm? Had as much happened to him as had happened to me? Was he still alive, had he been injured, had he been invalided home, found another girl maybe, another woman, was he perhaps a father twice over? I had met him for only a few moments, but I knew that if he was still alive, he would be faithful to Sam. We were opponents, rivals, in two senses now, he and I, but I still couldn't dislike him.

I returned to the Lamb, bathed and shaved and had my breakfast. I was at the station by seven forty-five, half an hour before the first Stratford train. I still didn't have enough petrol to use my bike.

Strictly speaking, I didn't need to go to Stratford, not to the Ag anyway. But I wanted to escape Middle Hill on this day of all days, when the hated board would be meeting. If I stayed, I knew that the hours would drag. At the same time, there were good-byes I wanted to make in Stratford, minor debts to clear up, the library book I had lent Sam to be returned.

Tonight would be my last night at the Lamb. I had decided to go to London straightaway, the very next day. It would give me more time to find a suitable hotel and I thought I would have a very short holiday in the capital, which I didn't know at all well. If I was going to be as overworked as Colonel Pritchard threatened, this might be my only chance for a while to see the sights, catch some theater, visit some seedy nightclubs, do a few exhibitions—all the things Izzy seemed so at home with. I should have gone to London via home, of course, to see my mother, as I had promised Izzy, but I knew that I couldn't just drop in on my parents for an hour or two. Better to steer clear for the moment.

At around eight the platform started to fill up. I nodded to the few villagers I recognized. I looked at the station more carefully than usual, now that this was my next to last morning. How would I think about Middle Hill in the future? There was a fine layer of soot on most surfaces. Was the whole countryside hereabouts being dusted in the same way? Not quite as bad as Birmingham.

The signal clanged down, in its gantry along the platform, and I looked toward it.

I saw Sam.

What on earth was she doing here?

She saw me and ran toward me. She stopped in front of me. She looked flustered and for once she wasn't wearing an Alice band. Her hair fell loose on her shoulders. I liked it. There was no sign of Will.

"I called in at the Lamb." She was breathing heavily. "They said you were here." Her skin was flushed. "I had to catch you, before—" She broke off. "That meant running—so I left Will with the land-lord's wife." She grinned. "Neither of them likes the arrangement."

I smiled but said nothing.

She drew me to the edge of the platform, near where the signal gantry was located.

"I haven't slept," she said in a half whisper and, now that I looked closely, I could see that there were sallow patches around her eyes.

"I've been up since five," I said.

"But I've made a decision."

The gantry creaked as the second signal clanged down. The train was nearby.

"You don't waste your time."

"That's because . . . if I were to take your offer . . . I couldn't do it after being dismissed by the board."

I frowned. "Why not?"

"It wouldn't be fair on you." She shook her head so that her hair was flicked off her face. "It would mean that I was just using you because some other course of action had failed."

"Maybe you see it that way, but I don't mind."

"I *do* mind."

I could hear the train in the distance. "So what are you saying?"

"I'm saying that—"

The train whistled.

"I'm saying that if I agree to your proposal . . . to your suggestion, I must do so not because I have failed at something, or been rejected by a board, but because I *want* to be with you."

The train was almost at the platform. I never took my eyes off Sam's face, but I could hear the squeal of the wheels, the hiss of escaping steam. The other passengers on the platform picked up their cases and bags.

"Go on."

She made a face, as if I were as young as Will. "You are a good man, Hal. Very good. And you are good for me. I said last night that I don't love you, and that's true. For now it's true anyway. But you're . . . I like being with you, I can talk to you, I like touching you, feeling you're there. Will's calmer, too, when you're around. You couldn't know that."

We were suddenly engulfed in steam. Everyone and everything else disappeared for a moment. I was reminded of what Sam had said about the mist on the canal, the night Will was conceived.

The steam cleared.

"I can't marry you, Hal. That wouldn't be right. Maybe . . . if I grow to love you . . . as I hope I can . . . then we'll see. But we'll have to pretend to be married. I don't know what I'm going to tell my sisters but I've had enough of the way people look at me in the village, and the way they look at Will, calling him . . . names . . . as if *he's* done anything wrong. At least in London we'll be more anonymous, people won't have to know . . . we can get on with living our lives."

She bit her lip. "If you can accept that, if you don't think I am using you, and if your offer still stands, I accept. But I'm not going to wait for that board to dismiss me. If your offer still stands, let's act on it straightaway. We can make a start for London right away; today, I mean."

She reached out and her hand touched mine. "I'll tell the school I'm resigning. The board can go . . . they can . . ." She grinned again. "I really don't care *what* they do."

Gas

NORTHUMBERLAND AVENUE, WHEN I FOUND IT, was gloomy be-yond belief. I mean the street itself. It led from Trafalgar Square to the Thames but was lined with vast stone-faced office buildings. And I mean the ministry too, or that part of the ministry that was housed there. At first, I thought I had made a mistake, swapping the tranquil, provincial landscape of Stratford for a metropolitan warren that made the Ag seem like the latest word in modern architecture. My sister had misled me.

Things didn't improve much when, eventually, and with some dif-ficulty, I located Pritchard. It must have taken forty minutes and three different escorts (all in uniform, with medals, all missing an arm or a hand) before I was shown into his office, at the back of the building on the third floor, across a small, stone-flagged courtyard. His was a windowless room containing two desks, though the other appeared unmanned for the present. At any rate there were no papers on it, no pencils, no cup for tea or coffee, no ashtray, no photographs of hus-band or wife, children or dogs. It was as barren as no-man's-land.

"*There* you are," he growled, scrambling to his feet. "No saluting here, by the way," he added as I raised my arm. "We don't go in for it in intelligence. Here, I have some papers for you to sign, confirming your appointment and your promotion. And the Official Secrets Act."

He laid them on his desk and I signed without reading them.

"Have a seat there," he said. "I'll brief you and then take you through to where you'll be working. Find a hotel all right?"

I nodded. "In Bayswater."

"Good," he said, lighting his pipe. He wasn't interested in where I lived. That suited me. Sam was looking for a flat.

I, of course, had been pleased—more than pleased, delirious, overwhelmed—that she had agreed to head south with me, right there and then, at Middle Hill station. She and I had had a good first weekend in London, even though it had meant lugging Will around the sights—Buckingham Palace, Parliament, the British Museum. But we'd found a cheap and cheerful restaurant near the hotel, where they made a fuss over Will and where a large Saint Bernard kept an eye on the proceedings. Will liked dogs.

"Okay," said Pritchard, once his pipe was safely alight. "For the first few weeks, at any rate, you're going to be doing some fairly routine stuff. Reading newspapers mainly—German newspapers that our agents have picked up, either inside Germany itself, and have smuggled out, or in Switzerland or Norway, and have shipped back here." He wiped his pipe with his handkerchief. "The papers are out of date, of course—maybe as much as three weeks out of date. But we're not looking for obvious secrets; the Germans have censorship just as we do, so it's unlikely anything obvious would slip through. No, I want you to read the papers in an oblique way, so to speak, to see whether the overall thrust of articles tells you anything about, say, German morale, general population movements, weaknesses or worries the population might have that we could use in propaganda. As days and weeks go by, you might notice changes in news coverage, and that might tell us something. It's thin, I know, but it's a useful way of starting, so we can double-check that you have the cast of mind we are looking for. And you'll learn, of course, from others who've been at this for months already."

He must have been able to see from my face that I was again beginning to think that I had made a mistake in leaving Stratford, for he reached across his desk and picked up a folder, made of thin brown card and across which was stenciled the word SECRET. He opened it.

"See this?" he said, lowering his voice and laying his hand on the sheets inside. "This is a report—very short, just two pages—about three newspaper references, in the Hamburg press, to a new class of destroyer. The newspapers are not allowed to give any details, but in the interests of boosting morale the papers were allowed to explain that Hamburg workers had beaten the work schedule for the first two of this new class of ship." He held up some more clippings. "Launch reports, a few weeks later. Nothing special, except the names of the ships. The *Albrecht* and the *Ewald*—mean anything to you?"

They did, but I couldn't put my finger on it. "Weren't they . . . weren't they eighteenth-century figures, sir? Theologians? Scientists? Sorry."

"No, no. You're halfway there. Good. Wilhelm Albrecht and Heinrich Ewald were, according to this report"—he laid his hand back on the papers—"famous professors at Göttingen University in the nineteenth century, and they were part of a particular group—"

"The Göttingen Seven," I breathed. "I remember now."

"Correct," said Pritchard. "Well done. Seven professors who objected to something the local prince had done and formed a protest movement."

He sucked on his pipe.

"So, this paper, this secret paper, argues that this new class of destroyer will very likely comprise seven ships in all." He closed the file. "It's not much, and it may not be true, but it gives our people something on the ground to work with. It helps them with what to look for, suggests what questions they need to ask. Do you see?"

I nodded. I supposed that you were more likely to find seven needles in a haystack than one.

"Now we work in teams of four—each team with a leader, a major. I divide up the work between the teams, and the leaders subdivide it further. The teams tend to have specialities, and we have about ten of them. Some specialize in German history, some in politics, some in economics, others in industrial relations. The science team is a bit short at the moment—I'd like you to go there."

It wasn't a request, so I said, "Yes sir, fine by me."

"Good. Now follow me, and I'll introduce you."

He led the way out of his office, along a narrow corridor lined with windows on one side, through two sets of double doors, down a flight of stairs that wrapped around a rickety lift, through two more sets of double doors, and into a room that resembled nothing so much as the school gymnasium where I had addressed the children back in Middle Hill. It was big enough to contain a badminton court with space left over, with high walls and huge round dish lights hanging on thick black cables. Bulky tables were laid out across the room, each one square and of such a size as to accommodate four people comfortably, one on each side. There was muted talk as we entered through the double doors, chatter that died as we descended the short flight of stairs. A pile of newspapers was stacked in the middle of each table.

Pritchard led the way through the layout of tables, toward one where I could see there was an empty chair.

"Sheila," he said to a woman seated facing the rest of the room. "This is Henry Montgomery. I told you about him. Injured at the Front, convalesced in Evesham, has done a few weeks at Stratford. Short, I know, but his family was in publishing—"

"Yes, I remember what you told me," said Sheila. She got up and came toward me. "Leave him with me. I'll hold his hand."

"Good." Pritchard turned to me. "Sheila was a professor of German at Liverpool University. She's not as ferocious as she looks."

"Oh yes I am," Sheila barked. "Don't mislead the poor lamb." She was smiling, but there was an edge to what she said. I was willing to bet she had been tough on her students.

"Come and see me on Friday morning," said Pritchard to me. "Let me know how your first week has gone. I just have to talk to someone in one of the other teams. Sheila will do the honors with everyone else."

He smiled at me, then at Sheila, and walked across to one of the other tables.

Sheila and I shook hands.

"Sheila Small is my full name," she said. "This is Colin Jardine and over there is James Leith."

We shook hands. Jardine was tall and lanky, Leith as wiry as a terrier and bald as a bullet.

"Colin worked for a shipping company in Hamburg," confided Sheila. "James was a railway man. He knows all about compressors, the physics of boilers, hard stuff like that."

"You?" said Jardine. Both Leith and he were Scots and he spoke with a soft lilt.

I brought them up to speed on my time in Germany and at the Front.

They didn't fuss but I could tell they were appreciative. Though I was young, I had the right kind of experience.

Sheila pointed to the vacant chair. "Plonk yourself there, Henry."

I nodded. "They call me Hal at home."

"Hal it is." She reached toward the center of the table, took a newspaper from the pile, and laid it in front of me. "Here's how it works. Colonel Pritchard probably explained to you that we read newspapers, German, Swiss, Hungarian, Rumanian, Polish, and Czech newspapers, on the lookout for anything we might turn into intelligence—yes?"

I nodded.

"Right. We'll soon see how good you are in that department. But there are two other things to bear in mind." She took off her spectacles and rubbed her eyes. "One, you have to read quickly. A lot of intelligence dates, so we try to read all papers within a month of publication—even if it takes them two weeks to get here. Clear?"

I nodded again.

"That means that we don't read the papers in the order in which they arrive, but in the order in which they are published, always trying to keep as up to date as possible." She put her eyeglasses back on. "Two, reading newspapers is the lowest of the low in intelligence terms. You'll soon get bored stiff by the whole thing. The good news is that a carrot is dangled in front of everyone in this room. Those who prove adept at reading between the lines in the newspapers are promoted—and given their chance at reading enemy interrogation reports, even captured enemy intelligence documents. If you're really good you are even sent abroad, back to the Front, to inspect fresh intelligence as and when it comes in." She looked about the room. "Not everyone gets sent to the Front, of course. Some are too old, too fat, like their creature comforts too much. It can be dangerous." She smiled a grim smile. "So someone your age may not find promotion so hard."

She went back to her seat. "Anyway, you're here on a month's probation in the first instance. Any problems, don't wait to ask. The hours are eight-thirty till six, lunch is twelve-thirty till one-fifteen, coffee and tea are brought round. No smoking in this room, men must wear ties, everyone must wear trousers, so we can all keep our minds on the job. If anyone makes a major breakthrough—as judged by Colonel Pritchard's superiors—each table gets a bottle of whisky. At the moment we average one breakthrough a month, though it has been falling off lately. This department goes round the corner to the Wellington for a drink after work on Wednesdays. You will be expected to attend."

I picked up the paper in front of me, a copy of the *Frankfurter Allgemeine Zeitung*, or *FAZ*, as I learned to call it, and the rest of the day passed rather more quickly than the days that followed.

I can't say I achieved a great breakthrough in that first week and what I remember most was the drink after work on the Wednesday, when I was buttonholed by several of the others in the department, who wanted to know who I was, how I had got my limp, how I had been recruited, whether I was married, whether I played bridge, how well I knew Germany, if I spoke any other languages, and, in one case, if I could lend them five pounds.

On the Friday morning at the end of my first week, I saw Colonel Pritchard as arranged. Or at least I turned up outside his office. He was just leaving as I arrived and merely said, "Everything all right?"

"Yes sir."

"Splendid. Sheila said you seemed a good egg, so don't let me down." And he was gone.

I went back to my chair and newspapers and worked on throughout the day. The War Ministry Intelligence Department was the only place I have ever been—apart from the Front, that is—where Friday afternoon was just like any other part of the working week. We sat at our tables, diligently keeping at it, until six o'clock on the dot. No one shirked, no one left early, no one gossiped about what they were doing at the weekend. In a way I was surprised that we didn't have to come in on Saturday and Sunday but Sheila said it would be counterproductive. "People need a break. The work is wearing as it is." She smiled one of her gloomy smiles. "You'll probably find that you can't bring yourself to read your usual newspaper tomorrow. There's a price to pay for everything. But try to have a good weekend if you can."

I had a better weekend than Sheila Small could have guessed. Sam and I found a flat. And not just any flat—a large flat, a vast flat, furnished, on the first floor of Penrith Mansions, a red-brick block overlooking the Thames in Chelsea. I was at first surprised that it had been so easy—until I realized that with so many men away at the war, and with so many dead already, there were empty flats and houses all over London, all over the country. It was sobering.

The flat had a huge living room, with two sets of full-length windows giving a view onto the river, a dining room, a kitchen, a bathroom, and four bedrooms, one for Sam and me, one for Will, when he got a bit bigger, and two spare. Sam had found the flat on Thursday, I saw it on the Saturday morning, and we moved in the next day. Between the block and the river there was a small patch of grass, a tiny park, where on good days Sam and Will would be able to sit out.

We spent the morning rearranging the furniture. During our stay at the small hotel in Bayswater, I had bought a gold band for Sam, so she wouldn't attract any unwelcome stares, as had happened in Middle Hill. And we had shared a room, which meant sharing a bed. We had been self-conscious to begin with. Embarrassed even, and of course nothing occurred. But when we moved into Penrith Mansions, she put her clothing and mine in the same chest of drawers and the same tallboy in the biggest bedroom, the one with the best view of the Embankment and the river. That held out the promise of . . . I was encouraged.

In the afternoon we took a walk, exploring the area. Chelsea is one of those places you hear about, but I had never been before and had no preconceptions. I was agreeably surprised. There were lots of small streets, lovely old houses—small, large, and huge—with more trees lining the pavements than I had expected. It felt more like a village than the capital of the empire. There were a couple of decent churches in the vicinity, the Lister Hospital wasn't far away, and, on our way back, we passed a picturesque pub, the Thomas More. It had a small garden, with rickety palings separating the seating from the street.

As we approached Penrith Mansions, on our return, I noticed a young woman sitting on the bench that was located on the patch of grass between the flats and the river. As soon as she saw us, she got up and moved purposefully in our direction.

"You expecting a visitor?" I said, turning to Sam.

She was fiddling with Will's clothing at the time. "What?" she said. "What did you say?"

"There's a woman over there—"

"Oh yes," Sam said. "She's early." And she waved at the woman. "It's my sister Charlotte. It's Lottie."

I could see now, as Lottie came closer, a faint family resemblance about the eyes. She was darker than Sam, shorter, a touch wider, but not unattractive, nowhere near as plain as I had been led to believe. She was wearing an off-white frock, flat shoes, and, like Sam, an Alice band.

The sisters kissed, Lottie kissed Will, who objected loudly, and then she looked up at me.

"Hal, this is Lottie . . . Lottie, this is Hal."

We shook hands. "So you're the hero," said Lottie. She had more of a West Country burr in her voice than Sam did.

"I was only in the war for—"

"I meant you taking on Sam and the boy. Much braver than shooting Germans." She smiled.

"I'm damaged goods, I'm afraid. Sam was doing me a favor."

"Rubbish," Sam whispered. "Now come on, you two. Will's getting tired—that's why he's making such a noise. I need to feed him; then he'll sleep."

"Let me carry him," said Lottie. "You must be tired, Sam, moving house *and* looking after the boy." She took Will and cupped her arms around him.

I let us all in through the door to Penrith Mansions and we trudged up the stairs.

"I'll make some tea," I said as I turned the key in the lock. "Sam, you do what you have to with Will, and then show Lottie around."

I noticed the sisters exchanging glances as I went through into the kitchen. The gas was on a meter but I had plenty of shillings. I filled the kettle with water and lit the ring. I readied a tray and took it through into the living room. The afternoon sun shone directly into the room and glittered on the river.

It took about five or six minutes for the kettle to boil and when I carried the teapot into the living room, Lottie was standing by the window, looking out.

"Sam's putting Will to bed," she said, turning. "I like the view."

"We were lucky with this flat. Sam did well."

"She did well, all right, finding you. Think this pretense marriage can work?"

She had been told the truth.

"It suits us both, Lottie, while the war lasts. Do you disapprove?"

She moved into the room. "Not if you really love her."

"Ah, well. There's no doubt there, I can promise you."

"And after the war?"

I shrugged. "I'll take my chances."

"Just like that?"

"I told you. I'm in love with your sister. There's a war on. Unusual situations are now normal, for the duration. I'm sorry if our arrangements seem wicked to you—"

"I didn't say that and I wasn't thinking it." Lottie sat down. "She says you are a good man. She's been through a lot, she's been a bit of a chump, if you ask me, and it's a good job our mother's not alive . . .

but if . . . she needs stability and she needs support, emotional, psychological, practical . . . if you can provide that . . . then for what it's worth, you have my blessing."

I started pouring the tea and as I did so Sam came through from our bedroom, and Lottie moved next to the fireplace. It had an elaborate, carved overmantel.

I flopped into a chair myself and said, "So, Lottie. What do you do? Are you married? Do you live near here?"

Instead of replying, she looked at Sam. They exchanged glances as before.

"What is it?" I said.

Sam drank some tea before saying, "Lottie's in a bit of a pickle . . . She's been working in the West End, in the theater, as an assistant to Todd Makepiece—maybe you've heard of him . . . he's a director?"

I shook my head. What was coming?

"Well, Todd's been asked to take a show on the road, to France, to entertain the troops. Of course, he can't say no—he doesn't *want* to say no. But the money's tight, there's some danger, and . . . the long and short of it is . . . Lottie's out of work. She's been living in the West End, in a tiny flat near the theater, but she can't afford it anymore." Sam put her teacup and saucer on the low table and looked up at me. "I thought she could maybe stay here for a bit, till she finds another job. She could have one of the spare rooms and maybe babysit, so you and I can get out now and then. Do you mind?"

Did I mind? It was a bit sudden. It was *very* sudden, but did I mind? I—we—now had Lottie's blessing.

"I don't know if I mind, Sam. You and I have spent exactly ten nights together so far. I'm not sure it's completely fair for you to spring this on me, *but*"—I raised my voice as she attempted to interrupt—"*but* . . . when I was at the Front, we had a show that had been sent out from London, and I can't tell you how much everyone loved it." I smiled at both of them. "So I'm not going to be hard-hearted about this. I'm sure Lottie will find another job soon. Of course she can stay here for a while."

At which Lottie jumped up, rushed across the room, and gave me a big kiss.

That night, our first night in Penrith Mansions, was different from all the other nights that had gone before, and we both knew it. The hotel in Bayswater had been a temporary stopgap but now, in the Chelsea flat, the flat where we would be living for the foreseeable future, as man and wife, we were sharing a bed and there was no hiding the fact.

I was sitting against the pillows in my pajamas, reading, when Sam came through into the bedroom from the bathroom. She smelled of toothpaste, and soap, and Will (she always smelled a bit of Will) and, as she took off her dressing gown, her nightdress underneath could not conceal the fact that she had taken off her camisole. I hope I may be forgiven for saying this, but although they were concealed by the pink cotton of her nightdress, her breasts moved in a way that I had never seen before. I thought I had been aroused enough for ten men on that hill overlooking Quinton Villa. How much more was I aroused now?

She went to the window and looked out at the river. "Will's asleep. Out cold. I think he likes it that there's more than just me around."

She pulled the curtains closed and slipped into bed. Her smell grew stronger.

I felt out of breath.

She leaned over and kissed my shoulder. "Not yet, Hal. Not long, I hope, but not yet. Sorry."

Dear Hal,

You were right, and I was wrong. War is every bit as bloody—bloody horrible, bloody tragic, bloody stupid, and just plain bloody—as you said it was. How I miss our cozy evening in that pub in Stratford, and how long ago that seems now. I especially miss the taste of a G&T.

I'm sorry I haven't written before. To be frank, this unit took a bit of getting used to, and to be even franker (is there such a word, bookworm?), we get a lot nearer the Front, the actual action, than I anticipated, and that has taken some getting used to as well. It's some comfort that I'm a nurse—not actually firing any weapons in anger. Our unit is saving lives, here and there, where we can.

Anger. I'm getting to know a little bit about anger. I've noticed that as soon as men who have been wounded learn that they are not going to die, their fear changes to anger. Not at the Germans—you will understand this—but at their superior officers. With the stalemate so stale at the moment, there doesn't seem to be any <u>point</u> to anything that happens out here. If their wound is bad enough to mean they're being shipped home, then fear quickly turns to relief. In a way, they are the lucky ones.

Our unit—you will remember my little lecture on blood transfusion, that night at Stratford—has had a mixed reception. To begin with, we were everybody's favorite. Blood transfusions save lives—and who can argue with that? But they also mean that some wounds, which beforehand would have meant the Tommy being shipped back to Britain, now mean that he can be kept in France and, after a break of only a few weeks, brought back into the lines. That is not what everyone wants.

Of course, we cannot save everyone and it is this that I have found most challenging. Dealing with the dead is wearing, harrowing—sad,

sad, sad. But, in a sense, it is the _dying_ who need us—need me—most. I say "me" not out of any sense of pride or in any egotistical (egoistical?) way. I am the only woman. Or, at least, I am usually. For these men who are dying—eighteen-year-olds, twenty-five-year-olds, forty-year-olds—I am their mother, their wife, their sister, their girlfriend, their daughter. You should see them, Hal. No one tells them they are dying, but one day, one night, early one morning, at some point, they realize that that is what is going to happen—and happen quite soon.

And then you should see the way they look at me. They ask me to wear lipstick, makeup, to wear perfume. I hope I can say this to you, Hal, and that you won't take it wrong, but I have to tell someone. They look longingly at my breasts. Yes, lustfully. These are men, nearing the end of life, most of whom haven't got the strength to get up from their beds, yet I am made love to, ravished every day, in their heads.

I don't pretend that it is _me_ that they are ravishing. I just happen to be the nurse who is here. But I tell you, if there were some way I could share myself out, if there were some way I could satisfy these men, _all_ of them, if the archbishop of Canterbury, or the pope himself, gave me some sort of sanction, I swear I would do it.

I have held men—boys—as they trembled themselves to death, those who cried right till the last, and those locked in a sullen, solitary, resentful silence, who hate this life and the fate that has brought them here. I observe that the ministrations of a priest can comfort some, but for most, I dare to say, the warm flesh of a woman is a far better pillow from which to start whatever journey it is that the dead undertake.

Sorry, Hal. I couldn't say any of this to Ma and Pa, or to my flatmates in London. You've been out here, seen what I've seen, so I know you'll understand.

I've been shocked by the number of men out here who can't read and

*write. Did you ever notice that? We expect people to die for their
country but can't give them a simple training that you and I take for
granted. Don't worry, I'm not going to get political, not in my first
letter anyway!*

*Hundreds of kisses. To think that I was frightened by an <u>owl</u>, and a
bull in a field!!!!!*

Izzy

Lottie's presence in the flat had a beneficial effect on Sam. I had
not realized, as perhaps I should have done, that in Middle Hill Sam
had been lonely, that the pressures she had put herself under, by allowing herself to become pregnant, had isolated her from others her
own age. Even her fellow teachers, who had been on her side, had kept
a distance until the board met.

In Penrith Mansions she was much more relaxed, and the flat rang
with the sisters' laughter. They quickly regained the camaraderie I
presume they had had together when their mother was alive. They
borrowed each other's clothes, finished each other's sentences and cigarettes, knew which foods they liked and loathed and how it must be
prepared.

When she moved her things into her room, Lottie brought with
her quite a few theatrical props that she had acquired over the years
and couldn't bear to be parted from—a policeman's helmet, a lion's
head, a birdcage, and an entire fake skeleton. "I call him George," said
Lottie about the skeleton. "He's been the only man in my life for
years now."

More laughter.

Will was frightened by the lion's head, however, so that was hidden away in the spare room.

Lottie, naturally, had a fund of theater stories and, as Sam had
said, she had a lovely singing voice and would, now and then, treat us

to a music hall number she knew by heart. But what I liked to hear most were their stories of their shared childhood.

"Remember that time," one sister would say to the other, "remember that time when—" and they would be off down memory lane, Lottie beginning the story, say, then Sam taking over, then handing it back to Lottie, back and forth till they reached the all too familiar punch line, which they delivered together. It would have been the perfect comedy act except that the punch lines were really only funny—understandable—to Lottie and Sam.

"Remember that time," said Lottie one Sunday morning not long after she had moved in and as we were finishing breakfast, "remember that time when the vicar came round—"

"You mean when he asked why we hadn't been to church that Sunday?"

Lottie nodded. "And Mum said it had been too nice a day for us girls to be cooped up in church, that we had been swimming in the river we used to go to, the Ryde, and that was much healthier than being in church."

"Lord, he was angry, that vicar. I thought he was going to hit Mum."

"And then Faye weighed in, and said, Church is boring anyway, whatever the weather—"

"—boring sermons, boring prayers, dreary hymns—" they chanted in unison.

"She really gave it to him."

"He never dared come back, anyway."

They were smiling at each other, thinking back to a time that Sam had told me was known in the family as B.T.: Before the *Titanic*.

After a pause, Lottie said, "Are you going to bring up Will religious?"

Sam was suddenly serious. "Left to me, no."

"What do you mean, 'left to me'?"

I was puzzled by that phrase too.

"I mean that, as Hal here knows, I have next to no faith, not after . . . what's happened. But . . . *but* . . ." She looked directly at me. "This is going to hurt you, Hal, but Wilhelm, Will's father, is a Catholic. And many Catholics have strong feelings—rules—about how their children are brought up."

There was silence around the table.

"Thankfully, I don't need to bother about it just yet, but I can't ignore the fact that I'll have to face it someday." She reached across the table and put her hand on mine. "I've made a mess of things and there's no escape, no simple way out." She sighed, withdrawing her hand. "This sort of thing is going to recur and recur. I'm sorry."

Lottie was looking at me. But I couldn't read her expression.

I had been at the War Ministry for two and a half weeks when I noticed an item in the *Berliner Zeitung* that I thought worth bringing to Pritchard's attention. The *Berliner Zeitung* was a small paper that circulated more in the north of the country than anywhere else and it reached us, I think, not via Switzerland but through Russia and Scandinavia. The copy I had was three weeks old.

The procedure, when anyone found anything he or she thought was significant, was first to explain one's thinking to one's team leader. If the team leader agreed that the item was important, it would be discussed with the rest of the team, and with one other team leader, from another table—this was as a form of "quality control," so that Pritchard was not constantly being disturbed by half-baked fantasies.

My idea passed these early hurdles and so, at about half past eleven on what I remember as a very wet Thursday morning, Sheila and I knocked on Pritchard's door.

"Come in!"

Sheila poked her head round his door. "I think Hal may have something, sir."

"Has he, indeed?" growled Pritchard, as we shuffled into his office. He fixed me with a look. "How long have you been here—two weeks?"

I nodded. "Nearly three."

"Not the quickest first idea, but not the slowest either, not by a long way." He turned to Sheila. "You've tried it on others?"

"Oh yes, sir."

"Good, good. Well, sit down." He waved me to a chair and himself slumped into another. Sheila was already perched on a radiator. She seemed familiar with it.

"Okay, now, what is it?"

I leaned forward with the newspaper in my hand. Pritchard understood German, of course.

"I'm tired, Hal," he whispered. "Tell me what's in it."

I looked at Sheila. Did she take precedence, was it her job to tell Pritchard? But she just smiled and lit a cigarette. "Tell him, go on."

I took a deep breath. This is what I had come south to London to do. "It's the *Berliner Zeitung,* sir. A small piece of news in an archaeology column."

"Archaeology?" Pritchard's growl grew deeper.

"Yes, sir. German archaeologists are the best in the world and there's been a bit of a fuss among them, because a new wartime institute has displaced an archaeological museum and, in the process of being moved, some priceless antiquities were broken."

"Ye-e-e-s?"

"The new institute is called the Haber Institute."

Pritchard didn't speak.

"Fritz Haber is one of Germany's most distinguished chemists, perhaps *the* most distinguished chemist. Among his discoveries, he developed the mechanism whereby we fix nitrogen from the air, producing the raw material for both fertilizer and explosives. It's partly because of Fritz Haber that German agriculture and German bombs are better than ours."

"I'm listening." He had lit his pipe.

"All that's important, but old hat. If he's been given his own institute, he must be on to something new, and something to do with the war."

"Do you have any idea what?"

I cleared my throat. "Haber's speciality, sir, is the behavior of gases—what happens when they are heated, cooled, compressed, what medical uses they may have, how they affect animals and plants."

Pritchard looked at me. "Are you saying what I think you're saying?"

"The Germans have started to use some poisonous gases at the Front, but from what I've read, they're not very effective and not very efficient. For Haber to have his own institute means the Germans have decided to improve this aspect of their weaponry—and that Haber himself, who is very ambitious, is convinced biological weapons can be improved." I hesitated. "It's not very pleasant, sir, but I think you should have our people inside Germany find out all they can about Haber's institute."

The long and the short of it is that, about three weeks later, the whisky came round. We were never told much, but obviously the institute had been checked out by our people on the ground and what I had inferred might be happening *was* actually happening. It was good news that I had put two and two together, but less good that Haber was turning his formidable brain to gas warfare.

From then on, I was an accepted part of the crew in the Gym and, when my probation period expired, the rest of the science table took me round to the Wellington for a celebratory drink. As they say in the Mafia, I had made my bones.

———

As soon as we had settled into the flat, Sam did the responsible thing and found a doctor locally, in case any of us should fall ill. He was also someone who, more immediately, could look after Will, check on his rate of development, and keep an eye out for the more common baby illnesses. It was while she had taken Will for one of these visits—early one evening—that Lottie buttonholed me in the living room as I was reading the paper.

"You didn't know Wilhelm was a Catholic, did you?"

"No."

"Would it have made any difference, if you had known? Would you still have made Sam the offer you did make?"

"Yes ... I think so."

"How much would it take to *make* a difference?"

"I don't know what you mean. What are you getting at?"

"I mean: Sam's life's a mess, she said so herself. How much messier can it get before ... well, before you regret what you rushed into?"

"I don't know—and I'm not sure I want to talk about this, Lottie. You're her sister, yes, but—"

"There's such a lot you don't know about Sam, about us Ross girls. She's really not—"

"Lottie, stop!" I closed up the paper and set it down on the low table in the middle of the room. "Let your sister and me get to know each other at our own pace, in our own way, and one step at a time—"

"I'm only trying to help, to give you an inside track—"

"I don't *want* an inside track, I don't *want* any help. I like things just the way they are, and if I get more things thrown at me—like the fact that Wilhelm is a Catholic—then I'll deal with them as they arise."

"But it's all been such a rush. Surely I can——"

"No. What happened, Lottie, wasn't rushed because we are both impetuous people; what happened happened quickly because there's a war on, and because I was offered a job, a job I couldn't turn down, in London. Your sister's not headstrong and neither am I. We are just making the most of the . . . unusual circumstances."

"But don't you want to be loved? Don't you want to be loved for who you are, rather than because . . . of what you have?"

I didn't reply straightaway. But after a moment, I said, "When we first met, that day you were waiting on the bench, outside the flats, you said you would give our 'pretense marriage' your blessing if I really loved your sister. You have lived with us long enough now, surely, to realize how much I *do* love her——"

"But it's so one-sided!"

"How do you know? How can you know what goes on inside a . . . even a pretense marriage?"

"Oh, Hal! I live here, I can *see*——"

"Yes, you do live here; you live here with my blessing. And, so long as you do, Lottie, I want you to keep your thoughts about Sam and me to yourself. I love your singing, I love your trips down memory lane with Sam, I love all the laughter and girl talk. I love it for itself and for the fact that Sam is so much more relaxed here in London than she ever was in Middle Hill. That's partly thanks to you and partly thanks to me."

I leaned forward, for emphasis. "Now let me ask *you* a question. You think you know your sister—yes?"

She nodded eagerly.

"But did you ever think she would get pregnant, and by a German?"

"Well, no——"

"There you are . . . you don't know her nearly as well as you think you do. People are not always an open book, even to themselves. Sam isn't a child anymore, she's no longer the young girl you used to know, and you shouldn't keep trying to fit her into the old mold."

We sat in silence for a while.

Eventually, Lottie said, in a much quieter tone, "But don't you want to be loved?"

"You shouldn't ask these questions . . . people hardly ever have simple motives for what they do. Let Sam and me make our life as best we can, given the raw materials. This war is not going to be over anytime soon, and anything can happen—*will* happen."

Another long pause. "Leave us be, Lottie, please . . . I do not want the subject raised again—ever. If you're going to stay, you must accept this one condition. Are we clear about that?"

She looked at me.

"Well?"

She nodded.

Just then, we heard Sam and Will on the stairs outside the flat, and we never had time to conclude our conversation properly. As I went to open the front door, I just had time to whisper, "I meant what I said. Never raise the subject again."

Treason

WILL TURNED ONE in March 1916. Five of us celebrated his birthday: Will himself, of course, though he didn't know too much about it; Sam; me; Lottie—who was still with us, babysitter in chief—and Whisky, a small Highland terrier puppy who was Will's first birthday present. Sam, Lottie, and I shared a bottle of Scotch and sang songs from a new revue we had seen in the West End, called *"Hullo!"*

Sam and I had settled into the flat, and flat routine, and Chelsea routine remarkably easily, considering we had come straight from Middle Hill. In fact, we hardly talked about Middle Hill or about Stratford. It was painful for Sam to look back—Wilhelm disappearing, and the school board ruling that never happened—and I now had two obsessions: intelligence analysis and Sam herself, and so I didn't look back either.

So far as our landlord was concerned, and the local shopkeepers, Sam and I were married, and Lottie played along.

We spent the winter exploring London, and here I have to admit Lottie came in very useful. It had soon become clear that she was going to find it very difficult to get another job in the theater. The music halls were doing well—in wartime, everyone wanted a good laugh, or to hear some familiar sentimental tunes. But the straight, or "legitimate" theater, as it was called then, and which was the theater that appealed to Lottie, was having a thin time. So the few weeks that she had been intending to stay turned into a few months. In fairness, she was most helpful. She always managed to have somewhere else to go at weekends, so that Sam and I could be together on Saturdays and Sundays.

We loved our weekends and, once we had bought a better pushchair for Will, we walked all over London. And not just the nice bits, the pretty bits, the parks and the areas with big houses, but the other places too, the industrial areas, the canals, the warren of forgotten lanes and wharves by the river. We got to know all the bridges, the railway sidings, the lock-up specialist shops underneath the railway embankments. We explored new pubs, the great Wren churches, the bits of Shakespeare's London that were still extant. We learned where the new omnibuses were garaged at night, where the police stabled their horses, the Jewish shops that were open on Sunday.

And, of course, we talked.

Sam talked about life in Bristol.

"It's a port, of course, which means there was no shortage of foreigners when we girls were growing up, and maybe that helped stoke my wanderlust. Early on, before he took to drink, our father told us lots of stories of far-off places—Lagos, Haifa, Montevideo. He had seen whales and crocodiles and polar bears. *Imagine!* He brought us dolls from Africa and jewelry from India." She bit her lip in the way that she had. "After he turned to drink and violence, we tore the dolls apart and threw the jewelry in the river."

Sam spoke a little bit about her mother, and her mother's singing voice, inherited by Lottie. "She knew *so many* prayers by heart, and so much poetry. The dresses she made were always meticulous—she invariably used the narrowest of ribbons, complicated stitches that few other people could do, and she chased all over the place for unusual silks and cottons; suppliers were always doing her favors because she was so pretty, and the dresses she made were so striking. And because of that, my sisters and I always won fancy-dress competitions at school. We became well known in the area where we lived because of the costumes our mother made."

She talked about how their father always blamed his wife for giving him four daughters and no sons. "Toward the end, or when he had been drinking, they argued about it, a lot, and it may have contributed to our father's drinking. But that was an excuse in my view. On the other hand, I did—do—miss having a brother. At teacher training college, my best friend was close to her brother, and she made it sound fun, just as your relationship with Izzy sounds fun. A family of all girls can be a bit of a hothouse, an echo chamber of petty rivalries and grievances."

Did Sam want me as a brother? It crossed my mind, of course, but on our walks she would put her arm in mine, we would hold hands; we grew closer gradually.

And we complemented each other. I knew a lot about science but, of course, Sam was very familiar with Shakespeare, his tragedies and comedies, his Iagos and Malvolios. She may not have seen the nightclubs of Munich or the trenches of Flanders, as I had, but her grasp of psychology was astute. Shakespeare had something to do with that.

On weekdays, Lottie offered to babysit as often as we wanted. That's when Sam and I went to the theater, to concerts, or to lectures at the Royal Institution or the great hospitals. And it was at one of the lectures in that spring of 1916 that Sam got talking to a woman who was a teacher. I never did know whether Sam offered her services or whether the woman, as Sam said, let slip that there was a vacancy at her school, and that Sam might just fill it.

She didn't say anything to me on the way home, or the next day, or the day immediately after that. But that Saturday, after Lottie had gone off to stay somewhere and we were taking Will for a walk (which is to say, I was pushing him along Chelsea Embankment), Sam said, "How would you feel if I went back to teaching?"

I looked at her without saying anything for a moment. Will was gurgling away.

"What about Will?"

"Lottie says she'll look after him."

"You've already discussed it with Lottie?" I was . . . I was out of sorts.

"It was Lottie who gave me the idea."

"What!"

Sam put her hand on my arm. "Don't get angry. I'm trying to be helpful and practical here."

"Practical? How?" I remember that this was the first cross word I had exchanged with Sam.

It didn't last. She raised herself on tiptoe and kissed my cheek, even though we were in the street, in public. "Hal, you've been wonderful to . . . to Will, to me, to Lottie. We can't go on just accepting your generosity—"

"I don't know why not—"

"No!" She said it softly, but insistently.

Will was looking up at us. The gurgling had stopped.

"I love having a baby, Hal, I really do. But I miss teaching too. Lottie's obviously not going to get a job anytime soon. The woman I met at the lecture the other night said there was a vacancy in their school and, well . . ."

She faltered.

"Well?" Why was I helping her out?

"I went to see them yesterday." She smiled. "The job is mine if I want it."

"Don't they want references?" That was my second cross word.

"They know the college where I trained, and it has a good name. I told them what happened at Middle Hill, and the headmistress was understanding. A big city like London is different—they have seen plenty of women made pregnant by soldiers. We are going to need all the people we can breed after the war. The headmistress said she doesn't have to tell the rest of the staff but, so far as she is concerned, it won't be a problem."

A horse-drawn cart went by and Will focused on that.

"And did you tell them who Will's father is?" I couldn't help myself.

Sam's face flushed. "Of course not. I told them I was married now." She still didn't raise her voice, but put her arm in mine. "You've got a sister, Hal. I've never met her but I've read her letter and I'm sure I'd like her. You'd do a lot for her, wouldn't you?"

I nodded.

"Well, think of the situation from my point of view. If I work, there'll be more money around *and* I'll be able to pay something to Lottie, for looking after Will. She'll have a bit of money to spend, to buy those books and magazines she likes, on the lives of the toffs, and she'll feel more useful, she won't feel she's sponging off us—off you—all the time."

She squeezed my arm. "And I won't become a drudge, weighed down by baby talk, baby habits, and baby timetables. And there'll be less pressure on you—after all, he isn't yours."

"Sam!" I shook myself free of her arm. Cross word number three. "How can you say that? I *love* Will—doesn't it show? Do you mean you want me to spend less time with him? What are you saying?"

Will had his attention back on us now.

"I didn't mean it like that, Hal. Don't react so."

"Well, what *did* you mean?"

She reached out again and took my hand. "It just seemed . . . it seemed like a good solution all round, that's all. It will be like when we first met—"

"No, it won't! Not at all. Don't you like the way things are?"

"Yes—yes, I *do!* Don't react so, Hal."

I noticed she didn't attempt to cancel the plan.

There was a silence between us.

Then she went on: "I don't want anything to change between us, Hal. But you're doing interesting work, and I want to do something too. Actually, it was that letter from your sister that set me thinking. She's more or less my age, and she's doing something useful, worthwhile. I can't just spend my hours with Will—I have to . . . I have to be more *active.* Remember our conversation in that station in Birmingham? When I said I wanted to get more involved in the war? I've rather let that drop since we've moved to London, but I haven't changed my view. Teaching in a poor area is more useful than teaching in Middle Hill and it's something I know. Also, the school has a lot of projects linked to the war, so I can be more involved, as involved as I want to be. You don't mind that, do you? You're doing important work now."

"Lots of women see raising children as a full-time job."

"If we had more than one, maybe . . ."

She said it softly, but it still cut right through me. I know I flushed. "I did tell you before—"

"Yes, you did, Hal. You've done nothing wrong. Nothing, nothing. I'm not criticizing you—how could I, after all you have given me. That evening, in the cricket field, when you asked me to come to London, you did say I could go back to teaching."

We walked on. Not very far, and then we turned back. Our appetites for fresh air had evaporated. Mine certainly had. But what she said was true. I *had* promised she could go back to teaching.

On the way back, after several hundred yards of silence, during which time even Will thought it safer to fall asleep, I said, "Where *is* this school?"

"Notting Hill."

"When do they want you to start?"

Without looking at me, she said, "I can start on Monday if I want."

"Does that suit Lottie?"

She nodded.

"So it's all signed and sealed."

"I'll be paid four pounds, six shillings a week, Hal. We can do a lot with that."

"We don't need money—"

"Lottie does, and I'd like some of my own too. I'd like to buy you presents, for instance, with my own money."

"I don't need—"

"But *I* want to give them to you."

We went to bed that night in silence. It was a first. While Sam was still in the bathroom, I put down my book, turned off my bedside lamp, and lay on my side, with my back to where Sam slept. I heard her come out of the bathroom, smelled the sweep of her as she got into bed and switched off her light. Suddenly I felt her body against mine and she kissed the back of my neck. As she kissed me a second time, I realized that she wasn't wearing her nightdress.

Dear Hal,

Short note. Just moving from Place A to Place B—can't say where, of course, but you know that. Did you go and see Ma and Pa yet? If not, you're a beast. I can't go, so you must.

Yesterday, we actually had a visit from a theater troupe—Todd Makepiece being the big name. Maybe you've heard of him (I hadn't). Anyway, they did Oscar Wilde's The Importance of Being

Earnest—*very funny, very silly, and very* <u>*English*</u>*, all cucumber sandwiches and railway stations and eccentric vicars. Everyone loved it. Will that England ever come back, once all this is over? I doubt it.*

Two of the women in the cast were very beautiful. It must be satisfying being an actress, and it will still be satisfying after the war. I wonder if what I do will still be as satisfying, or as important, after the war is over? Yes, your little sister is getting philosophical. Better stop.

Hundred and thousands of love,

Izzy

The Sunday after the night Sam and I first made love we went to take a look at the school in Notting Hill where she was scheduled to teach—I wanted to know what sort of place it was, what sort of life Sam would be taking on. We walked some of the way but there was a new motorbus route that went up Kensington Church Street. We took Will and Whisky.

The school, when we reached it, could hardly have been more different from Middle Hill. It was surrounded by high wire netting, part of it was next to a railway bridge, and part was edged by a canal, marked off by a row of palings in disarray. Rural it was not.

I pointed to the canal, the railway bridge. "You don't object to all this?"

"We're in the middle of London, Hal, not Middle Hill. The children here need educating just as much as there. Maybe more so."

Children were playing in the playground, even though it was Sunday. The wire fencing was far from complete. They were scruffy children, dirty even. I wasn't happy.

"I hope you know what you're doing, Sam. My mother would call this the rough end of town."

"Oh, it's rough, all right. That's part of the attraction for me."

She slipped her arm through mine. "When am I going to meet your mother, by the way?"

I was long overdue for a visit to my parents. I had not kept my promise, to Izzy, that I would get in touch with them more often.

"Don't change the subject," I said, but I squeezed her arm. They would have to meet Sam soon.

When Lottie came back to the flat that night, I could see she was nervous. She knew what had been going on and wasn't sure how I would react. She was, however, ambushed by Sam.

"It's all settled—Hal has agreed."

That considerably exaggerated what we had worked out—that I had agreed to a month's trial, in case the whole thing turned out to be a disaster. Sam glossed over that, and Lottie burst out smiling, in relief. As on a previous occasion, she rushed across to me and gave me a big kiss.

I have always liked numbers. Don't ask me why. Maybe it's their precision, the lack of doubt associated with them. Many *words*, certainly, are worryingly vague, ambiguous, or malleable—"justice," for example, or "God"; above all, "love." I mention this because it was my love of numbers that led me, in April of 1916, to spend time on the pages of German newspapers that few of the others in the Gym chose to linger over. I am talking about the financial pages and, in particular, the tables of stocks and shares. I concentrated on companies in the science and technology sector of the market.

Before the war, our family firm had published a book, a very technical book, by a German physicist, about tides, the nature of water flow, and the various tide races around the world. I knew, because it said so on the title page of the book, that he was a consultant to the

Bremerhaven engineering firm of STG, the See-Technik Gesellschaft, or Maritime Engineering Company. A few months after I had settled in at Northumberland Avenue, I happened to notice STG in the stock exchange listings of the *Berliner Zeitung.* Their shares had risen by two marks the previous day.

Now, this was a small thing in itself but it opened up a whole new world for me. I had assumed, I suppose—though in truth I hadn't really given any thought to it at all—that most if not all firms did badly in wartime. But, of course, a moment's reflection will tell you that such an idea is naïve. If you make uniforms, or weapons, or military ships, or medals, or coffins, or ammunition, or prayer books, or crosses for graves, your services are going to be in demand.

And that is what I noticed about STG: their share price was very healthy indeed. We didn't hang on to outdated newspapers in the Gym; they were shipped to the basement, where they were held for a while, then destroyed. Down in the basement, I found earlier copies of the *Berliner Zeitung,* and of other German papers that also carried stock exchange listings. Using these various titles I was able to plot the share price of STG over the previous four months. And very interesting reading it made.

I wasn't at my best that day—I thought I was coming down with a cold—but I showed the figures to Sheila and we discussed it with the team leader from the economics table. He agreed that my reasoning was sound, so Sheila and I went to see Pritchard.

"Yes?" he said, waving us to a seat, though Sheila, as before, preferred the radiator.

I took a sheaf of clippings from a folder I had created.

"Give me the headline," he said. "We're all busy, Hal, and we trust you."

"Not this time, sir." I sniffled as I said this. "You'll want to see the raw material for yourself."

He leaned forward and opened the file. "Stock prices? What *is* this?"

I gave him some background. "In 1912, our family firm published a book by a certain Ulrich Pöhl, a hydrologist, I suppose you'd call him. An expert on water, anyway—on tides, forces in water, underwater currents, hard science. He was a consultant to a Bremerhaven firm," I said and I explained about STG. "For that reason, I've always taken an interest in the company, and when I came to the Gym I looked it up." I pointed to the cuttings in the file. "I've been following it intermittently and if you go through those lists, you'll see that, over the past four months, the engineering sector has risen by, roughly speaking, two percent. STG, on the other hand, is up twenty-three percent. Something's going on there, and people in the know are buying shares."

Pritchard put on his spectacles and started going through the figures. He sniffed once or twice and licked his finger, to flick through the cuttings, but otherwise said nothing. Eventually he was done.

"You're right about the share price. What's your analysis?"

I glanced at Sheila. She smiled encouragingly.

"STG is a Bremerhaven-based shipbuilding company with a hydrologist as a consultant. I'd say that points to submarines. Either STG have invented something new—a faster, deeper, deadlier sub—or they've got a big order to expand production."

Pritchard was scribbling notes. "You've run this by the economics people?"

"Yes sir." Sheila was lighting a cigarette.

"There's no way of telling, I suppose, which of those scenarios is the right one?"

"Not really," I said. "But Pöhl's book came out in 1912. You could have our hydrologists check out what research he was doing in the years before the war—it might give us a clue. Also, you might have people check out the acknowledgments page in the book—he mentions by name other specialists he showed the manuscript to. Those names can be checked out as well. They might lead somewhere."

He took off his spectacles and rubbed his eyes.

"But we must have people on the ground in Hamburg, sir," I added. "That's still the best way forward."

Pritchard was cleaning his spectacles with his handkerchief. "I was in Bremerhaven once, years ago. Not my favorite port, I must say." He inspected the glass of his spectacles for dust and smears. "Submarines terrify me—I'd hate to be cooped up in a metal tube, all those feet below the surface, not knowing if, all of a sudden—*wham!*" He took an empty card folder from a drawer in his desk. "Well done, Hal. How's the limp?"

"Getting better all the time, thank you, sir."

"You'll keep an eye on the STG share price, yes?"

"Yes, of course."

"Maybe I should buy some shares myself."

He grinned.

Later that week, I fell ill. It was a severe bout of flu but I was bad enough to have to stay in bed for two days. And so, very quickly, I came to rely on Lottie, who was, of course, at home looking after Will. He moved around the flat in spurts now. Having just learned to walk, after a fashion, his habit was to run faster than his coordination allowed, so that every few paces he fell over and he would bawl out for a few seconds. Then, when no one took any notice—Lottie was very good like that—the bawling stopped, grunting and panting took over, and the serious business of getting back upright was begun, while he babbled to himself in some incomprehensible protolanguage. Whisky steered clear whenever these commotions were in progress.

I lay in bed, doing my best to sleep through his noise. I had a mild fever but nothing serious enough to trouble a doctor with. When Sam came back from school, she was alarmed to find me home and in bed on the first day, and fussed over me as if she were a nurse and not a teacher.

"When any of us caught the flu in Bristol," she told me, "we were given a sip of whisky, hot water, honey, and lemon juice. It made us sweat and sometimes it worked." She smiled. "That started to annoy our father, too. He said it was a waste of good whisky. Can you imagine anything more beastly, putting himself before his young daughters. What a man!"

Lottie came in very useful that day, I have to admit. Sam had found her first days at school harder than she had anticipated. Not hard physically, but hard emotionally. Unlike in Middle Hill, several of the children at the new school, St. Paul's Ladbroke Grove, had lost fathers in the war. As a result, they were disturbed, their families were broken, and poverty was an issue that it had never been in Middle Hill. Children arrived at school unwashed, unfed, and, in one or two cases, unshod.

"They're bewildered, Hal. You and I and Izzy have a problem understanding this war—think what it must be like for them. History, literature, and mathematics seem pretty useless, a long way from real life."

"Why not try some war poetry on them?" I said. (This was before I fell ill.) "One of the women at work is forming a collection—let me get some references for you."

"Oh, Hal, what a lovely idea. There's quite a good bookshop in Notting Hill—if you get me a few titles, I'll know what to ask for."

But the next day I was busy with the STG business. Then I fell ill, and so hadn't been able to keep my promise.

That night Sam cooked me some broth and gave me another fin-

ger of Bell's, hot water, and honey—though there weren't any lemons
in the shops. I couldn't finish all the soup but the toddy went down in
no time, and helped me sleep. Sam slept in a different room that
night. I could understand, but I missed her. I was getting used to sharing a bed with her and not just because we were now man and wife in
the full sense. We both found it comforting. I know because I overheard Sam and Lottie talking about it one time.

The next morning when I woke up, Sam had already left for
school.

I still didn't feel good, and I had a bad headache, but I knew from
past experience that I would feel a whole lot better if I had a shave.
Nursing my head, I got out of bed and went through into the corridor. The bathroom was two doors along, beyond the lavatory. There
were no locks on any of the doors and, too late, I realized the bathroom was already occupied. Lottie had just stepped out of the bath
and was toweling herself dry. As the door opened, she stopped rubbing herself and just stood there, totally naked, looking at me.

Then she stepped forward and kissed me.

Though undeniably flattered by Lottie's attentions, I was also profoundly shocked, and shied away as fast as I could, retreating to my
bedroom—unshaven—where I remained for the rest of the morning.
Lottie did not pursue me.

The next day, Lottie herself went down with the same flu bug I
had—and so did Will. The entire population of the flat in Penrith
Mansions, save for Sam, was laid low. Lottie wasn't shamming. I heard
via Sam that her nose was streaming, her joints were aching, and she
had a fever—all the symptoms I had. Amid this chaos, of course, Sam
had to take some days off from work and minister to the rest of us.

It never rains but it pours, they say, and while the flat was little more than a ward in a hospital, Sam's second sister, Faye, turned up. I didn't know it at the time—I was still ill and the news was kept from me. Only when I was on the mend, and the variety of voices and other noises in the flat could no longer be kept from me, was I put in the picture. As with Lottie, Faye had lost her job. As with Lottie, she had been unfortunate. She had worked in a park in North London, as a gardener, but the park had been requisitioned by the army for the duration, as a munitions and supplies dump, and the park was a garden no more. As with Lottie, Faye had been living in rented accommodations, her wages had been too low for her to build up any savings, and there wasn't much call for gardeners in central London in wartime.

One of the voices I had heard when I had been recovering from the flu, and knew that changes were happening without knowing what exactly, was male. This was explained now, in that Faye had arrived with her boyfriend, Tony. Tony was in basic training and about to be sent to France at any moment. He and Faye weren't living together— he was stationed in some barracks just off Sloane Square, which was an added reason why Faye wanted to live with us, to be near her man. All of which meant that Tony was at the flat as much as possible. That made five adults, plus Will and Whisky. What had been a flat, then a hospital ward, was now more like a railway station.

Here's the thing, though: I enjoyed it. Put it down to growing up with parents who were distant, or to the fact that I was besotted with Sam—whatever the reason, I *liked* living in a railway station. I didn't mind that the bathroom was permanently occupied and decorated with so much drying laundry that it put one in mind of flags at a regatta, or that the gas meter ate shillings as fast as Will acquired scratches and bruises.

By the time Will, Lottie, and I had recovered from the flu (Sam, miraculously, never succumbed), days had passed since the incident in the bathroom. Lottie and I never discussed it, and there was no repeat.

Part of me wondered what, exactly, Lottie had meant by her gesture, and pondered what one sister would do to another, but I never pursued the thought.

Faye, as I think I've said, was the second oldest of the four sisters. (Ruth, thank God, had a good job—as senior seamstress in a uniform factory—so there was absolutely no chance she would be asking to join us at Penrith Mansions.) Tall and slender, Faye lived life out loud. She was passionate, or at least emotional, about everything—about men, about children, about makeup, about politics (she was an ardent socialist), and, inevitably, about the war. Which meant that Faye was the one sister who had—or at least voiced—strong feelings about Germans as the enemy. She kept these feelings under wraps, as best she could, when she was in the flat, and I never could tell whether she approved of Sam and me living together. But, once or twice, I caught her looking at Will in a way that suggested she didn't entirely approve of Sam's behavior. She never said anything in my presence, not at the time anyway, but then she was living in a room that I was paying for, so she was very careful—polite and considerate—where I was concerned.

Tony's presence didn't help. He was a couple of years younger than me and came from Essex. He had shiny black hair, kept firmly in place by too much cream for my taste. He was slight and his uniform always seemed a shade too big for him—the arms of his tunic too long, the neck of his shirt collar too loose. Whenever I was in the flat he questioned me closely about the war, about what the Front was really like, what the casualty rates were, where exactly I had been hit and what the pain had been like and how long it had lasted. I came to the conclusion that he was frightened.

"Don't say that!" said Faye in her typically emotional way. "You make him sound like a coward."

"No, Faye." We were in the kitchen when this exchange took place, where Sam was cooking and Lottie and I were shelling peas, before lunch. "Being frightened is the only sensible reaction to this war. It will make him respectful, careful . . . and it may well keep him alive."

That Tony was frightened was reinforced when he came round one day not long afterward and said, in a subdued way, that his unit had been earmarked for France and had been told to be ready to ship out in ten days' time. He took Faye out dancing that night, they came back late and very obviously drunk, and he stayed the night. I didn't know whether he was breaking the rules of his unit, in staying out overnight, and it certainly wasn't my job to interfere, but when they appeared the next morning, a Sunday, they were engaged, and so everything was forgiven. Faye had a ring and I said that, provided Tony wasn't thrown in military jail for staying out overnight, we would have a celebration that evening.

If Tony *had* broken this or that regulation, his engagement seemed to soften military hearts as much as it had softened Sam and Lottie's and we had the celebration as planned. Which is to say, I bought some whisky for the men and some gin for the women and we all got drunk, not just the happy couple.

Twelve days later, Tony's unit did ship out and Faye, histrionic as ever, spent two days crying. Ruth came to the rescue, with the offer of a job in the uniform factory. Faye didn't move out, but she did begin to pay rent.

Dear Hal,

I'm at a place that the censors won't let me name but I've asked them and I can say that it begins with an "S." Someday S. will be known around the world. It's never been the first place where you would wish to spend your holidays, even if you could afford "abroad"; but I know where it is and I know what happened there. Tens of thousands were killed <u>in a few hours</u>!!

I tell you, Hal, this war—horrific in so many different ways—is stretching my ability to describe how terrible it is. And that's because we're having experiences we lack the language for. Or, more accurately perhaps, we are having to use language in ways it was never intended, just as we are having to think in categories for which there are no categories.

Take, for example, the reason I'm here: blood transfusion. When you train, you think of blood in terms of cubic centimeters, as something that fills a syringe or a test tube. If you prick a finger with a needle, or your nose bleeds, even though we say the blood "gushed" we don't really mean it, do we? Maybe two cc's are involved.

Already, in blood transfusion, we are dealing in <u>pints</u>!! But at S., even that way of thinking went out the window. Sixty thousand men were killed on the first morning!!! I'll repeat that, in figures: 60,000. Three times that number were injured. Half of those needed blood transfusions. <u>90,000 pints of blood, at least</u>. Eleven thousand gallons. Of course, we didn't have it. Where I was we had run out by ten-thirty that morning. We took another delivery about four in the afternoon, but had run out again by six-fifteen.

Here is an incident typical of what we had to do at S. all day long. A young boy—I remember he was called Sandy—was blinded by shrapnel. He had a white label looped in the second buttonhole of his tunic. That meant he'd been injured in the battle and had priority for treatment. We cleaned his wounds, gave him some morphine for the pain, and bandaged his eyes. Before he was shipped back to the hospital tent at the rear of the lines, I asked him, gently, if he minded if we took some blood from his arm. He said that if it would help save other men, then of course we could take it. I went to get my equipment. When I came back, Sandy had cut through his own carotid artery with his knife. He didn't want to live. The blood was still gushing out of him—and this

time I mean *gushing*. Hal, I didn't know whether to stanch his wound
or collect the blood that was pulsing out of him!!

I miss you, Hal. (I miss a good old-fashioned G&T too, but, you'll
be pleased to hear, I miss you more!) At night, when the shooting stops,
and when the sky is clear, I look up at the stars. The stars are the only
things that the war hasn't disfigured or obliterated. I think of our night
under the stars, when we slept out in the garden at home and pretended
to enjoy the sausages we had fried to a cinder. But I mustn't get
nostalgic or sentimental. There's no place for that here. Tomorrow won't
be any better than today. All we can hope for is rain. There is too much
blood in the soil to be washed away in any other fashion.

Izzy

Spending days reading the German newspapers, looking out for
something potentially significant, one naturally encountered a lot of
irrelevant information and pointless detail: sporting results, gardening
tips, the bridge column, birth announcements. But then, one day, I
came across something that had nothing to do with intelligence but
was of great interest to me. It was an article in the *FAZ* about the
Thirty-second Saxon Regiment—Wilhelm's unit. It wasn't military
information, of course; that wouldn't have been allowed. The article
didn't say what had happened to the regiment, or where it was—nothing like that. It simply said that a unit from the regiment had won that
year's drill competition. The Germans helped to maintain morale by
drill competitions, to which the public were invited. The crisp maneu-
verings of the companies taking part thrilled the public and boosted
their morale as well as the troops'. And this year a unit from the Saxon
Regiment had won.

This told me nothing about Wilhelm, of course, nothing at all.
No names were mentioned. But it put him in my mind. To tell the

truth, given my living circumstances he was never very far away, but seeing the name of his regiment in print gave me a jolt. In particular, I realized that his photograph was still in my wallet. I was suddenly worried that Sam would find it and so, that very evening, I transferred the photograph from my wallet to the briefcase I took to work. I had told Sam and Lottie that I had signed the Official Secrets Act and that my briefcase was therefore off-limits so far as they were concerned, that I could be sacked, fined, or charged with treason and sentenced to death if I violated the Official Secrets Act, especially in wartime, and they accepted that. The briefcase was safe and so was I.

I could have destroyed the photograph, of course, but I didn't. I didn't want my memory of Wilhelm to fade; it kept me on my toes. And without him I would never have met Sam. His photograph rooted me to the Front, reminded me that I had been at the sharp end and that, in a sense, I had *earned* Sam.

About a week or so after Faye began work at the uniform factory, under Ruth, we were sitting at the dinner table when Lottie said, "Faye! What's happened to your engagement ring—where *is* it?"

Faye looked flustered and blushed. She stood up. "Oh, I took it off when I had a bath and forgot to put it back on again." She slipped out of her chair. "I'll get it."

While she was gone, Lottie made a face at Sam. "I don't believe that story for a moment, do you?" She gnawed at some cheese. "I mean, you don't need to take a ring off, *ever!* Certainly not for a bath."

Just then Faye came back in. She held out her left hand, brandishing the ring on her finger. "There. See? It was sitting just where I left it, in my room."

There was an uneasy silence but we got through it. Then, a few days later, the same thing happened. Lottie drew attention to the fact that the ring was missing again, Faye went off in search of it, and Sam and Lottie exchanged words. After the fourth time, even Lottie stopped commenting on it. Faye took off her ring during the day, when she was at work, and put it on again when she came home.

It was therefore no real surprise when, two weeks after that, on a Friday night, she was picked up by a man, who was to take her dancing. He came up to the flat and introduced himself as Cyril, saying he worked in the same shop in the factory as Faye did.

He was a strange man, this Cyril. He was nearer thirty than twenty and well on the way to being bald, with a thin, wispy mustache. When he spoke it was barely above a whisper, and when he walked it was more a quiet shuffle than walking proper. I can't imagine what he was like as a dancing partner, but I took an instant dislike to him.

He didn't endear himself to me either when, on his first visit, he saw Will and said, "So this is little Fritz, is it?"

"His name's Will," I said.

"But he's German, right? Or has a Kraut father."

I felt my jaw setting to one side. "His name's still Will."

He looked at me, then shrugged his shoulders. "Have it your own way."

Fortunately, Sam was not present to witness this exchange, and I didn't tell her.

At breakfast the next morning, I asked Faye about Cyril. "He's not in the army, right? Any reason?"

Her mouth full of toast, she nodded. "Medical discharge. Trouble with his ears, getting over TB."

The ears explained his soft voice.

"Is he a good dancer?" Lottie, I could see, was longing for a fight.

"Better than Tony, that's for sure."

Lottie needed no more encouragement. "You might as well sell that ring, for all the time you wear it. Tony won't like being two-timed—"

Faye erupted—that was the only word for it. "You haven't even been one-timed, have you, Lottie?" She slapped the table. "What's it like on that shelf, Lottie? A good view of everyone else having fun, but lonely, I'll bet."

Lottie blushed.

"I'd *hate* being lonely," hissed Faye.

"Stop it, you two," said Sam. She turned to Lottie. "You can't blame Faye, not really. I know she's engaged but . . . well, face facts: Tony could be killed at any time."

"There's no need for you to stick up for me!" hissed Faye. "I can do my own defending, thank you very much."

Silence.

"So how was the dance?" I said at length, to cut through the atmosphere.

"Not much dancing, as it happened," muttered Faye, grateful, I think, for the change of subject. "Some of the men started arguing about the war and in no time a fight had broken out." She looked at me. "With the amount of blood spilled, your sister should have been there."

"What was the fight about?" I said. "I mean, was there something specific?"

Faye drank some tea. "From what was said, it had something to do with gas. Someone said only the Germans would use it, that they were barbarians, and then someone else pointed out that we have used it, that it's the poor people—the line soldiers on both sides—who get killed by it. That it's not only the British who are victims in this war." She spread more margarine on her toast. "That set everyone off—the idea that the Germans could be victims. I mean, people couldn't stomach that. Cyril went for someone, and in no time there was mayhem."

"Cyril started it?" said Lottie.

"He was one of them. Yes."

"And what happened?"

A pause while Faye chewed her toast. "The police arrived and he was arrested. I think he was kept overnight in the cells. I'm going down there later."

"Oh, Faye. Don't get mixed up in all that." Sam reached out and put her hand on Faye's arm.

Faye shook it off. "I can look after myself. In any case, I'm on Cyril's side." She glared hard at Sam. "We're not as barbaric as the Germans."

It was about now, I think, that we went to a concert at the Bechstein Hall, as it then was, in Wigmore Street. Later in the war its name was changed. All the property of the Bechstein Piano Company was seized by the government, and the hall auctioned off. Its original name was obviously too German for the times, and the new owners, Debenhams, changed it. (The change occurred virtually simultaneously with the royal family changing *its* name from Saxe-Coburg and Gotha to Windsor.)

Sam liked going to the Bechstein Hall, and she loved in particular the vocal recitals that were given there on Sunday afternoons. She was less enamored of the endless wranglings over whether it was unpatriotic to listen to German music, as some of the newspapers insisted.

"Brahms has been dead for decades," she would say, "Schubert for nearly a century. What have they got to do with the war?"

I could see both sides of the argument, but I didn't want a fight.

On the Sunday I am thinking of we were just leaving a concert where a Scottish soprano had been singing a variety of Schubert songs, and there were people outside the hall with placards, likening concertgoers to traitors and conscientious objectors.

Sam had insisted we come to this concert, so I asked her what it was that she especially liked about Schubert.

She turned her head toward me for a moment, then looked straight in front again. "He was Wilhelm's favorite and . . . well, I'm sorry, Hal, but it would have been—it *is*—Wilhelm's birthday today. I've tried to forget, but I can't. Not for now. Being here, I felt . . . I *feel* . . . that much closer to him, I suppose. I'm sorry, I wasn't going to say anything, but I don't want to lie to you and you asked me a direct question. Given how you and I met, our agreement, if I were found out lying to you . . . what would you think of me?"

She squeezed my arm. "It's not much, is it, Hal? Me promising not to lie to you. Not much of a commitment, I mean. But look what a mess Faye's life is—she's *living* a lie. I couldn't do that."

"What other favorites did Wilhelm have?" We had reached Baker Street, where we could catch an omnibus home. "If you tell me, I'll know what *not* to talk about."

She squeezed my arm again. "Don't be silly, Hal. We don't have to be so . . . regimented. But I can't just forget him. You can pretend, if you like, that he never was, but I can't. I won't. Every time I look at Will, I see his father—the resemblance is quite marked. You need to know that. I don't know how long Wilhelm will . . . you know what I'm trying to say, in a way that won't hurt you . . ." She trailed off.

I did feel hurt, but then I told myself not to be so . . . so one-sided, a phrase Lottie had used. I had told Sam a lie, a massive lie; in fact, I too was living a lie, just as Faye was. And what would happen if *I* was found out in my lie? What would Sam think of *me*?

———

I was promoted again that summer. It was due mainly to a combination of two factors. In the first place, I spotted something in *Die Zeit*, the Hamburg newspaper and probably Germany's best (and therefore more censored than most). In some ways it was unexceptional—a simple boast, on the front page, about the paper's rising circulation, the sort of thing all newspapers indulge in when recent statistics suit them. On an inside page, however, the paper gave a breakdown of its figures, according to the area around Hamburg where it sold. These figures showed that there had been an average increase in circulation, over the previous six months, of 4 percent, but that it had varied from -0.5 percent in Witzhave, to +1.3 percent in Moisburg, to +13 percent in Hetlingen.

As I say, I didn't know much about newspapers but what I did know was that, by and large, newspaper readership was fairly stable; it moved up or down by no more than a few percentage points every year. That made sense—readers are loyal to their papers and don't like to chop and change. But if those figures were true, then in one area of Hamburg circulation was rising by 13 percent a year, unthinkable normally. What could explain it?

I might not have followed through with these thoughts had it not been for the fact that the Battle of Jutland had recently taken place and I was aware of the debate in naval circles as to whether the British navy had done well or badly. Some said that the German fleet had run away; others pointed out that Britain had lost more ships—far more ships—than the Germans had. So naval matters were on my mind—on everyone's mind, come to that.

I therefore took the trouble to look up a map of Hamburg, and it was what I found on the map that caused me to involve Sheila again.

She brought in our naval specialist, who, as it happened, didn't agree with me. In cases like this, a table leader was entitled to go to Pritchard with the idea his or her table had come up with, but he or she had to take along the dissenting individual. Which is what happened that time.

"Ah! Another Hal special, is it?" said Pritchard, knocking the tobacco out of his pipe by tapping it on the heel of his shoe, his shiny shoe as it happened. "Julian, you here as well?"

Julian Mayhew was the naval expert.

"Julian disagrees with me, sir."

"Does he indeed?" Pritchard grunted and reached for his tobacco. "Okay. So be it. Why don't you all sit down and Hal can kick off."

We did as we were told, Sheila reverting to her usual perch on the radiator.

When everyone was settled I started on in, giving Pritchard the circulation figures for *Die Zeit.*

"Okay," said Pritchard. "The statistics seem fairly straightforward. What's your interpretation?"

"Sir, in Hetlingen there has been a massive increase in circulation. In my view that can be due to one of only two reasons."

I looked across to Julian. I shouldn't have. He had disbelief written all over his face.

"One, there was another newspaper published in Hetlingen, which has ceased publication, so that all the people who read it have transferred overnight and en masse to *Die Zeit.*"

"Or—?"

"Or . . . there has been a massive influx of population, in the last six months, since the previous set of figures were compiled."

"And—? I know you, Hal. You are busy making inferences. What is it this time?"

"Areas like Witzhave and Moisburg, which haven't seen much of an increase or have actually seen a *drop* in circulation, are all inland areas. Hetlingen, however, is on the coast—or, more accurately, it lines the estuary of the Elbe, Hamburg's river, which flows into the North Sea."

"Yes, I know about the Elbe and the North Sea," Pritchard said dryly. "Go on."

"Well—and here I'm guessing, sir—maybe the influx of population has to do with shipbuilding, a new shipyard, or the massive expansion of an existing one. I know it's a guess, sir, but—well, what with the Battle of Jutland being such a fiasco, for both sides, I mean, maybe this signals a change of military policy—"

"Hold on! Hold on." Pritchard held up his hand, the one with the pipe in it. "That's a lot to read into some circulation figures. Julian, let me hear from you."

"That's exactly my view, sir. I agree with you, and with Hal, that the circulation figures are interesting in themselves, and that there's a development that needs to be explained. But it doesn't necessarily have to do with population movement, and it certainly doesn't have to do with naval affairs. We've picked up nothing on naval matters for a few weeks."

"Hmm." Pritchard at last had his pipe going. "How big a jump *is* thirteen percent?"

"Massive," I replied. "I checked with British newspapers. Their circulations fall by plus or minus three to four percent a year—a *year,* not every six months. If a paper goes up or down by as much as eight percent a year, it's big news. A slump of eight percent and the editor would be fired. But, and this is the killer point, a big jump or slide always occurs *across the board*—everywhere the paper sells. We're not seeing that happen here."

"I don't see what Jutland has to do with this." Pritchard sat back now, his pipe well launched.

"As I read it," I said after a pause, "neither we nor the Germans can draw much comfort from that battle. We had several ships destroyed, the Germans retreated as fast as they could into harbor. I therefore conclude that the Germans must concede that they can't win this war at sea, as their navy is presently constituted. They must expand—and expand fast—their most successful and most fearsome vessel: the submarine."

"You mean—?"

"Yes. I think it's worth investigating whether the Germans have built a new submarine dry dock at Hetlingen and shipped in a workforce to build large numbers of vessels."

Pritchard turned his gaze on Mayhew.

"All this from a change in newspaper circulation?" Julian asked. "I think it's going too far. We have people on the ground in and around Hamburg—we must have or we are all lost. You can't just build a dry dock—several dry docks—without anyone noticing. If what Hal says is happening *is* happening, we'd already know about it."

Pritchard looked at Sheila.

"Hal's given us a target, somewhere to look, and a clue as to what to look for. I'd say it's worth acting upon."

"It's not that simple," growled Pritchard, "and I'm surprised at you, Sheila. Whoever we have on the ground there, they're not just twiddling their thumbs, playing with a sponge in the bath. They're busy, doing other things, worthwhile things. If I ask for them to be pulled off doing proven good work, to chase this . . . *theory*, we could be doing more damage to the war effort than help."

Silence.

He looked at me. "Anything else?"

"*Die Zeit* has a circulation of four hundred and fifty thousand. Of that, seventy thousand are sold in and around Hetlingen. If circulation has risen by thirteen percent, that represents nine thousand, one hundred copies. Say a third of the new readers are married—making twelve thousand people in all who've moved in. That's a huge factory by any standards. Can we afford to ignore the figures?"

Pritchard tapped his teeth with the stem of his pipe.

The rest of us waited.

"No. Not this time, Hal. I'm not convinced, not until we have something else. I'll keep the documentation here, in a file. But I'll not send it upstairs, not yet." He drew on his pipe. "That's all."

Sheila rolled her eyes at me and we trooped out of Pritchard's office.

Dear Hal,

Short note. You are in my thoughts because we have just treated a man who had been shot in the pelvis. He lost blood but we mended him.

You are also in my thoughts because, a few days ago, we received a batch of old, out-of-date newspapers. Among these were some copies of the <u>Times</u>. I was delighted to see that page 5 is still going strong. One paragraph, three lines long, said: "The Hampton Court crocuses are in perfect bloom. Now is the time to go and see them." Who writes this? What sort of subeditor chooses to put something like this in among the casualty lists, the battle reports, the new laws about rationing? Don't get me wrong—I think it's wonderful. Very few <u>Times</u> readers will live anywhere near Hampton Court, to be able actually to visit the flowers, but it's a paragraph of warmth, of sanity, in among all the darker events. Some anonymous journalist on the <u>Times</u> is doing us all a service. Reading those few words is the best thing that has happened to me all day.

Lucky you, getting a newspaper every morning.

Have to stop. Must write letters for some of the wounded.

Huge love,

Izzy

On nights when Sam and I weren't going to the theater, or to a concert, or to a lecture, and Faye wasn't going out with Cyril, we devised our own entertainment. Some evenings were devoted to hair washing, when Sam, Faye, and Lottie would all wander around the flat with their hair in towel turbans and I would read to them for an hour, sometimes recent novels I liked, sometimes poetry Sam had spotted, and sometimes from Lottie's magazines about the party life of the smart set in London. Sometimes we made respirators. These were pads of absorbent cotton wool between layers of gauze, about six inches long and three inches deep, to fit over the mouth and nostrils and fastened around the head by tapes. They were designed to help cope with a gas attack, should one occur, and we took any spares we made—over and above what we needed—to the local army barracks, for distribution.

And sometimes, when we really wanted to relax, we played charades.

Lottie, being a theater type, was the organizing genius here. She loved acting herself, though she had never dared try it on the professional stage. She would think up hilarious and often very clever phrases for us all to act out and, as the evenings wore on and the whisky began to take over, some of her ideas turned decidedly risqué.

I was by far the worst actor of the four of us. The sisters, of course, were used to the intimacy of large family life, their shared childhood, and had a string of in-jokes and in-talk that I simply didn't understand. They had borrowed one another's clothes and stolen one another's makeup for as long as they could remember, and their great triumphs and disasters, in the "men department," as they called it, were revisited every so often, accompanied by gales of laughter.

I loved the sisters' frankness and complete lack of embarrassment in front of one another.

"You're *such* a cow, Lottie," Sam would say after Lottie had made some cutting remark or other.

"I know," Lottie would agree eagerly, "but I can't help it." They would rib each other about the shape of their breasts, the ugliness of someone's ankles, or speculate freely about what they thought this or that politician was like in bed.

On one evening of charades, Lottie and Sam were playing against Faye and me. It was late, and Lottie and Sam were a game ahead, when Lottie set me to act out one final phrase. She took me to the edge of the room, so Faye couldn't hear, and whispered, "Premature ejaculation."

I laughed nervously. This was going to take some doing.

Lottie was already smiling, ready to laugh at whatever moves I might make.

It was hardly the most suitable phrase, given my predicament, but Lottie didn't know about that.

Or did she?

A horrible thought struck me: that Sam had shared this intimacy with her sister.

Sam was smiling too, but was she blushing as well? And was that because ejaculation was a sensitive subject so far as I was concerned, and she was worried I might be embarrassed? Or because she feared that Lottie had, in a roundabout way, betrayed a confidence she had been told?

I didn't know and I decided I didn't care.

I turned to Faye and held up two fingers.

"Two words."

I nodded. I put my fingers in my ears and led them down to my belly. This was a convention we had devised many nights ago in the flat, to indicate a stethoscope.

"Medical condition," said Faye.

I nodded again.

There was nothing for it, so I grabbed Lottie and lay her on her back on the carpet. She had got me into this; she could now help me out.

"At last!" breathed Lottie. "What kept you, Hal?"

All of us were laughing now, as I proceeded to lie on top of Lottie and started to simulate making love.

"Incest!" said Faye, laughing.

"That's not a medical condition," said Sam.

"Oh, I don't know."

"It's only one word, anyway," Sam went on.

"Do it twice, then," said Lottie.

"Is it my turn next?" said Faye.

Whisky suddenly came into the room, anxious to see what all the fuss was about. He started licking Lottie's face.

More laughter.

I suddenly stopped what I was doing and gave the best imitation I could of a climax.

"Poor you," said Faye to Sam. "Is it over that quickly every night?"

Sam collapsed into laughter, rolling about on the sofa. Lottie's frame heaved on the carpet.

"Oh God, I know what it is," said Faye, suddenly mock serious, trying to keep from laughing. "Premature ejaculation!"

"Yes!" chorused Sam and Lottie together.

"Brilliant," cried Lottie. "How did you guess? Hal's acting was terrible, as usual."

"I wasn't acting," I said.

Yet more laughter.

"If that's what you call sex, Hal, Sam really is in trouble." Lottie got to her feet and straightened her dress. "Seriously, Faye," she said, "that was a brilliant guess."

Faye shook her head, trying to keep from setting herself off again. "You don't understand," she said. "Hal's acting wasn't bad at all . . ." She looked from one sister to the other. "He reminded me of Cyril."

I should think they could have heard the laughter from Penrith Mansions across the street in the Thomas More.

Two days later, Sheila and I were summoned back to Pritchard's office. Mayhew was there again.

"Sit down," Pritchard said. "And Sheila, sit on a chair this time, will you. I want you in my direct line of sight."

We sat.

"This came in earlier today." He pointed to a folder on his desk, stenciled SECRET. "It's for my eyes only so you don't get to see it, I'm afraid, but you can take it from me it's a drawing. One of our people on the ground observed building going on north of Hamburg, on the right-hand side of the estuary of the river Elbe. She drew what she saw—and sent it to us. The scientists have looked at it. It's what they call a 'conning' tower for a submarine."

Silence.

"I was wrong. Julian, you were wrong. Hal and Sheila were right. Julian, close the door, will you?"

Julian got up and closed the door, which gave onto the corridor. He sat down again.

"Sheila, you're transferring downstairs to the Crypt, working on interrogation reports. You too, Julian. It's time for one of my periodic shake-ups. Hal, you'll take over the science table. You'll be a major from here on—but with a new set of sidekicks. The people there now have been in place longer than you have—they won't take kindly to you being promoted over their heads. So I'm giving you a new team. You two—" He indicated Sheila and Julian. "Go and get your things, and report back here. Hal, have the rest of the day off. Come in on Monday, and I'll have moved people around. I'm not being wet . . . I just don't want efficiency in my department affected by personal grievances, so do as you're told—right?"

I nodded. He was entitled to run the show his way.

Sheila gave me a kiss, I shook hands with Julian, and we left in different directions.

It never rains but it pours: have I said that before? What a day it turned out to be (and here I need some of Izzy's exclamation marks). After I left Northumberland Avenue, I had lunch by myself in a pub just off Trafalgar Square and then decided to walk home. I was in no hurry, the weather could have been worse, and I needed some exercise.

I walked along the Mall, enjoying the trees and the variegated shade they threw onto the pavement. A company of men was marching along by St. James's Park. They had no weapons or uniforms. They had been called up and formed into units—but the shortages were so bad just then they had to wait weeks for proper equipment.

I was a little light-headed, too, of course. Everyone likes being appreciated, and promotion was both the seal of approval to the work I had been doing and meant a little more money. I didn't exactly *need* more money from my job, but I wasn't so foolish as to turn it down, and in any case, without telling Sam I was putting something aside for a certain little boy I was growing fonder of day by day.

Just off Grosvenor Gardens I stopped at a secondhand bookshop and spent the better part of an hour looking over two or three things that appealed to me. Through a doorway, however, I was in for a surprise. It was a room full of old maps. There were framed maps, rolled maps, books of maps, maps of every age and size. Old maps of the world without Australia, because it hadn't yet been discovered, with India the size of a postage stamp, with Alaska and Siberia joined. Sam would love it here. I bought her a framed map of the Caribbean islands scattered in improbable places. It would go well with her map of the Orinoco; two maps meant she now had a "collection," I joked to myself. The shopkeeper wrapped it neatly.

One way and another, therefore, it had gone six by the time I got home.

Everyone else was there already. Will was trying to separate Whisky from his ears in the living room and the women were all standing in the kitchen, talking and drinking tea. I went into the dining room and left the package by the front door. Sam heard me pouring myself a drink—something she liked to do for me normally—and came through. She gave me a kiss. "How was your day?"

"I was promoted, to major."

"You *were?* Oh, Hal, that's marvelous. Well done." Another kiss on the cheek.

"One for you?" I said, holding up the whisky bottle.

"Not just—" she began, but at that very moment there was a rap on the front door.

"I'll go," I said. "I'm nearest."

It was the postman. He was holding a small brown envelope in his hand.

I signed for it, took it from him, stepped back, and closed the door.

Faye and Lottie had come out from the kitchen and were standing over Will in the living room. Sam was with them. The dog had disappeared.

I held out the envelope to Faye. "It's a telegram. It's for you."

Everyone stopped breathing. Lottie let out a soft scream: *"No!"*

My arm was still outstretched.

Sam breathed, "Do you want Hal to—?"

Faye stepped forward and took the envelope from me. As she did so, I noticed that—once again—she wasn't wearing her engagement ring. She gripped the envelope in her fingers, crumpled it up, and stepped across to the window. With her back to us, she fumbled with the envelope, ripped it open, and took out whatever was inside.

For a moment no one moved. Not even Will. The rest of us stared at Faye's back, now hunched over, as she reread the paper in her hands.

Then her frame began to shake, slightly at first, but with gathering force, and she threw back her head—and screamed at the ceiling.

"Nooooo!"

Sam and Lottie rushed toward her, but before they could reach her she had turned.

"Noooooo!"

Tears were streaming down her face; lines of smudged mascara covered her cheeks, making her look as though she'd just climbed out of a mine.

"He's dead! DEAD!" she screamed, webs of spittle forming at the corners of her mouth.

Lottie and Sam moved her to the sofa. I went through into the dining room and poured a large whisky into a glass, which I took back to her.

She was still sobbing, her frame heaving, tears tumbling down her cheeks.

Sam handed me the telegram she had taken from her sister. It was brusque:

+ REGRET • TO • INFORM • YOU • PVTE • ANTHONY • MCALLISTER •
KILLED • IN • ACTION • NEAR • VIMY + STOP + MY • CONDOLENCES
+ STOP + COL • WALTER • COLE + ENDS +

Faye gripped the whisky but didn't drink it. She simply stared at the carpet in front of her, rubbing her eyes with the ball of her hand. Lottie gave her a handkerchief for her runny nose.

After a few minutes, the sobbing subsided and I said, as gently as I could, "Would you like some water instead?"

Silently, she shook her head. She hadn't really heard me.

Then she said, "Where's the telegram?"

"On the sofa beside you," whispered Lottie.

I had replaced it there.

Faye took it and held it close. She read it again, and burst into tears again.

Sam picked up Will and carried him through into his room, shutting the door behind her.

Lottie and I waited for Faye to quiet down again. Lottie sat next to her, rubbing Faye's shoulder. I sat across from the fireplace, sipping my whisky.

Eventually, Sam reappeared and made a drinking movement with her hand. I went through to the dining room and poured her a Scotch. Then she sat on my lap and we waited.

Nothing much happened that night. After about another fifteen minutes, Faye got up and went into her room. We heard her crying again, but then she fell silent and we assumed she had gone to sleep.

The rest of us went to bed early and in silence.

In our room I silently handed Sam the package I had retrieved from near the front door.

"For me?" she whispered.

"To celebrate my promotion. I couldn't know what was going to happen the minute I arrived home."

She unwrapped the package.

"Oh, Hal," she said quietly. "It's lovely—a lovely idea." She stepped across the room and we embraced. We kissed but not . . . not ardently. She drew back and whispered, "Sorry, it's not—"

"I know," I said, putting my thumb to her lips. "It's not the moment. I couldn't know. Don't worry."

Sam shook her head. "You were wounded, Tony's been killed. Three children didn't come to school today—they stayed home with their mother because their father, away at the Front, has been killed." She touched my cheek with her fingertips. "How many men are going to be left, when this war is over?"

It was not immediately clear who she was thinking of . . .

"Our father liked the Caribbean," said Sam, placing her hand flat on the map. "He went there a few times." She sighed. "In fact, he liked it so much he changed the company he worked for, to one that only had ships going to the Caribbean."

She leaned over and kissed me.

As we settled into bed and I put out the light, she murmured, "That was a lovely thought, Hal. The map, I mean. It brought back a lot for me."

She turned and kissed my shoulder. "And don't worry, tonight's not . . . not the time. But I'll make it up to you."

The next day was a Saturday and Sam, Lottie, and I were at the breakfast table when Faye appeared. Her hair was disheveled, she hadn't washed the smudged mascara off her face, and she looked wrecked.

Will was again wrestling with the dog in the living room.

Faye sat down at the kitchen table without speaking, and Sam poured her tea in the way that she knew Faye liked it—strong and sweet.

"Toast?"

Faye shook her head. She sipped her tea.

Lottie leaned forward. "Don't take it so hard, Faye. There's always Cyril."

"Lottie!" whispered Sam urgently, but it was too late.

Faye jerked back, dropping her tea, which went everywhere.

"What do you know about anything, Lottie!" Faye shouted, getting to her feet, scraping the chair back and knocking it over. "How many men have you ever had, you sour-faced stage hag. Look at you! No job, no man, no brains—and no fucking hope in any direction."

"Not so loud, Faye," said Sam, softly but urgently. "Will might hear."

"Not in front of the little Fritz, you mean? The little sauer-fucking-kraut." Faye pointed her finger at Sam. "It was the fucking Germans who killed Tony. It was the fucking Germans who started this war and forced us to live like . . . like *this*." She slapped the kitchen table. She pointed at Sam again. "How could you, Sam—fuck a German, I mean? How could you *sleep* with the enemy?"

"Faye," I said, stepping forward.

"Don't you interfere, Hal. This is not your fight. This is not your family."

"Faye!" screamed Sam. "Take that back!"

"I'll take nothing back," growled Faye. She pointed to me. "He's not Will's father, he's not your husband." She glared at Sam. "Just because you've got yourself a war hero, Head Girl, a baby and a flat in Chelsea, you think you've got it made. How long do you think you can get away with it—eh? The boy's a German, a Kraut, a Fritz, a fucking *Kaiserkind*, and once the world knows, where do you think you'll be, Madame Mont-bloody-gomery. I'll tell you where you'll be. You'll be—"

And she burst out crying and collapsed against the kitchen wall.

Sam and Lottie went to her and shepherded her back to her room.

When they reappeared, Sam came up to me and kissed my cheek. "I am *so* sorry, Hal. You shouldn't have been put through that."

"I think she may have picked up some anti-German feeling from Cyril," I muttered. "And some of his aggression."

"I'll make sure she leaves today," said Sam, kissing me again. "Tomorrow at the latest."

I nodded. I didn't like Faye leaving under those circumstances, but at least it meant I didn't have to see the odious Cyril ever again.

The waiter shuffled across the lunchroom and leaned on the table when he reached us, breathing heavily and seemingly exhausted. He picked up the pad, on which my father had written our orders, and wheezed, "I'll send the wine waiter, sir." Then he launched himself on the long way back to the kitchen.

I had never liked the Athenaeum, bang in the center of clubland, in St. James's, wedged between Pall Mall and the Duke of York steps. I hadn't joined many clubs at Cambridge and when my father had asked if he should put my name down for his club, I had said no. I was developing a noisy home life, people came and went all the time, and the flat had now been christened, among our friends—and Sam's sisters and their friends—"Gare Montgomery." It was very different from my upbringing, but I loved it. What did I need a club for?

But with my job in the War Ministry, just off Trafalgar Square in Northumberland Avenue, the Athenaeum was a short walk from the office and it made good sense to meet my father there. He was spending one night in London.

My father was a brandy-and-soda man. He didn't drink to excess, exactly, but he thought nothing of a couple of brandies at lunchtime (and quite a few more in the evening). He rarely drank wine, so when the wine waiter arrived my father briskly ordered his "usual," which the wine waiter was expected to remember, and did; then he looked at me. I chose a small carafe of the house claret, barely more than a glass.

"Let me look at you," my father said, as the wine waiter retreated. "Your mother asked me to check on your weight, the shine of your skin and hair. She's worried you aren't eating properly. She wants to know if you've got a girlfriend yet."

I put out my tongue and held out my hands, palms down. I said, sarcastically, "Tongue clear, fingernails shiny, all vital signs good."

"Hmm." He nodded. "And the other thing, the girlfriend?"

"That's complicated, Dad. Why don't you tell me about Ma? Izzy told me she's not as good as she might be."

The drinks arrived. The waiter placed my father's brandy and soda in front of him and tipped half the contents of the carafe into a glass.

"Your mother is not well, Hal. That's true. Not at all well. Emphysema, it's called. In effect, because she smokes so much, her lungs are impaired—they're only about seventy or eighty percent efficient. That means she has to breathe two or three times as hard as you and me to get enough oxygen into her blood, and that puts pressure on her heart. She has this dreadful cough, which doesn't improve her mood—and as you know, her mood is not all that sunny at the best of times." He drank some of his brandy. "This damned war doesn't help, of course. She takes the stupidity of the military so personally." He helped himself to some bread from a small basket between us. "Speaking of which, tell me about this job of yours."

I told him what I could. That is, I told him I was in intelligence analysis, that I worked on a science team. I didn't tell him that all I did was study out-of-date German newspapers and try to read between the lines; nor did I tell him any specifics about the ideas I'd had. I told him I'd signed the Official Secrets Act.

He listened intently. "Sounds like useful work," he said, once I had finished. "And safe. There's something in that, I suppose."

"Why are you here, Dad? In London, I mean."

"Well, the official reason I'm here is because—and this is confidential—I have been asked to be one of the editors of the official history of the war. Because of my publishing experience, because I'm now retired, because I can afford to do it without payment, because I know someone in the relevant ministry who trusts me."

I sat back as the soup arrived. It had a brown intensity that would not have been out of place at the Ag.

"I'm impressed, Dad. Well done. But what happens if we lose the war?"

"We *can't* lose," he whispered. "Don't talk like that." He looked around the room, hoping that no one else had overheard what he took as my defeatism.

I changed the subject again. "If that's the official reason you're here, what's the secret reason?"

He spooned soup into his mouth, then wiped his lips with his napkin, nodding.

"Your mother, of course. We need another opinion on her emphysema, but it has to be someone who is willing to come down to Edgewater. You know I can't get your mother up to London."

The soup plates were taken away and the main courses placed in front of us. Chicken, which—apart from fish—was virtually all there was in those days.

"You're worried, Dad. I can tell. Is there anything I can do?"

"I *am* worried, yes. Your mother doesn't say much but of course I know her very well and she's fearful—fearful and angry—for Izzy mainly. Your mother loathes this war, as you know. She feels that it has already . . . well, taken part of you away, an important part. Grandchildren, for instance. And it might still kill Izzy. I don't think she could survive that."

"What news of Izzy?"

My father's features softened. "Doesn't your sister write good letters, Hal? They're slightly naïve, though like a lot of naïve people she tries hard to be worldly. But they are *so* vivid—she's got a real gift, I think. Her naïveté is part of their force."

Halfway through my chicken, I nodded. "We should keep them. You never know, after the war, *Letters from a Nurse.* People will want to read that sort of stuff."

He drank more brandy. "She sent us one letter the other day, in which she described a conversation she had overheard between two young soldiers who had been blinded by shrapnel. One had no wish to live. He did not want decades of life without being able to see, he said, and planned to kill himself. She understood that point of view, she said, she understood it very well. But the other man—a boy, really—was much calmer. He said he'd have to develop his sense of hearing and his sense of touch, that he would imagine, from then onward, that all women were beautiful. He looked forward to the sound of rain, to feeling sunshine on his cheek, to learning the different songs of birds. Once you thought about it, he said, there was a lot you could do, being blind.

"But here's the point." Father forked chicken into his mouth and chewed for a moment. "Here's the point. She got it wrong. The man who *seemed* calm was, in reality, just as depressed as the other man. But while the 'depressive'—let's call him that—was put on suicide watch, the other man was given back his uniform, including his pistol, for the journey away from the field hospital, back to Britain. The powers that be thought he was perfect hero material, stoically bearing his misfortune with placid fortitude and good humor."

Father paused for effect.

"First chance he got, he shot himself. The other man—the 'depressive'—was never allowed near weapons and his 'cheerful' colleague knew that, grasped it from the beginning. He knew he had to put on a show; otherwise he would have been isolated from the means to kill himself."

It wasn't the first time I'd heard stories like this from Izzy.

My father shook his head. "Izzy wrote all this with a sense of wonder, at what we are doing to each other, to ourselves, how people can be creative and cunning to the end, how we differ and yet are all the same, how willing we are to be misled by the poetics of the war, of death, of the impossibility of escape from the horror." He wiped his lips with his napkin. "Of course I'm keeping her letters. Don't tell her, though; if she gets wind that we think she's worth publishing, she'll change, and we'll make her self-conscious and kill her spirit. It's her unself-consciousness that is so attractive. We don't want to give her any complexes—not where she is, on the edge of danger."

He had finished—wolfed—his chicken. He placed his knife and fork together and wrapped his fingers around his brandy glass. "Speaking of complexes, or complicated situations, it's your turn. No ducking now. What are your living arrangements? Are you living with someone?"

I told him. I told him about Sam, about Will, about Lottie and Faye, about Whisky. I said that Sam had lost touch with Will's father, who was at the Front. I didn't say who Will's father was, what his nationality was, and I didn't say anything about Faye's bereavement and outburst.

He heard me out in silence. When I had finished, he moved his jaw to one side and said, "So it's as we thought. You *are* living in sin." He shook his head. "You are pretending to be married with someone whose man could come back at any time and reclaim what's his. Forget for the moment whether what you are doing is *right*, is moral. Is it *wise?* Do you love this woman? If you do, you could get very hurt." He shook his head again. "It's messy emotionally, Hal. And it's—well, it's hardly tidy, or clean, morally, is it?"

He looked at me for quite some time without either of us speaking. "Did your mother and I do something wrong, make some terrible mistake, bringing you up? I'm shocked and I'm disappointed. To be quite frank, Hal, I'm appalled—I can't deny it. I *won't* deny it. It's not at all what your mother and I had in mind for you."

His features were set in an icy glare.

"But I'm content, Dad. Happy. Very happy." In for a penny, in for a pound—I banged on, defending myself, making my own case. "It makes a kind of biological sense, too—you can see that, can't you? I don't think you should tell Ma, though. She sounds as though she's got enough to worry about, without a little bastard in the family."

He winced at my use of that word and nodded glumly. "At least you're not lonely. We were worried, both of us, that you would be . . . well, solitary in London."

I grinned. "No chance of that. The job is hard—long hours, anyway—and Sam has three sisters. There are always people coming and going at the flat—it's known as Gare Montgomery."

He almost smiled.

I think he was in part relieved that I hadn't become some sort of freak because of my sexual predicament, and in part disappointed, too, that I hadn't met a girl from a "good" family. Had Sam been a university lecturer, say, rather than a schoolteacher, he would have been far happier.

"I won't tell your mother just yet," he said. "You're right about that. Let's see what this other doctor has to say and we'll go on from there."

I nodded. Though they had been distant, I had always got on with my parents, and I wanted their good opinion.

But I wanted Sam more.

———

With Faye gone, the flat was a good bit quieter, emptier, less unpredictable than it had been. I thought I'd be pleased—and I *was* pleased that the odious Cyril was out of our lives—but I found that, if I didn't so much miss Faye herself, and her tempers, I did miss the extra level of busyness, of noise, bustle, and, yes, chaos that she had brought with her. Since she had been gone, Penrith Mansions was a little less of a railway station.

Sam felt differently. The arguments and shouting matches about Will's paternity had upset and wearied her, mainly because, I think, she realized that it would always be an issue among those who knew. Lottie never said anything, at least not to me, but she offered herself more often than usual for babysitting duty. On those evenings she still avidly buried herself in her books and magazines on the weddings and parties and affairs of the aristocracy. In my presence she never behaved as if Will were anything other than 100 percent British.

A few days after Faye had left, however, Sam tackled me. It was a Saturday, early evening, and the three of us—Sam, Will, and me—were visiting a fair in Battersea Park. There were about three of these fairs a year and we all loved going. They were, truth to tell, a bit tacky but they were a change from our normal routine, and Will—especially, naturally—was entranced by the bright lights, the music, the smells of candy floss, fried food, and the sheer exoticism of the occasion.

I had to keep my eyes open for him. He was as curious—as brave—as ever. If he could, he would walk—stumble—right up to machinery and peer in, oblivious to danger, poking his fingers where they shouldn't be poked, grabbing chains that shouldn't be grabbed, gurgling away triumphantly when we dragged him out of danger. He knew he'd gone too far and got away with it.

Halfway through the evening—it must have been eight-thirty, long past Will's bedtime (as he well knew, but kept very quiet about)—I bought him some candy floss. We were both standing there, our cheeks covered in laces of colored spun sugar, when Sam suddenly whispered, so that Will couldn't hear, "We've never really talked about it, have we—Will's father being German, I mean? Except that first day, in the rain, in Middle Hill. You didn't even say much when we had to walk through those placards outside the Bechstein Hall. Do *you* think I was wrong to do what I did?"

Faye's outburst was preying on her mind.

It wasn't easy replying, with so much sugar lace in my mouth, but I was grateful for it as a delaying device. This was not a subject I wanted to discuss. I made a show of chewing and swallowing.

"Sam, please. After your sisters, I am the first person you told about Wilhelm. Did I let it stand in the way then? Don't make yourself all . . . all upset about it. Have some candy floss."

But she wouldn't let it drop. She picked up Will.

"Why can't Faye see that it happened *before* the war. Wilhelm wasn't the enemy *then!* I mean, it couldn't have happened after war broke out. He had a brother and always wanted a sister, just as we sisters always wondered what having a brother would have been like. He said he was very competitive with his brother, whereas competition, although it was there, was always muted between us sisters. At school Wilhelm's brother got better marks, but Wilhelm was better at sport. Faye couldn't see—wouldn't see, *nobody* can see—that Germans are *just like us.*" She made a sound, somewhere between a groan and a sigh. "I hate it that she's gone and . . . well, that we've lost touch." She bit her lip. "But what she said to you was unforgivable and ungrateful."

"Well, she *has* gone," I said. "And taken the awful Cyril with her. Look on the positive side."

Sam wouldn't be comforted. "They can tell other people. That would be . . ."

"Who are you worried about?"

"Well, Hal, you work in a sensitive job."

I stepped forward and kissed her cheek, even though we were in public, even though my lips were sticky with candy floss. "Maybe I shouldn't say this," I whispered, "but I think I've done enough in my job to prove my worth, to show I'm not a spy or a German sympathizer or anything like that. But this is silly, Sam. The people I work with wouldn't care, if they knew. The people I work with are rationalists."

"Well, the people *I* work with are not!"

I was stunned.

She turned and started walking back in the direction of the flat. But the crowds were thick—it was Saturday night, after all—and I soon caught up with her.

"What is it?" I said. "What's happened at school?"

She bit her lip again. "Nothing. Nothing really. It's just that— well, one day last week, in the staff room, some of the other teachers were talking and one woman said that a child in her class had just had his father killed, at the Front, with her mother pregnant. She said that the child's family didn't know how they were going to survive—they were a family of three children, soon to be four, with no breadwinner now. That started everybody off. Oh, Hal, everyone was so anti-German, so vitriolic."

She put Will back on the ground and held his hand as we fought our way through the evening crowds. "I met Wilhelm at a fair like this—just like this," she said, straightening up. "We were standing next to each other, shooting pellets at something, and we got talking, laughing at how hopeless we were. It was the most natural thing in the world—or that's how it seemed then. Now," she sighed, "it's beginning to be a burden, the most unnatural thing I've ever done, falling in love. I know that the teachers at school . . . if they were told the truth . . . I'd be shunned, and out of a job in no time."

I took Sam's hand and led both her and Will to a quiet patch of ground away from the main walkway.

"Look," I said, brushing her cheek with my fingers. "The problem is with you, in your head, here." I tapped her temple with my finger. "Maybe you've still got some loyalty to Wilhelm—I don't know. Something that stops you from moving forward. But you're wrong to let Faye's behavior shape your life and Will's happiness. I don't know if you love me any more than you did when we left Middle Hill—I've deliberately not asked, so as not to burden you, as you say."

I touched her face again.

"But *my* feelings about *you* haven't changed, not one bit. If anything, they have grown. When you are ready, all we need to do is get married, quietly, and have Will christened; then you can change to another school, where you can tell everyone that I am Will's father."

"You'd still do that?"

"You know I would."

"But even at a new school I'd still overhear those conversations . . . I'd still *feel* the burden."

I let a short silence elapse. "Then it seems to me that you still can't let go of Wilhelm."

We walked home in silence.

In Middle Hill, that evening in the cricket field, the next morning at the railway station, it hadn't mattered that Sam didn't love me. If I was really honest with myself, that was no longer true. I still couldn't hate Wilhelm, but how convenient it would be if he were dead.

My new team at work consisted of Alan Brewster, a mathematician, brilliant but nearsighted, which banned him from active duty; Eve Palmer, an attractive (if vampish) forty-year-old actress who had worked in Munich—in a variety of cabaret roles—and had escaped just in time; and Genevieve Afton, the shy, blue-stockinged daughter of an earl.

At first, this new group was sticky. The relationship between the two women on the team—one flashy and worldly (and a little sarcastic), the other shy and academic—was tense, but I didn't have time to dwell on it, for Genevieve straightaway came up with something that kept us occupied.

She spotted that—on successive days, but in different newspapers—something interesting had got through the censors, because it was indirect and didn't immediately relate to the war effort. She didn't think anything of it until she came across the *second* reference that intrigued her. Then she sought me out.

"Look," she said, showing me an account of a brawl at a dance hall in a place called Bautzen. It was between some soldiers and the local men.

"Yes?" I said.

"I know Bautzen," she replied quietly. "I was taken there a couple of years ago, just before the war, when my father was invited to shoot by the local *Freiherr*, or count. It's not a military town."

"There's a war on, Genevieve. Everywhere has been militarized."

She shook her head. "Look at this."

It was a page of small ads from an edition of the same paper two days earlier. There was about half a page of notices, many for lodging houses advertising rooms, in several of which the wording specified that soldiers were welcome.

I got the picture.

"You think there is a military buildup in Bautzen, yes?"

She made a face. "I'm new at this. You decide. It's possible."

"Hmm. I'm skeptical." The reality is that I thought the two references too thin to support Genevieve's interpretation. I had to be careful, though. Bautzen was only thirty miles from the Polish border and if there *was* a military buildup there, it could signify the beginnings of a major push to the east, an important development in Germany's war strategy.

To be on the safe side, I shared Genevieve's ideas with Tom Black, who at that time ran the military table. A small man with a deep, plummy voice, he was incapable of whispering. He heard Genevieve out—and then whistled.

"Jesus, Gen!" he said, showing an informality that I found difficult. "If you're right, this is big—vee big." He talked like that.

"Is she right, though?" I still had my doubts.

"Hal, don't get me wrong, but this is too big for you and me. We're talking here about a major change in the enemy's war strategy. It's your show but if you want my advice, you've got to go to Pritchard—and you've got to go *now.* Get this one wrong and we would be letting the side down in a major—a massive—way."

So we went to Pritchard, all three of us—Genevieve, Tom, and me.

Pritchard was—surprisingly, perhaps—unsympathetic, and he took it out on me.

"Look, Hal, I expect more from you. You are a senior figure here now, and I expect better judgment. These are straws in the wind. You know what it takes for me to pull our people out of somewhere and deploy them someplace else. Yes, I can see that there are more soldiers in Bautzen than before. And maybe Bautzen *is* a strategically important location—but all that does *not* mean that the war is about to change course. Now, go away and do some more work and don't come back until you are convinced you can convince me." He smiled grimly, tapping his pipe on his desk. "I shall take some convincing."

Chastened, and in my case not a little irritated that I had let Tom get the better of my better judgment, we returned to our desks. For the next twenty-four hours, Genevieve was shier than ever but, as the days passed, more evidence began to build up. A small ad in the *Süd-*

deutsche Zeitung, the South German Times, announced that a Major Ritter of the Fourth Mecklenburg Field Corps would address the Bautzen (Obergurig) Boys Club. A butcher's shop announced that the meat ration was being cut—again—this time because bulk supplies were being directed to Camp Briesen, which we found was in a suburb of Bautzen. An ad in the Bautzen paper, for the local theater, suddenly announced that soldiers in uniform would be allowed in at half price. The same local newspaper started to print the emblem of the Fourth Mecklenburg Field Corps alongside its masthead. A school notice announced that the Field Corps Regimental Band would be playing at its concert.

I couldn't sit on this intelligence any longer.

This second time Pritchard was—to give him credit—more accommodating. But we had lost days without acting. Pritchard said he would see to it that the top brass were informed and that our people on the ground were moved into Bautzen to flesh out the picture.

Progress at last.

There weren't many similarities between Middle Hill or Warwickshire and London but, as it turned out, canals formed part of the landscape—*our* landscape—in both places. Because they were largely neglected in London, the canal banks were overgrown with grass and weeds and bushes—even a few trees—which at least made them oases of green and a refuge from the concrete and brick that otherwise dominated the cityscape of the capital. Not many people seemed to share our enthusiasm and, usually, we had the towpath to ourselves.

Will also liked canals. They were different from roads and there was always some sort of wildlife to be seen, as well as barges with interesting loads. Mostly, we saw water rats and moorhens, but there was the occasional duck or otter, sleek in the water but ungainly on land, with large hindquarters.

On one occasion there was particular excitement when we disturbed a family of rabbits who had quietly been munching on something or other until we came along. Will pointed, gabbled away, and would have given chase had he not been strapped into his pushchair.

"Remember how the children in Middle Hill hated it when you killed those rabbits at the Front?" Sam said, grinning. "I thought some of them were going to cry, right in the middle of your talk."

"I know," I said, grinning back. "I think some of them would have lynched me, given half a chance. Better to lose a war than kill some rabbits."

"Everyone should be so naïve," said Sam. "Though the children I teach now are not like that. They've seen too much . . ." She sighed. "So many fathers aren't coming back."

Silence for a while.

We both knew whom she was thinking of.

"That officer you met, in the Christmas truce . . . do you ever think of him? Do you ever wonder what has happened to him, where he is now, if he is still alive?"

What was she getting at? Did she suspect? Had she always suspected?

"Yes, I suppose I do think about him, from time to time." I tried to remain calm, not to make too much of it. "But only in a very general way. Our meeting only lasted a few minutes."

"Did you like him?"

"Oh, I can't say, Sam. It was an odd situation—intense, tense—you can see that. We'd been shooting at each other hours before, and would be again, very soon. No one acted normally."

"Didn't you swap anything, like others did? I've read all about it . . . buttons, cigarettes . . ."

What did she know? I was sweating. "We were officers, Sam. To an extent we had to set an example. So cigarettes, yes; buttons no."

"Where was he from? Remind me."

What *was* this, a test? Was she testing me deliberately?

"I can't remember. Hamburg, I think."

She shook her head. "Now I remember. You said Berlin last time."

I was still sweating. "Berlin, that's right. I forgot. I can't remember too much about the whole thing."

"I would never forget an encounter like that. It will be remembered, and recorded in the history books, forever."

She was right. Of course, she was right.

"And he had a brother, you said?"

Careful. "Did I? I can't remember. I remember we had a boy in our platoon who sang beautifully . . . he sang an aria from a Handel opera, accompanied by a mouth organ. Did I tell you that? Can you imagine a beautiful, crystal-clear boy's pure voice, in the cold night air, accompanied by a mouth organ. The Germans had nothing like that boy. I wonder what's happened to *him*."

That had moved the conversation on.

No, it hadn't.

"Wilhelm and his brother sang in a choir as boys. Dieter still did, when Wilhelm came to England, but he himself had ruined his voice—by smoking. He loved cigars but they played havoc with his voice. He was upset about it, but was hooked—he smoked one big cigar every day. I wonder if he can get them in wartime?"

"I shouldn't think so," I said. "The powers that be on our side send around cigarettes, but not cigars. Still, if the only hardship Wilhelm faces is a shortage of cigars, he won't be doing too badly."

I sounded reasonably calm, sane, or I hoped that I did. But as I said this, I was thinking—again—how convenient it would be if Wilhelm were dead.

A couple of nights later Sam and I went to the theater and Lottie babysat as usual with Will. When we came home, quite late, she was fast asleep in front of the fire, a book open on her lap. I gently picked it up, while Sam went to check that Will was still sleeping.

The book Lottie was reading was her usual fare—the doings of the "bright young things," good-looking aristocratic nobodies, so far as I was concerned, with more money than sense. Sam poured me a whisky, as she always did when we got in late, while I flipped through Lottie's book. And there, in the photographic section, was a picture of the Earl of Afton, Genevieve's father, taken at the gaming tables at a casino in the south of France.

"Not your cup of tea," murmured Lottie stirring. "How was the play?"

"It was American, *Mr. Manhattan.* Too unremittingly cheerful for most of the audience, unrealistic in wartime. But the songs were good. As it happens, this man"—I tapped the page with the photograph of the Earl of Afton—"interests me. His daughter works for us."

"Does she, poor girl?"

"Poor girl? She's an earl's daughter."

"But her father's a vegetable. Had a stroke four years ago, leaving massive gambling debts—"

Sam came in just then. Will was sleeping soundly, she said, handing me my whisky. Then the three of us did what we always did on theater nights: we had a bully beef sandwich with whisky nightcaps, before going to bed.

I woke at four-thirty A.M. This, in itself, was unusual, for I have always slept well, ever since I was a boy (save for that night in the tent, in the garden, with the owls, with Izzy). And I awoke vaguely troubled. Something that Lottie had said didn't add up. At first I couldn't work out what it was but after about an hour of twisting and turning, so that Sam once or twice gave me a shove, I finally nailed it.

Lottie had said that the Earl of Afton was a vegetable, having had a stroke four years before. But Genevieve had told me she had been taken shooting with her father—the earl—in Germany "a couple of years" ago, before the war. By "a couple" did Genevieve mean "a few," "several," or, more conventionally, two? If she meant the latter, how did that square with what Lottie had said? If the two accounts didn't square, what did it mean, what was I getting at? Come to that, why did I have a funny feeling in the pit of my stomach?

I got up and went for a walk along the Embankment. My bad leg was always stiffer early on in the day but exercise helped. The Thames, at five forty-five A.M. on a September morning, was misty, a perfect indistinct cityscape for a painter like James McNeil Whistler, or this Frenchman, Monet. The waters were sludge-colored, yellowy even. Black barges slid in and out of the mist like great beasts lurking in the jungle.

I remember that the zeppelin air raids over London had begun about then and the top half of all the streetlamps had been painted black, to curtail the amount of light they cast.

What *exactly* was bothering me? The truth is: I was reluctant—frightened—to put it into words. And what could I *do?*

My walk along the Embankment didn't help, but later that day, in Northumberland Avenue, we noted two more cuttings. One told of a local court case in which a soldier was accused of raping a Bautzen woman. The judge, in condemning the man, recorded that it was the fifth such case in recent months and signified a worrying trend. The soldier was given seven years in jail.

In the second cutting, the local beer was evaluated by a *Vizefeldwebel* (staff sergeant) named Eckart Müller. He was writing in the Sunday edition and comparing the local beer with the brew where the regiment was normally based, a town near Rostock.

I took Genevieve to see Pritchard, who considered these latest developments and managed to say, "Look out, Hal. I seem to remember it took you weeks to come up with a breakthrough. Genevieve has done it in days. She'll have your job yet."

Back in the Gym, I excused myself and went to the archive. I spent a few hours there but returned to my slot well before we clocked off at six.

That evening I did something I had never done before. I lurked in the large lobby of Northumberland Avenue, and when Genevieve left, I followed.

It wasn't easy, and maybe not wise, with my limp—though that had improved a lot by then.

It was madness, of course. I had been unable to warn Sam that I wouldn't be home at my usual time, and she would worry. Genevieve could have gone to any number of places—the theater, the hairdresser, to a library or a lecture, to confession (she was a Roman Catholic), on a long omnibus ride, or just home—wherever that was—and stayed in all night.

But she didn't do any of those things.

From Northumberland Avenue she walked to Trafalgar Square and turned right, north, up Charing Cross Road. It was on the chilly side, and coming on to rain, which didn't make my self-appointed task any easier. At Cambridge Circus, where Charing Cross Road met Shaftesbury Avenue, she turned left into Old Compton Street. This was the wartime West End—Soho—and, thanks to my own regular theatergoing, I knew the area well. Past Frith Street and Dean Street, she turned right into Wardour Street, still heading north. About a hundred yards along Wardour Street, she turned off left into a small dead-end street, Tyler's Court. As I reached the corner, I was just in

time to see her shape slipping down a metal staircase to a basement—
what looked like a club. At any rate, a small but brightly lit sign above
the steps announced: THE MATTERHORN.

I stopped. What should I do? Follow her in? That would—
perhaps—tell me who she was meeting, if she was meeting anyone. It
would—perhaps—tell me what sort of club or bar it was, if it was, in
fact, a bar. But then she'd know I had been following her. If I turned
up in a place like that, it would be too much of a coincidence.

While I waited, a plan formed in my mind.

I let a good ten minutes go by before making a move. In that
way, my arrival in the club could in no way be associated with Genevieve. Then I airily ran down the steps to the Matterhorn, as if I did
it every day.

"Can I help you?"

The man at the door was big, had close-cropped hair, wore a white
shirt and a tie with a black jacket, and he himself was very black.

I was disconcerted but said, "Yes," as confidentially as I could
make my voice sound. "I'm a private detective. I'm investigating an
unfaithful wife who, we think, frequents this bar—"

"It's not a bar, it's a private club. For Swiss and other people who
are neutral in the war. Strictly members only, plus their guests."

I did my best to recover. "Oh. I wasn't expecting this. A foreign
lover. The husband will scarcely be pleased." I winked. "Sorry to have
bothered you." I quickly turned back up the steps.

So Genevieve was consorting with the Swiss. Was that all there
was to it? (The Swiss were neutral, after all, and their expatriates
would want somewhere to meet in London while the war was still on.)
Or was there more to this business than immediately met the eye?
Based on what I knew so far, I had no idea. I decided to wait.

At the opening of Tyler's Court, on the corner of Wardour Street,
was a pub, the Eagle. I bought an evening newspaper from a stand and

went into the pub. I was able to find a seat by the window from where I could watch the front door to the Matterhorn and read the paper at the same time. My situation reminded me of the surveillance I had carried out on Sam from the Lamb in Middle Hill. This time I didn't have one of Wilhelm's cigars with me (I had two left).

Between six-forty and eight-forty I got through four half-pints of beer and two whiskies. I had read the paper from beginning to end and back again, all eight pages of it. The Eagle, I could see, had its share of characters. A man whose mane of long, lank grayish-silver hair suggested that he had once been a character actor in the West End theater had the voice of a Shakespearean senator, and at one stage he declaimed, in a full baritone boom, not the bard, as you might expect, but what I knew could only be Kipling:

> I've a head like a concertina, I've a tongue like a buttonstick,
> I've a mouth like an old potato, and I'm more than a little sick,
> But I've had my fun o' the Corp'ral's Guard; I've made the cinders fly,
> And I'm here in the Clink for a thundering drink and blacking the Corp'ral's eye.

The clientele heard him out, applauding when he had finished (or stopped) and moved on.

A gypsy woman in a long purple crocheted dress and lace-up shoes sang a song—frail, tender, embarrassing. Everyone let it go. If she had to sing, she had to sing.

I was seeing elements of Soho I had never seen before. Was the West End always like this, or was it a function of the war? Whatever it was, I liked it.

I dipped into the paper a second time, looking up every few seconds, keeping an eye out for Genevieve. With the evening paper gone through twice lightly, so to speak, there was nothing else to do but go through it again. I still couldn't concentrate, however, as I had to keep looking up every so often. Also, I knew that Sam would be beginning to worry, and that worried me. What I would have given for one of those new telephone things, there in the pub and at home.

Time passed. I had yet another beer, which I strung out till nine-ten—and then I saw Genevieve in the street. She was standing at the top of the stairs to the club, buttoning her coat. There was a man with her, older, darker-haired, thin. They both waved farewell down the steps, to the Negro at the door of the club, then linked arms and moved off.

I followed, at a distance. They turned south, on Wardour Street, then left—east—along Old Compton Street, back the way Genevieve had come, as far as Cambridge Circus, then on down Earlham Street to Seven Dials. From there they entered the other side of Earlham Street and, halfway along it, stepped into a brightly lit shop. Most shops had been closed for hours by now, but not this one, and I recognized it though I had never seen it before. It was a theatrical shop that Eve Palmer had mentioned, a shop that sold props, makeup, costumes, magicians' bits and pieces, and rented out dance shoes, clown's outfits, military uniforms, and so on. All the things that theatrical productions might need when things went wrong at the last minute. Presumably, Genevieve knew about it in the same way that I did.

The shop was far too small for me to enter it while they were there, so I waited near Seven Dials, where there was a convenient alleyway with no shortage of shadows in which I could hide. It was coming on to rain again and Earlham Street was a quiet place—you would never guess you were bang in the middle of the theater district of a major city with a war on. There were shadows everywhere and the hiss of the rain was louder than anything else.

Genevieve and her companion were in the shop for about ten minutes. I saw them come out, stand for a moment in the pool of illumination thrown by the shop lights as they pulled up their collars and wrapped their scarves around their necks against the rain. All that light spilling out onto the sidewalk almost certainly broke the law, but I was in no position, or mind, to do anything about it. Genevieve and her companion linked arms again and started out, back toward Seven Dials, toward me.

I eased back into my hiding niche. Apart from the sound of the rain bouncing on the cobbles, the street was empty and quiet, and I could hear the two of them talking as they came level with me. As they broached the corner of the brickwork at the alleyway where I was standing, in deep shadow, their voices suddenly washed over me, loud and clear.

"Trust me, darling. The right makeup can do wonders for a woman's self-confidence. You've made a good start. No need to be quite so nervous now."

Then they were gone.

I didn't move. What I had heard were simple words, innocuous, ambiguous, perhaps, an older man offering help to a younger colleague.

Nothing unusual in that.

Except that what the man had actually said was: *"Vertrau mir, Liebling. Die richtige Schminke kann wunders für Selbstvertrauen einer Frau tum. Du hast gut angefangen. Es gibt keinen Grund zur Nervositaet."*

The moment Sam heard my key in the lock of the front door to the flat, she came running. She flung her arms around my neck and gripped me hard.

I was pleased.

Lottie was down the hall. She was smiling, a smile of relief.

"Where *were* you?" cried Sam in a whisper that trembled with feeling. "I was *so* worried—we all were," she added, turning back to her sister. "What happened?"

"Is there any food?" I said. I was suddenly ravenously hungry.

"There's cold rice pudding," said Lottie. "It's either that or cheese."

"Cheese and whisky," I said. "In front of the fire, and I'll tell you everything."

I shouldn't have, of course. But I was so gratified by my reception, and so guilty at being late without warning, that I stood in front of the overmantel, warming my legs, and confided everything to them—why I had suddenly decided to follow Genevieve, after my conversation with Lottie about the Earl of Afton's stroke, where she had gone, the Matterhorn, the theatrical shop, what I had overheard.

They listened in silence.

When I had finished and while I was refilling my whisky glass, Sam said, "So Genevieve is a spy?"

"How *exciting!*" whispered Lottie.

"Thankfully, it's not my decision. I'll report tomorrow what I saw tonight and it will be out of my hands. Incidentally, you two had better forget what I just told you. When I joined the show in Northumberland Avenue, I signed the Official Secrets Act, and in saying what I've just said, I've violated it. So forget my little tale and save me from being shot for treason."

Later that night, in bed, Sam was as passionate as I'd ever known her. We had devised our own form of lovemaking—given my predicament—and that night was the best yet. We had been awkward at first. But, as she had said when we were taking tea at Snow Hill station that day in Birmingham, she came from a physical family—she liked touching, bodily contact, and during our walks through London, along the streets and canal banks, we held hands, strolled arm in arm, and, as we lay in bed, we curled together like spoons in a tray. Gradually, she allowed me to explore more of her body, slowly she surrendered, little by little she grew more relaxed, and then increasingly abandoned. Since she knew she couldn't get pregnant, she gave herself, eventually, without restraint. Her body was everything I had hoped for, everything I had imagined that first day when I had seen her on playground duty outside the school in Middle Hill, when I had realized that there was so much more to her than was revealed in Wilhelm's photograph.

Afterward, as we lay looking up at the shadows from the Embankment traffic, gliding across the ceiling, she said, "I thought some horrible thoughts tonight, Hal, when I didn't know where you were, and I don't want to think them again. Promise you won't do that again."

In reply I squeezed her hand.

"Will was worried too. He kept asking, 'Where Hal? Where Hal?' He wouldn't go to sleep until I assured him you would be there in the morning." She turned and kissed my shoulder. "Thank God you're here."

The next morning (having had Will arrive and climb into bed with us very early, just as Sam was suggesting we make love again), I went straight to Pritchard's office. He was already in a meeting, so I left word with his secretary that I had to see him on a matter of the greatest urgency as soon as he was free.

At my table they were all there—Alan, Eve, and Genevieve. Genevieve, I immediately noticed, looked slightly different today. Her face was less pale, had more color; there was an added dimension to it, so it seemed. Her eyebrows had more form, and there were hollows—shadows—in her cheeks. Under normal circumstances, I may not have noticed that today she was wearing makeup. However, after what I had witnessed and overheard the evening before, the change was obvious.

Why? Was she trying to make herself more desirable, to attract men in the department?

She had a cutting for me. It was again from a Bautzen newspaper. This time it was a story about a naming ceremony for a new locomotive that had taken place in the town's main railway station. There was no picture or engraving but a bottle of German sparkling wine had been broken over the front of the engine's boiler, and the mayor had named the locomotive the *Mecklenburg,* after the field corps that had moved into the area. Further evidence that there was a military buildup under way.

This at least gave me the excuse to leave my team and go off in the direction of Pritchard's office. I intended to wait outside until he was free—I couldn't sit at the same table as Genevieve anymore.

As it happened, I met Pritchard's secretary on the stairs; she was just coming down to get me. I walked into the colonel's office and closed the door. He was in the process of lighting his pipe.

"Hal?"

I sat down. "This will take half an hour and I need your undivided attention."

I waited while he got his pipe going and then told him what I knew, what had happened, what I had done—save for the fact that I had relayed everything to Sam and Lottie.

He heard me out in silence, but the set of his chin grew grimmer as I proceeded. It took closer to forty minutes before I wound up. I waved the latest edition of the *Bautzener Zeit.* "This is today's story. I think it's a step too far."

Pritchard read it.

He looked up. "Go on."

"It fits with the other stories, in that it's an indirect reference to military affairs that has escaped the censor and makes us all feel clever, because we've read between the lines to detect a buildup. But ask yourself two questions. One, is it likely that *all* these incidents would escape the censor? And two, more particularly, is it likely that a locomotive would be named in this way *before* the fighting starts? *Our* locomotives are named only well after the event, when something has passed comfortably into history, become a legend, because of a stunning victory or some other achievement. All these stories are phony. It's a setup."

Silence.

"You followed her to a Swiss club. The Swiss may speak German, some of them, but they are neutral. What you heard wasn't necessarily incriminating."

"Posing as a German-speaking Swiss is the perfect cover for a spy, sir. What has Genevieve Afton got to be nervous about, what has she made a good start *at?* She's just started with us. Remember how quickly she 'uncovered' this Bautzen business? It's all too convenient, sir, it's a setup. I repeat: her father's a vegetable. She cannot have gone to Bautzen with him as she said she did. She lied."

Another gloomy silence. "An earl's daughter. Can it be? What a scandal if it's true and it gets out." He looked at me intently, sucking his pipe. He passed a hand over his face. "You're right, Hal. Of course, you're right. I don't want to believe it but the dreadful gnawing I have in my gut says you're right. We've been too obsessed with our own cleverness to see that there have been just *too many* little stories put our way. She could have made a good start at learning to play bridge, or to paint. She could be nervous about driving her first car, or going to bed with our anonymous 'Swiss' friend. But somehow I don't think so." He breathed out. "You're right."

Another gloomy silence.

Then: "You've had longer than me to chew on this, Hal. Advice?"

I nodded. "Nothing precipitate, sir, nothing that gives the game away, nothing that shows we've rumbled Genevieve."

I lit my own cigarette. I only smoked when I was on fire.

"There are three aspects to this. One, they know our unit exists and have infiltrated us. I suppose they could have guessed that an outfit like ours must exist somewhere but they have found us and we need to know how they did that. The fact that they have located us will damage our credibility if it gets out, so we must put it right ourselves, and keep it quiet, to maintain our position.

"So . . . don't fire Genevieve or arrest her in a blaze of publicity. We check out her background and find a plausible reason for moving her from here—to a position where she can do no more damage. You must do it quickly but it must not arouse suspicion, in her, her German contacts, or in anyone else."

I blew smoke into the room.

"Next, have her German contact followed, see who he leads us to, and then, a month or six weeks from now, have them both arrested, for using drugs, or something like that. Have the police—not the army—raid the Matterhorn while Genevieve and her contact are there. Then, once they are separated from each other, throw the book at them.

"Meanwhile, and this is the second aspect, you will have been using the recent intelligence—'intelligence' in quotation marks—to move our agents into the Bautzen area. Withdraw the ones you have already sent and don't send any more. The Germans have been waiting for them, presumably watching for people who have been nosing around. Cancel everything, abort all operations in that area immediately.

"Third, though maybe this should have come first, you'll have to alert the top brass that our earlier intelligence, about a military buildup, was—well, wrong, that it was a feint by the enemy, but that we have now found out the truth. The brass are not going to like it, but the fact that we ourselves have spotted that we were being fooled may help a bit."

Pritchard nodded his agreement. "You seem to have thought of everything. The last two aspects are the most important, of course, but—thankfully—they are the most straightforward to put right. Moving Genevieve without attracting attention or suspicion, on the other hand, may take some thought—and thought takes time." He stood up. "Still, that's what I'm paid for." He held out his hand. "You've done your bit, Hal, and you've done it well. Now don't let me down for the next . . . however long it is. Keep up the pretense with Genevieve until I relieve you."

I went back to the Gym and congratulated Genevieve on finding the latest story. I then spent a difficult day trying to behave normally.

That evening, as I reached home, Will came running—stumbling—toward me and wrapped his little arms around my knees, which was as high up as he could reach, as if he would never let me go again. Sam wasn't far behind. It was all very gratifying.

Sam gave me a grilling as to how my day had been and, once again, I broke the Official Secrets Act and told her. Later, she was as passionate in bed as she had been the night before. She took the lead. Having been a fairly silent lovemaker, she was now . . . rather less so. The next morning, Will came into our room very early also. I think he was checking I was still there. I loved all of it.

I remember Sam was a bit on edge just then, because one of the girls in her class, a seven-year-old called Lily, had learned that both her brothers, a good few years older than she, had been killed at the Front. The girl had begun wetting herself in class.

"What it must be, to lose *two* sons." Sam held her cup of coffee to her cheek, warming herself as we had breakfast. "What must Lily's mother be going through?"

I knew what she was thinking, of course. "What was Wilhelm's brother called—Dieter?"

She nodded.

"Was he in the reserve, too?"

"I don't know."

"Did you not meet any of his family?"

"Of course not."

"Did he ever show you any photos of them?"

"Yes, once. His mother was tiny, *tiny*, yet she had given birth to two strapping sons." She paused. "What if they've both been killed, like Lily's brothers." She rinsed her cup under the tap. "What a war this is."

I reached the office that day at about eight-thirty, as usual, and set my mind to coping with a long day, trying to act normally with Genevieve. About nine-thirty, however, Pritchard appeared at our table. Without warning, so that my surprise was genuine, he put his hand on my shoulder and said, affably enough, "Hal, I'm sorry, and it's short notice—no notice at all, in fact—but I'm going to 'borrow' Genevieve from you."

We both looked up, perplexed.

Pritchard addressed himself to Genevieve. "Special request from General Hamilton, my dear, head of maps. They have a flap on—apparently our people have captured a whole cache of enemy maps, a lot of them with German handwriting on them. He says he knew your father before the war—used to shoot with him—and he needs a German speaker to help decipher the scribbles, in case they are important and comprise intelligence that might date. It's only for a few weeks—a month or so—then you can come back here." He turned back to me. "Can you cope with just the three of you, until I can find someone to replace Genevieve?"

"Do I have a choice?" I said as sourly as I could. "Couldn't you have found a replacement before taking Genevieve away?"

"I'm sorry about this, Hal, especially as we're in the middle of this

Bautzen buildup thing." He looked down again at Genevieve. "But there's some urgency, my dear, so I'm taking you away now."

He sucked his pipe and addressed me again. "I'm only a colonel, Hal. General Hamilton has three pips on his shoulder. You'll have to make do, I'm afraid. I'll be as quick as I can, I promise." He held out his hand to Genevieve. "Come along, my dear."

She got up, collected her few belongings—and that was that. If she was disappointed, or suspicious, she didn't show it, and in any case Pritchard had cleverly made it seem as though she was going to another "inside" job, where she could no doubt do yet more damage. She accompanied Pritchard out of the hall and no one made much of it. Neither Alan nor Eve seemed worried or bothered by the chain of events, so I concluded that, between us, Pritchard and I had pulled it off.

I later heard that Genevieve and her contact were arrested—by the police—during a raid on the Matterhorn, where at least a dozen people were held. A certain amount of hard drugs were found (or planted?) on the premises and the club was closed down for a while. Once Genevieve and the German were safely separated, Genevieve was charged with contravening the Official Secrets Act and with treason. Before the arrests, her German contact had been followed and three other German spies identified.

So Genevieve's hurried cover for herself—her shooting "expedition" with her father—had exposed her and brought about her downfall. It was a lesson I never forgot. In the end she had damaged the Germans almost as much as she had damaged us.

Dear Hal,

We've just had a bunch of journalists, war correspondents, who came to see what we do in our unit. All men. I suppose that's not too unusual or surprising but it did set me thinking. Maybe there'll be a bit

*of interest, after the war, in the journal I——as a woman——am
keeping. I'm sure a lot of soldiers, men, will write their memoirs, so
why shouldn't a woman? Will what I see and hear and feel be different
because I am a woman? You know how against the war Ma was——I
wonder, if she were to read what I have written, what she would say?
Most of what I recall is grim but not all——I have seen men behave well
out here. Not everyone loses their pride or their dignity. Far from it.*

*The journalists brought some papers with them and, I am pleased to
say, page five of the Times is still there, still doing its bit. Latest offering:
"The Plumage Act has failed." This act was introduced into Parliament
to stop women from wearing osprey feathers on their hats, the osprey
being rare and becoming rarer. Forget whether the flipping act passed or
failed, whether the act is a good thing or not. Where on earth did they
find the parliamentary time for such a debate? Wonderful!*

xxx

Izzy

The zeppelin raids on London had some effect on us. There were
one or two raids directly over the Chelsea and Kensington area, but
mostly they were more central—the Strand, Blackfriars, the City. As
we had discovered the new motor omnibuses, so we had extended our
exploration of London, taking a bus ride to begin with, then walking.
Will, especially, liked this new arrangement: from the omnibuses he
had a much better view of what was going on than from his pushchair.

We were on an omnibus one Saturday, going through Trafalgar
Square, where there was both a collection of captured German can-
nons on display *and* a crater formed by an exploding zeppelin bomb,
when he pointed and said, "Tolier."

"What?" I said. "*What* did you say, Will?"

"Tolier," he said again, pointing again.

Sam, sitting next to me, nudged me. "It's his word for 'soldier,' " she said in a low voice.

"Oh."

"Yes, I don't know where it comes from." She rearranged him where he was sitting on her knee. "Where *do* baby words come from? I can see that his word is a little bit like ours, but does he get it wrong because he can't say 'soldier' yet, has he misheard, does he *like* his word, has he heard other children use it . . . ? Does he *think* he's saying 'soldier'?"

Just then the conductress came to take our fares. All the staff on the omnibuses were women now, save for a few elderly men. The women wore leather gaiters to their knees and blue breeches.

"Don't you have any books about baby talk at school?"

"No. Everyone's too busy to bother about psychology. This new man, Freud, the Viennese doctor, says that a child's mother is all-important—for a stable childhood, I mean—but all the rowdies we have at school, all the bullies, all the ones who can't sit still for more than a minute on end, all the ones who answer back and are insolent . . . they are the ones whose fathers are away at the war, or have already been killed."

"Tolier," said Will, pointing again.

"If the father is at the Front, or dead, that puts pressure on the mothers. You, more than anyone, should know that."

"I do know that, of course I do. And I know that for me, for Will and for me, those pressures are so much less with you around, Hal." She squeezed my arm. "It's just that I feel we know so little about the psychology of children, of families. My own father was a drinker, and that proved catastrophic in the end. We know so little about the families behind our pupils, and the ones with the real problems are of course the very same tykes who don't want to talk about what's going on, or not going on, at home. So how are we expected to be able to help?"

"Has something brought this on, Sam?"

"No . . . it's been in my mind for some time. But the day before yesterday, late, the house of one of the families who send their children to our school burned down. A zeppelin bomb had dropped a little way away. Their house wasn't hit directly but it caught the blast of the explosion. It was a house without electricity—their lighting was gas, and the mantle was blown away and—"

"Mantle?"

"It's a light piece of plaster, where the flame of the lamp burns."

"Ah, yes. I've seen them. What happened?"

"The mantle blew away, the gas system lit back—and exploded, setting fire to the house."

"Anyone hurt?"

"That's the good news: no casualties. No physical casualties, anyway. But the family will have to go to the workhouse, they'll miss school, they've got hardly any clothes left, and no toys at all. Even if they do come back to school, they're going to be unteachable probably. We simply lack the means to cope with them, and they're not the first and they won't be the last."

"So what can be done?"

"I don't know." Will had fallen asleep, soothed by the movement of the bus. "I just feel there ought to be some sort of service; some sort of expertise ought to be developed, for these . . . well, victims really, there's no other word."

We got off the motorbus in a gloomy silence at Southampton Row and walked through Bloomsbury Square to the British Museum. When we arrived there our mood darkened still more. The gates were closed and a typed note, pinned to a placard, said that owing to the scarcity of curators, all of whom were on active duty, the museum was closed indefinitely.

"You look pale, Hal. You should get yourself a girl—a woman—to look after you." My mother had kissed me the moment I set foot in the house, and then she had stepped back. "Is your wound a burden to you? Do you . . . do you feel honor-bound to tell women about it? Does it . . . does it make a lot of difference?"

I'd been home less than two minutes and already she was grilling me. My mother was like that. At least it meant that my father had kept his side of the bargain and not told her about Sam.

Of course, my mother's questions were spot-on. Sam's predicament suited my predicament and formed part of the arrangement— and bond—between us. But I wasn't about to tell my mother all that.

"I don't tell women straightaway," I said. It was more or less true, in that it was the way I had played it with Sam. There hadn't been anyone else.

"But you have to tell them at some point, I expect, before it gets too serious."

I moved away without answering.

Fortunately, my father came in just then; he had been paying off the taxi man.

"Drink, Hal?" he said, going to the bar. "Whisky?"

"I'd love one," I replied. I was tired from the journey, but I was also shocked, knocked sideways, torpedoed, as Izzy would say, by my mother's appearance. Her complexion was florid—and not just her face; the skin on the backs of her hands was florid too. Her voice had deepened and she had lost weight. I did not like what I saw and I silently reprimanded myself for not coming home sooner. Izzy had been right to insist I make an effort.

Dad gave my mother her gin and me a whisky. As I think I said, he himself always drank brandy and soda, an old-fashioned drink that I had never been able to get used to. We were in the library, which was a good deal smaller than the drawing room proper, and which I preferred.

"I was just telling Hal he looks a bit thin, undernourished, and that he should get himself a nice girl. He needs to put on some weight."

"He's not the only one," said my father easily, and neatly moving the conversation away from me. "What are we having for dinner?"

"Chicken, of course. But a big one, one of ours, one of the few we have left. You won't go hungry, not for now." She sipped her gin.

"I'll take out a bottle of the Montrachet, then," my father replied. "It's a celebration of sorts."

"Yes," said my mother, setting down her glass on a small table. "Do try to get down here more often, Hal. It's lovely to see you, and I worry so—"

"Mother!" I growled. "Don't give me that. You are very definitely *not* the worrying kind, at any rate not for a grown son living in London. Now, I can understand you worrying about Izzy—"

"We had a letter yesterday!" she chimed in.

"Good, I'd like to read it later. When he was in London, Dad told me she has a man." He had let this news slip out, on the steps of the Athenaeum, as we were parting.

My mother sniffed. "He's married."

"That's unlike you . . . to be so conventional, I mean."

It was true. My mother knew her own mind, had her own arguments always, wherever they led.

"It's not a question of conventionality or otherwise, Hal. Married men only rarely leave their wives, so I do not foresee a happy future for your sister—*that's* what I mean. I would have thought she had more sense." She shook her head and sipped more gin.

After a short silence, she went on: "Seriously though, Hal, does your wound make things a problem with girls?"

"Mother!" I began, but my father got in first.

"My dear, Hal's twenty-five, a grown man who's been in a war and seen life. Don't treat him like a—"

"I'll treat him how I like, Arthur, I'm his mother. Because he's grown up, and fought on that stupid, evil Front, does not mean that I—or you, for that matter—will stop caring for him, or looking out for him."

She glanced at her watch. "I think I'll have a walk round the garden before dinner. I'll leave you two to talk men talk. Einstein!"

Einstein was the family Labrador, so called because, though adorable, he was monumentally stupid.

They disappeared through the door to the hall, and we heard them in the garden.

After another short pause, when both my father and I drank our drinks, I said softly, "I'm shocked, Dad. She looks really bad."

He nodded his head. "The worst of it is, she won't stop smoking. Your mother is so sensible in every other area of her life—as you well know. But the smoking clearly makes her cough worse. She has coughing fits that last for minutes on end, and if you think her skin is purple now, you should see it then. I don't know what to do."

"What do the doctors say? Did that man in Harley Street help?"

He shook his head. "They've washed their hands of her. If she goes on smoking, her coughing will only get worse, her lungs less efficient until . . ." He gloomily drank some brandy.

"Is there anything I can do in London?"

"I don't think so. We could have yet another opinion, I suppose, but . . ." He looked up at me. "You know, sometimes I think she's doing it on purpose—"

"No!"

"I mean it. I ask myself sometimes if she's . . . if she's trying to kill herself, if deep down she's depressed and wants to end it all."

"Depressed? Mother? She's always seemed perfectly sane to me—brutally so at times."

"Hmm. That's what I mean. She's been profoundly affected by this war—I mean, we all have, but your mother's *angry* about the whole show; the stupidity has really got to her." He lifted himself out of his chair, fetched the whisky and brandy decanters, and refilled our glasses. "You know she's always been fiercely moral—and, well, I rather think she feels this war is just about the most immoral thing that could happen. All those young men being sent to their deaths—and young women too. It's eating away at her insides."

"But that wouldn't make her clinically depressed, would it?"

My father shrugged.

After a pause, I said, "Perhaps I can help after all. There are one or two new psychiatric techniques about at the moment. Shall I try to find someone?"

"It's an idea," he said. "But whoever you found would have to be prepared to come down here. There's no way she will travel to London. How is your own situation?"

"Still the same. I'm still happy, content. You don't need to worry."

"I don't worry, but nor do I approve. What you are doing is not right, Hal, it really isn't. We can't tell your mother."

I let the subject drop. I could hear my mother and Einstein in the hall. Izzy had mentioned something about psychiatry, when we had dinner in Stratford, and Sam, too, was reading this Freud man. I decided to explore the possibility of a specialist when I returned to

London. It would make me feel useful. I had never dreamed my mother might be depressed.

> Dear Ma and Pa,
>
> When I had to stop writing last time, I was telling you about Alan. You, Ma, probably fell over at the point when I said he was married!! Try not to worry. (Though I know that you will!!) He's a lovely man and I didn't just meet Alan and fall head over heels for him. We worked together for weeks, for months, before anything happened! The feeling between us grew slowly and, now that we've talked about it, we know it was perfectly mutual.
>
> Blame it on the war, if you like. Our war—near the Front, dealing in so much blood every day—is not as dangerous as is the war of the soldiers who are stuck in the trenches, but believe me, what we do is quite wearing enough. In these circumstances—and I haven't mentioned the physical conditions: the mud, the lack of privacy, the lice, the smells it seems hardly right that we experience, the lack of fresh water (forget washing; what water there is goes to the injured), the sameness of the food, the intimate company of rats—in these circumstances it is only natural that our unit should grow closer together. We have special skills that set us apart, and me being a woman sets us apart too.
>
> Partly this is because in a few cases—in a very few cases—we can do something, save lives, give people hope. It keeps them going, but it keeps us going too. It makes us—and this may sound strange—more optimistic than many others. It is a relief being optimistic. To be here at the Front, as an ordinary soldier, even as an officer—like Hal was—must be the most soul-crushing experience anyone can have. Ma, Pa, I don't think any of us properly understood Hal's feelings when he found out that he couldn't have children. Now that I know what he'd been through, and then to have that news on top of everything, it must have been—I don't know what to say, but horrible.

Alan is a doctor—I think I mentioned that last time. Alan MacGregor is his full name. From Edinburgh, from a family of doctors. He's been married for six years, to a woman from the Highlands he met in Edinburgh, when he was at medical school there. I know what you are thinking and the answer is: yes, a baby son and daughter.

I hear you groaning and you're right, at least partly right. The existence of children doesn't make the whole business any easier. Part of me wishes this hadn't happened, but you will know, Ma, Pa, that these feelings just creep up on you. You relax with someone, talk to them, in our case you sneak away from the Front for a few hours, and you don't think anything is happening. Then you pretend nothing is happening. Then, before you know it, you __want__ something to happen. Then it happens. Then, before you can feel guilty, you feel so good, so alive, so joyful, that you are glad it has happened and you are trapped.

I'm not going to put down my feelings for Alan on paper, and I'm not going to go into any more detail. I know you won't be happy for me; I know you think it's all a mess and that it will end badly. All I will say is that being with Alan certainly makes this war a bit more bearable, and allows me to think about life afterward. After what I have seen here, even that is a luxury.

Please write, but if you do, please try not to lecture me. We're on a knife edge here.

All my love, Izzy (and to Einstein!)

When I told Sam about Izzy's latest letter to my parents, she pulled a face and shook her head. We were walking by the river, slowly, letting Will try his legs rather than have it easy in the pushchair.

"I envy your sister, being so near the Front, doing something practical. And I can see that emotions there can run very high. She couldn't help what happened to her—"

"My mother wouldn't agree."

"Maybe your mother . . . I don't know . . . maybe your mother hasn't been faced with a situation where . . . where she couldn't help herself."

I knew what she was thinking, of course. "But Izzy's situation isn't like yours, Sam. When you fell for Wilhelm, you didn't know the war was going to break out, but Izzy knew right from the start that this . . . Alan, was married. There's a world of difference. I know she's been working in a hothouse, been closer to danger than she ever dreamed possible, but . . . she could have kept her distance."

Sam didn't say anything for a moment. Some barges were going downstream and she lifted Will so that he could see over the Embankment wall. He pointed and said something in his incomprehensible protolanguage. She set him back down on the pavement again and we resumed our slow progress.

"Lottie's been in touch with Faye, and Faye's going out with a married man."

This was news to me. I knew that the sisters talked—Sam and Lottie, that is—but in general Sam kept me abreast of everything. Or so I'd thought. I would have assumed that had Lottie and Faye reestablished contact, Sam would have told me straight off. Maybe she was.

"Faye has had a lot more experience with men than Izzy has," I pointed out.

"True, and maybe Faye will handle her situation better than Izzy will handle hers. But ask yourself this: if someone knows in advance that someone they like, someone they feel strongly about, someone they could become attached to, is already married, and yet they go ahead anyway, doesn't that . . . doesn't that say something about the strength of their feeling, the force of their attachment? Is it something that, even in Izzy's case, can be avoided? Would it have made a difference to you if I had been married when you met me? In a sense

I *was* married—engaged, anyway—and it didn't seem to ... it didn't put you off."

"Sam, you can't compare me with Izzy or Faye. Come on! Had Wilhelm been right there, in Stratford, nothing would have—"

"I know. I know. I'm just saying ... before you condemn Izzy, remember how we all can get bowled over in different ways, blown this way and that by circumstances. I agree that, probably, in her case, and seeing it from my point of view, falling for a married man was not the wisest thing she has ever done. But you—we—don't know that. Treat your sister like an adult, with her own mind and sense of survival."

I let the subject drop. I could see that what Sam said made a kind of sense, but I wasn't fully convinced. And I could see that all our conversations of the emotional kind always came back to one thing: her encounter with Wilhelm.

Dear Hal,

I don't believe it! I heard from Ma and Pa and they said you had actually been down to visit. I'll ask how London is in a minute but first, do please write and give me your verdict on Ma. Pa wrote me a secret letter the other day—one she doesn't know he's written—to say how worried he is. Apparently her cough is "out of control," as he put it. Is there anything you can do, with your fancy connections? When you were ill, didn't you meet any useful *doctors or professors, or deans of medicine?*

If you've been home, then you'll know about Alan. Ma and Pa will have filled you in with what I've told them. I expect they're distressed—yes? Devastated, more like. They think I'm a silly girl who's lost her head with some older man, etc.

It doesn't feel like that. I'm not going to say what it does feel like, because I'm not sure I'm up to it, in pen and ink anyway. I'm trying to put it down in my notebook, because it's all so new, and so wonderful, for me, and we'll see how it goes. If I'm satisfied enough, I'll maybe show you someday.

I wish you were here, Hal. It was such a frantic time when I was in London, all us girls dashed about everywhere, doing everything, as I think I lectured you that night we had dinner. But although I thought my flatmates were friends, I don't think of them that way so much now. You're different. Your wound . . . don't take this wrong, Hal . . . your wound makes you somehow more—well, approachable. As an older brother you were always a bit like a god to me when we were younger. Now you're mortal. I like that.

Meeting Alan has changed everything for me. He's a scientist. Yes, I know, he's a doctor so he must be a scientist, but that's not what I mean. I mean that he looks out on life as a scientist, in a very rational way. He says this war is going to last at least another two years because of the numbers of men committed but that it's now not so much about winning as not losing. Fighting to avoid defeat, he says, is always the most vicious kind—we only have to look at animals defending their territory or their offspring.

Falling in love with Alan was never my intention—I ask you to believe that, Hal. But it has rescued me in more ways than one. The war was getting to me—I wasn't sleeping well, I found it hard to get out of bed, I wasn't finding the work as rewarding as I should have ("rewarding" isn't the right word, not in wartime circumstances, but you know what I mean). But that's all gone. I tell you, my life has changed.

Write to me, Hal. Tell me the truth about Ma, and tell me you are not distressed—not too distressed—by the news about Alan.

I haven't asked about you and London but that doesn't mean I'm not thinking about you.

Izzy

Later that year a zeppelin bomb dropped near the school where Sam taught. The school itself wasn't hit but the roads around it were cratered and the school was closed for a week, until the rubble could be cleared and the buildings that had been damaged made safe. I had accumulated a bit of leave by then and so I suggested to Sam that we use the opportunity to take Will out of London for a short break. The problems that many of the children in her school were facing were getting to her and she leapt at the idea.

"But where will we go?"

"I know where I'd like to go . . . I'd like to see where you grew up, in Bristol."

She was taken with the suggestion. "Can I bring Lottie?"

"If she wants to come, why not?"

But Lottie didn't want to come. She didn't say why; she just said she preferred to remain in London.

So the three of us took the train—the first train ride that Will remembered, and which he loved, though he was made a bit sick with the rocking of the carriages and the smell of smoke. We stayed at the Clifton, one of the best hotels in town.

"I never thought I'd ever get to see *inside* this place," Sam said as we settled into bed for our first night away. "It was far too swish for us when we were growing up."

The only part of Bristol I knew, of course, was the Baltic Wharf, but I wasn't about to tell Sam that. I did wonder if Crimson was still there.

Bristol proper was smaller than I expected, and hillier. Walking was quite arduous, especially when I had to push Will, which was normally the case after about half an hour under his own steam, when he conked out.

The next day we found the building where Sam's parents had rented their flat, we found the school the girls had attended, the church they went to on Sundays, and we found the tailor's shop where their mother had worked as a needlewoman. Nothing seemed to have changed.

Sam stood outside the school, slowly shaking her head. "Look how *small* it is. I remember it as a huge place—a cavernous hall, big heavy doors, a *vast* playground. As, of course, it seemed to a tot like me."

She recognized some of her erstwhile neighbors and school friends, but no one seemed to recognize her—she'd been gone from their lives for too long, and of course had grown up. It was only because they hadn't moved that she recognized them. And she didn't introduce herself.

She showed me a river nearby where the sisters used to go bathing in summer, an orphanage where the boys would chase them, and the warehouse where imported sherry was stored, with a back entrance the girls could sneak through to sample the "angel's share," the faint smell of fortified wine that escaped through the corks.

"As young girls we could get a little tipsy on the angel's share," she said with a guilty smile.

She was pleased we had come, I think. "I wondered, in the train on the way down, if all I would remember was our father." She looked serious for a moment. "But no. It has brought back my sisters in an earlier time, when we were all together. Before . . . before we grew up."

On the way back into the center of Bristol, where the hotel was located, we stopped off at a cemetery.

"I want to show you something," said Sam softly.

She found the grave she was looking for without any trouble— her memory was good.

"Look at that," she said.

From the names on the gravestone, which we could read only with difficulty, because it was so overgrown, there were about half a dozen people buried in this one plot, some of them named Ross, but not all.

"My father's parents and grandparents are here, and my mother's parents, and one of her aunts." She looked up at me. "We used to come here a lot, with my mother. She wasn't maudlin, or anything like that. She would come here, tidy the grave, clean it up, put fresh flowers in the vase, all the while singing to herself and talking to her mother and father as though they were still with us. No one thought it odd— everyone did it, and us girls would sit and have a picnic on the grass. It was what everybody did in those days; at weekends the cemetery was quite crowded, and there were picnics all over the place, children playing, making a noise, laughing." She smiled. "It sounds odd, but when I was growing up this cemetery was quite lively. Visiting the cemetery was part of our life, we did it every week, and in a way it was healthy. It showed us girls that death was a natural part of life, that life went on afterward, that grief eventually passes. We learned not to be afraid of death."

She made no attempt to tidy the grave but turned away, back toward the entrance and the road that led into the center of town. "Where will we be buried, Hal? And who with? That sounds crazy— right? What does it matter who you are buried with—you're not going to know it, are you? But I think a family grave is right, I think a family grave is a natural ending. With this war . . . with all those men, boys, being buried abroad, in some foreign field, with strangers, it's not right."

"Not strangers, Sam. Or not necessarily." Will had been poking around other graves and I lifted him back into his pushchair. "I agree it's not the same as being buried in a family grave, but many of the men killed on the battlefield will be buried with colleagues, comrades, others they knew, laughed with, smoked with . . . many will have come from the same town. And it's not dishonorable, is it, to be buried on the battlefield where you have given your life?"

"But will we remember them, one by one? I don't see how we can.

An anonymous death . . . doesn't that frighten you just a little bit? That if you'd been killed that day, and not just wounded, and you had been buried where your parents or Izzy could never find you, because your grave was unmarked . . . isn't that, don't you feel . . . doesn't it make you go *cold* just thinking about it?"

I didn't know what to say. The truth is, I hadn't thought about death very much, not then, not—perhaps—as much as I should have done. And what did she mean? Was she thinking of her mother's awful fate, of her own death, her sisters', of Will's—or of Wilhelm's?

She was thinking of Wilhelm, of course. She was thinking that if he was dead, she might never find out where. That he was lost to her forever. And that if he was dead, he had died not knowing he had a son and what a . . . what a cold, empty, desolate *King Lear*–type end that was.

I dug my hands into my pockets. I was playing a . . . well, not a dangerous game, exactly; that was the wrong word . . . I was . . . I knew enough to help her, to give her hope, to remove at least some of the dreadful coldness she felt in her heart. Should I tell her what I knew? If I loved her as much as I told myself I did love her, didn't I want her to be happy, to be released from the terror that gripped her? That was in my gift.

Love doesn't work like that. Love has its own logic. My sister had discovered that too. Instead, I told myself that maybe Sam was preparing herself for the fact that Wilhelm was probably dead, that she would never see him or hear from him again. That's what all this talk of death meant. I didn't really believe my own reasoning but it got me off the hook, at least for then. I said nothing.

Murder

THE NEW YEAR, 1917, was marked by another innovation: the air war—the first in history—was getting under way. On a personal level, I was glad to get the festivities over with. For obvious reasons, Christmas for me was fraught with mixed emotions. Without meeting Wilhelm, I would never have met Sam. At the same time, the course I had followed played on my nerves, more so at Christmas than at other times of the year. His photograph was still safely hidden in my briefcase but I never took it out now, to look at it.

That Christmas, at the end of 1916, we did something Sam had had at the back of her mind for a while without telling me. On the day after Boxing Day, she invited some of the poorer children in her school for tea at the flat. About half a dozen turned up and, from the way they wolfed down the food we provided—sandwiches and jelly, mainly—it was clear that they hadn't seen a square meal in weeks. All of us were eating less at that stage of the war, and we had all developed a craving for sugar. Meatless days once a week had been introduced by the government. To begin with, I had thought Sam risked being disappointed with her Christmas treat—that her approach was essentially patronizing—but, I have to admit, I was wrong: all the children seemed to enjoy their afternoon with "Miss," as they called her.

I was disconcerted when, after tea and without warning, she asked me to give a repeat of the talk I had given to the schoolchildren in Middle Hill—the one about the Christmas truce. What did she mean by it, I asked myself. Did she mean anything?

Anyway, I got through it, and the children left.

Later that night, however, we were reading in bed and I was half-way through the *Morning Post* when I shuddered. "Mannheim was bombed, according to this. How terrifying that must be, explosives dropping out of the sky. It must cause widespread panic, bringing killing miles behind the front lines, and affecting civilians as much as trained soldiers. What new horrors will this war bring us next? Didn't Wilhelm come from Mannheim?"

She didn't reply immediately; she was underlining something in the book she was reading. "Yes . . . yes he did. But how did you know that?"

I went cold. Too late I realized my mistake. I tried to remain calm, matter-of-fact. "You told me. How else would I know such a thing?"

"Did I? I don't remember. When?"

I had made a mistake, a bad one, and having been cold, I was now sweating under my nightshirt. But I had the sense, or the low cunning, not to make too much of it, not to overreact, not to be too specific, not to get into a protracted conversation, giving an elaborate explanation that Sam might brood on.

"You must have told me on some canal bank or other. Do you want to read the article?" I handed her the paper.

She took it, and buried herself in the account I had been reading.

I turned out my light, lay back, and waited for her to finish.

She did and turned out her light.

We watched the shadows from the traffic on the Embankment chase each other across the ceiling. As we often did, talking, before making love.

I waited apprehensively for her next question. Surely she could sense my heart thumping like a drum in my chest. Sweat had formed at my temples—but I daren't brush it away. That would show how tense I was.

In some ways it was extraordinary that I had not made any mistakes in my deception before now. But one error was all it took, one small foot wrong, one false move could destroy everything, could cost me my happiness, could raze and unravel and dismantle the whole careful choreography I had concocted. The pillow under my neck was damp with sweat.

Her next question would tell me if, in one unguarded moment, I had unwound months of effort. I daren't look in her direction.

And then I heard Sam's regular breathing, a rhythm I knew well.

She was asleep.

At the end of January and beginning of February, three things occurred together—though I am not attaching equal weight or significance to each. On the thirty-first, Germany announced unrestricted submarine warfare in the eastern Atlantic, even against neutrals, and immediately began sinking American ships. On the same day, Genevieve Afton was tried for treason. I gave evidence at the trial, which was held in a reserve court building just south of the river near Lambeth Palace, the official residence of the archbishop of Canterbury. The court had been bombed by a zeppelin a day or two before, and although the damage wasn't serious half a dozen soldiers were stirrup-pumping water from a burst main into the courtyard. I was cross-examined for about two hours and, I think, gave a good account of myself. Anyway, I found out later that Genevieve was found guilty and sentenced to death. I tried to put that out of my mind.

I was helped, to some extent, by the fact that a week later the third thing happened and I was promoted again and transferred from the Gym to the basement of the building, colloquially known as the Crypt. My job now was to read raw intelligence reports, reports that had come in from the field, and so had already been pored over by intelligence officers in France, or Flanders, or wherever they'd happened to surface. But we had access to all manner of material and the idea was that we were farther from the action, with a wider perspective, so that, perhaps, we could discern strategic matters in among the mass of material we had access to.

The Crypt was a step up in the career pecking order, but a definite step down in the life amenities department. The room was far more secure than the Gym and for that reason had no windows—the lights were always on, tobacco smoke of one sort or another was always swirling in and around the desks we worked at (no tables now), and the drone of a primitive air-recycling machine provided a steady hum that masked almost all other sounds. No chance of hearing the air-raid warning whistles that had been introduced.

The desks were arranged in concentric circles, facing a central glass booth where the commanding colonel sat, handing out the work. There was a good deal less camaraderie in this department than there had been upstairs, but in any case 1917 was a much more serious time. We all knew that the war could be lost at any moment; we would all have rather been at the Front in some more active role, though we knew that, at any moment, any one of us could come up with a crucial development. So we got on with it.

Upstairs I had been fairly lucky, in that I had made some sort of intelligence breakthrough reasonably early on. In the Crypt, however, it was different. I spent a very difficult two months scanning the paperwork I was given—captured documents, enemy morale reports, statistics of men and matériel provided by our side, interrogation reports—without, to be frank, spotting anything remotely useful. April came, and I was growing anxious.

What I remember most about that winter was not the cold or the rain or even the snow but the wind. We learned to dread the east wind. If there was an east wind in London, the chances were that there was an east wind at the Front—when the Germans would release their gas.

But then we were overwhelmed by the news that food riots had broken out in Russia, that the Cossacks had refused to fire on the rioters, and that the czar, faced down by railway workers, had abdicated. Russia was an ally, or had been—what was going to happen there?

That's when I spotted something that, at first, was a long way from Russia. It was a passing reference made by one of our agents in Zurich. Most days he took his midmorning coffee at the Café Odeon. This café, I knew from my general reading, was famous in Zurich as the home of the Dada artists' cult. It was frequented by Hans Arp, Frank Wedekind, James Joyce, Emmy Hemmings, and many other artists sitting out the war. In the account I am referring to, the agent happened to mention that he hadn't seen one of the celebrated regulars in a few days: Lenin.

That set me thinking. Incredible events—revolutionary events— were happening in Russia. Lenin was—or should have been—in exile in Switzerland. But surely, now that the revolution was happening, he would want to get back to his home? And wouldn't that spell trouble?

The procedure in the Crypt was different from upstairs. If you had an idea, you went straight to the colonel.

His name was Lockart, Hamish Lockart, and he was a Scot. He wore a mustache, had a mass of freckles and brilliant red hair. His rimless spectacles made him look like nothing so much as a Prussian.

"Aye?" he would say as you approached him. "What is it?"

A deputy shared his office, a major like me but of much more standing. His name was Frank Stanbury.

"Aye?" said Lockart, as I entered his glass booth. "What is it?"

I told him.

He frowned and didn't ask me to sit down. "And what do you read into that?"

"Maybe Lenin's gone back to Russia."

He shook his head. "How would he get there?"

"Via Germany."

"Why would imperial Germany allow a known revolutionary free passage?"

"Simple," I said. "Self-interest. Lenin's against all traditional authority. What he wants most of all is to pull Russia out of this war. If he did, think how many German divisions that would free up—to transfer to the Western Front."

"You know this Lenin person, do you?"

"No, of course not. But I read. He thinks—like a lot of people—that this war was started by governments and generals and that it is ordinary people who are being made to suffer. He thinks it's very likely that if Russia can pull out of the war, others will follow."

Lockart sat back in his seat. He exchanged glances with Stanbury.

"What do you think, Frank?"

Frank, it was clear, had got where he was by never expressing an opinion, certainly not one that could be contradicted all too easily.

"Difficult," he whispered, running his tongue around his lips—nerves, probably. "What do you think?"

It was like watching a tennis game, back and forth.

Lockart said nothing for a full minute. He stroked his mustache and kept his gaze on me. His calculation was always the same: not to bother his superiors unnecessarily, but not to stifle the supposedly brilliant ideas of his subordinates.

"Say you're right. What would our next move be?"

"Double-check whether Lenin's really gone, using our people on the ground in Zurich—"

"Which wouldn't be very expensive—"

I nodded. "Then, if he *has* gone, we need to talk to our people on the ground in Petrograd, warn them to expect trouble and to position themselves accordingly."

Another long silence. More rubbing of the mustache.

Then: "Very well. Come with me." He rose, buttoned his tunic, tightened his tie, and led the way out of the basement. We ran up a flight of stairs, strode across the internal courtyard, and entered the building through a set of imposing double doors, made of some fancy Indian hardwood from the empire.

Inside the doors, it was immediately quiet. A plush carpet, spongy as a cricket square, high bookshelves, crystal chandeliers, and the smell of polish, which, for some reason, I found comforting. Across from the double doors, at the end of the carpet and the bookshelves, were more double doors. We were clearly somewhere very senior indeed. As we approached those doors, as we passed a buttress, a desk came into view, with a forbidding-looking woman sitting at it.

"Margaret," said Lockart. "Is the brigadier free?"

She rose to her feet. She was an imposing figure, "stout," as my mother would have said, though she was tall enough to carry it. "Just a minute, I'll check." She tapped lightly on the doors and stuck her head through the gap she had opened. She turned back to us. "Give him a minute."

We stood without speaking. Lockart resumed polishing his mustache; Margaret went back to her typing; I watched dust particles dance in the shafts of sunlight from the windows.

The brigadier was as good as his word. After no more than a minute, the door opened, and he came out and shook hands with Lockart.

"This is Major Montgomery, sir," said Lockart.

"You new?" said the brigadier.

Before I could answer, Lockart did it for me.

"The major was a bit of a star in the Gym, sir. He's been with us a couple of months."

The brigadier fixed me with his stare and nodded. A light went on in his head. "I've heard about you." He nodded again and said, "My name's Malahyde. Come in."

His room was huge. Same plush carpet, same bookshelves and books as outside, plus a high window that gave onto a courtyard that until then I hadn't known existed. A lawn with trees.

He waved us to some chairs and himself sat on a sofa, with a low table between us. He crossed his legs, revealing expensive socks and elegant, slim ankles. Very shiny shoes.

"Got something for me, have you?"

Again, Lockart was first off the mark.

"It may be a long shot but . . . well, that's what we're all about in the Crypt."

There was a pad of paper on the low table. The brigadier took out a fountain pen and laid it on the pad.

"Fire away."

Lockart looked at me and nodded.

I told Malahyde what I'd told Lockart.

He didn't move and heard me out in silence. He didn't even blink. It was unnerving. When I was done, he leaned forward, picked up his pad, and made a few notes. Then he put the pad back down and put away his pen. He was a very tidy man.

"Well, you did right to come to me. It should be easy enough to check whether Vladimir Ilyich is still in Zurich or has disappeared. If he's still there but ill, or having a secret affair, that's one thing. If, on the other hand, he really has decamped for Russia, then that's a different kettle of fish entirely."

He addressed himself to me. "Major Montgomery, this is good work. If Lenin *is* on his way to Mother Russia, we'd have found out in due course, but obviously time is of the essence here and you've bought a few days, I would guess." He changed his tone. "But I have to point out that you have signed the Official Secrets Act. You must tell no one about this. Not even your wife, if you have one. Do you understand?"

I nodded. Of course I understood.

"What I mean is, no one likes the Germans at the moment—but they are a good honest enemy. There are, however, plenty of closet Bolsheviks in Britain who'd like to see revolution here someday. We don't want them making trouble, not just now anyway, with the war the way it is, and if they think Lenin is on his way to Russia that could cause all kinds of bother. Do I make myself clear?"

Again I nodded. I didn't want an argument and, whatever my politics, I didn't want Russia pulling out of the war—not for now.

"Keep at it, will you?" The brigadier got to his feet: we were being dismissed. He held out his hand for it to be shaken. "Now I need to get to work. See if I can build on what you have done."

We were shown out. As we retreated back down the plush carpet, I heard him bark at Margaret, "Get me Downing Street, will you."

At just over two, Will was noisier and more unruly than ever. He ran uncertainly around the flat, jabbed his fingers into any hole that would accommodate them, climbed every piece of furniture, burned himself once and scalded himself twice, through getting too close to the fire or the cooking stove. He seemed to have no fear and was as good-natured as a cat on a dairy farm.

Sam had long since settled in as a teacher at St. Paul's Ladbroke Grove. To begin with, as she had finally admitted, the children had been a good deal more unruly, and quite a bit more smelly, than the darlings of Middle Hill. "But they're just as bright," she assured me, before I could offer any criticism. "They've had harder and dirtier lives—but they've got such spirit, Hal. They fight a bit, call the teachers names—but it's not hostile. It's cheek, really. They know we know more than they do, but they don't think that makes us better than them . . . we're all equal. When we get on to the really interesting bits of a lesson, they all quiet down and concentrate. They know all about city life, of course, and, since they usually live in cramped conditions, there's little we can teach them about the raw practicalities—money, work, sport. We don't teach sex but we don't need to—they've seen all that, too."

"So what *do* you teach them?"

"History. Geography. Biology—how animals work, what happens on farms, which many have never seen, why the seasons change. Art— they love art. Many of them can look at pictures all day long."

"Do you prefer it to Middle Hill?"

"I keep asking myself that question. I loved village life, but I like my life here too. Growing up in Bristol, we had excursions—day trips—into the countryside. But although I enjoyed those trips, I never felt *part* of the countryside, never felt it was part of me. In Middle Hill I did start to respond to, you know, the wildlife, the seasons, I started getting to know the hedgerows, the copses, I learned the different breeds of cow and pig, I knew all the words for the different parts of horses' harnesses, I understood the diagnoses of the local vet—most of them, anyway. And yes, I loved it, all of it. But"—and her eyes shone—"I think the city is my natural habitat. Bristol wasn't London, oh no, but . . . your sister was right and I'm glad we are here."

We were in the kitchen at the time, making Will a hot drink. Having grown up with condensed milk, he didn't share Sam's or my revulsion.

"The real difference is the parents. In Middle Hill the parents were behind the children. Here, it's different. Once or twice parents have come in and said that their child is being turned into a dreamer, that we shouldn't fill their heads with far-off places. So I ask them to sit through a class. The headmistress doesn't mind. When they see how we teach—*what* we teach, how the children react—they change their minds, usually. Some of them become quite interested themselves. More and more parents are coming to the school—that has to be good. I say 'parents'—it's the mothers, of course."

Lottie, meanwhile, had found herself a man at last. His name was Reg and, when she had met him, he had been a trainee policeman. He was nice enough, if creepy-quiet—tall, thin, with very short-cut dark hair and a mustache. Why did Sam's sisters always seem to go for men with mustaches? Reg liked fishing, so Lottie and he spent hours on river and canal banks, on the edges of reservoirs, filled-in gravel pits, and so on. It got Lottie out at weekends, so that she saw a bit of the countryside on the edges of London. Reg lived in a police barracks and, after a day's fishing at the weekend, they would arrive home late, usually after Sam and I were in bed, and spend the night together. He would be gone at dawn the next day. I never knew if Lottie thought she was deceiving us, but neither Sam nor I cared. Lottie must find her happiness where she could.

But then Reg was conscripted into an army unit in Yorkshire. So, more tears as he made his farewells. He and Lottie did *not* get engaged before he went, so I hoped there would be no replay of the Faye episode. Still, it wasn't easy for Lottie.

Sam had made friends with one of the other teachers at the school, a woman called Ellen Smith whose speciality was science. She came round for lunch one Saturday and brought her fiancé with her. He, Edward, was an assistant harbormaster in the Port of London. I liked him immediately and we got on well. We went out to the pub but sat in the garden rather than the bar, because the weather had turned mild and we had Will with us. While Sam and Ellen talked, I asked Edward about his job.

"It's pure organization," he said. "I enjoyed math at school, especially geometry, and it's just as well. My job is all about timing and layout. Say a ship comes in, from the West Indies, for example. I'm told by telegraph when it's coming, what size it is, and how long it's going to be with us. So I allocate a berth. All well and good, assuming, of course, that it's in a convoy and doesn't get torpedoed. I arrange the customs inspection, handle any quarantine problems, make sure all the paperwork is in order."

"But . . . ? I sense a 'but' coming."

"Too right." He smiled. "First off, I don't control the rate at which ships arrive. If the port is full—and it happens—ships have to anchor in the estuary. That's expensive for them, and so is hardly popular. And it creates work for me, since I have to alert customs, who will keep an eye on them.

"Then, some ships overstay the amount of time they have told us. Ships are big things, so you can't just tell them to move. But if they stay, they are fined—and getting the money out of them can be a problem, though they know that if they mess us around they can't come back. Then, of course, sailors who have been at sea for weeks at a time are apt to go overboard when they reach the shore. They drink, go whoring, get into fights, get arrested, in some cases get sent to prison. I don't have to deal with all that but I do have to keep abreast of it, insofar as it affects when a ship leaves and we can bring in the ones waiting outside." He smiled. "As a job it's more interesting than it sounds, and I enjoy it. Of course, over time, certain ships and certain captains get a reputation and you learn to look out for them."

"Can you ban the black sheep from the port?"

"Oh yes, it happens all the time. We also impound ships that haven't paid their fees. That's always a lot of fun." He grinned.

"How many ships come in and out of the port each week?"

"There are between a dozen and two dozen major ports in Britain, depending on how you count. The Port of London is the biggest, of course. About thirty oceangoing ships—not coastal traders—come in and out every week." He pointed to my glass, which was nearly empty.

I nodded. "Thanks, I'd love another."

He picked up my glass. "If you're interested, come and have a look around one day. Ports are interesting places. They're a world all their own."

"I'd love that," I replied. "It would make a change from walking Will."

"I heard that," said Sam, standing behind me and placing her hands on my shoulders. "As punishment, you can take us for a walk this instant."

I hadn't been home for Christmas, but I did get down to Edgewater more often now. I still didn't take Sam. I didn't think my mother was up to it and my father continued to insist that he didn't approve of my living arrangements. *I* might be happy enough but they were a different generation and couldn't adjust.

My mother was not good. Her complexion was even more florid than it had been, the coughing fits were getting worse, and though she had always been a fierce character, she was now turning irascible, angry at everyone and everything, even Einstein. I had been as good as my word to my father and Izzy and had found a psychiatrist to examine my mother. She had steadfastly refused to be seen. Worst of all, her emphysema was now so bad that her walks were limited—forty minutes was all she could manage, twenty out and twenty back and that didn't take her very far. Einstein was putting on weight.

On one occasion, when we had walked down the lane near the house and were leaning against a wooden gate into a field, she had broached the subject I dreaded, which we all dreaded.

"Do you think you'll get married before I die?"

Fortunately, I was looking across the field at some rabbits when she dropped this little bombshell. I turned to her. "Of course, Ma. No hurry, is there?"

"You know there bloody well is," she wheezed. She patted her chest. "These lungs can't last forever. You'd better get a move on."

"Who'd have me?" I said in as pleasant a manner as I could muster.

"You must have been out with *some* women," she said softly. "London's a big place."

"Yes, of course," I said. "But, well . . ." I didn't want to lie.

She let a short silence elapse.

"I suppose, if I was a woman your age, and I got to know you, and liked you, and then it started to get serious—"

"Ma!" I cried softly.

"No, let me finish . . . I don't want to embarrass you." She put her hand on my arm. "It would obviously be a problem . . . I can see that. You would feel you had to say something . . . and that could be a problem for some women. A big difficulty. But . . . it's not unknown for some women to be unable to conceive. If you could meet someone like that . . . you could both adopt."

I didn't know what to say.

"It's such an important thing, infertility." She coughed, but not badly. "To be honest, children never interested me much, but I know your father would have been disappointed if we couldn't have had Izzy and you. Would he have married me if he thought I was infertile? Possibly not." She smiled ruefully. "There ought to be an agency where infertile couples can meet each other, don't you think? Maybe there is."

I was speechless. Why didn't I tell her there and then about Sam and Will? I don't know. I *do* know. It would have meant explaining why I hadn't mentioned it before. I might have told her about Wilhelm and our Christmas encounter. She might have insisted on meeting Sam and telling her everything—my mother was a law unto herself and I wasn't about to take any risks. So I said nothing.

"Can we drop it?" is what I did say.

"Promise me you'll check out if there's some kind of agency. Then I'll drop it."

I nodded and we headed back to the house.

On the way I turned over what she had said. I came to the conclusion that for her, in her condition, death had suddenly come very close and she wanted to see me settled. She was tidying up her life, or trying to.

I came home one evening to find Sam, Lottie, Will, and Whisky in the dining room, with bits of paper and cardboard and scissors and glue spread out all over the dining table. "This looks like a military operation," I said. I had poured myself a Scotch and I sipped it as I looked down and surveyed the chaos. "What *is* this?"

"It's Lottie's idea," said Sam, getting up to kiss me. "She found a shop selling travel posters and we're sticking them to boards, so we can decorate Will's room."

"Look," said Lottie, unrolling one. It was a railways poster, advertising Snowdonia, in Wales. "Here's another—" She spread open a second, advertising the Swiss lakes.

"Lottie knows all about my wanderlust—don't you think it's a clever idea, Hal? As Will gets bigger, he will understand more, and he'll ask questions and we'll be able to tell him all about far-off places."

"Let me help," I said, sitting down.

"Yes, you help Lottie, Hal. I must get started on dinner anyway." She went through into the kitchen.

Will came and sat on my lap, as he sometimes liked to do. I unrolled another of the posters—this one was for Imperial Cruise Lines, advertising the splendors of Bombay and Madras.

"That's a trip Sam would *love*," said Lottie, busy cutting cardboard to match the size of the posters.

"Not you, Lottie? You don't share her love of travel?"

She made a face. "After what happened to our mother? I don't think so."

"But you have a lovely singing voice . . . they have concert halls and theaters on these cruise ships, you know. You could travel *and* get paid for it. You never know . . . after the war . . . there'll be a lot of things you could do."

"You think there'll be many changes afterward?"

"Of course. Wars change people, entire countries. But you don't always know what will happen. For instance, you women will change—"

"Oh, how?"

"Well, for a start, women will do more jobs; I mean they will work at a bigger variety of jobs. They are doing so much already, because of the war—driving buses, lorries even. There'll be more policewomen after the war, more women doctors; more universities will admit women."

"I'm not so sure . . . Are men going to change, will they let women onto their turf?"

"They'll have to, Lottie, because there will be fewer men around. In that sense it won't be so much fun being a woman."

There was a brief silence as Will and I watched Lottie put glue at each corner of the piece of cardboard she had cut and begin sticking the Imperial Cruise Lines poster onto it.

"Will you go back to the theater, after the war?"

She nodded. "It gets to you, the theater. It seeps into your blood. The weird hours, the superstitions, the spiky rhythm of successes and flops, the smells, the tantrums of the actors and directors, the bitchy reviews, the backstage parties, the props, the music . . . I don't think I could do anything else."

One corner of the poster was giving her difficulty—wouldn't stay stuck down—and she leaned on it. "I'm very grateful for all the help you've been, Hal—you know that, don't you?"

I smiled.

"But I'm not sure I *want* the world to change. I *liked* the world as it was in 1914. I liked my life in the theater. London was the center of empire, and Soho was—is—the center of London. There!"

The poster had finally remained stuck down. She held up the card with the poster stuck to it. It was a brilliant blue, with patches of red and white—the imperial colors.

Will's large eyes stared up at it. He liked what he saw.

"What will you do after the war, Hal? Will you stay in the army?"

"With this wound? I don't think they would have me. In any case, no, I don't want to stay, even in intelligence. My family was in publishing till they sold out. I'd like to go back in. There are some new printing techniques about at the moment, producing new colors, so I think there's scope for a new kind of art book, showing what paintings look like. I'd like to try that."

"Do you think Sam and you will ever get married?" She had started cutting a second piece of cardboard.

"Sam knows the score. I'll marry her whenever she wants."

"You're willing to . . . you know, just hang around, waiting. Isn't that a bit . . . humiliating?"

"I don't see it like that. I love her. Surely you know that by now."

She didn't say anything for a moment, cutting away.

"One time, when we were girls, six or seven—"

"Remember our agreement, Lottie."

She nodded. "This is just a story, from our childhood. When we were nine or ten, Sam and I ran away from home. Our father was being particularly awful to our mother and neither Sam nor I could stand it. We took a change of underwear—that's all we could carry—and our savings, a few shillings each, and we walked to the Bristol docks. The idea was to catch a boat to somewhere far away, far away and exotic, of course, like Zanzibar, or Egypt, or Samarkand—I remember Sam was in love with that word. Once we were in this exotic and faraway place, we would become rich and powerful and come back to rescue our mother from our wicked father."

She looked up, but still cut at her cardboard.

"We got as far as the docks—we knew how to sneak in. We asked the man on the gangplank of the first ship we came to where it was going. Dublin, he said. That wasn't exotic enough for Sam. We asked at the next ship: Liverpool. And the next: Glasgow."

She grinned. "I can't tell you how disappointed we were. Well, Sam was disappointed. To tell the truth, the shine of the adventure was starting to wear off for me, and I was beginning to think about a change of plan—and going home."

Will was fidgeting and I let him down to play on the floor with Whisky.

"But not Sam. We stayed in the docks overnight—sleeping under some tarpaulin in an old tugboat in dry dock. Sam, although she was only a girl, knew the times of the tides at Bristol—it was part of her wanderlust—and she knew that high tide that night was about three in the morning. Sure enough, two boats slipped away in the night, and two other boats came in and tied up. The next morning, as soon as it was light, Sam was up and talking to the new crews."

Lottie finished cutting the second piece of card and started gluing the Swiss lakes poster to it.

"And . . . one of the new boats had come in from somewhere in Africa that neither of us had heard of, but was bound for Cape Town.

Sam was delighted—Cape Town for her was next to heaven—but I was thoroughly alarmed. I was hungry, my hair needed combing, I was dirty, and ships, I now knew, were big, smelly things full of strange men who were none too clean themselves. Cape Town was the last place I wanted to go. I had no idea how we were going to smuggle ourselves aboard ship and neither did Sam, but just then a policeman appeared in the docks. I saw him talking to one of the port officials; he was obviously asking if anyone had seen two young girls. At that moment, he saw us—and Sam saw him. She yelled at me, 'Come on, run!' And she ran back toward the tugboat where we had spent the night."

Lottie leaned on the poster, to make it stick to the card. "But I didn't run. I just stood there as the policeman hurried toward me. By then, I *wanted* to be caught."

Lottie looked at me directly. "Sam was the youngest of us sisters, but in some ways the toughest. Maybe she had to be tough *because* she was the youngest—she was the smallest while we were girls and had to assert herself."

A pause, while Lottie began work on the third piece of cardboard. Will was wrestling with Whisky under the table.

"I understand what you are saying, Lottie." I swallowed what remained of my Scotch. "Thank you for the warning."

She leaned across, placed her hand on mine, and squeezed it.

Dear Hal,

Full marks for going home again. As for what you say about Ma—well, to be honest, I knew it. Pa has taken to writing me secret letters, without telling Ma, so I know all about her condition and how worried he is. I should really try to get some leave but I've been told it's out of the question.

Alan has told his wife about me. I said I thought it was a bit premature, unnecessary even. I mean, what if he's killed tomorrow?

His wife will be doubly bereaved. And if I'm killed . . . well, she need never have known about me. But Alan's Alan. An upright Presbyterian with a fierce Highland conscience. To be frank, his conscience frightens me from time to time.

Since I can't get home just now, you're going to have to do the work of two and get home a lot more than you have been doing. Why don't you try and see old Dr. Barnaby and ask him what the prognosis is? I've asked Alan and he made a face. But I don't think he wants to alarm me and he is hundreds of miles away, with other things on his mind.

God, I'm getting gloomy. I'll try to be more cheerful next time.

Love XXX x OOO = XXXOOO

Izzy

I think it was about now, just after this last letter from Izzy, that we received a visit in Northumberland Avenue from the Blood Transfusion Service. They came round quietly and addressed us in small groups. They explained, as Izzy had explained that evening in Stratford, that there was a new science of blood, that the blood running in all our veins and arteries can be divided into four groups—A, B, AB, and O—and that, if someone who has lost blood, in an accident, say, or of course in war, was given blood of the same type, then his or her body would accept the new blood and not reject it. The man doing the explaining—a young doctor with melancholy brown eyes—said that a way had been discovered to prevent blood from coagulating, which meant that we, in the comparative safety of Northumberland Avenue, could now do something direct for the war effort: give a pint of our blood, which would then be rushed to the Front, to help our boys wounded in the trenches.

It was a stirring speech, in its quiet way, but even so people were a bit wary. A lot of people don't like injections, or the sight of blood, and a pint sounded like a lot. The doctor reassured everyone that giving a pint did not endanger the donor's life, that the only precaution that needed to be made was bed rest for twenty minutes after the blood was taken, to check there were no adverse reactions, and a cup of tea.

I was clued up more than most, of course, so as soon as he had finished his presentation, I volunteered. That encouraged others, I think, and he led a small group of us to a tent made of tarpaulin that had been pitched on the lawn of the central courtyard—the one I had not known existed until very recently.

He made me take off my jacket, lie down on a small bed, and roll up the sleeve of my shirt. As he slid the needle into my arm, and because I think he wanted to take my mind off what was happening, he said, "You were quick to volunteer. The mention of blood does funny things to some people."

I explained about Izzy.

"She's a brave girl," he said.

"War does funny things to people. She was my little sister; now she's . . . she's . . . really grown up . . . " I trailed away.

"Think how many lives she's saved," he said as he fitted a tube from my arm to a bottle hanging by the bed. "She'll be able to hold her head up when this is all over. That's more than can be said for a lot of people." He nodded across to the wall of the tent, where there was an army recruiting poster showing the head of General Haig.

I said nothing.

The doctor came round again a short while later, when the bottle was almost full, and disengaged all the equipment, removing the needle from my arm.

"Do you write to your sister?"

"Of course."

"Tell her about this, tell her what we are doing. It will reassure her. I was in a unit like hers—until I was promoted to safety. So I know how exposed she is feeling. Tell her the idea of transfusion is catching on. Lots of people are shying away—as I said, blood does that to people—but far more can see that it is a practical, if slightly grisly way to help the people at the sharp end."

"How often can one give blood?"

He made a face. "We don't know yet—we're still experimenting. Maybe twice a year, unless it's an emergency. But we've got all your details, and you'll get a letter from us in due course, thanking you for your help and telling you what blood group you are. Always remember the group you are; it's a useful piece of information and you never know when it might come in handy."

"What group are you?"

"AB—that's the rarest."

"The elite, eh?"

"Oh no, not at all. Quite the opposite, really. It means that if I am in an accident, or lose blood in an operation, or if I get sent back to the Front and am wounded, I can be given blood from anyone, not just AB. In blood transfusion, group O is both the elite *and* the commonest. More people are group O than any other group. And type O can be given to anyone, whatever their own group. People who are type O are common, but also the royals when it comes to transfusion." He grinned. "Now, I'll have the nurse bring you some tea. Condensed milk, I'm afraid."

Through her courtship with Reg, and with Reg being so mad about fishing, Lottie had discovered some unusual backwaters of London, canal and river walks that Sam and I would never have found for ourselves. At weekends we explored these almost secret places. They were often an unusual mix of wildlife—foxes, fish, water rats, exotic weeds and plants—and industrial bric-a-brac: coal barges, oily wharves, dead factories, char-à-banc parks. A landscape that, as Sam said, needed its own Constable but had never found one.

On these walks, Sam and I talked. She unwound after school and I—I have to admit—often told her secrets of my work that I wasn't meant to. The canal banks were not exactly overpopulated, very few German spies were in evidence, and I suppose I wanted her to know that what I was doing all day long was not exactly a waste of time.

It reminded us, of course, of the riverbank at Stratford, when we had first met. I also suspected that it reminded Sam of how she had first met Wilhelm, and been proposed to. But neither of us talked much about him now. Faye's outburst had affected us all.

However, my visits home had left their mark on me, and I remember one of our walks, a gray day when the wind gusted along the canal, creating patterns on the water, ripples in patches, dead leaves collecting in sodden masses against sticks and logs lurking in the weeds by the bank.

Sam had her arm in mine and, as usual, we were alone.

"Do you . . . ," I said, "have you ever thought . . . would you like Will to have a brother or sister?"

She squeezed my arm. "You've never asked that before. Why now?"

I shrugged. "It's a natural question, isn't it, in the circumstances? It must have crossed your mind."

Sam didn't say anything for a while, and we walked on. The canal curved just here and we were sheltered from the wind.

"We're doing all right, aren't we?" Sam squeezed my arm again. "I've never regretted my decision, Hal. You know that, don't you?"

"That wasn't my question."

"But that was my answer. I told you, that evening in the cricket field in Middle Hill, and again at the railway station . . . that I didn't love you, Hal. But we made a deal that suited both of us and, as I say,

I don't regret it, not one bit. You've been wonderful, to both Will and me, and to my sisters—though you'd never know it from the way Faye behaved. And the school I'm in is so much more . . . *real,* I suppose. I feel much more *useful* there than I ever did in Middle Hill. That was a surprise, in coming to London. I didn't expect that but I'm very grateful for it."

It was my turn to keep silent for a while. The canal straightened out and we approached a lock. We could hear the water sluicing through the gates as it began to fill up, to allow a barge to come upstream.

"I had hoped . . . I had dared to hope, for more than gratitude."

Sam stopped and pulled my arm, so that I was forced to face her. She raised herself on tiptoe and kissed my cheek. "I know," she whispered. "I know. But we get along, don't we? We're comfortable together. I've never said this before, Hal, but—I love what you do to me in bed. It took time, didn't it? But we got there. And it's so much better, not having to bother with messy contraceptives, or you . . . you know, you pulling out at the last minute and spoiling everything. You being the way you are—it's a bonus in a way. God, I make so much noise, these days—does that embarrass you?"

"No. Not at all. I find it erotic."

"Can't we be content with that, for the time being? I can't say what's not in my heart, Hal . . . you wouldn't want that, would you?"

I brushed her cheek with my fingers. "No. Do you think about Wilhelm still?"

She leaned her head on my shoulder. "Don't *do* this to yourself, Hal. We have our life now, and it's building. I was in love with Wilhelm, and part of me always will be, I suppose. When he spoke English, he had an accent, of course, but I loved it; it made him different, it made him *him.* And people always say Germans don't have a sense of humor—yet he could be very funny. He thought the Kaiser was a ludicrous figure—dangerously ludicrous, yes, but Wilhelm was always making fun of him. Still, the war's been going on for nearly three years now and who knows where Wilhelm is, whether he's alive and, if he is, whether he ever thinks of me. He's in the past, Hal. We are living here and now, on the bank of this cold canal, and we're making a life."

She lifted her head and looked at me.

"Remember you told me to read war poetry to the children at school? Well, I did, and that set me reading more poetry. There's a new set of verses by this Irishman, Yeats, W. B. Yeats."

"Uh-huh, I've heard of him."

"But I'll bet you haven't read his new collection, about the birth of this new political movement in Ireland—"

"You mean the IRA?"

"That's it. It has these lines, Hal: 'Wherever green is worn / all is changed, changed utterly: / A terrible beauty is born.' I'm not sure I have it exactly right, but don't you think that's a wonderful phrase—'terrible beauty'?"

I looked at her.

"Don't you think that's true—that some things can be both terrible and beautiful at the same time? What is beautiful for some is terrible for others? You and I were thrown together, accidentally, by this terrible war, both suffering, both maimed in a way. Both trapped, as you once put it. But, as I say, we're building, creating a better life than we had; it's not too fanciful to say that Will will have a more beautiful life than would have happened if you hadn't . . . if you hadn't come along."

I swallowed.

We stood and watched the barge, in the lock, gradually come into view as the water rose.

"Look at that," whispered Sam. "That barge, that filthy dirty barge, unlovely and belching black smoke behind it. Hardly a thing of beauty, is it? But it's going from one level to another, a new horizon as the lock fills. That's like us." She laughed. "Not my best metaphor, I agree." She leaned into me. "You can't hide the past, Hal, but you can detach yourself from it, up to a point anyway."

The lock doors opened and the barge moved toward us, and then past us. The man at the tiller nodded.

"Why isn't he at the Front, I wonder," said Sam in a low voice.

"Too old, too infirm, maybe he's transporting crucial cargo."

"Women are doing so many jobs now that only men did before the war. It's changing our psychology. Men and women will be different after the shooting stops."

"If it ever does stop. What effect will growing up in a war have on Will, do you think?"

Sam retied her scarf around her neck. "Children are more resilient than they sometimes seem. He'll be fine. For one thing, he has a man around. You're more important to him than the war, Hal." She squeezed my arm again and said, "Let's go back now," and we turned and retraced our steps.

Before we had gone very far, she said, "When am I going to meet your parents, Hal? Or are you going to keep me hidden forever?"

Now I squeezed *her* arm. "Would you like to?"

"It would be a step forward, don't you think? A step up."

"My mother would grill you for hours. It would be like being a prisoner of war."

"I'm a schoolteacher, Hal, in a rough school—remember? I can handle myself."

We didn't decide anything there and then. But, as we walked back along the canal bank on that dreary day, I suddenly felt brighter. Sam had signaled progress. She wasn't in love with me but things were changing between us, I was sure of it.

"Good morning, Colonel Lockart, and to you Montgomery. Sit down, please." Brigadier Malahyde was the same as always: immaculate suit, regulation length of shirt cuff showing beyond his tailored jacket, brogues so shiny you could comb your hair in the reflection, the crease in his trousers sharp enough to slice ham with. If you had any ham. "Got something for me, I take it?"

"Yes sir," said Lockart. "But . . . well, as is usually the case with Hal, it's out of the ordinary." He looked over at me. "It's your show and your neck."

The brigadier chuckled. "Oh dear, Hal. This had better be good."

I leaned forward and crossed my fingers. "Sir, my wife is a school-teacher and one of her fellow teachers, who has become a friend, has a fiancé who is an assistant harbormaster in the Port of London."

The brigadier rested his chin on his fist.

"Some time ago I expressed an interest and last weekend he invited me—us—to his office to see how the port works. I won't bore you with the details but I did notice something I think is worth repeating. Colonel Lockart here agrees."

Lockart made a sound, a sort of gurgle. The brigadier didn't move.

"One of the ships that was leaving the port that day—this would be last Saturday—was called the *Samuel Hood*. It had a cargo of insecticides and it was bound for South America, Uruguay, via Morocco. Samuel Hood is dead now but he was the founder of the Hood-Frankel Company, an Anglo-German chemicals outfit that, before the war, had offices in London and Hamburg. Of course, the company has not had any dealings—officially, at any rate—with its German counterpart since August 1914 but I wonder if, unofficially, the same thing is true."

The brigadier took his chin from where it was resting, on his fist, and sat back. "Go on."

"I looked up Hood in the stock lists—they are doing well. Their share price is up eight percent this year. According to the German papers, Frankel is also doing well. Now, before the war Britain exported thousands of tons of pyrethrum—that's the basis of an insecticide—to Germany, and Hood-Frankel had about forty-five percent of the business. But here's the thing: pyrethrum is isolated from chrysanthemum petals and, as well as being the basis for insecticides, it distils down to picric acid—an explosive."

"So you're thinking—?"

"Why is the *Samuel Hood* sailing for Uruguay via Morocco? I checked with the economic attaché at the Uruguay embassy here in London. Last year she imported precisely seven tons of pyrethrum—they get most of their insecticides from the United States. It occurred to me that Hood is selling pyrethrum to Frankel, exchanging the goods in Morocco, and in effect supplying explosives to the enemy. Who tracks if goods actually end up where they are supposed to?"

The brigadier did as he always did. He took out his expensive pen and began scribbling on the pad in front of him. "If you're right—"

"If I'm right, it means that people who *think* they are making insecticides in the Hood factories in Canning Town are in fact making stuff that is being used to kill our own soldiers."

"I realize that," said the brigadier. "That's not what I meant. I was going to say that a major shareholder in Hood is Sir Kingsley Draper, junior minister in the Foreign Office. He gave up his shares when he took on his official duties, but whichever way you look at it, this is a major scandal. If, however, we go public, we alert the Germans to what we know."

He looked at Lockart, tapping his fingers on the arm of his chair. The silence lengthened. Then: "In the first place, I think Hal should transfer to this office. I don't know how we're going to play it, but the fewer people who know about this the better."

On our way back from a concert at the Wigmore Hall one Sunday afternoon (the name change had taken place by then), Sam and I had reached Baker Street, where we normally caught an omnibus home. But this time, after waiting twenty minutes for a bus that, as sometimes happened in wartime, was obviously not coming, we decided to walk the whole way, and cut across Hyde Park.

We entered the park at Speakers' Corner. I knew about Speakers' Corner, of course, though I had never made a point of going to hear all the religious and political extremists and nutcases who made it what it was. Sam had her arm in mine and we drifted from speaker to speaker, comparing styles, smiling at the way they handled hecklers, invoked the Almighty, or thundered about the doom that was just around the corner. There were communists, Indian anti-imperialists, Zionists, Irish anti-British nationalists, and, inevitably perhaps, rabid anti-German zealots. When I realized that we had strayed into an anti-German orbit, I tried to hurry Sam out of earshot, but she wouldn't be rushed.

"No, Hal. Hold on. Let's hear what he has to say, and how he says it."

It wasn't pleasant. The gist of his argument, as I remember it, was that although the world had stumbled into war, in reality the Germans had started it, that they had wanted a fight, to prove their newfound industrial and military power and because "they think they are better than we are." It was probably what most people there that day wanted to hear, and I began to think he was being paid by the army recruiting services. But then he changed and broadened his argument, to say that this was a war quite unlike any previous war in history, because of the vast number of civilians involved as conscripts, and that as a result we were creating a generation of children without fathers and that, according to the new psychology—a Germanic psychology, no less—this too was the first time such a thing had happened in history and that as a consequence an entire generation would grow up disturbed, that the emotional effects of the war would last a long time, be far more severe than we yet knew, and that Britain would never be the same again. As a rhetorical flourish, at the end, he lifted aloft a baby, a baby in a shawl to which were attached, incongruously, two medals. The child, he said—he *declaimed*—was his nephew, his brother's son, a son his brother would never meet, because he himself was dead, shot to pieces somewhere in France. The medals were the baby's father's.

The speaker was beginning to rant, and Sam pulled at my arm. "Let's go," she said softly.

We wormed our way through the crowds and reached the open park proper. We headed southwest. Gradually the sound of shouting, and heckling, subsided.

Neither of us spoke for a moment.

Then Sam said, "Some of the children at school who have lost their fathers have begun wearing their medals."

"Do you approve?"

"I don't mind. Why wouldn't I approve?"

"Isn't it a bit like wearing your heart on your sleeve?"

"Oh no! Don't say that, Hal. These are orphans, or half orphans anyway. It's a badge of pride. Surely you see that. A badge of honor."

"Yes, of course, of course. But I was talking to Lottie the other night, when she was working on the posters for Will's room, and we were discussing how the war is changing us. There's never been a war like this one, as that speaker was saying, never one that involved civilians so much . . . it's changing our psychology and, I think, making us more emotional in public. We're not buttoning things up as much as we used to."

"Maybe that's a good thing!" she almost shouted. "Think how much I have to keep buttoned up."

Neither of us spoke for a moment. Had Sam said more than she meant?

"I mean, I can't tell anyone we aren't married."

I said nothing as three young children, chasing a dog, nearly ran into us.

"You can't tell anyone—anyone except Lottie and me—about Wilhelm, that's what you meant. And, assuming we don't lose the war, and if Wilhelm has been killed, you won't be able to unbutton even afterward. Will can never wear *his* medals."

Another pause. "No."

We walked by what had been, before the war, a flower bed. No money for such luxuries now.

I was buttoned up, too, of course, though Sam didn't know how much. It seemed that at every turn, these days, she was torn by her past, stranded by it, and I had it in my power, if not to remove her torment completely, at least to ease the burden. How simple it would be to tell her what I knew.

In the distance I could see the Albert Memorial. We'd be home in half an hour.

Two things came out of my meeting with Brigadier Malahyde, in regard to the *Samuel Hood*. First, as he had insisted, I was transferred to the brigadier's office later the same day, occupying a makeshift desk near Margaret, his formidable secretary. We soon found out that the ship was indeed unloading its cargo of pyrethrum in Agadir, and replacing it with dried olives before going on to Uruguay. Our people in Morocco produced photographs of both the unloading and the loading. But our side in London also uncovered the possibly even more revealing statistic that, despite the submarine attacks that were playing havoc with our merchant fleet, none of the Hood company ships had ever been attacked by German subs, let alone sunk. So the whole thing suddenly looked very suspicious.

The second thing I have to put down to the brigadier himself. He called me in one day, late in the afternoon, and offered me a whisky. He made it clear he was going to have one himself, so I accepted. It was a dismal day outside and the lamps in his office threw warm cones of yellow light, which winked in the golden liquid.

"That was pretty nifty thinking, Hal," he said after trying the whisky. "Just like your idea about Lenin. You've got a good intelligence brain. Well done."

"Thank you, sir."

"But we can't sit on our laurels." He fixed me with a look he had. It was halfway to a smile but it was a shrewd sizing-up glance as well. That look said, "Can you see where I'm headed in this conversation?"

I couldn't second-guess him. "Go on, sir."

"You yourself said that the Hood share price has been doing well."

"Yes sir, that's what attracted me to them in the first place."

"Very well. But think: if the share price is doing well, it means they are making a healthy profit."

I nodded.

"Which means they need a healthy income."

I sipped more whisky. Some things were obvious.

"So it's unlikely Hood would have *given* its pyrethrum to Frankel."

I saw what he was getting at. "Money will have changed hands."

His half smile became a 60 percent smile.

"But not in Morocco," I breathed. "Too risky."

He let a silence elapse, so I could digest what I had just worked out.

"If not Morocco, where?"

"America?"

He shook his head. "Too far away. Risky as well—they are allies, after all. Now."

"Uruguay?" But I shook my head immediately. "That's too far away as well."

"Which leaves . . . ?"

"Switzerland?"

"That's my guess," he said, nodding. He drank more of his whisky, stood up, retrieved the bottle from the cabinet, and gave us both a re-fill.

He sat down again.

"The photographs from Agadir confirm that what you thought might be happening *is* actually happening. However, before we go pub-lic, or put the directors of Hood in jail or the Tower of London, we need to box clever. If we barge in, we stop Hood from doing what they have been doing for God knows how long . . . But if we were to find out how they are paid, we might found out a whole lot more. Germany, we know, is feeling the pinch so far as raw materials are con-cerned. They must have some way of paying for illicit goods on the black market—and my guess is that such an operation, if it exists, must be in Switzerland."

"I agree with your reasoning, sir, but how would we ever close in on the payment mechanism? I, for one, wouldn't know where to start looking."

"Try this." He unbuttoned his jacket, something he hardly ever did. "Neither the Germans nor Hood would want a paper trail—too incriminating. It could be leaked at any time, even after the war. The

Hood people could never sleep soundly in their beds, for fear of the early morning knock from the police or MI5." He paused, sipped his whisky, savored the taste. "No, the transactions have to be made in cash. Someone from Frankel or some special German government 'front' organization must meet someone from Hood, who will be in Switzerland under some pretext or another."

I didn't respond. He had this worked out—he was that kind of man. I waited for the punch line.

"Anyone from Hood who went to Switzerland would need to go officially—because, again, it would be too risky not to. Which means they must have registered with our embassy in Bern. What we need, therefore, is someone from here to go to Bern—under cover, of course—check out the records, and see where it takes us."

It all dropped into place. The late hour of the meeting, the two whiskies, the unbuttoned jacket.

"But sir," I said. "I have a limp; I sometimes need a cane. I'm not properly fit."

He sipped his whisky and gave me a 90 percent smile. "It may surprise you to know that your limp has all but disappeared. But, in any case, take your cane if you want. That, to my way of thinking, is the perfect cover."

Sam didn't like this piece of news one little bit.

"Switzerland? For how long? Is it dangerous?"

"I don't know for how long, Sam. Until I get a result, I suppose. The only risk is in getting there. I have to travel through France—well behind the front lines—then cross Lake Geneva. Switzerland itself will be quite safe."

"Did you even *try* to get out of it, Hal? Will's going to be devastated. Remember how he was when you came home late that night?"

I nodded but tried to make light of it. "He'll probably forget all about me when I've been gone a week."

"Don't say that! He's surrounded by too many women as it is. Oh Hal, this is horrible—horrible, horrible, horrible!"

When we told Will, his first question was "Will come?" This was his way of saying "Can I come?" He had the habit just then of referring to himself by name rather than the personal pronoun.

When I gently told him he couldn't come, he went very quiet and clung to his mother.

Dinner was a dismal affair that evening and, later, as soon as Sam and I retired to bed, Will came into our room and slid under the sheets between us. He was exhausted, however, and as soon as he had fallen asleep, I carried him back to his own bed.

When I returned to our room, Sam had turned out her bedside lamp and had pulled the blankets right up over her shoulder.

"Look, Sam, I'm sorry about this, but . . . come on. It's the war. It plays with all our lives. You want me to refuse to obey orders? I could be prosecuted for treason, jailed. It would certainly be the end of my career, or my chance to be useful in the war. Don't be unreasonable—please. This is our last night together for . . . for however long it is. Don't spoil it."

She just lay there, not moving, not speaking.

"It's not as if I'm going back to the Front, being shot at. I'm not going into any real danger."

Now she did turn and face me. "How do you know? How can you be so certain? You'll be some sort of spy—I'm not stupid. I know you can't tell me why you're going—and I don't want to know, not really. But spies, in wartime, even in neutral Switzerland, kill each other." She sat up, her breasts rising and falling under her nightdress. "We were doing so well . . . now you're doing a Wilhelm on me, only this time it's on *us*, both of us, Will and me. What if you don't come back, Hal . . . I don't think I could bear that . . . to be left, to be abandoned . . . war-widowed twice. I've seen the children at school who've lost their fathers, I've seen what happens to them, how they close up, how they are diminished, smaller, less complete than they used to be, quieter, locked away somewhere, as if something that was inside them has escaped . . . Is that going to happen to Will? Please God, no!"

She gasped these last words and fell toward me. I put my arms around her and kissed her. Her cheeks were wet from tears. I found the slight salt taste arousing. I placed my mouth on her breast, under her thin nightshirt, and she cried out.

She cried out again and again that night.

I arrived in Switzerland four days later. I traveled by train—by several trains, in fact, changing every few hours at such backwaters as Langres, Saint-Amour, and Annecy. The brigadier had seen to it that I had some pretty impressive documentation to take with me, so although the journey was arduous, I was treated well. I had books to read but my thoughts kept straying to Sam. Our last night together had been a new experience for both of us, I think. We had explored each other's bodies with a . . . an almost violent intensity. We were more like animals than people that night. I had been slightly unnerved by the intensity we had shown and so, I think, had Sam. But, sitting in those French trains, with their smell of strong French tobacco, and watching the rolling countryside go by, I kept revisiting some of the things we had done. And I was aroused all over again.

Eventually, after three nights of being shunted from the shadows to the sharp end, and shortly after lunchtime on the fourth day, my train—my sixth train, as I recall—pulled into Evian, a spa town on the southern shore of Lake Geneva. Here I had a three-hour wait before transferring to a steamer. Switzerland's neutrality meant that, despite the war, the regular steamer service still circumnavigated the lake: Geneva, Evian, Montreux, Lausanne, and back to Geneva. It was one of the most popular routes in and out of Switzerland, used by spies of all nationalities.

I wasn't met. My only instructions from Malahyde were to act purposefully on arrival and to disembark quickly, as if I had made the journey many times before. If anyone was on the lookout for a spook behaving furtively they would be disappointed. I was to take a taxi to Lausanne station and board the first train for Zurich. The destination had been changed because although our embassy was in Bern, Zurich was the banking center of Switzerland. We didn't have an embassy in Zurich but there was a consulate, where I would be based. I was told the name of a hotel in Zurich—the Olden—where a room had been reserved. I arrived just after seven in the evening, unpacked, had a bath, then ate a solitary dinner at a brasserie near the lake. It was the lake featured in the travel poster that was on the wall of Will's bedroom, and it naturally made me think of him, and of Sam. Not that I needed any reason to think of them—this would be my fourth night without them, and their fourth night without me.

I could still hear Sam's cries from our last night together.

The next morning I was at the consulate promptly at nine, where I met my contact, a Major Gregory Gaimster. Not only was he my contact, I found I was also to share an office with him. It was cramped, on the second floor, with a small window that looked out onto a narrow street with tramlines down the middle. Directly opposite was a dingy joint, the Bar Venner.

"It's more interesting in the evening," Greg said. "There's a knocking shop over the bar. Some of the girls aren't bad." He was from Nottingham, which, it is always said, has the prettiest girls in England.

That morning I was introduced to one or two other members of the consulate; then Greg went into a small kitchen, made us both some coffee, and closed the door of our office behind him.

"I've had a wire from the brigadier, but there's never much detail in a telegram. Give me your version. No hurry. We've got all day."

I did just that. He sat and listened without interrupting, though occasionally he scribbled notes. He was a tall, emaciated man with sunken cheeks, hollows around his eyes, and a strong jawline. He wore a tweed jacket and a checked shirt with a knitted tie. He looked as if he were just off shooting, or fishing. I liked him.

When I had finished, he sat, drumming his fingers along his lips. After a while, he murmured, "May I ask you a question?"

I nodded. "Shoot."

"How many ships do you think Hood has?"

"I don't have to think. I checked before I left. Three."

"And if a ship goes to Uruguay, say, how long before it comes back?"

I shrugged. "I don't know."

"Guess."

"Say a week to ten days to get there. Four days to turn around. She'd be back in just under a month."

"Which means . . ." said Greg slowly, "that if the Hood people put their minds to it, their three ships could make three deliveries a month."

"But they don't. The husband of my wife's friend, the man who works in the Port of London, says that the *Samuel Hood* comes up the Thames only two or three times a year."

"She could transport pyrethrum from other ports."

"Unlikely. It would be wasteful, for Hood, to have insecticide depots spread out all over the country. And their extraction works *are* in the East End. The Port of London is convenient."

Again, Greg drummed his fingers against his lips. "That fits."

"Fits? What fits? Fits what?"

"We think it works slightly different from the way you have it."

"What are you talking about? What do you know?"

He pushed back his chair and lifted his feet onto his desk. His brown brogues could have been cleaner. "We're not complete turnips out here, you know. We recognize what Switzerland can be used for—that's one of the reasons we're stationed here in the first place. But your information could be the final link in the chain."

I didn't say anything immediately. He would explain in his own good time. "What chain?"

"More coffee?"

"Have we still got all day?"

He looked at his watch. "Long enough. It's your turn in the kitchen."

I made the coffee.

Again he made sure the door was shut.

He tried his coffee, winced, and said, "More beans next time. One of the perks of living in Switzerland is the coffee—can't get this back home, can we? So don't spoil it—and that means don't stint it. Okay?"

I nodded.

"Now, let me fill you in. It works differently in Geneva and in Lausanne, and even in Bern, but in Zurich and Basel we are very aggressive—discreet but aggressive—in our attitude to Brits in Switzerland. Yes, the damn country's neutral, but we want to know why every Brit who's here is here. A lot of legitimate business goes on during a war, of course, which means that some people are here for perfectly proper reasons. But some aren't."

He dolloped sugar into the coffee and that seemed to help, judging by the expression—or lack of it—on his face.

"We've infiltrated the Swiss border guards and their police, and so we get discreet lists of all Brits—and all others, too—arriving either by steamer on the lake or by train at Geneva. The police lists give us passport details and addresses inside Switzerland. We can't check out everyone, but anyone who stays in central Zurich or Basel gets our attention. Again, discreetly, of course. They are followed, their hotel rooms are, shall we say, *inspected* while they are out. Their contacts are followed too.

"A lot of it is a waste of time, of course, but now and then we turn up an interesting pattern. And we have identified one pattern that we don't fully understand but may just—just—fit with yours."

I drank my coffee. I didn't think it was so bad. But then I had been living in London. And it was good to have some sugar.

"One of the people we have highlighted is a certain Bryan Amery. He registered at the consulate in the normal way. He's in his early thirties, was born in Leamington Spa but has spent time in London. According to such digging as we have been able to do—at this distance and while there is a war on—Amery is a precious-metals man. He works for a small firm with headquarters in Hatton Garden and his job is to keep his ear to the ground in Zurich and give his masters back home advice on when to buy and when to sell gold, silver, platinum, and copper. We haven't actually faced him with this, you understand. This is all research on our part, back home."

"But you doubt that gold and silver are his real job?"

"We don't know. He has a small office here, in the Thuringstrasse, but we haven't been able to get in there yet. He has a suite at the Bar au Lac, the best hotel in town, overlooking the lake, and although we've taken a look, the entire suite is almost document-free. No use to us at all." He drained his cup and laid it on the desk in front of him.

"So what makes him suspicious?"

Greg made a face. "He meets a lot of people. Usually in cafés where they speak only in German. We have followed these individuals after the meetings and, although a lot of them are perfectly innocent Swiss, a handful of them—more than a handful, in fact—are Germans who are representatives of companies that are like Hood-Frankel. That is to say, Anglo-German firms that, before the war, were one and the same company or very close business partners."

Greg stood up and arched his back. "My spine seizes up if I don't do something like this," he muttered.

"It had crossed my mind," he continued, "that something very like what you say is happening with Hood is happening with these other companies. Why should this sort of deal be confined to just one outfit? If Hood has only three ships and makes, as you suggest, only around nine deliveries a year to the Germans, it would be expensive to keep Amery at the Bar au Lac full-time."

He stretched his back again.

"But, and this could be a big 'but,' maybe that's only part of the picture. Germany, we know, is short of raw materials. Say a handful of treacherous British firms are willing to profiteer from this state of affairs. That could mean that Amery uses his front to collect money on behalf of—what, half a dozen? a dozen? a score? of companies, taking a hefty commission along the way."

I was shocked by what Gaimster said. It simply hadn't occurred to me, as it should have done, that other firms than Hood could be acting in this way. "So why haven't you picked him up?"

"Three reasons, all of them good ones. First, we can never get close enough to overhear the conversations, so we can't be sure what the meetings are in truth about. Second, we have never observed any money being handed over. Occasionally they shake hands but never anything more. No one swaps bags or anything obvious like that. And third, we don't have any authority to pick him up. If we denounced him to the Swiss police, they would ask for evidence—evidence we don't have."

He sat back in his chair and laid both hands, palms down, on the desk in front of him. "If we ever *do* prove that Amery is trading with the enemy, or collecting the cash on others' behalf, if we can be certain of our ground, there's only one thing we can do. Very quietly, and very discreetly, and totally tidily, we have to kill him."

He let this sink in. "So, you can see, we need to be sure. Your evidence may help. If, in the next few days, he meets someone from Frankel, it will be very powerful evidence that what we suspect to be happening actually *is* happening."

He glanced again at his watch. "Come on. Amery usually has a prelunch cocktail at the Café Odeon. We'll stroll down there and you can take a look. Size up our man."

The Café Odeon, the famous home of Dada. I couldn't believe it. My very first full day in Switzerland and I was on my way there.

As we went, I asked a question that had been bothering me. "Greg, why don't the Germans just pay Amery direct into his bank account? Bank to bank."

"Too dangerous. One, there would be a paper trail, and two, the Swiss would hate it. They would see it as an abuse of their neutrality and they would close the whole thing down."

There was something else, too. "What does Amery look like? His name rings a bell."

Greg shot me a sideways look. "Really? He's small, shiny black hair, mustache, sideburns too long. Always wears a turtleneck pullover."

I shook my head. That description didn't ring any bells at all.

"If there's even a slight chance you know him, Montgomery, we don't want him seeing you. We'll sit right at the back of the café."

What a difference it was to be in Switzerland, after Britain and France. There was nothing drab about Zurich; it was throbbing with life. Looking around, you could see flowers, people sitting at cafés, eating ice cream and fruit; there were no soldiers framing every view;

the faces of passersby did not look weary. I had forgotten what peace was like.

The Café Odeon, when we came to it, was large, busy, with a polished wooden façade and bright red-and-yellow umbrellas outside. The waiters were dressed head to toe in black, with long black aprons that stopped just above their shoes.

We found a small table inside, right next to a pillar, behind which I could hide if I needed to. On the table, besides salt and pepper and an ashtray, was a small jug with fresh milk. Greg ordered beers and went to fetch two newspapers that were hanging on a contraption by the entrance, each with a wooden pole down its spine.

"How's your German?" said Greg, in German.

"Ich bin zweisprachig," I said in reply. "I'm bilingual."

"I think we should talk in German from now on," he said, sticking in the same language. "It will attract less attention."

"Sehr gut," I said softly. "Very well."

I leafed through the paper. The king had just returned to London after a ten-day visit to the front lines in France. Back home they were experimenting with air-raid sirens—until then the warnings had been sounded by whistle and the all-clear by bugle. The Americans had mobilized their National Guard.

But my eye kept straying to the lake. I have always loved lakes. For me they are more interesting than the sea—at least the open sea. I have never been able to understand the attraction of sailing. Being on a small boat, out at sea, with only the horizon for company is my idea of what the newfangled psychologists call sensory deprivation: nothing to feast the eyes on. With lakes, however, there is always something to watch: the far hills, yachts, the glitter of the waves—

"Here he is. On schedule. Amery's here."

I looked across in the same direction Greg was looking. A small man was pulling back a chair near a table at the edge of the pavement.

He was being helped by a waiter who clearly knew him and stood close. As a result, my view was partially obscured. The man sat down and looked up at the waiter as they conversed. At first all I could see was his neck and shoulders and I registered only that he had a large Adam's apple, which jiggled when he spoke. He was obviously giving his order because as soon as they had finished the waiter moved away. At last I got a full view—and immediately ducked behind the pillar.

With admirable self-control, Greg didn't flinch. "You know him, then?" he whispered. "You recognize him?"

"Yes," I whispered back. "I recognize him all right. But he's not Bryan Amery. His real name is George Romford."

"If he's here under an assumed name, then he's obviously up to no good."

Greg and I were eating lunch at a brasserie a few blocks from the Odeon—and we were tucked away at the back of the restaurant, where hardly anyone could see us, and completely hidden from view from the road outside. We had eased out of the Odeon by the emergency exit and left Amery/Romford to himself, for the moment.

After we had ordered—sausages, *frites*, a salad with fresh tomatoes, a Swiss red wine that Greg liked but I thought filthy—I had filled him in about Romford and me, Romford and Stratford, Romford and Pritchard.

"A lot of water under the bridge since then," replied Greg, gulping his wine. "For both of you."

I nodded. "And it explains why the name Bryan Amery was familiar. He was a fellow student at Stratford."

Greg made a face. "My money says this Amery person died and Romford 'borrowed' his identity. Easily done in wartime."

The food was brought. Too quickly, I thought. The sausages had not been cooked fresh. Greg didn't seem to mind; he had already started.

"I agree that an assumed name is suspicious, Greg. But is it enough to . . . you know . . . kill him?" What was I saying? What sort of talk was this? "Don't we need to understand the system a little more, if we are going to stop it properly?"

His mouth was full but he moved his head from side to side. "Maybe. Maybe not. I'll have to check with the brigadier. But, for now, what can you tell me about Romford? Can we get closer? What sort of character is he, what are his strengths, what are his weaknesses? You know him—or used to. You can be a big help here."

The sausages were not good. Maybe, just maybe, I could finish the salad and *frites.* And maybe a glass of red, if I could get it down.

"There are two and a half things I can remember about Romford that you might be able to use."

"Good. Go on. More red?"

I shook my head. "One, women. Romford is a bit of a slimeball who has never had much experience or success with women. If we are going to approach him, lure him, whoever does so should be a woman. Two, he's got a chip. He's from the East End and hates all toffs—or he says he does. I think he is secretly attracted by them, so that if you have a woman in the outfit who is an aristocrat—and looks and sounds like it—you, we, should choose her."

"And what's the other thing, the half a thing?"

"He was always self-conscious about his German. He learned it at school, has never been to Germany, so this trip in Switzerland is his first German-speaking country. If his German is better than that of whoever approaches him, he will feel more secure, show off more, and relax more, maybe give things away."

Greg stopped chewing. "I can see why the brigadier chose you. That's sharp thinking." He chewed on, then stopped again. "But I'm smart too, and I can use what you say."

He swallowed his red and immediately refilled his glass.

"Rebecca . . . Rebecca Berwick, that's who we need." He fixed me with a look. "How old would you say Romford is?"

"Early thirties."

"I'd say Rebecca is twenty-eight. Just right." He smiled. "She's lovely but she's terrifying in a way. Father's a viscount, owns huge chunks of the borders and half of Battersea. She has a degree—in math of all things, so she's one of our code breakers—and . . . well, she looks a million dollars, a billion. Not married—God knows why not. Her German's okay but she's a long way from bilingual—she sounds ideal for our little plan."

"Which is?"

"Operation Pillow Talk. The Honorable Rebecca Berwick meets Georgie Porgie, seduces him, for king and country, and learns all his secrets: who he meets, why he meets them, where the money is. Poor guy won't know what's hit him."

"Let's hope it's as simple as that."

"Hal, if you're right about Romford, I am certainly right about Rebecca. This two and two are going to make a very juicy four."

"When can I meet her? I can't wait."

"You'll have to. She's in Bern today, at our embassy. Back tomorrow."

That night, as I lay in bed in my nondescript hotel, I wondered what route Romford had followed from Stratford to Zurich. I had often wondered if our paths would cross again—and Romford himself had said he hoped as much during our last . . . encounter at the Ag. But I had assumed it would be in civilian life, after the war was over. Never did I imagine we would meet in such circumstances. And what had made him turn—assuming Greg was right and Romford was indeed working for the Germans? Was it all down to his chippiness? Was he getting his revenge on a system that, as he saw it, had held him back? Or was that too glib, too simpleminded? Would I ever find out?

Was this Rebecca up to the job? Greg was certainly sold on her, but the last aristocratic woman I had encountered in this war—Genevieve—had been anything but a heroine.

Dear Sam,

This is going to be a very weird letter. As you know, I can't tell you where I am or why I'm here, and I don't even know when or if you will receive this. All I can say, then, is that I am well, I arrived on schedule, and the people I am working with seem professional and agreeable. You are not to worry about me.

I miss you. The censor will read this letter before you do, so you will forgive me for not going into too many private details. Enough to say that our last night together was almost worth committing treason for—you will know what I mean—and I can only hope you feel the same way. It certainly felt mutual. And you can be certain that I will be home just as soon as I am allowed.

One good piece of news. I think that where I am is the home of one of Will's favorite toys. All being well, I can bring him something that will help him forgive me for going away. Give him a big kiss from me. And to Lottie.

Sorry this is so short but since there's such a lot I can't say, and since I haven't been here for more than a day or two, I hope you won't judge me too harshly.

Much love,

Hal

I'll say this for Greg: he knew his women. Rebecca was stunning. Besides going in and out—and then some—in all the right places, she had the most vivid blue eyes, hair the color of straw, skin that shone with health, and a soft, sibilant voice that seemed to enfold you in a secret cocoon, as if you and she were the only people in the world. On top of it the look in her eyes was intelligent, and her aristocratic demeanor—I can't quite describe what it was exactly but it was an amalgam of self-confidence and world-weariness, as if there was nothing anyone could teach *her*—was intoxicating, that's the only word for it. From the moment I met her, I had no doubt she could seduce George Romford.

Her first words, after Greg had outlined the full background to our plan, behind the closed door of his office, were: "So I have to sleep with him?"

"Not necessarily," said Greg, backtracking.

There was a short pause.

"Yes," I said. I surprised myself in saying this.

Rebecca turned her gaze on me. The tiniest of smiles appeared along her lips. Then she looked back at Greg, pointing to me. "I like him," she said in that soft voice she had. "He has more balls than you do, Greg." She looked back at me. "I'll do it. Just don't give me a medal if it works—there's only one thing worse than trading with the enemy, and that's sleeping with him. When do we start?"

"Now, today, tomorrow," cried Greg. "There's no time to be lost. As soon as we can work out a way for you to meet him."

"That's easy," I said in German.

"What did you say?" said Rebecca, turning my way again.

I nodded. "You wait for him to be seated at his table in the Café Odeon, then you sit at the next one. You look through the menu. Then, in your faltering German, you ask him if he can help you understand the wording. It will appeal to his vanity that he speaks better

German than you do. After that, it's up to you. Knowing Romford, it won't be difficult."

She looked me up and down. "Are you always good with women, Hal?"

"No. I just know Romford."

"Well, how do I follow through? Who am I? Why am I in Zurich in the middle of a war?"

"Yes," said Greg. "I was thinking about that. What do you think, Hal?"

"Invent as little as possible." I thought for a moment. Then I turned to Rebecca. "Do your family know where you are and what you are doing?"

"They know I'm in the diplomatic service and serving here in Switzerland. At least my father and mother do. They have been asked not to talk about it."

I nodded. "Get word to them. Tell them to say, if asked, that their daughter is a closed book, someone they refuse to discuss, full stop." I looked at Greg. "Can we do that overnight? Send them a wire?" I turned back to Rebecca. "Where do your parents live?"

"Kelso. But they have a flat in London."

"I'll send a wire in code to my people," said Greg. "I'll have someone go and brief them in person. Impress on them how important this is."

"Good," I said. "Now, Rebecca, what you tell Romford is this. You are a pacifist and conscientious objector. You are against this war and all it stands for, and you are sitting it out in Zurich, like a lot of other artists and writers. Let's make you a writer. If you were a painter, Romford might ask to see your paintings and your studio, which you don't have, and if you were an actress, he would surely want to come and see you act. As a writer, all you need is some notebooks and/or a typewriter."

"And how do I explain my poor German, when I've been here since the war started, two and a half years ago?"

"Simple: you had a Swiss boyfriend who spoke perfect English. He brought you here in the first place. That was convenient for you, but meant that you never had to improve your German. Now you are on your own—let that slip, but don't make it too obvious. Romford will think all his birthdays and Christmases have come at once." I smiled.

"Have you done this sort of thing often?" Rebecca said.

Greg answered for me. "No, he was shot at the Front in the early months of the war and has been in intelligence more or less ever since. The brigadier spotted him, but this is his first trip into the field. Do you think his ideas work? Are you comfortable with being a writer?"

"My brother's a writer. I'll adopt some of his mannerisms. And I've met one or two other writers through him. I think I can carry it off."

"Well, don't overdo it," said Greg. "Let Romford make the running. Don't come across too easily, but don't let him get away, either."

Our meeting broke up just then. Greg went off to send the coded wire, and Rebecca went back to her own office, which she shared with two others. Later that day, however, there were two further developments that made us all feel better. Greg received a coded acknowledgment of his wire to London, which said that Rebecca's parents were being informed that very evening. He also received a visit from one of his footmen, the people who followed the men Romford met at the Café Odeon. That very day, while Greg and Rebecca and I had been in conference, Romford had met someone for lunch at the café. After the lunch, the other man had been followed, back to the Hotel Grüben. Discreet inquiries at the hotel had revealed that this man, a Christoph Heyne, was a director of Frankel. The load of pyrethrum, which had obviously now reached Germany via Morocco, was in the process of being paid for.

That evening, Greg, Rebecca, and I had dinner together, at a restaurant a good way from the Odeon, the Grüben, and the Bar au Lac. We went over our plan of attack, scheduled for the next day, but we also discussed something else that bothered me.

"Greg, Romford is undercover, as Bryan Amery. Why aren't the Germans he does business with? Undercover, I mean. Come to that, if this operation is so important to the Germans, why isn't the whole thing organized by the government, centrally?"

"Ah, I wondered if that was bothering you," said Greg. "I can't give you a definitive answer, but I *think* I know."

We were waiting for our main courses and for a refill of the wine bottle—Greg certainly liked his booze—and we all sat back as the waiter brought the food.

"Don't forget the wine," Greg said, touching the waiter's arm.

Rebecca shot me a glance.

"Now," breathed Greg, reverting to the main topic of discussion, "always remember that the war is going against Germany, and that she shares a lengthy border with Switzerland. Britain, of course, is miles away. Which means British businessmen in Switzerland—because there are so few—draw attention to themselves. Why would they be here? It follows that the British side of this operation would want as few people here as possible, and that those who *are* here are under-cover. We can't be sure that Amery/Romford is the only one, after all. With Germany, it's different. This part of Switzerland is German-speaking; it has long and intimate links—commercial, banking-wise, cultural, educational—with Germany.

"We don't *know* that this whole operation *isn't* organized centrally, just that on the surface it doesn't look that way. And I can see why.

If it was organized centrally and was blown at any point, the whole shooting match would have to be closed down. It is, after all, an abuse of Swiss neutrality in a major way. If all the operatives were here secretly and their cover was blown, it would be very embarrassing and ruin Germany's access to raw materials at a stroke. But, run the way that it is, we have several—one might even say many—German businessmen coming here, under their own steam, so to speak, using their real names, ostensibly conducting transactions on an individual basis. Should any one of them be found to be contravening Swiss neutrality, he can be bundled out of the country but the operation overall isn't exposed and closed down. The system goes on."

The second bottle of wine arrived and, as Greg tried it, Rebecca and I sat in silence, digesting his argument. There was nothing to add; what he'd said made sense.

"So," said Rebecca, after Greg had refilled our glasses, "first I get to know Romford, then I get myself invited back to his room. Then what? What am I looking for? Stacks of cash? Little Alps made of Swiss francs?"

"Yes," I replied. "But what we need in order to move in is to observe the *method* of payment, *how* he is paid, not just how much." I let a short silence extend between us. "You may not find out everything on a first visit."

She nodded slowly. "I had worked that out for myself."

Another silence. Then I asked, "Have you ever had sex with a man you didn't love, or like?"

She stared at me. "Do you mind very much if I don't answer that? This situation is unique, after all—no?"

"Well, it's unusual, I grant you that," interjected Greg. "But I wouldn't like to bet on it never happening somewhere else in this goddamn war."

The silence around the table this time was profound, and gloomy.

"All I ask," said Rebecca at length, in a voice that was barely above a whisper, "is that you don't broadcast our little scenario to all and sundry. Can't we just keep it between us?" She looked intently at each of us men in turn.

Greg nodded.

I did too.

The next morning, early, Rebecca took me shopping. I'd told her I had a wife and son at home—I hadn't gone into details—and that I needed to bring them both something special. She showed me the main shopping streets, and a back alley or two where there were some specialty shops, mainly selling Swiss chocolate. Just then, chocolate was an unheard-of luxury in Britain. Our tour of the back alleys of Zurich reminded me of that Saturday morning, long ago, in Stratford, when I had first fallen for Sam. But, stunning as Rebecca was, I didn't fall for her. Walking the streets of Zurich, it became a habit of mine to look out for women wearing Alice bands.

As lunchtime approached, we decided that, since Romford knew me by sight, it was safer if I remained at the consulate, rather than keep hiding behind the pillar I had sat near on that first day. If I formed part of the team that kept Romford under visual surveillance, sooner or later he would spot me—and our plan would be in the soup. It wasn't worth the risk.

Rebecca made the approach, as I had suggested, and Romford bit like a fish that hadn't eaten for a month; according to Greg's account later, he all but raped her right there in the Café Odeon. In view of his evident keenness, Rebecca—in my view quite rightly—played it cool and rebuffed his advances. She even had her own plan as to how to proceed. She thought it would be less suspicious if she didn't turn up at the café on the following day, and did so only on the day after that with a friend of hers. This was another woman, a bit older than Rebecca and much slimmer, and darker, but still attractive in her own way. She was called Liesl, and was half Austrian and half Swiss. When Romford came across to their table in the Café Odeon, Rebecca was friendly in a polite sort of way but nothing more.

It was only on the third meeting between Rebecca and Romford, which happened two days later still, that she agreed to join him at his table and let him buy her a drink. The drink turned into lunch, and lunch turned into a dinner invitation two nights later. The fish had been well and truly hooked.

While we were waiting for the all-important dinner, Rebecca showed me more shops of Zurich, including one that I had been keeping an eye open for. There, I bought Will a very simple train set. It had a light at the front that lit up. I bought Sam a handbag and some perfume. Perfume was hard to get in London. And I bought two bags of sugar.

For dinner Romford entertained Rebecca at the main restaurant in the Bar au Lac, rightly calculating that she had never been there before. Added to that, it was just a short journey from the restaurant to his room upstairs. Romford behaved entirely in character throughout and shortly before midnight the couple walked into the lift. Greg watched from across the lobby. He came directly from the hotel to join me where I was waiting, in the Bar Venner in the narrow street that our office overlooked.

We sat in front of two whiskies like beavers at a dam.

"I hope Romford is content with straightforward sex," said Greg softly.

"Oh, it will be straightforward," I replied. "And probably over very quickly, in the first instance, at least. Romford doesn't have much experience."

We drank our whiskies.

"If Romford is doing what we think he's doing, and we manage to prove it to our satisfaction, what then?"

He leaned toward me, so that I could smell the alcohol on his breath. "As I said before, my dear Hal, you, Rebecca, or me is going to have to shoot him. Dead."

Dear Hal,

Your letter _did_ arrive, this morning. It was short, yes, as you say, but I was amazed to receive it at all, and of course delighted. Will has been looking up ▮▮▮▮▮ *on a map. He was very quiet for the first few days after you left. Of course, he doesn't yet have an adult conception of time, and so he doesn't really know what weeks and months are. You are just out of his life and he's perplexed as to why you have gone and no longer want to be with him, with us. It's entirely natural but it doesn't make it easy.*

Lottie is missing you too. She likes a man about the house, she says, and, worse, she's having to clean her own shoes! (I mustn't get like Izzy with the exclamation marks.)

And of course I'm missing you. ▮▮▮▮▮▮▮▮▮▮ *in which case we would never have known. Our last night together, which you mentioned . . . it's no one else's business, so I won't go into it. But it was unsettling and wonderful all at the same time. I had no idea . . . I'm going to censor the rest myself.*

We had another zeppelin near miss the other day, and school was closed for two days. You know, when the _idea_ of zeppelin raids was first announced, I was frightened, and so were a lot of people. The very thought of explosives from the sky was too horrible to contemplate. Yet,

*now that they have arrived, though they are hardly pleasant, we have all
adjusted. Remember our day at Speakers' Corner, and that man who
said we are living in a new kind of war? Well, perhaps we are, but
I don't think the zeppelin raids on London are anywhere <u>near</u> as
frightening as being in the trenches is frightening. We civilians just don't
have the bombardment, day in, day out, that people undergo at the Front.
I don't think people are being made mad by zeppelins, the way some people
are made mad at the Front. The psychology is different. (With you away,
I've been reading a lot in bed in the evenings. I like reading about
psychology and the unconscious—it explains a lot, I think.)*

*I have to finish now. The man who delivered your letter said he'd
come back for mine about now and I don't want to keep him waiting.
It's a bit like having our own private postal service. Be careful, Hal,
and* ▬▬▬▬▬▬▬▬▬▬▬▬▬▬▬▬▬▬▬▬

*All my love,
Sam (and from Lottie, Will, and Whisky, who is also confused about
where you've gone)*

It was half past eleven the next morning before Rebecca showed
up at the consulate.

"I had to shower," she said. "I had to get his smell off me."

"How bad was it?" I asked as gently as I could.

"Someday," she said, "someday, if you get me very drunk, I'll tell
you. But not now, not now or for a very long time. It was bad—don't
make me relive it."

"You have to relive some of it, Becky." Greg was insistent. "We
need to know what happened. Coffee?"

"Don't call me Becky—don't *ever* call me Becky. I hate it." She
shook her head, as if to free something caught up in her hair. "I'd love
some coffee."

Greg went off to make it. I didn't speak for a moment. When I did, it was to say, "War gives us the most terrible experiences, which become the most terrible memories. Is that what worries you—that you will never be able to expunge this memory, that it will spoil you for every other man who will be in your life?"

She looked at me.

"Is that another question you don't want to answer?"

A slight nod, so I let it go.

Greg came back in with the coffee. "Here we are. I've added a little whisky from my own private stash. Medicinal purposes." He smiled.

Rebecca sipped the coffee, then gulped it. "That's better," she murmured.

She leaned against a metal filing cabinet.

"Now, Hal here was right. Romford was fascinated by my background—by my family, I mean. How far back we go, which ancestors did what—generals, politicians, diplomats, bishops, Oxford dons. He couldn't get enough. I did most of the talking at dinner—we talked in English and in German. I made a few elementary mistakes from time to time, and he was quick to correct me, anxious to show off how good his German is. He asked me about my writing of course, my political views, how I got on with my father. I asked him about himself but he kept brushing that aside until I insisted—which I thought was only natural of me. To be interested in him, I mean. He gave himself away quite early in the meal—"

"What?" cried Greg.

"Not in the sense you mean, silly. I mean he rushed our dinner. He ate quickly, drank quickly, asked his questions in a rush—at times it was more like an interview than a conversation."

"So?" Greg looked mystified.

Rebecca looked at me. "Tell him, Hal."

"He wanted dinner to be over, so he could ask you back to his room."

"Exactly," whispered Rebecca. "Exactly."

"And . . . ? Go on . . . What happened . . . ?"

But Rebecca wouldn't be rushed. She drank more coffee.

"He had champagne in his room. We had a glass. Then he pounced on me. You don't need to know what happened, or how I handled him. Just that I did handle him. He was obviously not very experienced with women, but that meant I could lead him, teach him, reassure him when he needed to be reassured—as most lovers do." A sardonic smile crossed her lips. "All you need to know is that I satisfied him . . . in fact, I bloody well exhausted him."

She finished her coffee. "That was my plan. After we had finished having sex, at whatever time it was, he fell asleep—though 'passed out' would be a better description after what we did and the drink he'd had. That meant it was safe for me to look around his room."

"Brilliant," whispered Greg.

"Don't interrupt. I want to get this over with." She looked into her coffee cup but it was empty. "He has a suite—a bedroom, a bathroom, a sitting room, and a small hallway with a closet off it. I searched all the rooms, the chest of drawers, the drawers in the table in the sitting room, the closet, the bathroom, the wardrobe in the bedroom, the desk, his bags, under the sofas, behind the curtains, even behind the pictures on the walls."

"And—?"

"Nothing. Nothing at all. No money, no papers, no jewelry. A couple of train tickets, some restaurant receipts, a few cigars. But that's it."

"Shit!" hissed Greg.

A long silence elapsed in the room.

"While you were there, did anyone else come in?"

Rebecca looked at me. "Yes, room service. He ordered breakfast for both of us. As soon as he woke up he wanted to do it, so we did it. That made him ravenous, so he ordered breakfast. You press an electric button by the bed, the waiter comes to the room, you say what you want, and they bring it on a trolley. He wanted to do it again after that but I said I had to get on."

Another long silence, which Greg eventually broke with "Now what? Where do we go from here?"

He looked at me and so did Rebecca.

"I hate what I'm going to say, but I can think of only one way forward. First, however, let me make some more coffee."

I went to the kitchen and prepared three cups. Then I took them back to our office and closed the door. "We are pretty sure that Romford is the man these Germans pay. We know it must be cash, so the money must be brought to him. In that room. The fact that Rebecca could find nothing means that the paperwork is kept to a minimum— and somewhere else. More important, it means that the money doesn't stay with Romford very long *and not overnight.*"

"And so . . . ?" Greg spoke, but both of them were looking at me.

"We have to convert Romford's insatiable appetite for sex with Rebecca into an asset."

"What do you mean?" said Greg.

"How do we do that?" cried Rebecca at the same time.

"This is the bit I hate saying most. Rebecca, you must have dinner with Romford again, go back to the hotel room with him again—"

"*No!*"

"—go back with him again and this time . . . this time . . . you must tell him that he is one of the greatest lovers you have ever had—"

"You're joking—"

"—and the next morning you must say that you want to stay in bed and have him make love to you all day long. Say you are more experienced than he is—he will know that is true, somewhere inside him—but that he has this incredible effect on you. Put it down to the war, if you like, or your social differences, but say you've never known a man like him."

"And the purpose of all this is what, precisely?" Rebecca was not pleased. I hadn't imagined for a moment that she would be.

"You need to stay in his room for one whole day. See who comes, watch his routine, hope that it throws some light on what we want light thrown on."

"No. I've done enough. Fuck him yourself."

This sudden profanity surprised me but it wasn't out of place.

I smiled. "If he were queer, I would have a go. But he's not. He's fallen for you, Rebecca. You are our best hope. We can't change course now. You must see that. I know it's hard but—"

"You have no idea how hard it is—either of you." Suddenly she was close to tears.

I stepped forward but she held out her arm to stop me. "No, no . . . please. I'll do as you say. But don't ever say you understand. You don't understand, even one little bit."

Dear Sam,

How lovely to receive your letter, albeit censored in parts. (I'll keep it and bring it home, so you can tell me what the censored bits originally said.) I'm sorry that even Whisky is missing me—I can't tell you how much I am missing all of you (yes, even Lottie, you can tell her).

What I can say is that the reason I am here is approaching its climax so, all being well, I shouldn't have to be away for very much longer and can come home. I've done a bit of shopping, so I'll have one or two surprises for everybody except Whisky.

The memory of our last night isn't quite so vivid as it was, but still quite vivid enough and I hope that, on my return, we can re-create the mood of that time. I've seen quite a bit of the world, where I am now, and my days here have also given me a few ideas of my own, as regards what I would like to do after the war.

But first, I have to finish what I came here to do. This next bit might be censored but I can tell you that one of the people I have encountered was someone I last saw in that place where you and I had our first lunch together. How small a world we live in.

Masses of love to everyone.

Hal

Rebecca met Romford the next day, at lunchtime, and agreed to have dinner. This time they went to a club, the Astoria, and stayed late. Rebecca was clearly hoping that Romford would be too tired to make love that night. I never found out whether that was the case, but if so it made it slightly more plausible that she wanted to stay in bed all the following day. She must have said something like she was too tired the night before, but he was a wonderful lover, she wanted to make it up to him . . .

The way Rebecca told it, later, Romford didn't need to be asked twice. His sexual awakening might have arrived late but he clearly intended to make up for lost time. They went their separate ways around six that evening and she came directly to us, propping up the bar at the Venner, behind the office.

She looked ravaged. She swallowed a whisky at one go but it didn't seem to help.

"Would you like to take a bath?" I asked gently.

She shook her head, her body shuddering at the same time.

"No. No amount of soap and water could ever erase today."

Neither Greg nor I spoke.

At length, when she had gathered her strength, she murmured, "It has to be related to room service."

We looked at her.

"Can I have another Scotch?"

Greg signaled to the barman.

"Go on."

"We had three visits from room service during the day. Besides the maid who came to make up the room, and whom he sent away, Room service came twice, for breakfast and lunch, but only after Romford had pressed the button by the bed. They came to the door, knocked, came in, took our order, went away, and came back with the food."

"Nothing unusual there."

"No, but the other time there was just a knock on the door. Romford went to answer it. He hadn't summoned room service this time—I'm certain of it. He hadn't pushed the button—because I was with him, in bed all the time. The man just arrived. I could see the trolley being pushed into the hall by a small, bald man with rimless spectacles; then Romford closed the door between the bedroom and the rest of the suite. The door remained closed for about—oh, fifteen minutes and I heard the two men talking, though I couldn't make out what was being said. Then I heard the trolley leave—it rattled slightly. Romford came back into the bedroom and had with him a bottle of wine, which he said room service had brought, courtesy of the hotel management. Why would they need a trolley to bring a bottle of wine?"

"What time would this be?"

"Half past two."

Greg looked at me. "They bring the money in a tureen, Romford counts it, then off it goes to the bank."

"Maybe," I said. "That means at least one other person is involved. Where are the kitchens in the Bar au Lac?"

"In the basement, I expect," said Greg. "But I'll have it checked."

I put my hand on Rebecca's. "You did well, but it's over now."

"No, it's not," growled Greg.

Rebecca and I looked at him. "If you stop now he might suspect something. One more time, I'm afraid."

Rebecca looked shattered and turned to me.

"Don't worry," I said, smiling in what I hoped was a comforting way. "Just have dinner. Over the cheese contrive to take offense, have a fight—and walk out. Easy."

Rebecca brightened. "You bet!"

Because it was next to impossible to follow the people from room service every time they left the kitchen and went up to the rooms, *and* do it without being noticed, we stationed a man outside the kitchens, which was easy enough to do because there were a lot of people milling around there, visiting storerooms, the barbershop, the lavatories, or the boiler room, and we put someone else on Romford's floor. At first this proved puzzling because, when we checked the times later, we found that the arrival of room service at Romford's suite did not always coincide with the times that the trolleys had left the kitchen.

It took two days for the penny to drop.

Every so often, a "room service" trolley arrived at Romford's room that did *not* come from the kitchen.

The following day, therefore, we had a man on every floor. This too was easier than it sounds because they were dressed as hotel staff—carrying towels, fresh sheets, flowers, that sort of thing—and because the Bar au Lac is huge: its corridors extend for hundreds of yards, the staff almost as numerous, and as anonymous, as the guests.

What our systematic surveillance eventually showed was that, once or twice a day, "room service," always appearing from room 306, on the third floor, transferred first to another room—a different one each day and on different floors—and then made a second journey, always to room 411, Romford's suite. The trolley remained in 411 for about fifteen minutes (our observations agreed on this point with Rebecca's) and then always returned to room 306. *This trolley was never taken anywhere near the kitchens.* Sometime later, the occupant of room 306 reappeared, now dressed in a sober suit and carrying an attaché case. He was followed and invariably went to the Haller & Kuhn Bank on Westheimstrasse.

It didn't take Greg long to establish that the occupant of room 306 was a certain Rolf von Maltzen, that he was Swiss-German, and that he was a representative for Scholz-King, an Anglo-Swiss steel company.

The system revealed itself. After the inital meeting with Romford, in the Café Odeon, his contacts moved into the Bar au Lac, for one night only. They never met Romford again. The cash was collected from them, in their room at the Bar au Lac, by von Maltzen. He took it to Romford, to be verified and counted, and then trolleyed it back, hidden in the great silver tureen, to his room. There he changed into his banker's outfit and carried the money to Haller & Kuhn.

"Why," said Rebecca at one point, "does Romford need von Maltzen?"

"Because no money is actually leaving the country," I replied. "That would attract attention and create a paper trail. Smuggling so much cash regularly across borders, in wartime, is much too risky. Scholz-King is a big, multinational company. They receive payment here in Zurich. Romford confirms to the U.K. that the money has been paid, and von Maltzen confirms to his bosses. Then the Swiss in London pay Hood and others like them. There'll be a paper invoice created, for transporting their steel, and so on. A hollow transaction."

"How do you know all this?" said Rebecca.

"I don't. I'm working it out as I go along." I turned to Greg. "What do you think?"

"As you do. It must operate something like that. And I'm now go-ing to wire the brigadier. You and I need to work out exactly how we get a look at the money—to be doubly, triply certain we have our man. But, once we do, I want his authorization to act immediately."

"Are you really going to have to kill him?" I asked.

"Hal! Think what he's doing! He's helping fund the German war effort. Not indirectly, but very, very directly. He *deserves* to die."

I looked at Rebecca.

She took a deep breath. "Can't come soon enough for me."

That evening I had promised myself I would write to Sam one more time but, with the denouement of our plan so close and its resolution so . . . so terrible, I was on edge and unable to concentrate. Greg had gone off to draft and encode his wire for the brigadier, so I asked Re-becca out for dinner.

She shook her head. "I'm having supper with Liesl." But then, see-ing how cast down I was, she said, "Why don't you come too? Though I warn you: it's a Dada club and quite shocking. Be prepared to be shocked." She added with a smile, "I'm smiling but I'm not joking."

I told her about my prewar days in Munich.

"Not bad as a warm-up sort of place, Munich. But this is the real thing. Dress casually—corduroys if you have them, no tie, be ready for a late night. We'll meet in the Venner at nine. Bring money."

I did as I was told. I had one pair of corduroy trousers with me, as it happened, but that was as bohemian as I got. For the rest, my en-semble was a blue shirt and a blazer.

Rebecca and Liesl were already at the bar when I arrived. They were both wearing trousers, both smoking, and both had on lots of makeup. I didn't know Liesl but these were all innovations so far as Rebecca was concerned.

We had two drinks at the Venner, then caught a taxi to the club. It was in the Zäune part of town and called the Club Pantagruel. Inside, it was crowded, the air thick with the reek of tobacco, and a saxophone was playing slow, sad, reedy music. Despite the crowd, Rebecca and Liesl seemed to be known to the management, and a table was found. It was very dark but as my eyes became adjusted to the gloom I began to make out some very unusual ways of dressing.

The next thing I noticed, after registering that the quality of musicianship in the band was extremely high (a virtuoso pianist was now ripping through a much faster tune), were the pictures on the walls. They were very modern—collages of sorts—and appeared to be made of wood and paper. They were very assured and I immediately liked them.

"They're by a painter called Kurt Schwitters," murmured Rebecca. "He's a friend of Liesl's."

A waitress appeared. Or was it a waiter? He/she was very slim, very good-looking, wore lots of makeup, and spoke German with what I could swear was a Munich accent.

"Red or white, whisky or gin?"

"Champagne—and a bottle of Scotch," replied Rebecca with a laugh. "We are going to get very steamed."

He/she disappeared.

I looked around again. This was definitely what you would call a bohemian club. There were some very beautiful women and some very beautiful men. Almost all were dressed casually, exotically even—low-cut dresses, high-cut skirts, very high-heeled shoes, long cigarette holders, feather boas, makeup by the mile. Dark glasses. Military jackets together with tight leggings. They were arguing, canoodling, kissing, dancing, stroking. One or two, I saw, were sprinkling powder on the backs of their hands and sniffing it.

I have to say I was glad I had come. I wasn't part of this scene—no way, not yet, and probably never would be—but at least it was *alive.* After all I had been through, in here the war seemed a long way away.

What would Sam make of all this, I wondered. There had been no nightclubs in Middle Hill or Stratford, and in London, mainly because of Will, I suppose, we had hardly sampled the clubs the capital had to offer.

I'm sure my sister would have loved this club, I told myself. She and her flatmates would be right at home here—how did she put it?—dancing, flirting, drinking, and even, as she had said, trying drugs.

I turned back to Liesl and Rebecca. Under the table, Liesl had her hand on Rebecca's leg, stroking the inside of her thigh. They were kissing ferociously.

They sensed me watching and broke apart. Rebecca laid her head on Liesl's breast. "Now do you see why what I did for you was so hard?"

We stayed until after three. The champagne went quickly but the whisky lasted longer and our supper (*truite au bleu* with *frites*) was wonderful. We got gloriously drunk, all danced with each other, and all danced together. I got to know Liesl, who was Rebecca's flatmate (of *course*) and, I discovered, a painter of no small repute herself. One of her collages was on the walls of the club.

Rebecca and Liesl made me think of Sam and *our* living arrangements. Back home, people—those like my father who knew the truth, that Sam and I weren't married—disapproved of how we were living. Had more people known, they would certainly have told us we were "living in sin"—that was the phrase used so often, and still is. What, then, would they have thought of Rebecca and Liesl? Yet here in Zurich, in the Club Pantagruel, a safe, nonjudgmental habitat, they were happy, content, free. What could be wrong with that? Who made these rules, anyway? I thought of my mother. If she thought I was happy with Sam, she wouldn't object. It really was time I took Sam home.

The only shadow on our horizon—for me, at any rate—was Wilhelm. Was he still alive?

Later in the evening, by which time we were all very affectionate with one another, leaning on each other, kissing each other, and breathing alcoholic fumes over each other, when I was enjoying the smell of Rebecca and Liesl, and when our speech was just beginning to be a little less clear than it had been, Rebecca said, "We should go shoon. I need Hal to be sober tomorrow. He'sh going to kill Romford." She gave me a big wet kiss on the ear. "Don't let me down, Hal. Romford hash to die." She made a pistol shape out of her fingers.

"Boom! Boom!"

"Not here, Rebecca, *please*."

She placed a finger on my chest. "You'd be easier to fuck than George Romford, Hal. Why wasn't it you? Why do I prefer women, anyway? Liesl, take me home."

Then she threw up in my lap.

The next day I could have felt better. My headache had my full attention for most of the morning.

Greg looked at me with sympathy. "I deliberately didn't tell you about the Pantagruel because I know the damage it can do. Did Rebecca take you?"

I nodded.

"And?"

"And what?" What did he know?

"Did you get lucky?"

He didn't know. "I can't remember the last time I had any luck. Unless you count the time that I was shot and not killed." I changed the subject. "Have you heard from the brigadier?"

"I have."

"The verdict?"

He pushed a telegram across the desk.

I looked down. It said: +VPMGOTQSMFYRTOMSYR·OPMSI173+

"Meaning?"

"Confirm and terminate."

"And the rest—the digits?"

"Office of the Prime Minister, Secret Instruction Number 173. That will protect us after the war."

I said nothing.

"Are you sure you are up for this?" Greg murmured.

I took a deep breath. "Oh yes. I don't like it, I feel ill just thinking about it—but, yes, I won't let you down. I've come this far; I'll see it through."

"Good man. Well, the plan is simple. You and I spend the next however many days it takes on the fourth floor of the Bar au Lac, posing as staff members, carrying towels, sheets, and so forth. Whatever it takes until we see von Maltzen arriving at room 411. Then, when he leaves, we intercept him. The minute we clap eyes on the money, the cash, we overpower him. We can't shoot von Maltzen first—that risks alerting Romford and he might escape. Holding von Maltzen is the tricky bit, but we've got to make it work. Just think of the damage they're doing." He looked at me from head to toe. "Now, I'm fitter and stronger than you—yes?"

"Ye-e-e-s, I suppose so."

"Is that a yes or a no?"

"It's a yes or a maybe."

"Not good enough. Yes or no?"

"Very well. Yes."

"Right. That's settled. And it means that the logic of the situation dictates that I take on von Maltzen. You knock on the door to 411 and when Romford appears, you shoot him."

I said nothing.

"I repeat: Think you can do it?"

"Yes."

"Sure? You're not too familiar with him?"

That might once have been true. But not since last night. Not since I had discovered quite what a sacrifice Rebecca had made.

"I'm sure."

Dear Hal,

I don't know if you'll get this, or if you are on your way home already. So I'll keep it short. Will, poor thing, has mumps. The doctor has been and confirmed the diagnosis. He was miserable anyway, with you being gone, and now he's even more out of sorts. He won't sit still to be read to, he torments Whisky, and, in short, life in the flat isn't what it was before you left for ▇▇▇▇▇▇▇▇▇▇▇▇▇▇▇▇

I've started sleeping on your side of the bed — it makes me feel closer to you and sometimes, just sometimes, I talk to you as though you are still here. Is that an odd thing to do, do you think? Am I going a little bit mad? I don't feel as if I'm mad; in fact, it feels natural.

When am I going to meet your parents, Hal? You don't know how lucky you are, to have both your parents still alive. I know that my own mother, if she were still here, wouldn't speak to me, because of Will. Even so, I miss her, more so with you being away.

Oh, for proper letters, proper conversation, not these emaciated

exchanges we are being forced into. I want some __real__ contact, like our
last night together.

Come home soon.

Xx

S

A hotel the size of the Bar au Lac must have hundreds of people on staff. This can be the only explanation for the fact that, the next day, Greg and I prowled the fourth floor of the hotel, dressed in short white coats and black bow ties and carrying towels or sheets or bottles of disinfectant, for hours on end without anyone questioning who we were. Between the two of us, we managed to keep the door to room 411 under surveillance at all times. I maintained a good distance, however, in case Romford himself appeared.

Nothing happened that first day, or the next.

At about eleven on the following morning a man pushed a trolley out of the lift and turned toward room 411. He was wearing a white coat like we were, but there could be no doubt: he was bald, small, bespectacled. That fitted Rebecca's description of von Maltzen.

He knocked on the door and was admitted.

Greg and I, suddenly on edge, stood near the lifts. Greg leaned against the wall, chatting easily to me, giving the appearance of a gossip, while I made a show of folding the towels I had been holding. Standing helped Greg's back. We conversed in German. It seemed to work; a couple of guests passed by without giving us a second look. A maid—genuine, I supposed—also went by. She did give us a doubtful look but still went about her business.

Ten minutes passed, twelve, fifteen. Von Maltzen was still in there. Seventeen minutes.

"Must be a big stash of money," Greg whispered with a grim smile.

I was halfway through smiling back when I heard the door to 411 open.

The trolley appeared, then von Maltzen.

Then Romford!

They were talking, obviously feeling secure.

When they saw us, they stopped. Romford stared at me. Then, without a word, he turned and bolted down the corridor.

This wasn't in the script. I dropped the towels—in fact, I threw them at von Maltzen to stop him from reaching for his gun, assuming he had one.

I edged around the trolley and ran after Romford. Not easy: my leg still ached from time to time. At the end of the long corridor he turned left into a smaller one. I knew, from my previous reconnaissance, pretending to be part of the staff, that the emergency exit lay that way.

I reached the turn and peered round the corner. Romford was just disappearing down the back stairs, shiny stone steps that led to the emergency exit.

I followed.

As I reached the back staircase I could hear his footsteps below me. I went after him. I couldn't see him but I could hear him and I assumed he could hear me. We descended one flight, two flights; he would soon be on the ground floor. Was I gaining on him or losing him?

Suddenly I heard him gasp, then a rattling/clattering noise, followed by a groan. I slowed and looked down, over the stair railing. He had fallen. His body was in a heap two landings below.

As quickly as I could, I skipped down the rest of the way. As I passed the intervening landing I again peered over the railing. Romford was bent in two, clutching his ankle. He must have broken it; he was clearly in a lot of pain.

I had my gun out and took the last few steps carefully—this is where he had slipped. I approached him nervously. Gregory had provided my gun and shown me what to do, but I had never fired the thing.

Romford looked up. "Mont-fucking-gomery. I knew we'd meet again someday. I had hoped you'd been killed."

"Major Romford," I said quietly. "Trading with the enemy."

"Who says?" He winced.

"We've been watching you. We know everything."

"Oh you do, do you? You're still a smarmy fucker, I see, who knows all the answers."

I took two steps forward.

"I suppose you're a general by now. All those connections of yours—"

"What's it to you?"

"I was fired from Stratford." He was sweating with pain. "You, of course, got promoted out of it. But I was sodding sacked, all because of some cheap little tart of a secretary who said I'd . . ." He stopped. "It doesn't matter." He smiled, more of a smirk, really. "But the Germans were clever. They put a spy into Stratford, to see who they could hook. When I was fired . . . they hooked me."

At first I was puzzled, but then a light went on in my head. "Rollo West!"

I could tell from Romford's expression that I had hit the nail on the head.

"I should have guessed. He tried to stop Bryan Amery and me from helping our fellow students—he was, in effect, trying to sabotage the translators' course. And he knew the German for lots of fancy cricket terms, which he had researched, but was thrown by LBW. So he turned you, did he?"

Romford glared at me and thrust his chin out. "I've done pretty well, made money, avoided the trenches, enjoyed the women of Zurich."

"Yes, we know."

He glowered at me in bewilderment.

I smiled. "Rebecca . . . one of ours."

His features registered disbelief. "*Jee*-sus!"

How different Romford was from Wilhelm, the last enemy I had come this close to. Wilhelm had been civilized, elegant, generous. All things Romford was not.

"Why do you think she stayed in bed with you all day?"

"You fucking—"

"How did you get into this, anyway?"

He reverted to smirking. "They're clever, the Krauts. I remember you always said that. They always knew raw materials would be a problem someday. This outfit was set up early. It's worked a treat— until now. What rank are you?"

"Does it matter?"

"I'm an *Oberstleutnant*."

"A lieutenant colonel? Is that what they've told you?"

"I'll stay here when the war is over. I've made good money."

"Colonel, Major, whatever you are, for you the war *is* over."

He stared at me. Then adjusted his gaze, to look over my shoulder.

I hadn't heard any movement, but then I hadn't been concentrating. Was he bluffing, or was von Maltzen really behind me?

Did doubt show on my face?

I couldn't hear anyone else. No sound of breathing, no footsteps.

I saw the glint of gun metal as Romford pulled a hand from his pocket.

So I shot him.

I shot him through the head. I shot him for Rebecca. I shot him because he was a traitor. That's what I said later. But I really shot him because I was suddenly frightened—terrified—and thought he was going to shoot me. Or that someone behind me would get me first.

But no bullet ripped me apart, no fire seared my insides. There was no pain explosion as my shoulder blade, or pelvis, or skull was cracked into a thousand smithereens. Romford *had* been bluffing and we were alone in the stairwell. For the time being.

He lay, his head against the wall, blood now mingling with the mustache I had hated so much. His leg was turned at an unnatural angle, and his finger was in the trigger guard of his gun. George Romford was as ugly in death as he had been in life.

You can't hide the sound of a gunshot, so I didn't hang around. I clambered back up the stairs to the fourth floor, gingerly peered around the side corridor into the main one. I was sweating because—well, although we *believed* there was cash in the tureen on the room service trolley, I hadn't actually seen it. And I had killed Romford.

I could see Greg along the corridor, kneeling, with a body lying on the carpet beside him.

I approached warily. The man beside Greg wasn't moving, so I gained in confidence as I came closer.

Greg stood up. "I broke his neck," he whispered. "Quieter than what you did. We'd better go."

"What about the money?"

He lifted the lid of the silver tureen.

"That's more money than you'll ever see again."

And so, I killed a man. I killed a man. That takes some saying. Yes, I had spent however many months it was in the trenches and had, I am sure, shot several Germans on the other side of no-man's-land. But they were a proper enemy, in uniform, on a proper battlefield, nearly a hundred yards away. I had never actually *seen* anyone I had killed, even assuming I had done so. But now I had killed someone I knew, who was not ten feet away from me, wearing a jacket and trousers just as I was. And I had seen him go from living and breathing, looking nervous but still a cocky little Cockney as he had always been, to being slumped in a stairwell, unmoving, his head at an awkward angle to his body, his ankle mangled in a misformed twist, and patches of black-red blood on his shirt and face.

Yes, he was a traitor in wartime and he would have killed me without thinking twice if I had given him the chance. It doesn't make any difference. I knew next to nothing about Romford, whether he'd ever had a family, a wife, children—people who loved him, who depended on him and would miss him, whose lives would be changed out of all recognition by what I had done to him. Part of me didn't care, part of me did. I was shocked, exhausted, drained.

Greg and I didn't hang around after our own little war-within-the-war. Still wearing our white coats, we took the trolley down two floors and, while no one was about, slipped into the men's lavatory and removed our disguises. We took the bag with the money, left the trolley, and went back into the lift and dropped down to the ground floor. We strolled out by the main entrance.

When we reached the consulate, Greg took me to the Venner and sat me at a table. He gave me a large whisky and murmured, "Stay there."

He was back minutes later, with Rebecca, who sat next to me and gave me a big kiss. "Well done!" she whispered. "Now I can start to feel clean again. You've released me, Hal. I can't thank you enough."

I just looked at her. I felt washed out and, yes, now that she had raised it, unclean.

She leaned against me and took my hand in both of hers. "You look beat up." She turned to Greg. "He can't go back to his hotel in this state. I'll take him to our flat. Liesl and I will look after him to-night."

I thought I saw a flash of envy sweep quickly across Greg's face but all he said was "Fine by me. I think we got away without being seen. In any case, I've got to write up my report, and encode it. Having the office to myself will help."

Rebecca and Liesl's flat was obviously occupied by women. It had all those little touches—flowers, photographs, fancy silk cushions, small woollen animals—that only women take the trouble to acquire and spread around in all the right places.

Liesl was already there, and when Rebecca gave her the news about Romford's death, she came over and also gave me a big kiss. I was made to take a bath, with another whisky to go with it, given a huge toweling bathrobe, and then, for lunch, we all had a bowl of hot soup in the kitchen. Then they put me to bed. Liesl closed the curtains, Rebecca turned out the light, and they quietly closed the door.

It felt odd, going to sleep in broad daylight. It was like being back in childhood when, in summertime at least, Izzy and I were made to go to bed long before it got dark and much to our displeasure. Hearing our parents up and about, even giving dinner parties, was to Izzy and me just about the cruelest thing imaginable, when we were tucked up in boring bed.

I tossed and turned for about twenty minutes, but then dropped off into a profound sleep. I slept for hours and when I woke up I couldn't at first remember where I was. Then it all came back to me and the sick feeling in my stomach returned.

I had killed someone.

I lay on my back and looked at the shadows on the ceiling. It was a molded surface not unlike the one in our flat in Penrith Mansions, where the traffic on the Embankment cast moving shadows on the ceiling there too. Would Sam be lying in bed now, wide awake, as I was, and on my side? Would she be reading her psychology books, or would she have Will in bed with her? Had she allowed that habit to grow while I had been away? Was he over his mumps by now? Was he going easy on Whisky?

How I missed home, and what extraordinary things a home is made up of.

How was my mother?

But at least I was now free to go home. Maybe, as I traveled back by the many trains I had arrived on, I would begin to forget that I had killed a man.

The noises and the ambient light told me two things: it was night and it was raining. I didn't know how late it was so I got out of bed and went to stand by the window, to catch the light from nearby streetlamps. From my watch I could see it was just after midnight.

As I gazed down at the wide boulevard that Rebecca and Liesl's flat overlooked, I heard a sound. It was softish. Were the women still up, or was there an intruder in the flat? Surely not? With a jolt I was suddenly afraid all over again. Had someone on Romford's side found out where I was recovering and come for revenge?

I opened the door to my room and peered out. The corridor was empty. There was light coming from the doorway to another room, but from its intensity it was probably a streetlamp from outside.

I heard a whisper.

Now thoroughly alarmed, I eased out into the corridor. I had on the terry-cloth robe, and my bare feet made no sound on the carpet that ran the length of the passageway. What was I going to do if I *was* being stalked and there *was* someone in the flat bent on revenge? I had left the gun with Greg.

As I passed the second door I froze.

Light from the street outside streamed amber across the room. Liesl, totally naked, lay on her back on the bed. A shaft of light fell across her breasts, leaving her stomach in shadow. She had her eyes closed but was whispering.

"Yes . . . oh yes . . . there, please, *there!*"

In deeper shadow, Rebecca had her head between Liesl's thighs. She was naked, too, half on and half off the bed, the runnel of her spine visible as a still darker shadow down her back.

I shouldn't have been there. But Liesl was very beautiful, in the half-light, her skin smooth and honey-colored in the glow from the street. She moved languidly—her shoulders, the swelling of her breasts, the backward arch of her throat as she sobbed in pleasure, the way her lips closed and opened, the flat smooth expanse of her belly. I was transfixed.

I didn't notice that she had opened her eyes and was looking at me. When, finally, I did realize that she was gazing straight at me, I blushed, though I doubt she could see that in the dim light. But she hadn't moved. Instead, she raised one arm and, with her fingers, beckoned me into the room.

Sensing movement, Rebecca turned her head in my direction. She smiled. "You slept for ages," she said softly. "We wondered whether to wake you. Come in."

She moved up the bed, turned, and lay next to Liesl, her arm around the other woman's shoulders.

Two very beautiful women, naked, lying there before me on the bed, in the dim glow thrown by the streetlamps. A gentle rain falling outside.

I had stopped blushing but my face still burned. My whole body burned. It was an exotically erotic scene and the juices in my body were flooding my system. But, suddenly, it was Sam I was longing for. Longing? The German word, *Sehnsucht*, says it much better. It was Sam

I wanted, Sam's flesh I longed to . . . People back home might disapprove of us living together, but what did they know? I wanted Sam, violently.

Liesl ran her fingers up the inside of Rebecca's thigh and she moaned. She opened her legs slightly and as she did so her arm fell over the side of the bed, in an attitude—in that light—reminiscent of Romford's arm in the stairwell earlier in the day, after I had shot him.

I gripped the doorknob with my clammy hand. "Thank you," I whispered. "Good night." I closed the door behind me and returned to my room.

At breakfast the next morning, Liesl wore a silk kimono as a dressing gown, Rebecca a long man's shirt. No one referred to the events of the previous night, but they were exceedingly affectionate toward me, lavishing attention on me, touching my hand or cheek in very tender ways. Rebecca was taking real risks for her country and what she had done with Romford had been a terrible ordeal, and they wanted me to know that in killing him, I had put something right with the world—with their world anyway.

I stayed in Zurich a few more nights, to allow time to elapse between the killings at the Bar au Lac and my departure. Von Maltzen had been a Swiss citizen, after all. The maid at the hotel who had looked so doubtfully at us could have given the police a description. Had she noticed my slight limp, the accents with which Greg and I spoke German? Would some clever Zurich detective put two and two together?

But no one came looking for us and, after the best part of a week, we judged it safe for me to leave.

The last night I spent in Zurich, I took Liesl and Rebecca to a very smart restaurant by the lake. We had too much to drink and we all, I think, got a little maudlin. At one point Rebecca kissed my ear, then nibbled it, and said, "Have you ever been to bed with two women, Hal?"

"No."

"Do you want to tonight?"

Liesl leaned forward and put her hand on my thigh. "Our farewell gift."

"I'm flattered," I replied.

"You weren't flattered the time before. You turned us down."

I didn't take that up either.

What I did do was tell them about the Christmas truce, my meeting with Wilhelm, the business with the cigars and the Christmas pudding, the photograph he gave me, my meeting with Sam, what I had done and not done—everything. I told them I had almost confessed all to Sam that day in Hyde Park, how I had made a mistake in referring to the fact that Wilhelm came from Mannheim—I got it all off my chest. I was never going to see them again, they would never meet Sam, and it was good—cleansing, purgative—to be able to tell someone, to listen to myself tell the story and see their reaction.

They didn't judge me. I suppose I knew they wouldn't, and that's why I felt able to talk to them. They didn't judge Sam, either.

"Look at me," said Rebecca. "I'm sleeping with the enemy, too. Liesl's half Austrian."

I shook my head. "You're not deceiving each other. Everything between you is honest, out in the open . . . clean."

"But it wasn't always," said Liesl. "You can't think it's easy, being a lesbian. Zurich's only tolerant now because so many extraordinary people are sitting out the war here. It's only become bohemian recently."

Rebecca put her hand on my knee. "Find your happiness where you can, Hal. It's a pity Romford wasn't Wilhelm. You could have solved everything in that stairwell."

"I couldn't have killed him, if he'd been Wilhelm."

"How do you know? What has happened, has happened. Make the most of it. War allows you to . . . to step outside the normal boundaries. We did."

They were different boundaries, of course, but I didn't say so. We drank more wine and went on to the Pantagruel, where we smooched on the dance floor and kissed and drank some more.

I was sorry to leave them. They were good for me. The next day they came to the station to see me off, and Rebecca slid a small package into my hand as I stepped onto the train. They then stood on the platform, waving as the train pulled away. Those wartime friendships were very intense, as Izzy had warned me.

As the train for Geneva picked up speed, I settled into the carriage and unwrapped the package Rebecca had given me. It was a book and fixed inside it was a note: "I never told you about this. I stole it during my ordeal with Romford. Maybe it will help. xx R."

Puzzled, I opened the book. It was, to my surprise, a sketchbook. Romford, it appeared, liked to make sketches as he went along—and he wasn't bad, not bad at all, revealing a hidden talent I'd never dreamed he had.

The book fell open at a sketch of Rebecca; he was good enough with his likenesses that there was no doubt as to who it was. Rebecca, asleep in bed, naked, her breasts visible above the sheets. Is this what she meant? Was this drawing in some way intended to help me? Did she think the drawing indicated a deep lust or love for her, on Romford's part, and that had I not done what I had done, she would have been tormented by him until she went out of her mind?

I leafed through the book, backward toward the beginning. Scenes of Zurich, scenes of London, scenes that I recognized as Stratford-upon-Avon.

And then I saw what she meant.

A drawing of me. There was no mistaking who it was: me on my motorcycle. Except that Romford had made a caricature of my features. My teeth were fangs, my fingers—gripped around the cycle's handlebars—were talons, and there were two small horns sticking out from my forehead. It was a drawing filled with loathing.

I snapped the book shut. Romford had been a traitor and a boor, but in his sketch of me was he entirely wrong?

The train was picking up speed now, as it hurried along a narrow valley between two mountains.

Though Rebecca and Liesl had done their best to reassure me, my behavior in Stratford and Middle Hill still troubled me, still hovered at the back of my mind. My deception hadn't eaten at me enough yet to prompt me to tell Sam the whole story, from Plumont to Sedgeberrow to the change of plan that had formed in my mind that day when I had sat in the Lamb in Middle Hill, after I had seen her on playground duty. But nor would the cloud that shrouded my conscience go away completely. My position was so . . . so ramshackle. If, during the weeks I had been away, Sam had looked in my briefcase, she would have found Wilhelm's photograph, and my whole deception would—even now—be exposed. I might be going home to a bloodbath. But that was my own fault. I had no choice but to live with the lie I had manufactured. It had brought me great happiness but a happiness that could be destroyed—vitiated, ravaged—in a moment, in a flash, at any time.

Shortly afterward, the railway line broke out of the valley and skirted a lake. I opened the window of the carriage and hurled the sketchbook as far as I could. I never saw whether it reached the water.

My reentry back into Penrith Mansions was low-key. Sam, I think, was a bit upset that I had not been in touch more often but was content to see what I had to say now that the censor wasn't there to intervene. Will was quiet, too. He had missed me and he liked well enough the train set that I gave him on my return, but he was not going to rush back into my arms until he could be sure there was no risk of me disappearing all over again.

The sugar went down well, though.

The flat itself hadn't changed much. Lottie was still there but very worried. She hadn't heard from Reg for weeks and was living in dread that, any day now, a telegram would arrive with the news we all feared.

In truth, after the excitements of Zurich, life in London was a little dull, or would have been but for one bright spot. On my return, and in view of the success of the operation in connection with Hood-Frankel, the brigadier had seen to it that I had been promoted—to lieutenant colonel, the same rank as Romford.

On my first day back at Northumberland Avenue, a Thursday, the brigadier had another surprise up his sleeve.

"I've got a big job for you, Hal, but I'm not going to tell you what it is just yet. Can you drive?"

"Yes, of course." I was mystified. Was I about to become a driver to some very important person?

"Good. Now I want you to take a long weekend off. Today's Thursday; don't come back till Tuesday. I've managed to borrow a car for you for the weekend. Get out of London, take your woman and boy. Get to know them again. Understand?"

Of course I understood. Sam was a bit tricky about leaving her charges in school "in the lurch," as she put it, but Will was excited about going on a car journey, and I piqued Sam's curiosity by saying, "I've got the perfect place for a weekend away."

"Oh yes? Where?"

"Stratford-upon-Avon."

Stratford hadn't changed, or not much. We stayed at the Crown, where Sam's friend Maude was still a waitress. The food was still hardly better than it had been at the Ag. There were more military types around, now that the airfield had opened just outside the town, and so prices—for food especially—were markedly higher than they had been before.

It was all very different from Zurich—so rural, so unsophisticated, so much less stylish. We walked along the bank of the Avon. Cows still munched the dandelions and buttercups, but I made certain that we turned back well before we came in sight of the kissing gate where Wilhelm had asked Sam to marry him. She didn't seem to notice.

On the Saturday, we drove to Middle Hill. We passed the air force base, which was now up-and-running. We took a drink in the Lamb but it was not really a success. There was a new landlord who I didn't know, and of course he didn't know me. One or two of the regulars showed the glimmerings of recognition and smiled, but that was all. We walked down to the cottage Sam had lived in to find three children playing outside in the front garden, which was now a complete mess. Sam shuddered and whispered, "Let's go."

We hurried away, the smell of the pig farm strong in our nostrils.

It being Saturday, the school was closed and we walked on past, into the churchyard and across the stream with its moorhens. We passed through the kissing gate that separated the churchyard from the cricket field, where there was a game in progress—it must have been one of the last of the season. We sat on the grass and Will took a keen interest in the proceedings, which I tried to explain to him. I think it was this, as much as the prolonged proximity in the car on the drive up from London, that started to bring our relationship back to where it had been before I left.

Sam and I talked a lot, of course, during the Stratford trip. On the cricket field, I gave her a blow-by-blow account of the whole Romford operation. Will was out of earshot, sitting by the boundary, hoping the ball would be hit his way.

Sam was aghast at what Rebecca had been through. "I couldn't sleep with someone just because a superior officer told me to. I couldn't. It's beastly! *I just couldn't!*"

"I don't think you'll have to, so don't worry."

She shook her head, hard, so that her hair twisted violently in the wind, as if she was trying to get clean on Rebecca's behalf.

"I think it was harder for her than for other women—"

"How do you know that? How can you possibly—?"

"She was a lesbian."

Sam stared at me. "Oh *dear!*"

Will was suddenly up and running. The ball had been hit for four, in his direction, and now was his chance to handle it. He reached the ball first, picked it up, dropped it, picked it up again, and ran toward the cricketer who was nearest.

"Thank you, young man," said the fielder, doffing his cap and grinning.

Will came back toward us looking pleased with himself and puffing, as if he'd been out at work all day. I'd have to buy him a bat and a ball. He looked more and more like Wilhelm but Sam never said anything to me.

I went over the killing of Romford again with Sam, describing in detail those few horrible moments in the stairwell of the Bar au Lac. I did it as much for my own benefit as for hers. Only by facing those moments would I eventually be able to expunge the horror.

Sam listened, keeping her gaze on the cricket, so she could also keep an eye on Will. When I had finished she said nothing for a while. But then, softly, she murmured, "What if you hadn't shot him first?"

"But I did."

"This war ... God, how it's played with our lives. When will it ever stop? If you'd been killed, what would have happened to Will and me?"

That evening, Sam put Will to bed and then took a rest herself before dinner. I went down to the residents' lounge of the hotel, ordered a whisky, and made myself comfortable in an easy chair to read Izzy's letters. Four had arrived during my absence and I was eager to see how she was getting on. A fire had been lit in the lounge (September was almost over and the weather kept pace). No one else was there. I lit a cigar, one of Wilhelm's, put water in my whisky, and sat close to the fire so I could feel its warmth on my legs.

Dear Hal,

Good news and bad news. Finally, Alan and I were given some leave. We had four days off, or that was the plan anyway. Originally, we were going to Paris but then we thought we would spend most of our time traveling there and back, so we decided instead to go to Reims, where I am writing this. We are staying in a hotel and, can you believe it, <u>have two baths every day</u>!!!

The French still manage to cook up a storm, despite everything that has happened and is happening, and we drank some great wines too. (We didn't stint on the G&Ts either!) However, in the middle of all this food, wine, cleanliness, and G&Ts came the killer—literally. A telegram to Alan that his wife has tried to commit suicide!! Slit her wrists in a bath of warm water.

Now here's the thing. This woman has two children, two young children. Why would she commit suicide—assuming she meant to do it and not get discovered at the last minute—and leave two lovely creatures to be brought up by God knows who? Does this mean that she loves her husband more than she loves her children? Does it mean that "love" for one's husband—mate, spouse—is a different "love" from that for a child? Were I in the same situation, which way would I jump?

To my mind it all goes to show that I was right to begin with: given the danger we work in, there was no need for Alan to tell his wife about us, not for a while certainly.

Anyway, Alan was granted compassionate leave to rush home and be with his wife. She may have had an ulterior motive, of course. If she really did intend to kill herself, that's one thing. On the other hand, if it was a gesture, to bring him home and get him away from me, then that's another thing entirely and they need to talk it through. But he can't really tell until he's face-to-face with her.

Oh dear, Hal. What a state we are all in. There is no chance we will have a replacement for Alan in our unit, so I am going to have to run the show till he gets back. This was supposed to have been a relaxing break, but it has turned into a nightmare.

Much love xxx000

Izzy

Dear Hal,

I'm back now amid the mud and blood, the bodily fluids and broken bones, the screams in the night and the shivering bodies as they slip away to God knows where.

No word from Alan. In his absence, I have discovered something about myself. I have become bossy. I feel it. In a war, a great big messy war like this one, the army runs everything and you would think, therefore, that life is regimented, everyone knows their place, their rank, who is above them and who is below. That's how it should be. But the chief fact of life, even this far into the war, the main characteristic, the dominant element of our existence, is confusion. No one has the _faintest idea_ of what is going to happen. Most of the time we don't even know what is happening right now.

And so, in these terrible times, in this awful, godforsaken place, I have found that what the people around me want is certainty, any kind of certainty. That's why I have become bossy. I tell people what to do. I don't necessarily know what's best for anyone in any particular situation, but people seem to prefer my style to anyone else's. No doubt being a nurse gives me some authority, but it's more than that. I settle minor disputes. They come to me and they accept what I say. As I move about the trenches, I tell the men to tidy up this, clean up that, rearrange something else. They do it. Why do all these men obey a woman so easily? It's weird.

Some out-of-date British papers came our way. I see you are getting zeppelin raids over London—thank God Ma and Pa·are where they are. I read that Max Bremner was killed. The name may not mean much to you but he was one of the war correspondents I mentioned who visited our unit. A funny man and a good writer. He was forty-two and was gassed. What a waste.

I haven't heard from you for a while. Are you all right? Let me know. That's an order!

xxxooo

Bossy Izzy

Dear Hal,

You haven't written, you beast. What kind of pig are you? Are you so grand now that you can't be bothered with your little sister, now not so little? I suppose it's just possible that you are off on some mission you can't tell me about, and if so, I forgive you. But if that's not the reason, you are now, officially, in the doghouse. Way below Einstein in the pecking order.

Alan's back and he's not the same. He <u>says</u> that his wife's suicide attempt was not a real attempt. Oh, she slit her wrists all right, but he says she made sure there were people around who were more or less certain to find her. But the way he behaves, the way he is toward me, the little tendernesses that we used to exchange, the intimate sillinesses that people share when they are in love . . . all those have gone, certainly for the time being. He's also lost a lot of the forcefulness that I liked about him; it's as if his intellect has been dulled by going home. His idealism is dulled too. Maybe, perhaps, just being back in Britain got to him; maybe it was too depressing but he won't talk about it, and I don't like that.

(Several hours later.) He just talked about it. He saw me writing this letter, leaned over me, and read what I was writing. And it's cleared the air a bit.

Alan says it's true, that being back in Britain depressed him. The view of the war is so different there from the way it is here at the Front. In Britain, he says, people are bullish, aggressive, very anti-German in a simplistic kind of way. He says it's not so much London, which is very involved in the war, obviously, but in the countryside, where people are able to lead their lives as if the war is miles away, which of course it is. He says people still play cricket, visit the pub, fish in rivers and canals. He knows that normal life has to go on—otherwise all is lost, people need an escape from war. Even so, the gulf between the Front and the British countryside is <u>enormous</u>. He says that, after this war is over, the big difference between people will be between those who have been at the Front and those who haven't. It will be a big divide in our society, and it will disfigure us.

I have no way of knowing if this is true, but I trust Alan. He's not here right now and can't see me writing this, so let me add something: I don't think this is a complete explanation for how he has been a different

man since he has been back. There's something more personal too, though
I don't know (yet) what it is.

Write, you brute.

Izzy

Dear Brute,

   This will be short. You deserve only short letters until you respond.
   Alan is back in Britain, in Scotland actually, for his wife's funeral.
   *Yes, that's right. She tried to commit suicide a second time, and
succeeded. He received a telegram two days ago. Before he went, he told
me that he realized he'd been awkward with me and the reason was
guilt. On his first trip home, it was clear that his wife really loved him,
more than she loved her children, and that, contrary to what he told me,
her first attempt was not a "cry for help" at all but a warning to him,
that if he didn't come back to her she would keep trying until she really
did do away with herself. The children were devastated, he said, but . . .
and this was the real dilemma facing him: he, too, loved me more than
he loved his children. Hal, what a terrible thing. Is it an unnatural
thing for both parents to love someone else more than they love their
children?*

   *I'm back in charge, being bossy all over again. But inside I'm
churned up.*

All love.

xxx (still only three at the moment).

Izzy

The following day, Sunday, after a late start, Sam and Will and I
drove out again toward Middle Hill but stopped short of the village.
We climbed out of the car and strolled along the canal. At first I
thought it was a mistake. It was the same stretch of water where we

had walked that day in the pouring rain when I had first realized that Sam had a baby and she had confessed to me, in the shelter and darkness under the bridge, who Will's father was. Did I really want to remind her of all that?

But all she said was "Remember that wonderful tea shop near here? Shall we see if it's still open?"

It was.

The prices had gone up, there were more people at the tables, but the scones were still as good and, amazingly, they had managed to get some cream to go with the jam. No prizes for guessing who ate two scones, covered his cheeks in jam, then promptly fell asleep.

On the way back to the car, with me carrying Will, I told Sam about Izzy's last letter, the one where she had discussed the difference in love between adults and between a parent and a child.

"Is that what you were reading last evening, by the fire in the hotel, while I was sleeping?"

"Yes. How did you know?"

"You were quiet last night at dinner."

"Guilty."

"Nothing for you to feel guilty about. But you've been quiet ever since you came back from Zurich. I assumed it was because of that . . . you know, the Romford business. It would be natural."

"It did have an effect, Sam. It is still having an effect. But Izzy's letter had its effect also."

She stretched out her arm and wiped away some crumbs that were still on Will's cheek. "I don't have much experience, of course, but I can say that the love for a child is nothing like the love I felt for Wilhelm." She stopped and turned to face me. We were on the edge of the canal. "That was like a bolt from the blue. I could do nothing to control it."

She shook her head. "What is it that sparks love? In the winter months he always wore a scarf, loose about his neck and shoulders—

was that it? I thought it was stylish and . . . languid, that's the word. He was a languid person in some ways—he didn't rush me, and I liked that. He was always very gentle with me but firm about his aim in life, to go to America and work in something like wine growing or tobacco growing. I loved that mixture of languid easiness and self-confidence. I couldn't help myself falling for him."

She was fiddling with her Alice band. "Incidentally, that cigar you were smoking last night—what make was it?"

"Cuban, of course. Cohiba, I think. Why?"

But I knew. The sweat on my neck told me, the fist of solid stone in my stomach told me. I had made another mistake.

"It smelled like the cigars Wilhelm used to smoke, that's all. You don't smoke cigars normally, do you?"

Some sort of clever—but not too clever—reply was called for, and to be convincing, it had to be immediate. "I started smoking them when I was in Munich, but I gave up when my mother's cough got really bad. I treated myself to a box when I was in Zurich. Do you like the smell? If you don't, I won't smoke them."

She squeezed my arm. "I just thought you'd like to know . . . they remind me of Wilhelm, that's all."

I was still sweating but . . . I had got away with it again.

She returned to the conversation we were in the middle of. "I could do nothing to stop myself from falling for Wilhelm, and I can do nothing to control my love for Will, either, but it's very different. He needs me, I'm helping to form him—just as you are." She smiled. "Have you noticed how he's even started to worry about his shoes being shiny? The whole color, the whole tone of my love for him is different."

We walked on and, after a little while, she continued: "I can understand what Izzy's lover's wife did. I hope I'm never in the same situation—but yes, I can understand her feelings and her actions."

We walked on a short distance more until she put her hand on my arm again and we stopped. She turned to face me. "There *is* a third sort of love, you know. I thought about it a lot while you were in Zurich. I *am* falling in love with you, Hal. It's not a thunderbolt, I can't say that—and I hope that doesn't hurt you. It's more . . . more like the gentle unfolding of a flower as spring warms into summer. Will, of course, he loves you like . . . oh, I don't know, like . . . like he now loves a cricket ball!"

We both laughed so much that Will woke up.

That night as we put Will to bed, he asked for his "cocoa book."

"Oh, Lord, I've forgotten it," said Sam.

"What on earth is a 'cocoa book'?"

"One of the things that happened while you were away in Switzerland. The *Times* produced a new dictionary for children—with a new printing technique that means they can do pictures in color. The book has a tin of cocoa on the cover and Will, as you know, loves his cocoa. Even more now that he has some sugar."

I smiled. "I'm interested in color printing myself—the Swiss are quite advanced. I'd like to see this cocoa book. What else happened while I was away?"

"Apart from the zeppelin raids, you mean? Well, the king wants us all to drink less alcohol—especially at home; he thinks we're all becoming closet alcoholics. Telegrams are now ninepence, not sixpence. I had my fortune told. Oh—and I went to a lecture, with Ellen, given by a psychiatrist, on how being in the trenches drives some people into shell shock, while it is the making of others."

"Doesn't sound like my idea of fun. No theater?"

She tucked Will up in his bedclothes.

"You're wrong. The lecture was very interesting—the man who

gave the talk was from a hospital in Scotland. Some of the injured, the mentally injured, are really hard on their wives when they return. I hadn't expected that."

She kissed Will good night.

"As for theaters, you're out of date. Since the zeppelin raids, the theaters have been closing down at night. The only performances for now are the matinees, and I can't get away. Even then the theaters advise people to bring their knitting or something to read in case there's a daylight raid in the middle of a performance."

She took hold of my hand. "Now, since I've forgotten the cocoa book, you'll have to help out."

"Oh? What do you mean?"

"You've just been abroad, traveling. You can tell Will a story. Come to that, you can tell us *both* a story."

On the Monday evening, when we returned to the flat, there was a surprise awaiting us, and a very pleasant surprise indeed. Instead of Lottie having received a dreadful telegram in our absence, who should have turned up but the man himself, Reg, as thin and as creepy-quiet as ever. He'd been given some leave, he said, but had had an eventful journey back from France. The train he'd been on had been shelled, the railway line itself knocked out of action for a few days, and then the Channel boat he was due to sail on had never arrived. It had been one fiasco after another and it would have been comical if so many people hadn't been killed in the process and if it hadn't taken so long for him to reach Lottie.

Still, Lottie was out of her mind with relief and Sam was delighted for her sister, who hadn't had much joy in the men department. While we had been in Stratford, Lottie had seen Ruth and invited her oldest sister and her man, Greville, for a "party" on that Monday evening. So the six of us shared some pasta and whisky, Reg told us stories about the Front, Lottie sang, and Ruth kept us amused with some stories from her factory, where something always seemed to be going wrong. Ruth and Greville stayed late, very late, and Sam and I made up the spare room. All the men went to bed, and the sisters stayed up, talking.

I reached our room feeling content. What Sam had said the previous day, by the canal, had warmed me inside.

I had just got into bed when Will came through. As sometimes happened, he couldn't sleep and wanted company. I took him back to his room and read him a story, or I read as much of it as I needed to before he was fast asleep. I put down the book, tucked him in, savored the soap smell that always clung to him in bed, and went back to our room.

On the way, I could hear Sam and Lottie and Ruth still talking. I wasn't eavesdropping exactly but as I went by the door to the living room, I couldn't help but overhear the word "Wilhelm."

I froze. I stopped breathing. I listened hard, letting my hearing adjust to where I was, to the faint sounds of their voices.

Ruth was speaking. She had a louder, more authoritative voice than her sisters. ". . . long time now. And what does Will think?"

"He thinks Hal's his real father, of course." I'd know Sam's voice anywhere.

"How long can you keep that up?"

"I don't know. The longer the war goes on, the harder it will be to tell him the truth. We were playing with his latest cocoa book the other day, and I showed him some pictures of uniforms . . . there were British uniforms, French uniforms, American uniforms—and German uniforms. Will took his crayon and scratched through the drawings of the German tunics." She made a sound like a sigh. "It's only natural, I suppose. But still . . ."

She paused, but then more than one person was speaking at the same time and I didn't catch what she said next.

"... think Hal's a lovely man." This was Lottie.

"But Wilhelm really got under Sam's skin." Ruth said this more gently.

I could hear no reply. Was Sam nodding her agreement?

More talking all at once, then: "... I know you both think I'm foolish—to have fallen for Wilhelm, I mean, and to have slept with him ... but I did, and I wouldn't have it any other way. Those weeks with him were so *intense*, I didn't know life could be so ... *vivid*. I thought my heart might stop at any moment when war broke out and I realized I might never hear from him again. I felt so sure he would find a way to let me know where he was and that he was safe. Hal came into my life too soon, really. I did a good job, I think, of not letting him see how inconsolable I was, how much I missed Wilhelm."

"And now?" Lottie again.

"I don't feel quite so overwhelmed by Wilhelm's absence, as I did. Hal and I sleep together and it's ... it's better than it has a right to be, in fact. Hal's a considerate lover—he's a considerate man—and when we are making love, I forget everything else. I never imagined I would need sex so much, but I do."

"Lucky you," growled Lottie.

"The funny thing is ... I would be a lot fonder of Hal, but for Will."

"How do you mean?"

"The older he gets, the more he resembles his father—"

"Isn't that natural?"

"Yes, of course, but what's also natural, but in a different way, is that he has adopted some of Hal's mannerisms. He's become— becom*ing*—a perfect mix of Wilhelm and Hal. He doesn't realize he *is* a mix, of course, it's all unconscious, but I can't help but notice. Hal can't know just how much Will looks like his father, and I'm not going to rub it in, that would be unkind. But I have to face this mix every day and it cuts through me. What am I going to do?"

A pause.

"If I were you, I'd throw in my lot with Hal."

"Lottie's right," said Ruth. "Even if Wilhelm makes it through the war without being killed, can you ever . . . a German husband . . . it wouldn't be easy."

I never heard Sam's reply. Just then I heard a movement behind me. Will, his pajamas crumpled and awry, was standing in the corridor, watching me. How long had he been there, I wondered, what had he heard?

I lifted him up, took him back to bed, and read him the rest of the story.

"What's wrong with you?" Those were the brigadier's first words when he clapped eyes on me the next day.

"My sister-in-law's fiancé came home from the Front, on leave. Family celebration." It was just a white lie, about Lottie being engaged.

He nodded. "What regiment is he in?"

"The Yorkshire Fusiliers."

"He's lucky. They're at the sharp end, just now, near Bertrix. I thought all leave had been canceled. Anyway, was your break worth it? Was I right about that?"

"Yes sir."

"Good, now follow me."

He got up, came round his desk, opened the side door to his office. Through the doorway was a small room with a desk, at which sat a woman of about thirty. She was dark-haired, slim, and wore spectacles. She was dressed in trousers and a white shirt.

"Hal, this is Nadia, your new assistant. Nadia, this is Hal, Colonel Montgomery."

Surprised at this turn of events, Nadia and I shook hands.

"Now come through into your office." He led the way to the other side of the room and opened a door.

Beyond was a space about twice the size of Nadia's, with a desk, a window looking out onto the fabled lawn, and—I could not believe my eyes—on the desk stood *a telephone!* I was to have a job that needed a telephone.

I picked it up and put the earpiece to my ear.

"Oh, it works all right, don't worry about that. You'll be shown how all the kit works in due course. Now, put down your things and come back into my office. We have a lot to get through today."

I did as I was told and trooped after Malahyde back into his room. He sat on the easy chair and beckoned me to the sofa. On the low table in front of him was a buff-colored folder.

"Before I get to the heart of the matter, Hal, let me just say one thing."

"Yes sir."

"Will Nadia be the first assistant you have ever had?"

"Yes sir."

"In which case, please, don't have an affair with her. It will make all our lives so much less complicated."

"Yes sir, but—"

"I know nothing is further from your mind right now, and I don't require you to respond at all, you're an adult; just bear in mind what I say."

I nodded but said nothing.

"Right. Now here is your new responsibility." He took out his expensive pen and played with it. "We are entering the final phase of the war. The Americans are in, and in the next year or so, the fighting will end. When the end comes, almost certainly, there will be a peace conference—a peace conference to end all peace conferences, I should say. And the hardest wrangling will be over who should pay what to whom for starting the war in the first place, who should have to dig deepest for nearly bankrupting one country after another. I want you to be in charge of calculating and masterminding our arithmetic on what the war has cost us."

I looked at him.

"The cabinet has a Reconstruction Committee, Hal, but we need a proper audit of the war. Not just how many people have been killed but how many weapons and how much ammunition we have turned out, at what cost, how much legitimate business has been lost as a result of the war, what the expense is going to be for looking after families where the father is dead, what the cost of rebuilding damaged buildings is going to be, what the cost of medicines has been, how many ships have been sunk and what it will take to replace them. What we owe the Americans. I'm just mentioning the obvious things, of course. I want you, with Nadia's help—she's a statistician, by the way—to amass figures for everything. You have a head for this type of thing. I can't be sure how cleanly we are going to win the war but sure as hell we don't want to lose the peace. Do you understand?"

"I understand, sir, but—"

"But what?"

"Aren't people kind of busy just now, to provide such figures?"

"Ah! A good point but your authority comes from the prime minister, Lloyd George himself. He will tell the cabinet about your new appointment and role this very week and senior figures in all relevant departments will be expecting to hear from you and will be under pressure from the P.M. himself to respond promptly. Don't worry about that. This is important work. Top secret, of course."

It was so top secret that I can't put some of my findings down on paper even now. But it is fair to say that over the next few months, Nadia and I became, so far as I know, *the* most well-informed individuals on what the war had cost the country. The brigadier was as good as his word and Lloyd George's instructions to the cabinet produced the intended effect. I found that my name was known around Whitehall even if my face wasn't. I learned to use the telephone, and senior people—very senior people, indeed—took my calls, or returned them promptly.

Our first task was to establish what Britain's level of economic activity was in August 1914. That wasn't too difficult. Finding out what had happened since wasn't anywhere near as straightforward. I suppose the best idea I had, on this front, was to ask each permanent secretary—the civil service bigwig in the relevant departments—to recommend one individual whom they trusted and I could deal with. That way I wasn't passed from pillar to post, and no one could hide. In effect, I had about a score of people working directly to me.

It was exhilarating work and there were two consequences. One, I paid far more detailed attention to the news. The nearer the end of the war seemed, the more pressure there was on me. And two, I started to arrive home later and later. Sam was not pleased.

"You hardly see Will in the mornings, and he's in bed before you get home. I know that what you're doing is important, but Will is important too. Can't you get home early on, say, two nights a week?"

"I'll try." I meant it. I had enjoyed telling Will stories and he, I think, enjoyed hearing them.

The following night I did come home early, only to be met not by Will but by a very irate—in fact, a spitting mad—Lottie. As I let myself into the flat, I heard a scream and she came charging down the corridor, her arms outstretched. As soon as she reached me she lunged forward and tried to run her sharp nails down my cheeks. With difficulty, I held her off—she was much smaller than I was but she was clearly fired up with some grievance or other. That gave her strength.

Sam was not far behind and grabbed at her sister. "Lottie!" she cried. "Stop it! *Stop it!*"

We didn't so much calm her down as pin her against the wall between the two of us.

"What . . . what the heck is going on?" I managed to breathe at length. "What am I supposed to have done?"

"The military police came here today," said Sam quietly. "They arrested Reg. Took him away."

"Why? What's he done?"

"Deserted," breathed Sam.

"And you told them!" screamed Lottie. "You gave him away, you lousy *bastard!*"

"I did not!"

"You *did!* You're the only one who could know his regiment is still at the Front—"

"Lottie, please. I didn't do anything," I said.

"You did, *you did!*" she screamed. "You're a smoothy civil servant sod. You shopped my lovely Reg, the only man I ever had. I hate you!"

She burst into tears and slumped down the wall by the tallboy in the corridor.

We all sat on the floor, breathing heavily. By some miracle Will was asleep.

At length, after a long silence broken only by our breathing and Lottie's sobs, Sam said softly, "Hal . . . you didn't, did you—?"

"Sam! How could you even ask?" I was shocked. Was blood still thicker than water with her? "How could you ask?" I repeated. "Even when someone in the office said he thought that the Yorkshire Fusiliers were still at the Front, it never crossed my mind . . . How could you?"

"I'm sorry."

Again, we sat in silence.

"What . . . will happen to him, Hal?" Sam asked the question that was on Lottie's mind.

"If he *has* deserted . . . *if* he has . . . he'll face a court martial."

"And?"

I said nothing.

"And?"

"It depends on the verdict. I'm sure it won't—"

"If he's found guilty?"

They were both looking at me.

"He could be shot."

Lottie screamed, "Nooo!"

Lottie moved out. She could not be convinced that I had not betrayed Reg and insisted that she no longer wished to share the same roof with me, nor accept my hospitality. And for the first time, she also had some harsh words to say about Sam's romance with a German, and what the war had done to their family.

Sam was distraught, Will confused.

I was annoyed, more than anything. I had most definitely *not* done what Lottie accused me of doing, and her leaving meant that Sam had now fallen out with two of her sisters. On top of everything, Lottie would no longer be there to babysit. The flat—once Gare Montgomery—felt strangely empty.

We found a daily woman fairly quickly who could clean and look after Will, but it wasn't the same as having Lottie. There had been no charades since Faye had gone and now we didn't even have Lottie's obsession with the smart set to complain about. There was no singing in the flat.

One good thing among this mess: I had bought Will a (very tiny) cricket bat after the Stratford and Middle Hill trip but he had lost interest, the way children do. The bat and ball lay strewn around his bedroom along with all his other half-forgotten (though jealously guarded) toys. But following the story I had made up for him in Stratford, I had begun reading to him, and he seemed to enjoy that. And so did Whisky, who would lie on the bed during these sessions and go to sleep when Will did. So cozy did these moments become for me that I looked forward to them and began keeping more regular hours, as Sam had asked, leaving work between six and six-thirty so I could see Will and read to him. It also helped keep my relationship with Nadia on a fairly formal basis. Twice she asked me out for a drink after work, but after two refusals she gave up.

Sam and I slipped into an easy, comfortable way of life, staying at home most evenings. She had found that the daughter of the local pub landlord would babysit at weekends and so we didn't miss Lottie as much as we might have done. We resumed our visits to the West End theater, though Saturday matinees lacked some of the atmosphere of evening performances.

Dear Hal,

Hal-lelujah! Thanks for your letter. When I saw your handwriting on the envelope, I kissed the man nearest to me!

Your letter didn't actually <u>say</u> much, did it? But it is good to know you are alive, back from wherever it is you have been, and are all in one piece.

Latest dispatch from page 5 of the <u>Times</u> (papers are getting through from time to time): a paragraph headlined "The War and the

Dressmaker"—can you believe it? Two sentences tell us that "afternoon gowns are very popular still, but there is no market for evening wear." I think we could have worked that out for ourselves but I _love_ the headline. Full marks to the backstage stars of the _Times_.

Now: I've had another top-secret letter from Pa. Ma is sinking fast apparently and a terrible thought has hit me. _I may not see her again_. I may not see her again—ever.

Which means, Hal, you have got to start being a presence in her life, enough for the two of us. I told you earlier that I can be bossy. Well, I have never bossed my older brother but I am doing it now. As they say in those dreadful telegrams they send out:

+GO•AND•SEE•OUR•MOTHER•SOON+STOP+XXX+IZZY+

The Kissing Gate

THE ONLY FACE-TO-FACE MEETING I HAD with the prime minister took place in January 1918.

Christmas had, as usual, been a bit tense for me; I was self-conscious for the familiar reason.

There was a lot of news just then out of America, which was experiencing its first Christmas under arms since 1864, the Civil War.

The brigadier gave me barely twenty-four hours' notice about the meeting with Lloyd George. I had just arrived at the office one morning when he came in and said, simply, "This part of your report . . . the section on what we owe America . . ."

"Yes sir?"

"The prime minister wants to discuss it."

"Oh."

"Eight A.M. tomorrow. Be here at seven-thirty. We'll walk across to Downing Street together."

"Yes sir. What . . . what in particular does he want to discuss?"

"I don't know and he doesn't have to tell me in advance. He's the prime minister, for Christ's sake. Don't be late."

It was a glorious winter morning—bitterly cold, sunshine as bright as butter—when the brigadier and I walked up Whitehall and turned into Downing Street. Inside, No. 10 was bigger than I'd expected, and we were taken to a room deep within. Lloyd George didn't keep us waiting but we weren't his first meeting of the day, far from it. We heard others leaving the next-door room; then the P.M. came through to us.

He was smaller than I'd expected and his hair was whiter in the flesh, so to speak, than it seemed in the engravings in the newspapers, and his mustache was bushier. His eyes shone up at me as we shook hands, and he then waved us to a seat.

"Colonel Montgomery," he said. "That was a fine operation last year in Switzerland. I expect it took some getting over, killing a man in cold blood—I mean, someone who wasn't a stranger?"

"Thank you, sir. All I can say is I did it, and that I still dream about it."

He nodded. "I can understand that. War twists all our lives. But you'd have cracked by now if you were going to. Think of that. You are doing an invaluable service now, with all these figures. And you will be rewarded after the war. A knighthood, I should think. But keep that to yourself." He smiled. "Now, our debt to America. It is of course colossal—not just materially but morally as well. The material side is easy to calculate—well, not easy perhaps but doable. But what about morally?"

"I'm sorry, I don't understand."

"Your report set me thinking. Our debt to America can't be measured only in material terms. Their support means we have a moral obligation as well. That's what got me going." He brushed his mustache with his thumb. "We know how much a submarine costs, a tank, we know what it costs to replace a building that has been shelled or bombed. But how do we calculate the value of a life?"

"I'm not sure we can."

"But that's what I'm asking. The brigadier here says you are a very imaginative man. You are working on these costs. As you go along, I want you to give some thought as to how we might—might—try to calculate the cost of a life." He held up his hands. "I know that may sound crass, crude, may offend religious people. But this war has been terrible in its human costs, and even if we don't get the enemy to repay everything, calculating what has been lost in human terms, what the dead *could* have achieved, created, earned, how many doctors we have lost, how many inventors, how many brilliant businessmen, actors, writers . . . We need to have some idea, if we can, of who and what has been lost. *Quality* as well as quantity. How many books would have been written by our people who have been killed, how many pictures painted, songs and symphonies composed, concerts given. When I say 'our,' I mean our side, America included. We need to show our appreciation of their help. In its way it will be a great monument to the war. Now do you see what I mean?"

"Yes, sir. I think that's an exciting idea, if it's doable."

"That's what I'm asking. Let me know in a month whether you think it's doable. I don't want it done by then, just a feasibility report. Can you do it? Will you do it?"

"I'll give it a go, sir."

"Good. Good man. And don't leave out the women. Don't skimp on what they've done for us. There's going to be a female emancipation bill some time soon. Remember that."

"No sir, I won't."

"Good. Thank you. Now I have other things to discuss with the brigadier, if you will excuse us."

I was shown out into the street.

One evening after I had begun work on the moral costs of the war, Sam and I went to a concert at the Wigmore Hall. The singer was, I remember, an up-and-coming soprano—from Bristol, of all places—and one of the songs she sang was the aria from Handel's opera *Rinaldo,* "Let Me Weep." It was just as haunting, just as sad, in its clear, slow notes, as it had been during the Christmas truce.

It brought back a lot, of course. Not just the voice of the young man who had sung for us in the trenches and the sound of the mouth organ, but it brought back the smell of ammunition, the snow crystals on the dead trees, the sounds of the dying men crying out in no-man's-land, the shrill squeaking of the rats gorging on the dead, the ragged crosses we had built of wood as we buried men that Christmas Day. And, of course, it brought back my meeting with Wilhelm.

There was still a campaign running in the newspapers not to allow German music to be played at concert halls and Handel divided people more than most. Yes, he was born a German, but eighteenth-century Germany was not the Kaiser's country and, in any case, Handel had spent years in Britain, in London, where he had composed a lot of his music and found real fame. There was a case for saying that Handel was as much an English composer as a German.

At the end of the concert, we braved the placards being brandished outside the hall and tried not to listen as the demonstrators called us "traitors."

"That was the song you told me about, right?" said Sam as we left the demonstrators behind. "The song the young man sang, the night of the Christmas truce?"

I nodded.

"Did it bring everything flooding back?"

"Not everything," I said, mindful of the conversation I'd overheard some nights before. "Even the most vivid memories fade. You can remember too much."

She squeezed my arm. "You were part of something extraordinary, Hal. You shouldn't allow it to be forgotten. You should write it down and keep it. Will might like to read it someday. It would let him see that the English and Germans can be friends."

"How long do you think it will take, once the war is over, for the British and the Germans to . . . to get back on civilized terms?"

"Do we have to talk about it? Let's talk about Handel and his lovely music. Wouldn't it be wonderful if Will inherited my mother's voice."

"No, Sam, hear me out. I've been thinking. The war won't go on forever. We're in the last phase. When it does end, when it's safe, would you . . . would you like to go to America?"

"Oh Hal! Do you mean it? What a lovely idea—as a holiday, do you mean?"

"Well, I thought we might try a holiday there in the first place, but while we were there we could see what we thought of it, consider whether we could live there . . ."

She said nothing.

"It would take you away from your sisters, of course. But in the long run, and given that there will be anti-German feeling in this country for . . . well, for quite some time, it might be easier for Will. It might be easier for you."

She put her arm in mine. "You are a good man, Hal, to think about us, Will and me, thinking *for* us. America!"

She didn't remind me, then or later, that Wilhelm and she had once thought of emigrating, and I didn't mention it either. But I could see she was excited by my idea and left it at that.

When we got home I paid the babysitter, and Sam went through to check that Will was sleeping and then on into the dining room to pour us our whisky nightcaps, as usual. I went into the living room to check that the fire was safe—and there, in front of the fireplace, was a jumble of papers and photographs, *including Wilhelm's.* What was going on? The entire contents of my briefcase had been tipped out. The briefcase itself was lying there, open and empty, by the coal scuttle.

I could hear the chink of glass on glass as Sam poured the night-caps. Will was obviously sleeping soundly and she hadn't lingered in his bedroom. She would be through to the living room in a matter of seconds.

I stooped, grabbed Wilhelm's photo, and quickly slid it back into the briefcase.

Even though I only had time to glance at the photograph, Wilhelm's face and uniform belied what I had told Sam—they brought back the Front and the Christmas truce vividly: the rabbits, the mudflats, the smell of no-man's-land. What a world away that seemed now. If Wilhelm was still alive, how had he aged? I didn't wish him dead, exactly, even now, or so I told myself. But with Sam's feelings about me beginning at last to . . . change . . . how convenient, how much easier all round it would be if he was.

As I started on the papers, the door opened and Sam, whisky glasses in hand, appeared. "Good grief! What happened?"

"Will's been doing a little spying, breaking the Official Secrets Act." I tried to make light of it, but I was sweating. Would Sam notice? "He's been going through my papers." I smiled. "He'll get me shot."

"Let me help," she said, putting the glasses on the mantelpiece and kneeling down.

"No, no, don't worry. I can manage."

But she started shuffling the papers and handed them to me.

"I blame myself," I said. "Lottie knew not to let Will play with my briefcase. I never explained to the new babysitter."

"She should have known not to allow it. Common sense."

I put the papers back in the briefcase and snapped it shut. I was still kneeling on the carpet in front of the fire. Sam handed me my whisky and stooped down next to me. We sipped our nightcaps.

"You're very imaginative, Hal. America, what a lovely idea." She took back my whisky glass and set both of them down on the floor. Then she kissed me. Both our lips were wet and smelled and tasted of Scotch. "But I'm imaginative, too. Why don't we make love, right here, in front of the fire."

"I like her, Hal. Why didn't you bring her down before?" The bossiness of my bossy-boots sister had finally worked and I was making a visit to my parents in Edgewater. It was early March and I had finally thought it time to take Sam, who was currently off with my father, looking at his books. But we had decided to leave Will behind; there would be fewer awkward questions without him around. We had found a new babysitter, or Sam had. She had been unhappy that the previous one had let Will ransack my briefcase and I was in full agreement with that. It meant there was one less person around the flat who had seen Wilhelm's photograph. As it was, Will might refer to it at any time. The new babysitter was the daughter of the local vicar at the church in Old Church Street. Wilhelm's photo was now safely under lock and key in my desk in the office. I couldn't quite bring myself to destroy it. ·

Theoretically I was out for a walk with my mother, but her emphysema was now so bad that it was all she could do to walk around the garden. We were sitting on a bench with Einstein in front of us, his tongue flopping out and his tail thumping the lawn. He had expected a proper walk—so what was *this*?

"Well, we have been living together since . . . since I left Stratford, but we aren't married."

She looked at me. "Hal, you know that sort of thing doesn't bother me overmuch, not if you are genuinely fond of each other. But do you mind me asking why not?"

I shrugged. "She has a young son, whom we didn't bring, by a man who went off to the war and hasn't been heard of since." No lies there, I told myself. "So—"

"Hmm," said my mother. "Not ideal, is it? You *pretend* to be married, in London?"

"Yes, most of the time. Her sisters know the truth, of course."

"Do you love each other?"

"I think so."

"You *think* so! What kind of answer is that? Do you or don't you?"

"Well, *I* love *her.* She's . . . I think she's coming round to me."

"I'll try to understand," she cut in. "You are a family at the moment, but the father may reappear at any time. Is that it?"

"Sort of."

"So she doesn't love you, not the way you love her?"

My mother was always brutally honest and to the point.

"She didn't love me to begin with, no. I knew that. She was very much in love with the man who went to the war. But I think she's learning to love me. And with the boy, of course, it's different. I am the only father he has known."

"Dear Hal." My mother was suddenly very tender. "We thought you would be lonely in London, solitary anyway, your father and I. But you're not lonely, are you? Does your predicament make it better or worse, I wonder?"

"Ma, it's not a predicament! What a horrible word." I blushed inwardly. I had used that word myself.

She didn't reply, not immediately. And when she did she changed the subject.

"Bring the boy next time. He'll love this house and this garden. Do you have a dog in London?"

"Yes, a—"

"There you *are!* He'll *adore* Einstein."

She looked up as my father and Sam came out of the house, into the garden, but they turned away to inspect the roses.

She coughed, an alarming rumble in her chest.

"I didn't love your father, you know, when we were married."

Why was she telling me all this?

"I was in love with someone else but, well, to be honest, he was unsuitable in all sorts of ways." She threw Einstein's stick, so he would retrieve it and get some exercise. Even that seemed to tax her. "Women are practical, you know. Much more so than men. Your father offered more—and, I must say, he has given me far more—than . . . my other lover could ever have done. And yes, slowly, I learned to love your father. But in any case, I think that what counts in life is for women to be loved and men to love. It works better that way round."

Einstein brought back the stick and stood in front of us, panting and wagging his tail. He was so adorable and so stupid.

What my mother said was a surprise but heartening nevertheless. She had learned to love my father and their relationship still worked beautifully.

Now it was my turn to change the subject. "I received a letter from Izzy, Ma, about the wife of her doctor friend, Alan, killing herself. She—the wife—said she loved Alan, her husband, more than her children. Did you love Father more than Izzy and me? Is that still the way you feel?"

My mother took off her spectacles and cleaned them using her skirt.

"Don't get trapped in the words, Hal. We only have this one word—'love'—which we use for all sorts of things. People say they love fishing or the theater, and I'm sure they do, in their way." She patted my knee. "Parents love their children, of course they do. But not in the way they love each other. When you've made love with someone . . . when you have discovered true intimacy, when you have trusted someone in the way that you have to trust them when you are making love . . . you discover that no other love matches that. Look at a parent's love for a child. It is not based on intimacy so much as protection. That must be true because children don't love their parents in the same way. That's quite natural because children will have to make their own path in life someday; that's the way we are made, so parents love their children more than children love them back. I feel sorry for parents who never realize that, because they are bound to be disappointed, bound for sorrow."

"But what about——?"

"I'm coming to that. I can understand that woman in Scotland, the wife of Izzy's doctor lover. She felt a failure, unbearably lonely, rejected, unloved. If a child fails in life, a parent may feel some of the blame but never all of it. If a child turns on a parent, or leaves the family, there is a hole, yes, but intimacy remains between the parents. Two people together are much stronger than two individuals separately. That's what you must tell yourself, that's what you must build on. Two individuals together are a whole world—no one can touch you. When you fall in love immediately, that whole world is conferred on you. When you fall in love gradually you have to build it. It's not the same, but it can be as wonderful."

"Did Father fall for you—I mean, immediately?"

"Oh yes. He'd had quite a few girlfriends before he met me but he had no doubt once he saw me."

"So what did you do?"

"I played hard to get for a bit, just to test him."

"And the other man?"

"He emigrated, to America."

"Brokenhearted?"

"Let's just say he worked hard in America, made a small fortune, and, three years later, came back for me."

"And?"

"I told you, women are practical, unromantic. I had a son by then—you—and Izzy was on the way. I was happy, your father and I had a splendid life. Harold—that was the other man's name—didn't try very hard to win me back. I think part of him just wanted to show me he had got over me and that his life had turned out well. He returned to America and I never saw him again."

"Did Father know any of this?"

"No. Your father is like you, very self-contained. He doesn't need to be loved and is much better at loving. He's been wonderful to me. He still is."

"You don't think I need to be loved?"

"No. Am I wrong?"

"I don't know. I find what you say slightly disturbing."

"Don't. It means you have the capacity to make others very happy, but that you will never yourself taste the real heights of happiness *or* the depths of despair. It's the way you are made, the way most men are. Rejection will never crush you, as it crushed the wife of Izzy's doctor friend."

I couldn't think what to say then, and was relieved that my father was approaching.

"Darling, let's go in," he said to my mother. "It's going to rain." To me, he said, "Sam is cutting some roses, for you to take back to London. What a beautiful woman, Hal. And from what she's been saying, she seems very fond of you. I take back any criticisms I may have made. I'm quite bowled over."

I have to hand it to the prime minister but also to Sam. Since our visit to Edgewater, she had managed to persuade the daughter of the vicar in Old Church Street to look after Will on Saturday afternoons as well as Saturday evenings. This meant that we could resume our walks around London and along the canals before going straight on to the theater, which, now that the zeppelin raids had died down, had reinstated evening performances. On one of these walks, in June I think it was, along the Vauxhall canal, I was telling Sam about Lloyd George's plan for assessing the cost and quality of a life. I'd made quite a bit of headway but I asked her if she thought it was a crass idea. I shouldn't have—it was still top secret—but the cityscape of the canal put me at my ease. So much of my time with Sam had been spent on the banks of canals; I felt safe there, in the familiar surroundings.

Sam had her arm in mine and squeezed it. "I'm sure you'll be criticized by some people, Hal. But I think it's a wonderful idea. We were doing a similar sort of exercise in school only last week. If one of us teachers—in peacetime of course, not now—were to take out life insurance, then that's exactly the sort of calculation you would do: work out the amount of money someone would earn over a lifetime, work out what the average length of life for that sort of person might be. We did it for teachers, and the amounts of money involved are staggering."

I had a bit of a cough just then and cleared my throat. "I suppose I could contact all professional agencies, find out how many lawyers, teachers, doctors, bricklayers, postmen, plumbers, and writers have been killed, and go on from there to work out the earnings that have been lost. Is that the cost of a life, though? Is one life worth more than another?"

"Don't call it the cost of a life," she said, "or the price of a life. Call it the cost of death. It would be very powerful, Hal. Depending on how you phrase it, how you present it, the whole country will want a copy."

The canal where we were was very run-down. Sheets of paper, algae, rubber tires, old clothes all disfigured the water.

"Remember how you used to say these scenes needed their Constable?" I asked.

"Yes, and they still do. A proper painter would find beauty here. Don't change the subject, Hal. If you did this statistical exercise, it would be very valuable, but why not contact some special associations and ask them to send you any details of specific people—postmen who were brave and won awards and then were killed, bricklayers who showed exceptional bravery but who *didn't* win awards but were still killed. Calculate how much *they* would have earned had they lived. Do the same for doctors, teachers, writers, actors, train drivers, zoo workers ... make it a memorial for everyday people, as well as stars. Specific examples would bring it home. Think of all the families—like Will and me—who don't have someone like you to complete their lives, to bring in money. I think Lloyd George is right. Let the archbishops say that putting a cost on life is crass or even blasphemous; I think most people will understand and approve. And you're in the right place at the right time to do it. It would sell like hotcakes. Hot scones, remember?"

She laughed, stood on her toes, and kissed me.

And so that is what I did. I updated my report for the brigadier and Lloyd George, arguing that any document should contain more than just brutal statistics that might be useful for the peace negotiations and, furthermore, that a more popular version should be prepared, with specific examples from a wide variety of professions, to bring home what losses, and what *kinds* of losses, the war had inflicted on so many people. We would, I said, be able to calculate how many fewer musical tunes had been composed in an average year during the war, how many jokes had been lost by comedians being killed, how many babies had gone unborn.

It might be crass but, as Sam had instinctively grasped, altogether it would be very moving.

I heard back from Lloyd George inside a week, before June was out, when the brigadier called me in. It was late one day and he asked me to sit down and offered me a whisky. He was his usual dapper self.

"The P.M. thinks your idea is brilliant and has given the go-ahead. When can you have it ready?"

"I don't know. A year maybe."

"You've got six months."

I grimaced. "Why the hurry?"

"Propaganda before any peace conference."

I shook my head.

"Hal, you've crossed an important line and don't appear to have realized it. Lloyd George knows who you are now. For the moment, he thinks you can do no wrong. But that has its downside. Failure isn't an option. Or, I should say, failure would be fatal. For you—and for me." He paused, to let that last phrase sink in. "Fighting the peace is going to be as hard as fighting the war has been. As things stand, you are going to play an important role in that. Don't shoot yourself in the foot."

One Saturday in early July I was standing at the window of the flat, looking out, when I saw Sam and Will coming back from the shops. I frowned. Unless I was very much mistaken, and I wasn't mistaken, Will was limping. What had happened? Had he been injured? If so, when? He'd been perfectly able when he and his mother had left the flat, and all they had done was walk to the shops and back. But he was very adventurous, curious, as I have said before, always getting into scrapes. I was immediately worried.

However, as I heard them entering the flat, the gas meter suddenly gave out and I hurried to refill it with shillings. Sam was cooking something or other and the water had to be kept boiling.

I had just finished feeding the meter when she came through into the kitchen.

"Where's Will?" I said.

"In the loo," she replied.

"I watched you from the window," I said. "I saw him limping—what's happened?"

Sam put her finger to her lips and whispered, "Shhh." She looked round. The boy was nowhere to be seen. "I told him the other day that tomorrow is your birthday. He's planning a little surprise. Say nothing for now.

"By the way," she added, as an afterthought, "after I told him it was going to be your birthday, he looked hard at picture frames in the shop. He said you had a photo of someone in your briefcase, in among your official secrets, and he thought a frame would be good. But we couldn't find what he said was the right size. What *is* this mysterious photograph? I've never seen it."

I went cold. I'm sure I blushed. But I had anticipated that something like this might happen. "It was George Romford, the man I killed in Zurich. I had to write a report and his photo was part of that. The report was top secret and so was the photo. I had to write it up so I can't be prosecuted after the war. Hardly the kind of photo you'd want to frame, even if you could."

Did I sound convincing? Sam didn't like being reminded of my time in Switzerland, when I could have been killed, and so she said nothing.

When Will came out of the loo he had lost his limp. I scooped him up, ready to read him a story.

The next morning, very early, he came into our room carrying an envelope and a small package.

He held out the envelope and package and said, "Happy birthday, Hal."

"Thank you," I said, taking both. "What *is* all this?" Whatever was inside, I was touched. Even if it had all been his mother's idea, he'd had the grace to hand me the items himself.

I opened the envelope. Inside was a piece of folded paper. It was covered in squiggles in different colored crayons, an attempt at some figures, and what could have been guns, together with some kisses and the words "Happy Birthday, Hal," obviously written by Sam.

"It's wonderful," I said. "The best birthday card I ever had." I meant it. "I'm going to keep it on my desk at work." I leaned over the edge of the bed and kissed him.

He picked up the package from the bedcover and put it into my hands.

I opened it.

I laughed and said, "Will, that's very thoughtful." I looked at Sam and smiled.

"It was his own idea," she said. "When we were in the shop."

"Are you sure?"

"Sure I'm sure."

"He's got a very adult sense of humor for a three-year-old."

Will had given me a tin of shoe polish.

I turned back to Sam and said quietly, "And what about the limp thing?"

"Oh yes," said Sam. "Will, what about the limp?"

He made a face and gulped. "I forgot."

"Oh no!" his mother said, grinning. "Come here, climb on the bed, and let's tell Hal what the plan was."

Will clambered onto the bed and settled down between us.

Sam did the talking.

"About a week ago, Will and I were at the shops when we saw a blind person with a white cane. Will asked why the man had a cane and what it meant to be blind and I told him. Now, it so happened that a couple of weeks before, at school, we had done an exercise with a young class, to get them to understand blindness and deafness. For a couple of hours we had them moving around the building wearing masks so they couldn't see."

She paused as Whisky joined the party, jumped on the bed, and settled next to Will.

"We did the same with deafness, giving the children big ear mufflers for a couple of hours. The aim was to teach the children about blindness and deafness in a vivid way, so they will have sympathy with those conditions and understand them."

She shoved Whisky, who had made himself rather too comfortable between us.

"Anyway, I told all this to Will and it was his idea—his, not mine—to limp along with you today for a whole day, your birthday, to see the world as you do."

I looked at Will.

He shrugged theatrically. "I forgot. I'm sorry."

"I'm touched anyway," I said. "That was very thoughtful, very sympathetic. Now, I'd better get up and shine a few shoes."

"I'll get mine," said Will, and scrambled off the bed and ran to his room. Whisky barked and scampered after him.

"Here," said Sam. She handed me a package. "Happy birthday. It's only one thing—your parents would approve."

It was a book. As she well knew, I only ever wanted books, at birthdays and at Christmas, and at any other time of the year, come to that.

"I hope it's not too serious," she said. "But it's by a Swiss, and with your time in Switzerland . . . I thought it might appeal to you."

I took off the wrapping and read the title: *Psychology of the Unconscious.*

"I've read it," said Sam, "and it's fascinating. Ellen Smith told me about it at school. It's new, a new theory, showing how we all have hidden reasons for why we do things, why we think and behave in certain ways without being aware of it. The author's a Swiss called Carl Jung."

So I didn't get up straightaway, after all. Since it was my birthday, and since I had a new book, I lazed in bed for an hour, reading. Then I ate a leisurely breakfast and had a lingering bath. I went out to get the Sunday newspapers, read them for a while, and only then did I start to do what I did most Sundays: clean and polish all our shoes.

Will, although he liked shiny shoes almost as much as I did, had never shown much interest in cleaning them but today he sat with me. I gave him a cloth with a smidgen of black polish on it and he made a halfhearted attempt to clean one of his little boots. I was concentrating on what I was doing and I only noticed just in time that he had lost interest in shining shoes and had somehow managed to open the tin of polish he had given me as a gift.

He was about to lick what was inside.

"Will!" I cried. "No! You'll be sick. Smell it if you want to but no licking or eating."

Affected by the urgency in my tone of voice, he did as he was told and held the polish up to his face.

I couldn't resist it. Quick as a flash I tapped his hand that was holding the tin—and a smudge of black polish attached itself to the tip of his nose.

He gurgled with laughter. Laboriously, he got to his feet and held the tin in front of my face—and then did the same to me.

I lifted the cloth I had, dipped it in the polish, and drew two lines of black down his cheeks. "You look like a Red Indian."

He did the same to me.

In no time our faces were covered in black, so that we resembled a couple of Africans more than Red Indians. I lifted him up and we stood in front of the mirror.

Will loved it, and his gurgling laughter grew louder. He ran his little fingers down my cheeks, drawing squiggly patterns not unlike those on the birthday card he had made for me.

I gave him a mustache and a pointed beard.

He insisted on doing the same to me.

"Hal, oh no!" Sam stood at the end of the corridor, looking appalled.

"Don't worry," I said. "We're Red Indians with beards and it's only shoe polish. Nothing a good bath won't get off."

"It's not that," she said. "Have you seen the time? It's a quarter to one."

"So?"

"I've arranged a surprise birthday lunch for you. Ellen Smith and her husband, people you work with. They'll be here any minute. Oh, Hal!"

I ran a bath and Will and I got into it together. He loved that.

In truth, however, getting the polish off was a good deal harder than I had imagined. I had to use almost a whole bar of soap to remove everything, and Will didn't make it any easier. He so loved being in the bath with me that he wouldn't sit still.

It was not until one-thirty that I was ready to face the guests Sam had invited, all of whom had arrived by then. But she had told everyone why Will and I were missing, they all thought it was very funny, and that helped the lunch go with a bang. The guests stayed until about five, by which time Will was flat out, and Sam went to rest.

After the guests had gone, I read her birthday present for a couple of hours, every so often getting up to check on Will. He was still fast asleep, exhausted by the day, and he reeked of all the soap I had lathered on him during the bath we had shared. He usually smelled of soap when he was asleep in bed. I had grown to love that smell.

In the early evening Sam got up, wearing her dressing gown. "How would you feel about another birthday gift?"

"I'm happy with one. I was brought up that way, you know that."

She was smiling. "But you don't know what this gift is."

I looked at her.

"Will gave me the idea. I don't think you and I have ever taken a bath together."

Throughout the war, we hadn't seen much of Ruth, Sam's eldest sister. A seamstress, helping to run a factory in North London, making uniforms, she was always very busy and it was obviously important work, and much in demand. In July 1918, however, we got a letter from her inviting us to her engagement party. Sam quickly accepted.

The party was held in the factory—not as bizarre as it might sound because as well as uniforms, Ruth's factory made tents for the army, and so they had no difficulty in erecting a big one for celebrations.

I remember the event for three things. One, there was a slight awkwardness because Faye and Lottie were both there and we were all involved in an elaborate piece of choreography, carefully avoiding each other throughout the evening. (It wasn't too difficult; there were more than three hundred people there—Ruth really did have a big job.) The second thing was that, at one point, Ruth drew us away from the crowd and took us into the factory proper. "I have something to show you," she said to Sam.

She led us into a small office and drew open the doors of a large cupboard. "This is a new line we are introducing. You can have one free if you want."

In front of us was a line of infantry uniforms, but in children's sizes. I could see why Ruth had brought us here all by ourselves.

Sam was flustered. "Can I think about it, Ruth?" she said.

"Of course," said Ruth softly. "They'll be in the shops in about a month. I just thought I'd . . . you know . . . let you have a private preview."

"Thank you," said Sam.

We went back to the main party.

Ruth's fiancé, Greville, was a wiry Welshman from Aberystwyth, with hard gray eyes and a long neck.

"They're something, these Ross sisters, eh?" He grinned, looking from me to Sam. He had prominent cheekbones, too, which made his face seem longer.

I nodded. "Four firebrands."

"You're in the War Ministry?"

"Yes," I replied. "You?"

"Security. Can't say any more."

"I understand. How did you meet Ruth?"

"She helped me with a case."

"Oh yes?"

"You bet. I can't say too much about that either, but we needed to put some men behind the German lines and for that we needed German uniforms. We had captured a couple but nowhere near enough. Ruth was able to copy them perfectly—how she got the right material, and the right color, and the right stitching, and so quickly, I'll never know, but she did and the operation was a success. She'll get an honor after the war—one of these Labor Medals I should think."

"Are you having a honeymoon?" asked Sam.

"No. Neither of us can get away. Plenty of time for that sort of thing later."

"Family?"

"I hope so. You have a son, right?"

"Yes," Sam said, squeezing my arm.

"Does he want to be a soldier?"

"He's barely three and a half. By the time he's grown up, this war will be long over."

"I hope so," breathed Greville. "God, I hate Germans, don't you?"

Toward the end of the month we went to the Battersea summer fair again. Will was now nearly three and a half (as he would say seriously whenever anyone asked him) and the fair was probably the first thing he remembered from one year to the next, so vivid was the experience for him, and so different from anything else in the rest of his short life. He was still a bonny boy—he had not yet thinned out—and guns were now his favorite toys. Three mornings a week he attended Miss Allardyce's infant school—kindergarten was too German a word in those days—and he was making friends with other boys. While both Sam and I were pleased about this (he seemed to be popular), I know that Sam was less pleased by the jingoistic atmosphere at Miss Allardyce's. War games were by far the most popular form of entertainment at the school—the lessons, at that age, were not very arduous. Everyone wanted to be British soldiers, and no one, naturally, wanted to be German. Sam, I could tell, though we never talked about it openly, was apprehensive as to how this might rebound on Will in later years.

Her predicament was made more poignant for me by the fact that Will more and more resembled his biological father. Save for the different colored hair, Will had Wilhelm's eyes and nose, his lips, and the general thrust of his chin. From time to time, when I was alone in my office at work, I would take out Wilhelm's photograph to double-check that this really was true. And true it was. Will had some of my mannerisms, but there was no doubting whose son he was. Not if you had met the father.

Will was a bright child and curious too—curious to a fault, in fact, as I think I have said before. He would stand too close to the bank of a river or canal, or approach too close to a railway engine, too close to horses, studying their muscles. Sam and I were always pulling him back. He climbed furniture without fear and was fascinated by fire. Perhaps all children are.

At Battersea that year there was a new attraction. It was a sort of horizontal wheel in which the chairs, as well as circling at the circumference, as the wheel turned, also spun on their own axes. Will was much too young to be taken on this contraption—I don't remember what it was called—but he would have jumped at the chance if Sam or I had said yes.

As it was, while we were watching, he somehow slipped his mother's notice, and mine, and got closer to the wheel than he should have. There was a crowd gathered, and for a moment I lost sight of him. A whirring sound started up, music began to play, the wheel slowly got going, and the chairs began to rotate. Women strapped into the chairs held on to their hats or tied their scarves more tightly about their heads, as the momentum increased. The wheel turned once, twice, three times, until it was going quite fast and the chairs were spinning at a dizzying speed. I saw Will at the front of the crowd and pushed through the people toward him.

Suddenly, there was a loud *crack!*—and a shout went up. From where I was, easing my way through a multitude of bodies, I saw a cable under the wheel snap, snake free of its moorings, unfurl in a kind of lazy whiplash—and slice across Will's tiny body. I gasped as I saw blood spurt from his little arm as his frame fell to the muddy grass. I shouted—and was with him in no time. Sam screamed behind me but I had my tie off and was pulling it tight around Will's upper arm, above the cut. The cable had severed an artery and I had to stop any more loss of blood. I knew about severed arteries, ever since the murder in our village when I was a boy.

There was blood everywhere—on Will himself, on my clothes and face, sprayed across the grass around us. Women were screaming as the wheel ground to a halt and the music faded.

But I knew what I had to do. I lifted Will and began to run.

"Where are you going?" screamed Sam.

"Follow me!" I yelled over my shoulder, saving my breath. I ran between the new wheel and the great slide, and hurried to the edge of the park. I could hear Sam running behind me. My leg was hurting but not badly, not yet.

At the edge of the park I turned north, across the bridge over the Thames. I didn't know how much time I had but I knew it wasn't much. My tourniquet was an amateur affair and wouldn't hold forever. Will's face was pale and he looked frightened. So was I but I tried not to show it.

I reached the north end of the bridge and hurried across the road. I scared a couple of horses in the process and was shouted at by their riders, but I pressed on—I knew what I knew. Diagonally across the road from the park was the Lister Hospital. Sam and I had walked past it countless times on our jaunts through London.

I rushed in. "Quick!" I shouted at the first nurse I saw. "The boy's severed an artery at the fair. He needs it cauterized, and then he needs a blood transfusion."

The nurse—barely eighteen—stared at me.

"Get your sister—*now!*" I bellowed. "She'll know what to do."

Just then an older woman in a dark blue uniform appeared. "What's going on?"

I told her. Sam arrived, panting. She just stood there, terrified.

"There's no doctor here at the moment," said the sister. "He's been called out to an accident."

"Then you'll have to do it."

She glared at me. People didn't speak to sisters like that.

"There's no blood."

"I'm type O. Take it from me."

The sister looked from me to Will, who was pale. Then she looked back to me.

"You're right. Follow me."

The operating theater was all the way at the far end of the corridor.

I laid Will gently on the table. His eyes were closed, his face was still pale, and his skin was caked with dried tears and spatters of blood. I was close to tears myself.

The sister replaced my tie tourniquet with another one, made of rubber tubing. It was neater and more tightly applied—it would hold.

Calmly, she set up a saline drip, fitting it into one of Will's veins in his good arm with a needle, and then set about cauterizing the artery. The smell of singeing filled the room. Will began to cry out.

"I'm here," I whispered. "The pain won't last long."

The sister finished what she was doing, put a swab of cotton wool on the wound, and tied a bandage over it. Then she loosened the tourniquet and watched for a moment.

There seemed to be no escape of blood so she straightened up and turned back to me. "Take off your jacket and roll up your shirt-sleeve. How much blood do you think he lost?"

"I don't know. Take what you need."

She selected a needle for her syringe, tapped the vein in my arm quite hard, so that it stood out, and, to judge by the smell, wiped some form of alcohol on it.

Sam was holding the hand of Will's good arm.

The sister inserted the needle and led blood from my vein into a bottle. The red, sticky liquid poured steadily but the bottle still took several minutes to fill.

Sam looked on anxiously, between Will and me. She had never seen anything like this before. Hardly anyone had. I only knew about it, of course, because my sister was doing this every day at the Front and because of the blood transfusion session we'd had at the ministry. I had received a letter not long afterward informing me that my blood group was O.

Finally, the sister was done with me. She took the bottle, suspended it upside down next to the saline drip, and led a fresh tube down to Will's good arm.

The young nurse gave me a patch of cotton wool, soaked in alcohol, to hold over my wound.

The sister murmured to Will, "You're going to feel a pinprick, young man. It will hurt a tiny bit but not for long. You've been very brave so far, so you're not going to make a fuss now, are you?" She smiled.

Will, looking serious, shook his young head and half-whispered, half-cried, "My shoes are dirty."

Sam and I looked at each other. She was crying and smiling at the same time.

The nurse inserted the needle and Will whimpered.

Sam kissed his forehead.

We watched the level of blood in the bottle fall as the liquid entered Will's body.

Suddenly the door to the operating theater burst open and a man in a white coat strode in. He was tall and thin, and his hair drooped over his forehead. In a moment he took in what was happening.

"Where did the blood come from?"

"Me," I replied. "I'm type O."

"How do you know?"

"My sister works in an experimental unit at the Front, giving blood transfusions. She told me about the technology. I work in the War Ministry and gave blood. They told me I am O."

"I hope you are," said the doctor. "Now, will you all wait outside, please. It looks like Sister Wakefield has done an excellent job but, under the law, I am responsible for patients here, and I need to double-check her work."

The junior nurse led us back outside as the doctor bent over Will.

I put my arm around Sam as she sobbed. Then she looked up. "Will he be all right?"

"I think so." I was more nervous than I looked.

"How did you know about—what's it called?"

"Transfusion? It's what Izzy does in her experimental medical unit in France. They are giving transfusions all the time to men at the Front who have just been injured. Apparently it's very effective." I told Sam about the session at the War Ministry. It certainly took her mind off Will for a few moments.

The young nurse brought us some tea. "Not many people know about blood transfusion," she said. "It's a new technique."

We sat sipping our tea.

Suddenly a policeman appeared. He took off his hat and came up to me. "Excuse me, sir, are you the man who ran off with the young boy who was injured at the fair?"

"Yes." I pointed to the operating theater. "He's in there with the doctor."

The officer nodded. "I won't bother you much, sir, but we will need a statement from you, in case the fairground company is to be prosecuted for negligence."

"Yes, of course."

"Just your name and address, for the moment, then."

I told him and he wrote down the details.

"Was anyone else injured?" asked Sam.

"I don't think so, ma'am, not seriously anyway," he said, putting his notebook in his pocket and making his farewells.

"More tea?" said the young nurse, but just then the doctor appeared.

He came up to us. "You are the mother?" he said to Sam.

"Yes."

"What's the boy's name?"

"Will."

He softened his tone. "Well, Will's going to be fine, ma'am. Not immediately, not for a few days. He's in shock and he's going to be a bit weak. But you were fortunate that the accident happened where it did, near a hospital. And your quick thinking saved his life. I've given him a junior sedative and he's asleep. Just help the nurse with the paperwork and you can go and sit with him."

He looked at me. "Lucky you knew about this new blood transfusion business, sir, and that you are O. And lucky that the Lister is one of those hospitals involved in the initiative you mentioned. You are quite certain that you are O?"

"That's what the medics told me."

He nodded. "You're the boy's father—yes?"

"No," I said.

"Yes," said Sam at the same time.

One evening in August I came home from the office and, as I was approaching the flat, I saw a figure rise from the bench in the small patch of green between the buildings and the river. The outline of the figure—small—was familiar and I had no difficulty recognizing who it was.

"Lottie!"

"Don't worry, Hal, I'm not going to scratch your eyes out."

I smiled. "This is like a film rerun. The first time I saw you, you were sitting on that very bench, when we first found the flat."

She nodded. "I remember. But I'm only here because Sam won't let me in—don't worry, I don't blame her."

"Really? So why *are* you here?"

"Reg was shot today."

"Lottie, I'm sorry—"

"No, no, Hal, I didn't come for sympathy. I came to apologize."

I looked at her.

"There was a court martial, as you said there would be. I wasn't allowed to go because Reg and I weren't married, but one or two of his friends gave evidence, and through them I found out who shopped him, the bastard who gave him away."

I still said nothing.

"It was Greville."

It took me a while to realize that this was Ruth's man, the secretive security type whom I had last met at their engagement party at Ruth's factory.

"Lottie," I whispered. "How terrible. I am so very sorry."

"Just kiss me, Hal. On the cheek, I mean. To show that you forgive me. This war, this bloody war, has divided family against family."

I kissed her cheek. "Does this mean you're coming back to live with us?"

"No, Hal. I loved it while it lasted. You are a good man, and you helped save me. But I'm back in the theater now, where I truly belong. Make-believe all day, every day. I'll get by. We are—or were—one family, Hal, four sisters, and look what has happened to us. You have forgiven me, but how much forgiving is there still to do? Will we ever get over it? Good-bye Hal."

I turned away.

"You're with the wrong Ross, you know."

I turned back. "What? What did you say?"

She stood next to the bench. She hadn't moved. "You never saw it, did you? You only had eyes for Sam."

"I don't—"

"She doesn't love you, Hal. There'll always be that bloody German in the way. But I . . . I . . . remember that day in the bathroom, the day you were ill . . . I didn't follow up . . . I've always wanted you."

"Lottie!"

"I never showed it, not after that. No. I was a guest—and I could see how . . . how far gone you were over Sam. But I know her, Hal, better than you do. Be careful. She likes you, she likes what you can do for her. But does she love you—?"

"Stop!" I cried. "Stop. Don't say any more. Please. We had an agreement. Whatever you think you know, keep it to yourself. I'm sorry for what happened to Reg, but don't spoil our life, Lottie. Please go. Don't say any more."

I held up my hand, my fingers outspread. "Please!"

She nodded, turned on her heel, and walked away.

When I reached the flat, Sam was beside herself with rage.

"I saw you! I *saw* you! I watched everything. You kissed her! You forgave her, didn't you?"

"Yes . . . yes, I did. Was that wrong?"

"Forgiveness comes easy, for you, does it? You heard what Lottie had to say about Will's parentage when she left? It was no better than Faye's insults all those months ago. How do you think that makes me feel? I can't forgive her. Nor can I forgive Ruth."

"For what?"

"For letting you take the blame when it was Greville all along who shopped Reg. They just . . . they just sat back and let you take every-thing. That's so . . . wait till I see Ruth tomorrow. She'll think Hin-denburg's a marshmallow compared to me."

"Sam, listen. Do you think you should take on Ruth? Do you think you should fall out with *all* your sisters?"

She came up to me then and took my hand and kissed it. "Some-times I don't think you know me at all, Hal. Remember that early morning at Middle Hill station? I gave up everything then, to go with you to London that very day." She squeezed my hand. "That wasn't done without a lot of thinking, and it wasn't done lightly. I'm a delib-erate person, Hal, you must have seen that. And I have never regretted my decision. *Never.* Do you understand? I have always known what I have to do. Ruth hid. Ruth let Lottie think it was you who betrayed Reg. That is unforgivable."

I pointed out of the window. "Down there, Lottie was lamenting how war divided family against family. You don't have to do this." I was confused. Did I believe Lottie, the unkind and unpleasant things she said? Was it true, or had her grief made her spiteful, jealous of her sister? Did I believe Sam?

"What does Lottie know? Yes, I do have to do this, Hal. I'm yours now, *yours.* We have *our* family. The three of us and your parents . . . and the dogs, of course." She grinned. "That's our family now. You saved Will's life, Hal. You're his father. We can't go back. He even has your mannerisms. He loves shiny shoes and puts his jaw to one side when he's irritated—have you noticed?"

She paused, and then added gently, "I've let Wilhelm go, Hal. See-ing you and Will in the bath together, with all that shoe polish as war paint, the blood thing in the Lister Hospital—that's what childhoods are made of. You know, I actually think Will loves you more than he loves me. Maybe that's natural—you are a man, after all. And Ruth put all that at risk. I can't have that."

She put her hand on my arm. "I tell you—Ruth won't know what's hit her tomorrow. Poison gas is too good for her!"

Darling Hal,

I know, an extravagant beginning but I'm feeling generous today. The sun is shining, and, of course, we are all anticipating an end to the war soon.

I heard from Pa that you took your lady down to Edgewater for a visit. Great. What's her name? Pa didn't say (he's hopeless at important details like that).

Alan has asked me to marry him. <u>Do not tell Ma!</u> Not yet anyway. I'm not sure and I haven't given him an answer (yet). Alan's a curious Scottish Puritan. I'm sure he does love me but . . . <u>BUT</u>, somewhere in among his motives at the moment there is guilt, guilt over his wife's suicide. I can't quite explain it but it's as if the Puritan in Alan can't abide <u>waste</u>, and if we don't get married after all that has happened, then his wife's suicide will have been an even bigger waste than it already is (has been?). This is a Puritan conscience working overtime. If he doesn't marry me, it is almost as if he has made a fool of her—she killed herself for nothing. What a moral mess.

I daren't ask how his children are. I'm sure he'd tell me if there was (were?) a problem.

Write and tell me how long you and your lady have been together. Is it bliss, sharing a comfy bed every night? (I won't ask about sex, you always get shirty if I do.) Crikey, half this letter's been in brackets. But do tell me all about "married" life! Pa says she's very good-looking—I think he was quite envious! (At his age! There I go again, with the brackets.) You are a lucky man.

One tricky thing. I can't tell this to Alan just yet—he might look upon it as treason—but I have to tell someone. I'm not sure I want to be a nurse forever. Being in this war, I've seen so much blood, death, and mutilation that it will last me a lifetime. Life is going to be different after the war, especially for women—we'll have better and more varied jobs, I am sure, and that has set me thinking. I'd like to be a journalist. Is that too ambitious, do you think? I don't think so. I've enjoyed writing my journal and these letters have taken me out of myself (and the letters I've written for others). I enjoyed it when we had a visit from those war correspondents. They were so knowledgeable, so interested in events, even though it seemed as though they had seen everything. They were funny, too—witty, I mean.

What do you think? It would be a varied life, I'd have to keep myself informed, learn to use one of these typewriter things, brush up on my punctuation and subjunctive, but it does attract me. By the time the war is over, I shall have done my bit— and then some—as a nurse.

Huge love. (Still feeling generous.)

Xxxooo

Izzy

(P.S. Just reread the above before sending it off—and you know what? I'm going to finish this letter and accept Alan's offer right away! I'm telling you first. But I won't tell him about the journalism thing for now.)

About a week later, I was sitting in my office working on my "Cost of a Death" report, as it had come to be called. I have to admit, Sam had been right. It was alarming how much wealth goes out of a country in a war, in terms of lost careers. The real problem we had, in making the overall calculation, was the remarriage rate. Normally, in Britain at least, before the war, most women who were divorced—and it wasn't that many—remarried sooner or later, and their prospects, having taken a dip, picked up again. But, of course, circumstances are now very different. How many women will be able to remarry when—

for a time at least, for a generation anyway—there will be so few men available? As Izzy had reminded me, it is sobering just to think about it.

While I was working on the problem that day, Nadia, my assistant, poked her head around the door. "The brigadier wants to see you. He says can you come through now."

I frowned to myself. This was a shade on the brusque side. Normally, the brigadier was politeness itself.

I went through.

He was seated in his usual easy chair and he had someone with him. Malahyde introduced him as a Colonel Roland Moore.

"Colonel Moore is from one of our secret security outfits. I know which one but you don't need to. I want you to listen to what he has to say. It appears you may have broken the Official Secrets Act."

He said this as I was lowering myself onto his sofa. I allowed my frame to slump the last few inches. This was a shock.

Moore came straight to the point. "Our understanding is that you shared information with your wife that you should not have done. And that your wife has had a child with a German national."

Naturally, they were both gazing intently in my direction.

"Am I allowed to know who made these statements?"

Moore ignored the substance of my question. "I notice you say 'statements,' not 'allegations.' "

"You're splitting hairs."

"Answer the question."

"My wife, as you call her, is not married to me, though we have lived together since 1915. She was made pregnant by a German teacher in July 1914, in Stratford-upon-Avon, and he went back to Germany before war broke out. He hasn't been heard of since. He doesn't know he has a son. I may have mentioned one or two things to her, in the course of the past three years, but nothing that could be compromising or helpful to anyone else."

"Hmm. We'll have to see about that. Did your . . . lover tell you about the German?"

"Yes, of her own free will."

"Did you ever meet him?"

"No," I lied. "He had gone back to Germany more than a year before I met Sam—my lover, as you call her."

"Why did you take her on, so to speak?"

"I fell in love with her. I can't have children, because of a war wound, and she had a child without a father. It was convenient on her part, love on mine."

"You didn't do this out of sympathy with the German?"

"Of course not. I'm not a rabid nationalist but I know where my interests lie. What information am I supposed to have given away?"

"It is claimed that you gave away the identity of a German spy here in London, a certain Genevieve Afton, and that you told your wife and her sister before you told your superiors in the ministry."

"That's true," I said. I explained what had happened that night, how I had been tired and shocked by what I had overheard, that my domestic relations had been important to me, and that in a moment of weakness I had described my evening. "But it was something that my wife's sister—let's call her my wife, for convenience—it was something that my wife's sister had said that drew my attention to the spy in the first place. Without my wife's sister pointing out something about the spy's father, something that didn't agree with what Genevieve Afton claimed in the office, I would not have spotted that she was a traitor in the first place."

I took out a handkerchief and wiped my lips.

"Also, I know who gave you this information. He is Greville

Muirhead and he is the fiancé of my wife's other sister Ruth. The sisters fell out last week and had a flaming argument, because Greville shopped her sister's lover who had deserted—"

"Yes, I was coming to that. Apparently you knew this man was in London but did nothing about it."

"Because I never imagined he had deserted! Even when the brigadier here told me he thought that this man's regiment was still at the Front, I didn't put two and two together. What's more, why is Muirhead coming forward? Not really out of a concern for security, but because of a domestic row between his fiancée and my wife, her sister, that's why. Genevieve Afton was shot for treason months ago. Yes, I shouldn't have told my wife what I did tell her, but it hasn't affected anything."

"Hal has a point, Colonel," said the brigadier quietly. "He *did* expose Genevieve Afton, she *was* executed, and he *has* himself killed another traitor since then, on the instructions of the prime minister. His loyalty is not in doubt. At the highest levels."

The colonel didn't say anything for a while. "Yes, he told his wife he was going to Switzerland, when he shouldn't have done. Another black mark." A pause. "Brigadier, you are ultimately responsible for this audit of the war. It would be . . . disastrous if the main author of that audit turned out to be . . . well, a traitor. Are you quite happy with this man?"

"Yes," said Malahyde quietly. "I am. I have no doubts."

Another silence. Then: "Very well, sir. Since you vouch for him, I will take no further action. A report of the matter will, however, remain on his file—is that clear?"

I nodded.

"Please," he said, getting up, "the Official Secrets Act means what it says. Wives and girlfriends are off-limits. It would be embarrassing— worse than embarrassing, much worse—if you were caught again."

I nodded and he left.

The brigadier walked with me back to my office. "I once told my wife something I shouldn't have."

I looked at him. "And?"

"She comes from a very old, diplomatic family—ambassadors, private secretaries, that sort of thing. Used to running the country. She said that if I did it again, she'd divorce me." His eyes twinkled. "It was very tempting."

After its summer break, Miss Allardyce's school got going again in September. In the second week, the headmistress held a cocktail party to meet all the parents. Because the school didn't accept children until they were three, Will hadn't been able to attend until the spring, so we had been ineligible for the party the year before.

The school, when we reached it, was in reality little more than a four-story house with large gardens front and back. The front garden looked directly onto the road: Queensgate.

Parents and children were scattered all over the house. Sherry and beer were offered, plus lemonade and, of course, water. Sam had a sherry; I stuck to beer. In the course of meeting several sets of fellow parents, I lost sight of both Will and Sam and was surprised when a small, wiry, and very energetic gray-haired woman buttonholed me. I guessed she was Miss Allardyce herself.

She was wearing a woolen three-piece with a set of expensive-looking pearls at her neck. Were we paying too much in fees, I wondered.

"You must be Mr. Ross," she virtually shouted at me, fixing me with the sort of stare a teacher reserves for a miscreant child.

I hadn't a clue what she was talking about and was about to deny it when I saw movement off to my left as Sam's head jerked round in my direction. She had heard Miss Allardyce and knew what she meant before I did. Sam came toward us.

"Er . . . yes," I muttered eventually. "That's right." It had been so long since we had used Sam's maiden name that I had all but forgotten it.

Sam joined us.

"He's a bright boy, your Will," Miss Allardyce said. "I can see the family resemblance," she added, looking at me. "He's a natural leader, you know. The army would suit him very well as a career."

"Don't you think it's a little early?" I said as forcefully as I could without sounding rude. "He's only three and a bit."

"Yes, but you can always encourage the little ones. They never forget what they learn early on." And she was gone; there were other parents to meet.

Sam looked at me. "I'm sorry," she whispered. "I should have warned you. When I brought him here, to register, I never thought . . . I thought it might burden you if I used your name."

"You'd better make up your mind soon," I replied sourly. "His name is going to mean a lot to him before long. You'd better decide what it is." And I walked off.

But not far. There was a commotion in the front garden. The children were crowding by the fence, with some of the parents standing not far off. It soon became clear what they were looking at. Some grenadiers were marching in the road, the scarlet stripes down their gray trousers very vivid in the sunshine. As they drew abreast of the school, and with a stylish flourish, the sergeant major at the front of the men suddenly barked out, "Eyes right!"

As one, the soldiers turned their heads to acknowledge the schoolchildren.

Some of the boys, impressed by this, uncertainly saluted back to the men. Will was one of them.

"Eyes front!" The grenadiers marched on and out of sight.

I turned. Sam was standing behind Will. She looked at me, mouthed that she was going home, and pulled down Will's arm, the one that was saluting, so that she could lead him away.

> *Dearest Hal,*
>
> *News of an "incident." An incident that would make a good report in my new "career" as a journalist (I still haven't told Alan).*
>
> *We were working well behind the lines the other day, in a lull in the fighting, taking the opportunity to clean our kit and do other maintenance jobs, when a Frenchman appeared. He was in his thirties and told us he was a doctor from the nearby village of A. How he had evaded our security system I don't know, but he had. He was in a state. He said that his wife had just given birth a short while before and that she had hemorrhaged and lost a lot of blood—could we help? He had obviously heard something about blood transfusion and our unit, but at that moment the military police turned up, together with the local commanding officer. They arrested the doctor—or at least they tried to. As they moved toward him, to take hold of him, he pulled out a gun—a pistol. Standoff. In no time at all, there we were in a small tableau: the doctor pointing his gun at Alan, and the military police, three of them, pointing their guns at the Frenchman.*
>
> *The commanding officer said we couldn't let him have any blood—it was reserved for military use. The doctor replied that we were in France and that we were all fighting to preserve France and the French way of life, that we were guests in his country, and allies. However, I am making it sound all rather more polite than it actually was—the exchange was very heated. Alan let it go on for a while, until the argument had more or less run its course, then said that he sided with the doctor, that there was a lull in the fighting and that two or three pints of blood would not affect the war effort one way or the other.*

He then took some bottles of blood and stepped in front of the doctor, so he was acting as a human shield. He said that he was going to leave, with the doctor, and walk to A. if need be, to help with the transfusion. He was a doctor, he said, and if he could save this woman's life he would.

It was very dramatic. Alan and the Frenchman walked past the three guns and on toward the village. No one did anything to stop them. I ran after them and the three of us hurried unchallenged into A.

When we got there, the woman was dead. She had bled to death while we were arguing. The baby, a boy, amazingly, was alive but there was nothing we could do for the mother. We did what we could to console the doctor, who was also the father, of course. Then Alan and I returned the way we had come.

When we were a few hundred yards from the village we heard two shots. You can guess the pitiful truth: the doctor had killed himself and the baby.

So now we have made enemies of the local villagers.

When people think that wars are black-and-white things, that there is good on one side only and bad on the other side, how wrong they are. War throws up these confused situations in profusion. I was proud of Alan, that he did what he did, but it took it out of him. He has been on at me, saying we should get married. The romantic in him says that a marriage in wartime, at the Front, would be something very poignant. I tell him no. I want to get married in our tiny church in Edgewater, with my parents there and my lovely brother, with lots of flowers, masses of hymns, and our mother's sisters in their awful frocks. Weren't you sweet on one of the vicar's daughters at one stage? I remember you always used to go bright pink whenever she was near. Maybe you didn't notice but the rest of us did!!

Speaking of Ma, I also think, secretly, that having a wedding in Edgewater will give her something to hold out for—I hope so anyway.

*She wrote me a rather tough letter the other day, asking if I felt any
responsibility for the death of Alan's wife. All I can say is that I was to
blame at some level, but I never wanted Alan to tell his wife about us;
he didn't need to, not yet anyway. I will have to meet the children at
some stage, I expect, and that won't be easy. But an Edgewater wedding
is what I think about most now. With the Germans on one side, and
now the hostile villagers of A. on the other, I badly need to get back to
the peace and friendliness of home.*

*But . . . the war is almost over, or it looks like it. What a time it has
been for all of us. I now see why our side is called the "Allies." Will we
still be friends when the peace comes?*

This is <u>far</u> too serious for a letter.

Who do you think I should choose as bridesmaids?

Huge love: xxxooo

Izzy

"You've got a letter." Nadia, my assistant, was standing over me, a
cup of coffee in one hand, an envelope in the other.

"You make it sound unusual."

"This one is. It's not internal; it's from the great unwashed public."

I saw what she meant. Being in a top-secret unit, we got all our
post from other departments of government—the few departments
that knew we existed—and it arrived via the internal, civil service,
Whitehall-based postal service. The envelope Nadia was holding was
white rather than brown, had what looked like a normal postmark and
stamp, and had been slit open by the censor.

"If it got through the censor, it can't be very important," I said. I
held out my hand and she passed it to me.

I slid my finger into the envelope and took out what was inside. I
looked at the signature first: it was from Lottie. Why was she writing
to me, and why was she writing to me *here*?

I took the cup of coffee that Nadia had made me and settled down with the letter. Its thrust was, as she put it partway through, a "double olive branch." The first item of news was that Faye was getting married. Being Faye, it was a whirlwind romance, with an actor she had met through, of all people, Lottie; the two sisters were friends again. Faye had seen Sam and me at Ruth's engagement party, felt ill at ease in not talking to us, and wanted to resume "normal relations," as Lottie put it. Therefore, we were invited to Faye's wedding, to be held at St. Martin-in-the-Fields three weeks hence; afterward there would be a party on the stage of the theater where her actor fiancé was appearing. Faye wasn't sure what reception she would receive if she approached Sam directly, so she had asked Lottie to intervene with me.

At the same time, Lottie said, she was offering an olive branch of her own. She was sorry, she wrote, for the things she had said outside our flat that day when Sam had not allowed her in. She was sorry, she said, because they weren't true; she'd just been "hitting out" at Sam because Sam wouldn't forgive her.

"Some of what I said was true," she wrote. "Like the fact that, yes, I always did have a soft spot for you and, had we met under different circumstances, what fun we might have had. But I had no right to say what I said about Sam. Of course, I do know her better than you—at least, I have known her far longer. But she never discussed you and your life together with me, and I <u>never</u> asked, please believe that, Hal. I said what I said out of spite and I am sorry and ashamed and, for the second time, ask you to forgive me. I hope I will see you at the wedding."

I sat, sipping my coffee and rereading Lottie's letter. The business with Faye's wedding posed no problems. Sam would either agree to go or she wouldn't. The rest of the letter, however, was far from straightforward and posed as many problems as it attempted to solve. First off, did I believe Lottie? Had she undergone a genuine change of heart, and was what she was saying now a truer version of events than what she had told me—in a heated exchange—outside Penrith Mansions? If so, why had she changed her tune, and why now? I had no idea. I did know that part of her letter was demonstrably untrue. Sam had discussed our life together with her sisters, because I had overheard them the night Will couldn't sleep, after the party for Reg. Second, what was I going to say to Sam? If I said that I had received a letter from Lottie at the office, she would think that very odd and she would want to see it, and I didn't want that. But if I didn't show her the letter, how had I come by the information that Faye was to be married and that we were invited? I couldn't duck that.

Lottie had landed me in it.

As the week went on, I couldn't decide what to do. On Thursday, Sam said, "Will's playing in a school football game on Saturday. He wants you to take him and to stay and watch. I have things to do. Do you mind?"

"Of course not," I said.

But the very next day, when I came home in the evening, after she had poured me a whisky, Sam took me to one side, away from Will. "Saturday's game is off."

"Why? What happened?"

"Oh, Hal. I went to see the headmistress, Miss Allardyce herself. It's the first time Will's been selected and they type out the team sheets for these games and post them on the school notice board. Knowing that, I said to the headmistress that Will's name wasn't Ross but Montgomery. She asked me how that could be—and I told her. That we aren't married, I mean."

Sam looked at me. "She was shocked. Shocked and very upset. Spitting fire. She said I had cheated and she's asked me to take Will out of the school." Sam was close to tears. "I feel so wretched—it's all my fault, and Will is going to be devastated." She looked distraught.

I thought for a bit. "The game is the easy part. I'll take him to a proper game—you know, at Woolwich Arsenal or Tottenham. He'll be thrilled and that will take his mind off what was going to happen."

"Oh, Hal, you *will*?"

"As I said, that's the easy part. How are you going to explain changing schools—and what are you going to tell the next one?"

She came across and sat on my lap. "Ellen Smith, at school, will help me find somewhere else." She handed me the whisky. "She knows about us. I'll tell the new school we're married, of course. I can't put Will through this again—or you."

While I was still mulling over what to do about Faye's invitation, I was let off the hook. On the Monday morning of the following week, in the post at Penrith Mansions, there arrived a printed invitation to Faye's wedding, plus a note from her begging forgiveness and asking if Sam would allow Will to be a page boy. Faye added that Ruth would be making her wedding dress, those of the two bridesmaids, and Will's outfit.

I was delighted by this turn of events. "It's an olive branch," I said over breakfast that morning, "the perfect way for you all to get back together again."

Sam felt differently. "No," she growled. "Not under any circumstances. Not after the way Faye behaved toward you, and the way Ruth behaved toward you."

"Sam!" I said. "Don't be silly. You can't do this. They are your sisters, your family, your blood."

"Blood!" she almost screamed. "Don't talk to me about blood. My father was flesh and blood, and look how he behaved. Sir Mortimer Stannard wasn't flesh and blood and he was always much more decent to my sisters and me than our father ever was. You've been better for Will than any of my sisters ever have." She finished her tea and put the cup and saucer in the sink. "So don't tell me blood counts for *anything!* Hal, how many times do I have to tell you: *you* are my family now, *you* are Will's father, it's *you* I am with. My sisters know they've done wrong, done wrong by Will, by you, and by me, and they are trying to . . . trying to slide out of it."

"Meet them halfway, Sam. They have made the first move—"

"And the last move, so far as I am concerned. Will is not being anybody's page boy, not for now. Faye's marriage won't last, anyway. You know what she's like."

I let a pause elapse. "If you really think I'm Will's father now, I say we should meet Faye halfway."

Sam looked at me. Her features were set. "No."

At the end of October my mother died. It was scarely a surprise but it would come hard on Izzy, I thought, upsetting—devastating—her wedding plans. Ma died on a Thursday. This was fortunate in one way: it meant that my father's telegram announcing the news reached us on Friday and we were able to get the vicar's daughter to look after Will for the entire weekend.

It was a gray morning as we boarded the train at Paddington down to Edgewater. Both of us were in a mood to match the weather but, in a funny way, Sam took the death of my mother harder than I did. I knew my mother as an unsentimental person, someone who held her emotions inside, and I was much the same. Sam, on the other hand, had thoroughly enjoyed her first visit to Edgewater, she looked upon my parents as a new family, and the prospect of a second visit in very different circumstances did not sit well with her.

The train was fairly empty and we had a carriage to ourselves. We talked about all sorts of things and Sam raised the business of my meeting with Colonel Moore and the brigadier.

"I dropped you in it, didn't I?" she said. "I gave away too much in my fight with Ruth. After all you've done for me and my family, this is how I repay you. I'm so sorry."

The train was passing some reservoirs. We could see men training to be divers.

"I've thought about that myself, from time to time. How did the subject crop up in the first place?"

"Oh, I said that Lottie had helped catch a spy and that Ruth and Greville had no business shopping her man. That Lottie had been as useful to the war effort as Ruth has, and that letting you take the blame in Lottie's eyes was despicable. One thing led to another and Greville was listening in. What a pig he is."

She leaned forward and touched my hand. "I'm sorry."

I lifted her hand and kissed it. "No harm done. I was just rapped across the knuckles and told not to do it again. Anyway, the war's nearly over. Not much chance now."

"Yes," she said after a moment. "The war *is* nearly over. And when it is over, Hal, would you mind—would you mind very much—if I tried my hand at something other than teaching?"

I stared at her. I couldn't think what to say for a moment or two. First Izzy wanted out of nursing, and now Sam wanted a change too.

"Do you have something in mind?"

She nodded. She went to speak but the train rattled over some points and she held off till we were back on smoother rails.

"Haven't you noticed how interested I've become in psychology?"

I thought. "My birthday present, that Swiss chap and the unconscious."

"Jung. Yes. But before that the lecture by the psychiatrist from Edinburgh, and before that I suppose I first got interested in the different ways the war has affected families, especially the children."

"And where does all that lead?"

"Well, first I'd like to do a course on psychology—"

"You want to be a psychiatrist?"

"Nnno . . . that would mean six years of medical training, more. But there's a one-year course on psychology that I can do at London University. That will tell me whether I'm cut out for it, and it will also show me what sort of jobs are—or might be—available."

"What sort of job do you want?"

We rattled over a bridge and the noise of the train deepened for a moment.

"Trying to help people, I think, in a more personal, more technical way than teaching. Helping children who have been disturbed by the war, lost fathers, been totally orphaned in some cases."

I told her about Izzy's change of heart over nursing. "She finds it too much, too overwhelming. You might find the same."

"Oh no, Hal. Your sister's been in a war, blood and death and horror for twenty-four hours a day, seven days a week, for more than three years. What I want to do—well, what I *think* I want to do—is nothing like that. And there's going to be a need for it after the war."

Another train went past, going in the opposite direction. The smell of smoke was briefly intense.

"Well, I don't have any objection if that's what you really want to do. I just hope all the grief you'll encounter doesn't get you down."

"I've got you to keep me on an even keel," she said softly, reaching out for my hand and kissing it.

We dozed for a bit then, even though it was morning, lulled by the swaying of the carriage. Later, as we were pulling out of High Wycombe station—the railway tracks lined with beech trees—she asked, "Are you nervous? How will your father have taken it?"

"Stoically, I am sure, in the Montgomery family tradition." I shook my head. "No, I take that back. Mother, Father, and I are stoics. Izzy isn't—she's the opposite. It shines out in her letters. Her bubbliness makes up for the rest of us."

As the train headed west, the weather deteriorated. We went through a cloudburst near Lechlade but by the time we reached Chalford, where we got off, it had stopped. I had wired Dad which train we would be on and he'd sent the car, driven by old Dr. Barnaby's son, Trevor, who did odd jobs while he waited to go to Cambridge after the war.

The boy had the understanding to make himself scarce when we reached the house, though at first we couldn't find my father. We shouted and shouted until Sam suddenly cried out, "There he is, in the garden, on your mother's favorite bench."

"Father!" I called out softly as we stepped into the garden. Now that we had arrived, I *was* a bit nervous. He didn't move but sat hunched on the bench.

As I approached I could see that he was weeping. I was alarmed. Such a display of feeling was surprising, to say the least, and most unlike my father. I immediately sat next to him and put my arm around him. That was most unlike me.

But he didn't flinch. Instead, his frame continued to shake softly as he sobbed and tears ran down his cheeks. I was disconcerted.

I noticed Sam scrabbling in the gravel under the bench and then she was holding a piece of paper. I paid no attention.

I took out a handkerchief and handed it to my father. He accepted it but just held it in his fist, in a ball.

Sam held the piece of paper out to me. "Hal."

I glared at her and shook my head. "Not now," I whispered. "Dry your tears, Father. Let's go in. It will rain again soon. You'll catch a chill."

"Hal, read this. *Now!*" Sam still had the paper before my eyes. I glared at her again but then noticed that the piece of paper was a telegram. I snatched at it with one hand and scanned the lines:

+ REGRET • TO • INFORM • YOU • SENIOR • STAFF • NURSE • ISOBEL •
ELIZABETH•MONTGOMERY•DIED•TODAY•OF•SHRAPNEL•WOUNDS
• RECEIVED • IN • ACTION•EARLIER • THIS • WEEK + STOP + LETTER
•FOLLOWS + STOP + ALAN • MACGREGOR + SURGEON • COMMAND-
ING + STOP +

I have never cried before or since. Yes, as a child when I fell out of a tree, or crashed my bicycle. But not for long and never, never as an adult, except then. My father and I sat together on Mother's favorite bench, weeping. My lovely sister, a bundle of bossiness, my lieutenant in so many adventures, the one person who could talk to me in total candor, who could be embarrassingly honest *and get away with it,* was no more. Was dead. I would never see her again. I would receive no more letters from her. Those outraged exclamation marks and breathless underlinings were gone forever. Her lovely languid brown eyes, her button of a nose were now just a memory. No more dinners with her. I would never again taste the envious glances of men who thought I was her lover. I now had no chance of meeting her flatmates. No wedding, no nieces and nephews. No chance to mix her her beloved G&Ts. She would never meet Sam or Will or Whisky. They would never meet her.

How I hated the Germans.

Sam, I think, went into the house, ostensibly to make some tea or to pour some whisky, but in reality to leave us alone.

I had been prepared for the death of my mother. I had hoped she would live for Izzy's wedding, but neither she nor my father nor I had any illusions about where emphysema would lead, and in taking Sam down to Edgewater on our previous visit, I had known, as my mother had known, that we were acknowledging the beginning of the end. It had been a suitable gesture and had, I think, made it easier for my mother as she faced oblivion.

But this . . . Izzy's death, Izzy's too premature, tragic, and violent death . . . I wasn't prepared and had no mechanism to cope. Since the depression I had endured after my injury at the Front, I had done well, I thought; I had handled what had been thrown at me, both professionally and personally, and had come out pretty much on top.

But not this time.

I was wrecked.

How I hated the Germans.

I don't really remember what happened during the rest of that day. I think that Sam had Trevor fetch old Dr. Barnaby, and he may have given both my father and me a sedative. Or we may just have drunk endless bottles of whisky. I don't remember.

I, we, got through that day, and the Sunday afterward. Like most doctors, as I think I said, Liam had been equipped with a telephone, and I was able to call the office on Monday morning from his surgery and speak to Malahyde. The brigadier was understanding, more than understanding. He gave me the week off and used his authority to ensure that Izzy's remains were sent on to us immediately.

Alan MacGregor was as good as his word. A letter was hand-delivered on Tuesday. MacGregor told us that Izzy had been gassed—mustard gas, the gas developed by Fritz Haber at his institute in

Berlin. Little had I known, when I'd first made the connection, that it would have such devastating personal consequences for me. I later learned that, in the course of the war, mustard gas killed some 135,000 Allied soldiers. But it didn't kill Isobel. It burned her and blinded her, as it has burned and blinded so many, and in her distress she blundered around and took shrapnel in her head from an exploding shell. She was invalided home but died on the way, at Ashford in Kent.

At least the circumstances of Izzy's death meant that she wasn't buried in France, or Flanders. Thanks to the brigadier, her remains reached us on Wednesday.

Sam had gone back to London on Sunday. She had to look after Will. But she returned for the funeral.

When my father and I could bring ourselves to face up to the dreadful truth, sometime on Sunday, we decided that a joint cremation would be seemly. And so, on Friday, we held a funeral in two parts. First, there was a ceremony at our local church at Edgewater, the church where the previous vicar had five daughters, when I was a boy, one of whom caused such a scandal. The church where Izzy had hoped to be married.

Sam had managed to leave Will with the wife of the vicar in Old Church Street, who, when it came to it, helped us out in our hour of need. My mother's two sisters came, as did a few friends. Alan MacGregor did not come. No doubt he was back at the Front. He, poor man, had lost both of the women in his life. The church ceremony was well attended by all the locals, all the traditional hymns were sung, and I paid for a chorister to come from Gloucester Cathedral to sing Handel's "Let Me Weep." My father didn't object—he was too grief-stricken—and he agreed it matched our mood perfectly.

But there was no wake. A small group of us then went on to Stroud, where there was a crematorium. After that, my father, Sam, and I went back home, where we left him alone to do as he wished with my mother's ashes.

I knew what I wanted to do with Izzy's remains, and my father agreed. I took Sam with me. We turned left out of the house, right just past the church, and walked down a rutted lane until we reached a barn, beyond which a field rose to a small copse of trees.

"Remember the bull?" I said. "This is where he was kept." The field now looked as though it was sown to potatoes, more useful for the war effort. I took Sam forward, to the iron fence that marked one edge of the field. It was now all overgrown but we found the kissing gate that had featured in the great game of "Bullrush," and let ourselves through. I walked round in a circle, spreading Izzy's ashes on the ground. "This would have appealed to her," I said. "Outlasting the bull."

We just stood for a while, without speaking, looking at the field, feeling the breeze, listening to the birds, brushing off the insects that landed on us. Izzy's ashes had already all but disappeared. It might not be a family grave but she was home.

Though I was sad that day, sadder, I think, than I had ever been, I was also angry, still choked with loathing for the Germans. Handel had made that lovely music but it had been a long time ago, and what had the current crop of Germans done—produce ever more deadly forms of gas, zeppelin sky bombs, and torpedoes. Faye was right— how could Sam have fallen in love with a German? How could she, after all these years, after all that had happened, after her own family, and now mine, had been devastated, how could she still hold fast to Wilhelm? She didn't mention him much now but he was there, he was there, in our minds, filling our thoughts, like a mine buried but not too deeply, ready to explode and destroy all around it with one false step. My mother's death, Izzy's death, the funeral, seeing my own father weep for the first time . . . none of that made me depressed the way I had been all those months and years before; instead I was fired up, burning with loathing, bristling with contempt, gorged on a hot rage—and part of me, I could admit it now, was angry with Sam. I never thought I'd feel that. I was angry, livid, that she still felt . . . whatever she felt for Wilhelm. Whatever she felt, it was too much, it was *wrong*, he was the enemy, he bore some responsibility, some blame, for what we had been through. I had to tell her that, and at the same time she should know what I had done, how I had deceived her . . . but also how I had *delivered* her from the limbo, the no-man's-land, the *wilderness* she would have inhabited for the rest of her life, had I not come along. The play had gone on for long enough. It was time she was told. I would sit her down at home, this very afternoon, in Izzy's room, a room Izzy would never return to, and let Sam know what I had done, how I had tried to steal her love, so she could decide where to go next. I didn't care anymore.

I took one last look at the field where Izzy's ashes were now part of the landscape. I wouldn't be coming back.

I led the way back to the gate and then let Sam go first.

She stepped into the angle but then blocked my way by holding the gate firm.

"Those are beech trees over there, right?"

I nodded.

"Is that where the badgers live, where the bluebells grow in spring?"

I nodded. "And the foxes."

"Is this the time of year for the Severn Bore?"

"You remember that?" I was surprised. "I don't know."

"I remember everything," she said, reaching out and stroking the lapel of my blazer. She leaned forward and laid her head on my shoulder. "And I remember telling you, back on the platform of the station in Middle Hill, just after you had been promoted to the war ministry, that I didn't love you. I said I didn't love you but that I might learn to love you."

She kissed my shoulder. "I didn't believe myself when I said those things and I've always felt guilty about saying them. Everyone I've ever liked—you know, in that way—I've liked right off, right from the start." She raised my hand to her lips and kissed it. "Well . . . I was wrong." She lifted her head from my shoulder and looked up at me. "I have learned to love you, Hal."

She took a deep breath.

"So much has happened to us. Because of the war I've fallen out with all of my sisters, one by one. Two of them have lost their men. You've lost a sister." She took another breath. "I didn't hate the Germans, not to begin with—and I know you felt the same way."

She licked her lips with her tongue.

"But now, after all the pain, all the blood, all the turmoil . . . it's hard not to let some . . . bitterness creep into your heart."

I nodded. She was right. Isobel had never harmed anyone.

"And I've been thinking about Will. Does he really have to know who his father is? There's so much hate now, everywhere . . . it will always be hard for him, once he knows the truth. He thinks *you're* his father. He adores you. Why can't it stay that way?"

She climbed onto one of the iron rungs of the gate, so that her face was level with mine. "I know that when I mention Wilhelm, Hal, it hurts you, so I'm going to mention him one more time—and then never again. He asked me to marry him at a gate just like this. The one by the river at Stratford, where you and I once walked. He loved these kissing gates—they don't have them in Germany—I think I told you that. He said he had me trapped, just like I have you trapped now. He said he wouldn't let me go until I gave him an answer. I never hid Wilhelm from you, Hal, but maybe I hid the depths of my feelings, when we first met. In a way you came into my life too soon after Wilhelm. There were times, early in the war, when . . . when I hoped our side would collapse, just so I could have Wilhelm back. How terrible is that?"

She brushed wisps of hair from her face. "But he's been gone years now. You've been wonderful to me, and to Will, and to my sisters. We can't go on living in this halfway world, not being married, holding back at least some of the time, waiting . . . Waiting's not living."

She smiled. "We've been here before, you know."

"We have? I don't— What do you mean?"

"Remember that day on the platform in Middle Hill station, amid all the steam and clanking signals? I told you that if I was going with you, to London, I had to say so before the school board met, before I found out what their verdict was; I had to *choose* to be with you . . ."

I remembered but I didn't say anything.

"It's the same now. What I'm going to say, I need to say before the war is over, before I find out, one way or the other . . . whether Wilhelm's alive, whether . . . what his feelings are . . . I need to *choose*, to decide, all by myself."

She took off her Alice band, threw it away, and let her hair hang loose. "So, here on this gate, this is the best way I can think of to prove to you that I mean what I am about to say." She kissed my hand again and stroked the lapel of my blazer. "You said, that day in the cricket field when you asked me to come to London with you, that we were both trapped. You meant it in a different way to Wilhelm but you were right and . . . and that played its part in persuading me to go with you. But I don't feel trapped anymore." She raised herself onto her toes, on the iron rung of the gate, and kissed me on the lips. "If you still want to marry me, Hal, dearest Hal, the answer is yes."

The wind blew her hair across her face. I could smell Will's smell on her.

All my anger had gone.

"You're not just feeling sorry for me?" I kissed her hair. "All this grief."

She didn't move, other than to shake her head. "You saved Will's life. That's when . . . I think I've loved you since then."

She turned her head to mine and we began kissing. I kissed her lips, her cheeks, her neck. Our tongues interlocked. I whispered, "Look, Sam, I'm flattered and honored by your offer, but the war will be over soon. If you want to wait for six months, in case—"

She put a finger to my lips. "*Shhh.* You haven't been listening to what I'm saying." She brushed my cheek with her fingers. "It's you I love now. Will's always loved you. It took me a whole war."

She stepped back, so I could go through the gate. "Now come on, let's not leave your father by himself anymore."

One thing I was wrong about. When we returned to Penrith Mansions from the funeral, there was a letter waiting for me—from Izzy.

Dear Hal,

Strange times. Now that the war is nearly over, men are taking fewer risks, officers are sending fewer men into exposed positions. Result: our workload has lightened. Not by huge amounts but significantly. Some sanity in the world at last.

Now, I'm going to set you a challenge. You've been in London for a few years so you must know what the best restaurant is. I know there's been rationing and fantastic shortages but even so there is bound to be a place that everyone swears by. Somewhere with a piano bar and plenty of gin, where the slimmest women and the tallest men go. And I want you to take me there. I can't wait to get out of this uniform.

Once I had admitted to myself, after weeks of denying it, that I had

had enough of nursing, I felt released. I really do want to be a
journalist—I'm sure that writing can be just as noble a calling as
nursing, and just as satisfying. Alan doesn't mind, amazingly. He said
I could always write about medical stuff but I told him no: it's all up
with me and blood. I want to write about anything <u>but</u> blood. Which
will look best in print, do you think, Isobel Montgomery or Isobel
MacGregor?

Huge love

Izzy

As it happened, Sam and I didn't have time to get married just then. Izzy's death and my mother's were too close to do anything immediately, and then events—and what events—intervened. Later that week, less than a fortnight after Izzy's death, the Armistice was signed. No sooner was that done than plans were announced for a peace conference to be held in Paris in early 1919. Before that, however, there was a preconference conference in London, and the brigadier and I were fully involved in that. My *Moral Cost of the War*, as it had been retitled, was released at the same time. It created quite a stir.

On 14 December, the female emancipation bill was published. Things really were going to be different now that the war was over. Izzy would miss all that.

Sam and I did travel down to Edgewater to be with Dad on his first Christmas alone, and this time we had Will and Whisky with us. My father took to the boy immediately. Moreover, Will loved the rambling old house. Physically, Will was quite recovered from his fairground injury but psychologically he had lost a good deal of his curiosity. In fact, that's where my father's house was perfect for him. It was so much bigger than the London flat and, over the few days we were there, Will expanded his horizons, but within familiar territory. He and Whisky took to Einstein, and Einstein, still perplexed by my mother's sudden disappearance, was grateful for the company. The three of them did everything together. They also took my father for long rambles across the wolds, which Will also loved. Although he had been born in Warwickshire, all his memories were of London, and the beech woods and streams of the Cotswolds were a new world. I think my father needed those rambles as well.

He and Will would come back with birds' eggs, shards of terracotta—the remains of pots found near a Roman villa in the vicinity—and stories of monks they had seen in the nearby monastery. One day Will came back and announced proudly, "I had beer."

"What?" gasped Sam.

Dad chortled. "Don't worry. He had one sip. So did Einstein."

Over Christmas lunch Dad made an announcement. He said that he had decided to give up the house. Some years previously, he said, he had bought a cottage elsewhere in the village. It had been intended for my mother, assuming that Dad would go first.

He looked at me, at us, really. "Do you want the house? It's yours, if you do. Otherwise, I'll sell it. You'll get the money, of course, in time."

Neither Sam nor I knew what to say, but Will did.

"You mean we can live here always? With Whisky and Einstein?" His eyes were rounder than ever.

I could see that Sam, although she didn't say anything, was taken with the idea, but I didn't push it.

"You'll need weeks—months—to dispose of all your junk, Dad. We'll try the idea on for size."

"I've already got rid of most of your mother's things," he said sadly. "I'd have done more, but this official history of the war is taking up quite a bit of my time just now. I'm just about to start on Izzy's belongings—will you help me with the books, at least, while you're here?"

I nodded, but in the event I didn't. My leave was cut short by a telegram and, two days after Christmas, I was ordered to Paris, where I was to form part of the team preparing for the peace conference. I couldn't say no: after my brief stint at the Front and my rescue from the Stratford backwaters by Colonel Pritchard, the peace conference would be the crowning achievement of my wartime career.

Peace

FOR SIX MONTHS AT THE BEGINNING OF 1919, Paris was the center of the world. More than eight million soldiers had been killed in the war and now hundreds of politicians, diplomats, bankers, professors, economists, lawyers, and journalists came to Paris to try to fashion a lasting peace.

There were statesmen from many nations—more than thirty countries sent delegations—but the real work was done by what came to be called the Big Four: France, Britain, Italy, and the United States. The British staff alone consisted of four hundred people. It was an extraordinary time: new borders were drawn throughout central Europe and the Middle East, and there was, to begin with, a sense that all was now possible. By the second week of January, all delegations were in Paris.

Paris: beautiful and sad at the same time. There had been a lot of rain and the Seine was in flood. People were mournful for the sons and lovers they had lost; half the people wore black, while the other half, mainly the women, did their best to look elegant, *chic.* There was a gaping crater in the Tuileries rose garden and a captured German cannon on display in the Place de la Concorde. Along the grand boulevards there were gaps in the rows of chestnut trees, where some had been cut down for firewood. Coal, milk, and bread were in short supply.

We had very little time off in the early weeks but we did have a spring break for a month while President Wilson went back to America to try to persuade Congress to be more accommodating to his idea for a League of Nations. During this break I—like everyone else on the delegation—was allowed to bring my family, Sam and Will, to Paris for a few days before the conference restarted.

Our delegation occupied five hotels in Paris, all near the Arc de Triomphe, and centered on the Majestic, where I was billeted. However, security was tight; our own Scotland Yard people were on the doors and our own kitchen staff cooked the food. Wives and girl-friends weren't allowed to stay in the official hotels, so while Sam and Will were in town (Whisky was living with Einstein now) I moved out, to the Hôtel de Sèvres, near the Invalides, so we could all be together. The German delegation had not been allowed at the peace conference proper, but was expected in town any day now, to be presented with the Allies' demands.

By then, Paris was humming. There was more in the shops, the weather had turned cold but the races at Saint-Cloud had got going again, *La Bohème* was playing at the Opéra, and Sarah Bernhardt appeared for a charity gala. In the bars the new American cocktails were becoming all the rage, and the Majestic Hotel even held poetry readings. The dances at the Majestic also became notorious, featuring the tango and the brand-new fox-trot. Tours were organized to the battlefields, where German helmets and empty shell cases could still be found, as souvenirs.

The visit by Sam and Will should have been a golden few days, and in many ways it was. Sam was traveling at last, at long last. We tired ourselves out—at the Louvre, the Eiffel Tower, the ruins of the Tuileries, Sacré-Coeur, Les Halles. We boated on the Seine, tried exotic French foods, gave a sip of French beer to Will (he made a face but pretended to like it), and even risked a fun fair, though I kept a firm hold of him at all times. We found a babysitter one night and I took Sam to Larue's, a rather risqué nightclub.

Toward the end of their stay, we also had a day out at Versailles.

By now I knew my way around the palace, its great gardens and lakes. Sam seemed to enjoy it but it was all a bit much for Will. After a couple of hours, we went in search of a café, to have lunch, and on the way we came across a large crowd of people just standing in the road. They all seemed to be staring at one building, which I knew as the Hôtel des Réservoirs. When I asked what was happening, we were told that the people were hoping to catch a glimpse of the enemy. The Hôtel des Réservoirs was where the German delegation was staying— it had arrived the day before.

I hoisted Will onto my shoulders for a better view but neither he nor I saw anything. Inside the hotel the Germans could see out, but we couldn't see in.

We didn't stay long. Will was wilting (he liked that word; he thought it had been coined with him in mind) and we found somewhere for lunch.

I have to say, though, that I sensed a change in Sam during those days in Paris. It was difficult to put my finger on. It crossed my mind that, after all her *talk* of travel, the real thing, the real Paris, was a disappointment. But I dismissed that. She wasn't cold exactly, or distant, nothing so specific. But, undoubtedly, some of the intimacy had gone out of our relationship. She now preferred to read to Will herself rather than have me do it. She never once mentioned her new interest in psychology. Maybe I was being touchy—I *had* been away in Paris for a couple of months, after all. But still . . .

She did, however, bring me a precious—an intimate—gift. It was a notebook, a journal, the journal written by Izzy.

"Your father found this, in the box of things the Medical Corps returned after . . . after she was killed. He says it's quite well written and, if suitably edited—by you, perhaps—could be offered to the old family firm. He thinks there'll be quite a market for this sort of thing, now that the war is over."

I accepted it gratefully. Remembering Izzy's letters, I looked forward to reading it. Her memoirs would be vivid, funny, compassionate. She shouldn't have kept it, of course—there were rules about that sort of thing—but then that was Izzy all over.

The day after the trip to Versailles, I saw Sam and Will off, back to England, from the Gare du Nord. One of the privileges of my position meant that they had good seats in a first-class compartment. I helped Will up into the carriage and kissed his forehead. I turned and leaned forward to kiss Sam. In a movement that was the complete reverse of an earlier moment, she turned her head at the last second so that, instead of kissing her lips, I kissed her cheek.

She looked me in the eye but I couldn't fathom her expression. "Will you write to your father about Isobel's manuscript?" she said.

"I will, but it may take some time. Now that the German delegation is in town the hard bargaining begins and I'll be pretty tied up."

She nodded.

Whistles blew, steam hissed, a hooter sounded down the platform, and the train eased forward. Sam held Will as he leaned out of the window, waving. I waved back, waiting till the train had quite disappeared from sight.

That afternoon I moved back into the Majestic. For the next forty-eight hours I was frantically busy, helping finalize our position papers for the resumption of the last phase of the conference.

Lloyd George was in buoyant mood, despite having to cope with labor unrest at home even as great events were under way in Paris. He disdained the Foreign Office staff and preferred the use of his own people, which meant there was always plenty for us to do. I remember that one of our main problems just then was to curb the jingoistic mood among the French. We found that our allies had wired the rooms at the Hôtel des Réservoirs and always knew what the Germans were thinking. Some among the British delegation thought this was unsporting and bad form, but the full peace terms hadn't been agreed yet, only the Armistice, so who were we to complain? In a sense the war was still on.

There was also a big disagreement between us and the French about how much reparation the Germans were to be forced to pay. The French had their own war-audit unit, similar to ours, though they had concentrated on the naked financial costs of the fighting, rather than the moral costs. Their calculations of loss were much, much higher than ours and, privately, I didn't think that the Germans, much as I had come to loathe them, had a hope in hell of ever repaying what the French wanted.

No amount of money would bring Isobel back.

Normally, we broke for lunch each day around twelve-thirty, a compromise between the American and French desire to stop at twelve and the British and Italian wish to eat later. I usually had a quick sandwich, a glass of water, and a smoke and then, because we were sitting all day long during the negotiations, took a brisk walk in the Versailles gardens. There was more peace among the chestnut trees and rhododendron bushes than in the palace itself.

At the lunch break on the second day of the German session, I was walking back from the Jardin de France, admiring the façade of the Petit Trianon, when I scuffed my shoes on the gravel. There was a fountain nearby, surrounded by a circular pond with a stone rim. I stepped across to the pond, taking a handkerchief from my pocket as I did so. I rested my shoe on the stone rim and bent to wipe my toe cap. As I was doing this, the bottom half of two gray trousers appeared in my line of sight and a voice said softly, "Hal? Is that you?"

I looked up.

It was a German officer, an *Oberstleutnant*, or lieutenant colonel, the same rank as me. I recognized these things now.

I straightened up, uncomprehending at first. We'd had nothing to do with German officers yet, or at least I hadn't. They had only just arrived. How did he know my name?

Who am I fooling? Whatever my head said, my body told me straightaway. A bolt of recognition shivered down my spine.

Despite the lines on his face, the tired, liver-colored patches under his eyes, the exhausted expression, the longer but better-cut hair, the different uniform, my skin burned, my heart seemed to swell, my throat turned dry and it hurt to swallow.

Wilhelm had survived the war.

His cheeks were sunk; he didn't fill his uniform properly. He was still handsome but he had lost his dash and swagger.

But Wilhelm had survived the war.

I had read that day in Northumberland Avenue that the Saxon Regiment, his regiment, had won a drill contest. Not with Wilhelm they hadn't. He was a shadow of what he had been.

Did I salute? We had shaken hands in no-man's-land and, as he took off his cap, we did the same again.

For a moment, neither of us said anything. My blood was pulsing through my ears. The back of my neck was damp with sweat. I felt my chest would explode.

"What happened to you?" I managed to breathe in German.

He smiled and, speaking in English, said he had eventually made it to major in his regiment, then been taken up by General Ludendorff, as an adjutant on his general staff, where he had shown a talent for propaganda. In 1917, he had been seconded to the army propaganda outfit and was here, in Versailles, as liaison officer with the German press.

"And you, Hal? Did I see you limping?"

"Yes, I was shot, here——" I pointed. "It happened about a week after . . . after the truce. Hospital, convalescence, military intelligence at the war ministry, economic intelligence in Switzerland. I'm here as an expert on reparation——what the war has cost us." I made a face. "I delivered your photograph," I lied.

"Yes, I know."

"What? What do you mean? How do you know? Have you been to England already? I know you said you would, as soon as the war was over, but . . . have you seen Sam?"

He shook his head. "No, of course I haven't been to England. Like you, I'm part of our official delegation. This is my first time out of Germany for more than a year. But I have seen Sam, yes."

"You *have?* Where? When?"

"Three days ago, when all three of you stood outside the Hôtel des Réservoirs, where our delegation is staying. I was inside. You didn't see me but I saw you, and I saw Sam."

I was flustered. Did this explain Sam's behavior while she was in Paris? It couldn't——she had been . . . changed ever since her arrival, since before she could have seen Wilhelm. "Why didn't you . . . why didn't you come out?"

He shrugged. "Be realistic. In the first place, if I had come out, I'd probably have been lynched——the crowd you were with was quite aggressive. They stood outside the hotel for the first three days, shouting at us all day long." He played with his cap; he was more nervous than he looked. "More personally, don't forget that I used to be very much in love with Sam." He swept a hand through his hair. "And, to tell you the truth, I still am, seeing her here, in beautiful Paris of all places. I had always promised to bring her here and . . . well, it was hard to bear."

Carefully, I said nothing.

"But the main reason is that you looked so complete, as a family. Your young son looked tired, sitting on your shoulders, but he looked content; so did you—and so did Sam. I couldn't . . . I couldn't interfere. It wouldn't have been right." He ran his tongue over his lips. "We are all four years older—it's nearly five since I last saw Sam. If I'd . . . if I'd introduced myself, who knows what ghosts would have been let loose?"

I couldn't believe what I was hearing. Had he not recognized the likeness between Will and himself—the eyes, the jawline? Perhaps we had been too far away.

"You don't feel . . . you don't feel I've stolen Sam from you?"

I had said it.

"Did you? Maybe you did, in a sense. But it was I who asked you to give her my message. It was a risk—you would see how beautiful she was. But it was a risk anyway—if she didn't hear from me for years, didn't know whether I was alive or dead. And she was in love— I hope she was in love; anyway, she told me she was—with someone who was now the enemy. There was a war, I could have been killed, you were there . . . life has to go on. You met her through me, you told her about me, and if she preferred the certainty you offered, the Englishness, how can I complain?"

He smiled ruefully.

"I spent a lot of the war in propaganda, devising ways to make people hate the English more and more. And I can tell you, it worked. So, perhaps, by now, Sam hates the Germans, and hates the one German she once loved, or said that she did. It would be natural."

He swallowed. This wasn't easy for him.

"I survived but at one point our unit was heavily shelled and my quarters caught fire. My tunic was burned, with Sam's photograph in it. I thought I had begun to forget what she looked like—but now I've seen her again and no, my memory was good. She was just as beautiful the other day as she was in Stratford all those years ago. And you've made her happy—I could see that. You've made a family together, and your side won." Another effort at a thin smile. "My country is ravaged by strikes, violence, revolution. That's not Sam's world at all. If I'd introduced myself the other day, if I'd risked those crowds outside the hotel, how many wounds would I have reopened, including the one in here?" He pointed to his heart. "And what would it do to that boy's life? What's his name, by the way?"

I could barely get the word out. "Will."

"After Shakespeare, naturally." He nodded, smiling again, congratulating himself on working it out. "I've often wondered whether we would meet again, and how it would be." He took a cigar from his pocket and offered it to me.

I shook my head. "I've still got one left over from the three you gave me before."

"It was something, that truce, eh?"

"Sometimes I think it's the only sane moment in the past four years. I lost my sister. Gassed."

He shook his head. "We didn't like firing those shells, you know." He paused. "But we did. My brother made it. But still, the war was better for you than for me, I think. My country is devastated—and all for nothing." He put his cigar away. "And at this conference the French will humiliate us. Already they make everything difficult. No staff in the hotel, bad food. Perhaps it is what we deserve."

What did any of us deserve, I wondered.

The garden was emptying. The afternoon session was almost ready to begin.

"Shall we meet again?" I felt I had to say it.

"No," he whispered. "Now that the horror is over, I'm not going to look back. I could, if I chose, say that I lost twice over. I was on the losing side in the fighting, and not there when Sam needed me. But I tell you, Hal, anyone who was in this war, at the sharp end, and survived . . . you can't call that losing."

His voice almost broke. "Think of the people—the parts of people—that you and I buried between us, in our short stretch of the war, on just one day." He shook his head. "I'm glad we met during the truce, I'm honored we were part of that, you and I. I don't regret it, despite what has happened. I'm comforted to know that you told Sam about me and that she made her decision. I am sad, but I am free at last. I'm pleased we met today. What you have told me has freed me." He put his cap back on and held out his hand again. "We shared a few moments of that precious truce, and now a few moments of the peace conference that will shape the world for Will and all the other children. How many can say that?"

He turned and walked away.

That encounter, and in particular my part in it, must count as the other really low point in my life. Now I had in effect betrayed Wilhelm twice: once in not giving Sam his photograph as I had promised, and a second time in not telling him of my first betrayal and not coming clean about his son.

How I got through the rest of the conference that day I don't know. As soon as it was over I rushed back to the Majestic and collapsed onto the bed. I was shattered. Naturally, I kept wondering whether Sam had seen Wilhelm in Versailles but I kept coming back to the conclusion that she couldn't have: her changed demeanor, her subtly different attitude had been there from the very first moment she arrived in Paris, well before our near encounter at the Hôtel des Réservoirs. It occurred to me that she was the way she was because she had always hoped to be introduced to Paris by him—he had said he had always planned to bring her, and maybe it had reawakened her memory. But if that was the case, then at least part of Sam had never got over him, and she had been lying to me when she said, in the field at Edgewater, on the day we scattered Izzy's ashes among the potatoes, in the field of the bull, that she had learned to love me.

Izzy. I couldn't sleep that night and so, around two A.M., I picked up my sister's journal and started to read. It was vivid—I'll give my sister credit for that. It started off, in a girlish way, as you would expect, written with more enthusiasm and élan than skill, but that changed after war broke out. I found that she could be much more acerbic about her brother on the page than in the flesh, but by then Izzy's voice came through with such painful verisimilitude that I could forgive her anything. Her reflections on the early disasters of war were original, pertinent, and often darkly funny. The journal was roughly chronological but was also full of asides, flashbacks, ruminations on things that took her fancy—how people decorated their uniforms in the trenches to mark out their individuality, the smell of the Front, the various accents, some of which were mutually incomprehensible: this was Izzy at her funniest. Some of the episodes I was familiar with already from her letters. Having been initially skeptical, I began to see what my father meant about the journal being published.

I reached an interesting section about her role as a nurse at the Front. She had of course sent me several letters in which she had described some of the horrors of what she had seen, and her multiple roles as a medical orderly, letter writer, part-time girlfriend, and confidante of the dying. But there were also some completely fresh reflections on the differences between the hospitals at the Front and those back home. I now learned that she—and my parents—had originally been misinformed about my own injuries. At first, they had been told I had lost a leg, even both legs, according to one account. She was beside herself with misery, railed against the war, and decided she would devote her life to taking care of me. Her relief when she found out that my injuries were much less serious than she'd thought was palpable, and she couldn't understand why I was so depressed when my plight could have been so much worse. She thought it a mistake that I had been brought back to England, maintaining that if I had remained in France, among men who were much worse off than me, I would have recovered more quickly and never have been brought so low.

Even here, though, I have to say, she was at times bitingly funny. Some passages needed editing but my father was right: Izzy's journal was definitely publishable. All this and God knows how many lives she had saved, how many girlfriends she had written to, trying to console the inconsolable. On the platform at Stratford that morning I had told her I was proud of her. How pleased I was now that those had been my last spoken words to her. And how pleased I was, now, that she had fallen in love with Alan. Izzy had banged on about sex during our dinner at the Crown in Stratford, but there is a world of difference between sex and love and the fact that she had experienced love before she was killed . . . I was pleased for her for that. She had told me at Stratford about this new psychiatrist ("Sigmund somebody" she had said, meaning Sigmund Freud). Well, I'd read one of his books on her say-so (before Sam discovered Jung), and this Freud says that for a satisfying life we need two things and two things only: useful, productive work and love. Izzy, more than anyone, did useful work—not just giving blood transfusions but all that support for men about to meet their maker—and she also loved and was loved. My lovely sister, however short her life, had experienced the best of what this world has to offer. That was something for me to hold on to.

Then I read the next section and . . . well, this is the beginning of the end of my story. In addition to her vivid prose style and cheeky sense of humor, Izzy had an excellent memory. The section I was reading was a frank—and very full—account of her visit to me when I was recovering from my operation in Sedgeberrow, including how, out of boredom, she had gone through my belongings, making the discovery that caused her to think that I was homosexual. Naturally, she then wrote up my explanation and description of the Christmas truce. She had read many of the press accounts of the truce and had neatly placed my experience in the wider context—my meeting with Wilhelm, our exchange of gifts, his request for me to give his girl-friend his photograph. Which she assumed I had done.

And Sam had read her account.

It was about half past four when I reached Izzy's visit to me in Sedgeberrow. Outside, in the Avenue Victor Hugo, it was raining, wa-ter lashing against the windows. I could hear the clatter of horses' hooves on the wet cobbles of Paris, the occasional swish of automo-bile tires through the puddles. I recalled that day when it had rained equally hard as Sam and I walked along the canal in Middle Hill.

That Sam had read Izzy's journal explained a lot. It explained everything. In particular it explained her manner with me while she had been here in Paris, for the break in the peace conference. The more I thought about it, however, the more puzzled I became. If she had read the passage, as I was sure she had, if she had decided that I had behaved—well, beyond all humanity—why had she come to Paris at all? Why not just turn her back on me and disappear, taking Will with her? Or why not have it out with me, there and then, in Paris— one hell of a fight, with every blunt truth aired? That she hadn't fol-lowed either course of action didn't make sense.

Five A.M. came. I stood at the window, looking out at the rain. There were a few stragglers going home from their revels, uncertain on their feet, but most of the people I saw were the solitary night people—policemen, off-duty waiters, newspaper deliverymen, early morning bakers who had no choice but to be up at this sad hour. Will would be fast asleep now, the smell of soap about him. Occasionally, he would turn in his sleep and absently rub the scar on his arm where it had been slashed at the Battersea fair. I had watched him do that on countless evenings when I stood over him, before silently bidding him good night.

Five-thirty came, five forty-five. Was there a possibility still that Sam *had* learned to love me, and loved me even now; that she liked our life, looked forward to living in my father's house; and that she understood my actions—that with a war on, with all the danger and uncertainty it implied, what I had done was forgivable? That I deserved some credit for saving Will's life?

Then I asked myself again the question I had framed many times over—whether love, the slow burn when you have learned to love someone, is ever the same as the explosion of love at first sight?

Six o'clock came. I took a bath and, while I was in the bath, I finally realized what Sam had done.

Everything at last, and for the first time, was out in the open between us. Now she was saying: Hal, you have to decide what to do. You, the man who wrote the book on the moral cost of the war, have shown an amorality beyond all conscience. She had kept her promise and had never mentioned Wilhelm's name since that day in the field when we had scattered Izzy's ashes, not even in Paris. So she was saying, in effect: Your actions got us into this situation, this predicament, this love story of sorts, and all via dishonesty, opportunistic deception, and luck. What are *you* going to do?

Except, of course, that Sam *still* didn't know everything. She thought she did, at long last, after a wartime of not knowing. But once again, and ironically—bitterly ironically—she didn't have all the facts. But *I* did. I knew that Wilhelm was still alive, still in love with Sam. *I even knew where he was!* Once again, as before, at the very start, I was the only person who knew everything, who had the whole picture.

Sam didn't know that Wilhelm had been in Paris, where he had promised to take her, at the same time she had. Wilhelm, having seen us, thought we were a family and because of that wouldn't go looking for Sam, as he'd once vowed—to her and to me—that he would. If I pretended to Sam that I hadn't yet had time to read Izzy's journal, if I could spin it out for even a week or two, it would soon be more than six months since the Armistice. There was chaos, violence, and talk of revolution in Germany. Once the peace conference ended, Wilhelm would go back to Berlin and our lives would diverge forever. If I did absolutely nothing, nothing at all, the attractions of life with me would continue to grow even as Wilhelm's prospects receded still further. Will loved me. I was engaged in work of historical importance, and Sam knew that. I was to be knighted; Sam could become Lady Montgomery if she wished. Life with me was a much better life than no life and was I *so* bad to do what I had done? Wilhelm was the enemy, and the enemy had killed my sister, killed Faye's fiancé, and, in a sense, killed Lottie's Reg.

All that happened a week ago. That morning I got out of the bath, put on my bathrobe, sat down, and began writing this story.

It is for you, Will, and now I address you directly for the first time. It is for you, though I do not doubt that your mother, Sam— Sally Ann Margaret—will read it first. She, after all, is the one who, following one of our visits to the Wigmore Hall, told me to write down my memories, for you to read one day.

I didn't go back to the peace conference. I wrote to Malahyde to say that I wasn't well, and since then I have stayed in my hotel room to set down this account. Now that I am reaching the end, I want to say three things more.

First, I want you, Will, and your mother to have the house in

Edgewater, plus anything else that my father leaves me when he dies. I shall write separately to my father but I ask, second, that you show him this account. I don't want to be excused for what I have done, but I do wish to be understood. I am saddened that my mother will never read this. She always understood me instinctively—better than my father certainly—and, having had plenty of time to think it through, I grasp now that she fully appreciated the effect my wound might have on my life. She understood, as perhaps I did not, that few women could love a man—or wish to be a wife to a man—who could not have children.

She was always secretly concerned that I would lead a solitary life. And I know now, from talking to one of her sisters who came to her and Izzy's funeral, that the story she told me during the last conversation I had with her, on her favorite bench, about her not really loving my father when they met, was a total fabrication. She made up a story that she thought would warm and comfort me inside and set my mind at rest. Is that a mother's love?

Third, I ask that you do not try to find me, ever, not even if you have inherited your mother's wanderlust. By the time Sam reads this, I shall be aboard a ship bound for somewhere a long way away—Australia maybe, Canada, Chile even. Who knows? I shall decide when I get to Le Havre and find out where the next ship is sailing for.

Sam set me a task, to decide what to do, and this is my decision, my reply, to set you and your mother free—free financially, free emotionally, free of the past, free of me. Seeing you sitting on my shoulders, thinking you were my son, freed Wilhelm, he said, to move on. I can't allow that. It would be a false freedom: you are his son, not mine.

You will find the fact that I am not your father a terrible shock, a brutal blow. I am sorry for that, but it is why I have written this story. And you will, as time goes by and you grow older, learn that having a

German father in England, or an English mother in Germany, is not easy. I hope that the arrangements I have made will help ease the pain that you, your mother, and your father will have to go through. Your mother realized, at the end, I think, that anti-German feeling in England would not end with the war. That explains a lot.

Your mother . . . I have loved your mother, Will—oh! how I have loved her. Nothing will ever replace her in my heart. But I have loved you too. When I worried that you would die, at Battersea fair, on Chelsea Bridge, in the Lister Hospital, I thought I had discovered something worse than war itself. In your short life, my dear boy, you have had two sips of beer, and you gallantly pretended on each occasion that you liked them, for my sake. When you came into our bed, the morning after I had arrived home late, when I had been following Genevieve Afton, when you wanted to make sure I was still there, I felt the wriggle of your body, the clutch of your tiny fingers digging into the flesh of my shoulder, as you climbed over me, your small wet lips kissing my ear, and I suffered a bolt of electricity, a shock so vivid, so intense, so wonderful, that I realized I had only been half alive until then.

Who would have thought that a war, of all things, could bring me such a gift?

So, more than the fact that I have loved you, Will—dear Will— *you have loved me.* You are perhaps the only person outside my family who I can be sure *has* loved me. One day you will know what that means, but you will also learn that the love of a child is not the same as the love of an adult, of a man for a woman, or a woman for a man.

When your mother first told me, on the cricket field in Middle Hill, when you were crawling all over the blanket, that she didn't love me—well, I decided I could cope with that, that her kiss on our previous meeting held out a promise, and that I had a whole war to change her mind. When I saw how much she missed me, the night I stayed out late unexpectedly, shadowing Genevieve Afton, I told myself that our relationship was deepening. When we were by that lock on the canal, watching a filthy barge rise from one level to another and Sam said our horizon was expanding in a similar way, I believed her. When, by another canal, this time in Middle Hill, she said that her love for me was unfolding like a flower in spring—again I believed her. I thought it was a wonderful thing to say. When we made love the night before I left for Switzerland, and she cried out again and again, I thought we had reached the limits of intimacy, an intimacy neither of us had achieved before. When she wrote to me in Switzerland to say she was sleeping on my side of the bed, I thought that was a spontaneous gesture that confirmed our intimacy. When she suggested we take a bath together, on the evening of my birthday party, when you and I had been playing with the shoe polish, she convinced me that, yes, she would one day be able to love me. When she cried out, at the Lister Hospital, and said without thinking that I was your father, I was touched and, yes, I thought a line had been crossed. When she fought with Ruth, after Ruth and Greville had allowed me to take the blame in Lottie's eyes for Reg's betrayal, your mother was—was she not?—putting "our" family, as she described it, before her own. When she lectured me about "blood" not being everything it is cracked up to be, I saw no reason to disbelieve her. When she stood on the rung of the kissing gate, in the field where we scattered Izzy's ashes, and told me she would marry me, I believed her, and all my anger dissolved in an instant. I am sure she meant it, and all the other comforting things she said, when she said them.

I am sure she *tried* to love me. I was as much a gift to her as she was to me.

But . . . I cannot shake my recollection of how uncomfortable she felt when Ruth showed her the children's uniforms her factory had made, or when you saluted the grenadiers at Miss Allardyce's on the day of the party. Why had she registered your name at Miss Allardyce's under "Ross" and not used mine?

Our predicaments suited us, both of us. But with me the way I am, there was never any chance of another child—a brother or sister for you—and the complications that might bring.

Did your mother love me, Will, or—I repeat how hard it is to write all this—*or* was I . . . ? No. You will understand what I can't bring myself to say.

I recall with vivid but sad pleasure the walk in the back streets of Stratford, that Saturday in July 1915, when I fell in love with your mother right there and then, among the saddleries, foundries, and blacksmiths. I, more than anyone, should know that the internal explosion, the furnace of fire when love swells to fill every organ and every cell of your being, when the juices of your system are warmed by this sudden charging and changing of your physiology, a transfusion that floods your arteries and veins with electricity, is very different from the slow glow that Sam says grew inside her, in regard to me. An adagio is not the real thing.

Until last week, I thought I had been clever and had fooled everyone—Sam most of all—with the way I had contrived to meet her, and then build a life, a family, a love, all derived from a daring calculation, a neat juggling of our joint predicaments, the fortuitous way we had both been trapped by dramatic events and ironic circumstances. But the only one I was fooling was myself.

The peace conference will last a few more weeks, so when she reads this your mother will know where to find Wilhelm. The idea that Wilhelm's child, the enemy's offspring, but the enemy who wasn't the enemy, should be the one person whose love I could know, is strange, is ironic in itself, but the world is as it is.

And, in making you free, Will, and in making Sam free, I hope that I am making myself free. I can see that now. Your mother could not have known, when she sent me Izzy's journal, but the great events that put this whole story in motion have also helped bring about its resolution. At least I hope so.

It is getting late and it is still raining outside. In a few hours I leave for Le Havre.

Unlike Izzy's splendid journal, my story is not for publication. If Sam reads it, if my father reads it, even if Wilhelm reads it, that is as it should be. But first and foremost it is a gift for you, my dearest boy, because in war and in peace I have been happy, joyous, and, yes, privileged to have been, for however short a time,

Your father

FROM THE *LONDON TIMES*, 12 MARCH, 1926:
BRITISH VICTIMS IN BERLIN CLUB FIRE

BERLIN—Police here yesterday named more of the victims in last Saturday's arson attack on the Pelikan Cabaret Club in Schillerstrasse in the Wedding District of Berlin. No charges have yet been brought, though the attack is believed to have been orchestrated by the National Socialist Party and was targeted at the work of the Swiss-Austrian Jewish Expressionist artist Liesl Seide.

Apart from Miss Seide, whose body was identified on Sunday, the 17 victims are now known to have included three British nationals: Piers Pargeter, the saxophonist with a New Orleans jazz band on tour in Germany; Rebecca Berwick, second daughter of the Earl of Berwick and Alnwick; and Colonel Henry ("Hal") Montgomery. Montgomery, aged 34, was born in Edgewater, Gloucestershire. After being injured at the Front in the Great War, Colonel Montgomery had a distinguished career in military and political intelligence, and formed part of the British delegation to the Versailles Peace Conference. He was the author of a popular study on the "moral costs" of the war, which became a best seller in 1919. In Berlin he worked as a publisher of artistic prints, Liesl Seide being one of his most popular artists. He never married.